A PLACE OF LIGHT

A PLACE OF LIGHT

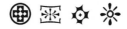

Kim Silveira Wolterbeek

Cuidono Press
Brooklyn

ISBN: 978-0-9911215-0-2

Front Cover: Marigolds and Fontevraud Arch
© 2013 Sydney C' de Baca

Cuidono Press
Brooklyn NY

www.cuidono.com

AUTHOR'S NOTE

In the spring of 1101, with the backing of Peter II, Bishop of Poitiers, and the financial support of members of the aristocracy, including Philippa, Countess of Toulouse and Duchess of Aquitaine, the priest Robert of Arbrissel established Fontevraud Abbey, a double monastery where Robert and his male followers served the nuns. While this book draws upon actual people and historical events, it is a work of fiction.

THE MIRACLE AT ROUEN

✝

The sky shuddered and exploded. Deep in the forest of Craon, Robert sprinted for cover beneath the branches of a hawthorn tree. Weak from fasting, he lowered his sodden cowl and dropped to his knees. "O Lord, show me the way." Sharp stones jutted up from the soil, piercing his flesh. Less than a stone's throw from where he knelt, lightening touched ground. Amidst a cascade of blue sparks, a woman hovered above a knoll, completely unaffected by the storm. Transfixed by her presence, he stumbled to his feet.

"Robert," she said, in a calm voice that was audible above the tempest. "Help the women."

He wondered if she was an angel sent by God or one of Lucifer's minions come to seduce him. He did not think her human, for no earthly being was ever so exquisitely formed. Her sheer linen gown hugged her breasts, flared at the hip and skimmed her bare feet. A disconcerting thrill mingled his desire for Parisian whores with his passion for the Word. Before he could say a word, hail the size of chickpeas thundered from the sky.

"Use your gift to save women in need. Shelter them in safety and serve them diligently as the Evangelist served Mary."

Even as he struggled with her meaning, he understood that God had granted him a revelation. When he opened his mouth to give thanks, the woman vanished, the rain ceased and the air grew balmy. Sparrows preened in the bushes and squirrels chattered from the branches of trees.

Raising his eyes to a sky of shifting colors, he watched pale blues meld with yellows and magentas and held his breath when the swallows mounted and rode the heady currents, gliding and falling in ecstasy. Looking to the heavens he placed his faith in the Blessed Virgin and left the forest for the bustling market city of Rouen.

A dozen women sat before an open hearth scorched black from the flames of countless fires. Woolen rugs blanketed the clay walls and a single window covered by oilcloth funneled twilight into the room. The proprietress, a massive woman in her forties, sat facing the fire on a barrel chair, the cowhide hammocked to fit the spread of her rump. It had been years since a man mistook Marie for one of her girls.

Marie wore a gown lined in rabbit fur for warmth beneath a quilted waistcoat and burgundy tunic. Her feet, the only portion of her body not affected by time, rested narrow as an aristocrat's against the warm stone. In the days she had worked alongside her girls, men had licked the pink arches and sucked the tiny toes. Now those toes curled around the shaft of a metal rod, for while the girls worked the bellows, only Marie manned the poker.

The women rested on straw trusses and cloth-covered pallets. Bertrad, who had recently given birth to a son, and Beatrice, who for five days would be spared the bother of accommodating men, wore dresses of rough serge. The rest wore their underclothing, long lengths of linen pinned at the back. The twins, Agnes and Arsen, held hands and whispered their gibberish, a secret language of incomplete utterances that Marie thought made them sound dumb as cattle. Most of the others talked quietly or took turns playing jacks and string games with Florence's two daughters, Emma and Esther, while the younger children finished their dinner of beans. Only Madeleine, a girl of sixteen with strawberry blond hair and pale, freckled skin, sat slightly apart, lost in a daydream. While Marie did not approve of flights of fancy, she understood that in Madeleine's case they provided temporary escape from unpleasant obligations and a troubled past.

Madeleine's father had spent ten years beating his frail wife, as disappointed by the rise of her bread as he was by her performance in bed. After she died giving birth, he had buried their stillborn son, left his two daughters with Marie and ran off to join the crusades. Like every man Marie had ever known, he thought his needs worthy of special consideration. And while Marie found such egotism annoying, she knew that the real evil in men was their ability to elicit hope. "Never trust a man," she warned her girls. In response, they met any gesture of male kindness with suspicion.

Studying Madeleine's distracted gaze, Marie knew a profound satisfaction. Sex had long ago lost its power and its revulsion for Marie. In its place she discovered a ferocious maternal love for women. If not for her, these girls would likely have died at the hands of indigent fathers and uncles. God, she felt certain, would forgive her sins.

Outside, a barefoot and cassocked figure sidestepped pigs and chickens picking through piles of kitchen rubbish. Stopping beneath a banner depicting a rose, the stranger made the sign of the cross and took the knocker in his hand.

Marie sighed. Every evening the family life she had created ended abruptly and the other began. "Let's go, girls," she said, straightening her tunic. A rumbling cough seared her lungs and left her gasping.

Florence scooped up jacks and slipped them into her pockets, promising her daughters a bedtime story if they moved quickly. Bertrad rose so abruptly that her son lost his hold on her nipple and began to howl. Beatrice shooed the older children behind a tapestry of a white unicorn with a spiral horn thrusting three hand spans from his forehead. The tapestry, a gift to Marie from a grateful lord, separated the communal area from Marie's bedroom. Agnes and Arsen dropped hands long enough to adjust their shifts and assume expressions of haughty indifference. *What*, Marie wondered, *did God have in mind creating two identical beauties that were so ugly mean?*

"Maddy," Marie said, "see who it is."

Madeleine tucked a sprig of periwinkle behind her ear and unlatched the door to a tall, well-formed man with vivid blue eyes.

"Come in, sir," she said, for Marie insisted her girls address men with respect.

The man lowered his cowl. Firelight haloed his bearded face. Wavy black hair brushed his shoulders. "Do I know you?" he asked Madeleine.

"Perhaps." She shrugged in a suggestive way.

"Friends or strangers," Marie commented from her place of privilege by the fire, "what all men want is the same. Isn't that right, mister?" Her lungs had settled into a tolerable burn, and she did not want to risk a sudden move. So while she was curious to get a look at the man, she remained seated with her back to the door. "Come warm yourself," she said.

"Thank you, my daughter," he replied, but made no movement towards the fire.

"Daughter?" she grumbled. "You won't find your daughter here." Bodkins, a stringy tabby, threaded her ankles. Marie knuckled the sinewy hollow between the tom's shoulders until he rattled a purr.

"You are *all* my daughters," he said. Although men of God seldom entered houses of prostitution, Marie pegged this one for a hair shirt, albeit one with a compelling voice.

"Two pence," she said, holding out her palm. "Then you may choose one of these ... daughters ... to accompany you upstairs."

Placing his hand on Madeleine's shoulder, he whispered, "I choose you."

PART ONE

✝

The world is slippery, full of slime. A man cannot long remain steadfast within it, and once he falls, rarely if ever does he rise. You have risen in this world as if it were a high mountain, and for this reason you have turned the eyes and tongues of men toward you. But standing on your mountain, beware that you do not fall, nor, practicing a form of martyrdom virtually unknown to the holy martyrs, that you bequeath a stain of infamy to the beginning of a religious life.

Geoffrey of Vendôme, Letter to Robert of Arbrissel
Vendôme, c.1099

The moment Robert touched Madeleine's shoulder he grew dazed and disoriented. Backlit by the blaze of the fire, her sheer linen shift revealed a shapely body that tightened his belly and set his heart pounding. Her solemn grey eyes reminded him of the hovering beauty who had answered his prayers. The fire sparked blue, a blast of cold air whistled under the door, and for one confusing moment the whore before him and the woman from his vision merged into one graceful form.

Robert followed Madeleine to the stairwell, mesmerized by the swell of her slender calves as she mounted the steps above him.

Mint, lilac, and straw covered the planked floor of the second story. Casks and barrels stood along the walls. Madeleine lowered herself onto a sack of grain and fixed the candle on the floor. Robert prayed for divine direction, but his mind snaked into that dark cave where impure thoughts coiled and writhed. Instead of concentrating on the woman's soul, he studied the curve of her lips and recalled the whores he had known in Paris, a sinful city where temptation walked the street in scarlet tunics and bare shoulder. His favorite, Black Mary, had been a solemn dark-haired girl of few words and an insatiable appetite.

"What would you like, sir?" Madeleine asked now.

"Like? I would like to help you," he whispered, appalled by his own audacity. Who was he to offer help? He had been entering brothels for weeks, preaching the word without success. Despite his good intentions, he was a sinful man with no safe haven to offer anyone.

"Help me? I must work for my two pence," she said with a startled, vaguely derisive laugh, undoing her braid. "Let me bathe your feet while you—help me.

He watched the muscles in Madeleine's forearm tense as she scooped water into a bowl. In his youth Robert had imagined a benevolent God scooping sinners into His large forgiving hands and felt the weighted need of humanity in his own palms. As he grew older, this vision intensified—fueled his life, gave it meaning and fostered in him a calm serenity and an enormous guilt. Knelling before our Lord, he confessed to being repulsed by the blemished skin of old men and the sour smell of colicky babes. No matter how hard he tried, he seldom felt drawn to the singular burning soul. Likewise, the need that welled up inside of him now had nothing to do with his love of mankind.

"You wear the robes of a holy man. Are you a monk?" She dropped to her knees and swirled lemon rind and mint into the water. "Why don't you tell me your story?"

Robert's breath caught in his throat. Repentant sinners asked forgiveness, young men for direction, and old women for clarification of the Word, but no one had ever asked him for his story. More seductive than her flower-scented hair was the power of her question.

"My name is Robert. I grew up in Arbrissel, a village southeast of Rennes, in the vicinity of La Guerche de Bretagne and Craon. I attended seminary in Paris." He blushed remembering the nights spent stalking lust in alleyways. "Several years after I was ordained, Pope Urban commissioned me to reform the corrupt church in Rennes."

"What is Rennes like?" she asked.

Encouraged by her question, he continued. "Rennes is a dangerous city still reeling from the Viking attacks a generation ago," he said. "Longhaired men wearing animal skins roam the streets brandishing knives." She listened, wide-eyed and unblinking. He did not think her interest feigned, but the moment she placed his feet in the bowl of warm water he lost the thread of his story.

"And the place where you grew up?" she prompted.

"I grew up in a bleak town of stone," he said and then faltered as she began humming. He began anew. "Arbrissel is a town of slate houses, cobble streets and barren countryside."

Madeleine furrowed her brow and touched the blossom tucked behind her ear. Water rained in rivulets down her arm and splashed a ripple in the bowl at Robert's feet. All around them, the air churned with the grunting pleasure of men.

He resumed his story, but whether to please her or to distract himself from temptation, even he did not know. "My earliest memories involve accompanying my father to visit the sick and dying or to assist an ailing cow or pig or even to prescribe a cure for an infertile field. I remember standing at the bedside of a dying farmer while my father performed the last rites. My father heard his confession and tried to calm the man's fears, but as the moment of his death approached, the farmer reached for my hand. My family never questioned my future vocation. Like my father and grandfather before me, I entered the priesthood."

Madeleine nodded and began massaging Robert's feet. He noticed that the pinkie nail on her right hand had been blackened by some accident. Had she pinched it in a drawer? Grazed it with a clabber? Robert's mother had soothed his scraped fingers in her warm mouth, and now he wanted to do the same for this woman. His breath quickened and words failed him. *Please God*, he prayed, *show me a sign that I am justified in taking his woman from the only life she knows.* For the second time that night, the present moment in the brothel and the sacred one in Croan became one.

The pitched ceiling of the whorehouse gave way to a bank of clouds. There, nestled in misty skies, a fountain bubbled near a white stone church. Before he could take in the spectacle before him, four domes formed the blue steepled roof of a nave. Dorters, a novice house, priory and convent broke ground and stretched in glory. Floating above the abbey was the woman of his vision. "Robert," she said. "Gather your followers and journey to Vendôme. There your old friend Abbot Geoffrey will help you realize your dream."

As suddenly as the spectacle had formed, it vanished.

Robert crossed himself and composed his thoughts. "My daughter," he said to Madeleine, "I would like to take you away from this life of sin and give you a new life where you will be free." Now that he had a plan, his voice swelled with confidence.

Madeleine abandoned his feet and leaned back on one arm. Her hair fell away from her face. "What is this place?" she asked.

He heard resistance in her question, a cynical hesitancy that prompted him to pray for eloquence. If he stumbled in his persuasion, then surely he would lose her soul.

Wishing to avoid her arching brows, Robert dropped his eyes and discovered a strawberry birthmark in the shape of a butterfly, fluttering the pulse of her neck. "There is a majestic white-walled building," he said, "a place of light with a blue roof and lofty spires that reach towards the heavens."

A look of startled recognition crossed her face. "Where?" she asked.

"The place is not yet built," he said, leaning forward to touch the darker corpse hair plaited in her own, "but it's as genuine as the sorrow that floods your heart and real as the place where all that we love and have loved abides. Come with me. Together we will build a refuge for women, a holy place of contemplation and prayer."

She sighed and shook her head. "Look around you, sir. This is no nunnery. The likes of my kind are not found in any holy place." She drew herself up onto her knees.

"Please do not dwell on sins of the past, except so much as they may be named, confessed, and absolved. Declare your faith in God and be released from the chains of your dark prison." Below them a door slammed, as if from a great gust of wind. The sound of booted footsteps and raucous laughter drifted up the stairwell.

They sat for a moment without speaking, Robert resigned to

failure, and Madeleine lost in thought. "Trust me," he said. She did not respond except to study the empty air around his head and shoulders. Whatever she saw seemed to reassure her. She smiled faintly, her expression shifting from resignation to confusion to hope.

"I have seen this place of light," she whispered.

Robert's breath caught in his throat. He felt the hand of God against his spine.

Accustomed to men who fawned apologetically or swaggered in lust, Madeleine did not know what to make of Robert's composure. When he chose her and placed his hand on her shoulder, she felt exhilarated. And though she reminded herself that men were greedy, self-involved creatures, she wondered if this one might be different. Certainly his colors glowed brighter than any she had seen before. No single shade dominated; instead, a muscular rainbow knocked against his shoulder and pulsed the length of his body.

Madeleine had always possessed an unusual sensitivity to her surroundings. As a child, the world came to her in a jumble of separate notes that bled artlessly into noise. Slowly, and with enormous effort, she learned to distinguish her mother's shushing presence from the ping of rain. The first time Madeleine saw colors tucked in around her mother, she thought that the delicate green that fluttered like the wings of a cabbage moth marked her mother as a saintly woman. But unlike the fixed halo in the statue of the crucified Christ that hung in the cathedral, her mother's colors stretched, pooled and transformed on an hourly basis.

As she grew older, Madeleine became aware of the fields of

color surrounding all people. The blacksmith, a mean-spirited, contentious man, vibrated angry reds whereas her even-tempered sister Ruth shimmered pink and lavender. Madeleine did not discuss her ability to see colors, at first because she thought all people had the same capacity and then, later, because she knew they did not. She told no one when the fishmonger's muddy orange disappeared the day before he died, but she spent hours wondering why. Madeleine had always been interested in why— why one man wanted this and another that, why the moon smoldered red on certain evenings, why snails left trails slick as egg whites, why the syllables of speech held more meaning than the hum of a treadle wheel. Curiosity, not fear, prompted her to hide behind a cask of grain whenever her parents argued.

Robert sighed and Madeleine heard only the soothing whisper of his breath. Looking into his eyes, the darkest shade of blue she had ever seen, Madeleine felt both exhilaration and fear. But no matter how unusual Robert might be, he was a man like any other man. And since experience had taught her that most men liked a brief conversation before settling down to business, she dragged a three-legged stool from the corner of the room and placed it in the round spread of candlelight. "Please, sir, sit down," she said, and prepared herself for the usual verbal fumbling regarding failed dreams and ungrateful lovers. His talk, however, proved more personal.

Far more troubling than the nightly violations of her body, Robert's words rubbed up against her soul and left her feeling vulnerable. She touched the amber lock of corpse hair woven into her lighter strawberry-blond braid and imagined that the strands of her dead sister's hair tethered her to this world even as she prayed to join her in the next. Lowering her eyes, Madeleine slowed her breathing and retreated into solitude. Without even trying, her mind entered a grand portal into a sweet-smelling place of light where tall white columns rose to the heavens. She was making her way down a marble aisle towards an altar fragrant with gladiolas and carnations when Arsen's companion's grunts pulled her back to the smoky whorehouse. Marie said that Madeleine's daydreams contained songs never sung, paintings never painted, stories never told. "Maddy girl, you're an artist without an art form trapped in the body of a whore!" she pronounced, her voice bitter, her eyes wide with awe, a response held in reserve for the rare human desire she did not fully comprehend.

Madeleine herself grew up in a household where the few objects of beauty—a carved crucifix and a trunk full of quilts—were functional, intended for worship and everyday use. One of her earliest memories was of her mother teaching her to quilt. Madeleine hastily cross-stitched Satan, with great curving horns that grew beautifully from his high forehead, harpooning a sinner. Using a precious bit of scarlet and orange thread, she shaped a row of eternal flames that flared brilliantly against his cloven hooves. Her mother shook her head when she saw the square. A look of disappointment and wonder flickered across her face. "Remove the stitches carefully," she said. "Mind the linen and save the thread."

"I offer you salvation," Robert said now. His voice reminded her of the belly fur of Marie's tabby cat!

Candlelight played on the water at his feet and buffed the glazed bowl into toasty iridescence. Dropping to her knees, Madeleine began working his feet with her hands.

"There is a place of light with soaring while columns and marble tiles…"

She sucked in her breath. How could this man know the details of her daydream?

Suddenly, she wanted to tell him everything—how an older girl with coaxing hands and almond-tasting lips taught her to pleasure men, how she learned to leave her own body whenever she lay beneath a man, how earlier in the year she had lost her sister to hard work and pleurisy, and the loss had left her vulnerable and sad. She had to bite her lip to keep the words from spilling.

How did this haloed man know her heart with such clarity? For while he may have guessed her losses—there was not a girl living at Marie's that had not suffered loss, else why would she be there?—reading her dreams was another matter entirely. Robert's voice radiated love, ensnared her heart, and marked him as a man who understood how to shape feelings into words. Calm took hold of her, and quite suddenly everything about this stranger felt familiar. Even the silence that separated his words she had known always and forever. Only her own galloping pulse surprised her. That and the miraculous way their colors mingled, swirling madly, bumping starlight, and emitting a scent like musk and apricot. She thought of the sudden still that heralds a storm, the muscled intent that announces a cat's leap. She thought of skylarks positioned for flight.

"Come with me," Robert said, his face lit by candlelight.

Madeleine heard the wail of Bertrad's babe, a random gust of wind, and the scrape of a stool. Each sound seemed to resonate with some larger meaning.

Robert's temples throbbed with biblical injunctions and gospels of persuasion. An hour's worth of words—the ones he had spoken and the ones he had swallowed whole—grated against his throat. Even his eyes hurt, each grainy blink a reminder of the smoke-filled air and feeble candlelight. Despite his fatigue, he straightened his shoulders and descended the brothel stairs with Madeleine at his side. Together, they would battle Marie in service of the Lord.

He had known many madams over the years. Cynical, jaded women, they had carved out thriving businesses that exploited the vulnerabilities of the men they despised. Marie, he understood, would not be so easily convinced to follow him down the path to redemption.

Madeleine entered the communal room first, dropping to her knees beside Marie's barrel chair. "This man is a prophet come to save us!" she said.

Marie examined Robert's flushed face and damp feet. "If you were a prophet, you would know what kind of woman has been bathing your feet." Her laughter rumbled up from her belly.

Robert took a measured breath. "Oh, but I do," he said. "She is the kind of woman who has loved many people, her mother and sister among them. She is the kind of woman who receives God's grace."

A loud, urgent rap sounded at the door. Madeleine rose to answer it, her fingers trailing the back of Marie's chair. A spasm of loss tightened Robert's chest.

"If loving many is all that's required to receive God's grace," Marie said, picking up the poker and jabbing a log, "then my girls must be ablaze with His glory!"

The fire popped and flared. The cat, asleep at her ankles, startled awake and leaped to his feet. The sharp howl of a colicky baby erupted from behind the wall hanging, momentarily drowning out the gruff voices of bartering men and the giggles of the whores.

"If you're not wanting another girl," Marie said, "the door's over there." She lifted the poker and pointed, an imperial gesture that seemed at once grand and threatening.

"I will leave you now, Mother," an exhausted Robert said, signing the cross, "but I'll be back."

"Every man's entitled to his two pence," Marie said and shrugged dismissively.

The following evening Robert returned to the brothel carrying his two pence.

"Well, if it isn't the prophet! Have you come back for another one of your… daughters?" Marie asked, thrusting out her palm to receive his coins.

"It's not the young women's bodies I'm interested in," he said, scanning the room for a glimpse of Madeleine. "It's their souls."

A stewing pot of pork greased the air with animal fat. A mouse scuttled along the baseboard and disappeared into a darkened corner.

"Blessed is the man who stands up under trial," Marie said, her voice curdled with sarcasm. "Don't look so surprised. I wasn't always an old whore. I lived for a while with a missionary and his wife. I know my Bible stories," she said, delighted to have taken him off guard. "Madeleine's upstairs, if that's who you're looking for."

Black bile burned the back of Robert's throat. In truth, he both despised and envied the men who bedded Madeleine.

"No? Then pick another. There are plenty of…souls…to choose among," Marie said, a note of boredom flattening her tone.

Robert nodded to a young woman with a scooped out face and a spotty chin. Without a word, she rose from her straw truss and mounted the stairs. The frayed hem of her linen shift swayed against the backs of her calves, drawing Robert's attention to her slim ankles and the dirty soles of her feet.

Once upstairs the woman led him to a pallet that was foul with spent seed. "What is it you like?" she asked in a sweet, fluid voice that surprised him.

"To sit," Robert said, pointing to the stool.

Her face, as vacant as a melon, revealed nothing. Loosening the tie that bound the neck of her shift, she shrugged the garment past her shoulders. It gathered in folds against her breasts.

"No," he said, raising one hand. "I want only to talk. Light the taper please." Robert lowered himself onto the stool. He did not look beyond the pool of candlelight, for fear of seeing Madeleine in the embrace of a filthy farmer or greedy merchant.

The woman frowned, retied her shift and lit the candle before settling at his feet. She recoiled when he reached into his pocket. "It's my Bible I'm after," he explained. The young woman stared boldly at his crotch, impatience tightening the skin around her eyes, until Robert stumbled upon a psalm that pricked her interest. "Deliver me, O Lord, from wicked men; protect me from men of violence…"

She slid to the edge of her pallet and grabbed the hem of Robert's robe. "How can He do that?" she asked "Can you tell me how?"

"Forsake your evil ways. Embrace the Lord. I will take care of the rest," he said.

By the end of the week he had climbed the stairs a dozen times, each time with a different girl at his side. Looking past their flirtatious giggles and swaying hips, he asked the girls questions, as mindful of their mannerisms as he was of their responses. For Robert believed that much could be discerned in a toss of the head or a downward glance. Once he had discovered their hidden thoughts and feelings, he said whatever it took to open their hearts.

On Robert's final evening in Rouen, he asked for Agnes and Arsen. Marie held up four fingers. "Four pence for two girls," she said curtly. Robert's knock had awakened her from a nap. She sat slumped sideways in her chair and did not even bother to look at him.

Upstairs, the twins sat on a pallet and motioned Robert to join them. He declined, taking his usual stool. Every head tilt, every finger curl offered its own obscene allure. "What would you like, sir?" they said in one voice. The dimples bracketing their mouths drew attention to their enormous eyes. Together they examined him with confident stares that seemed to reflect his darkest desires.

"We will do anything you can imagine…"

"Only better…" they whispered tossing their dark hair and licking their lips. Robert felt the heat of their bodies and smelled their caramelized scent. Studying the candle's flame, he directed his thoughts back to God.

"Tell me about your family," he said, hoping their responses might give him an opening into their lives. They looked at each other and smiled. Still, he did not give up. Leaning forward on the stool, he described the better life he could give them if only they would follow him, but Arsen merely scratched her arm and Agnes looked at him with the placid gaze of a cow.

As the hour wore on, he grew tired and frustrated, and despaired that he would ever find a connection with them.

Then, just before dawn, as sleep began to overcome Robert and he faded in and out of consciousness, the stench of sulfur jolted him awake. The smell prompted the disturbing sensation that he was in the presence of evil. In desperation, he began telling the twins about Saint Pelagia the Harlot, the most beautiful courtesan of Antioch, who moved even religious men to despair.

At first Agnes and Arsen combed their fingers through their dark hair and yawned unabashedly. Distracted by footfalls on the stairs, they glanced over their shoulders before readjusting themselves on the pallet, stretching their legs and rolling their shoulders.

But once Robert began describing the depths of Pelagia's beauty, they stilled their bodies and turned their faces towards him, listening attentively when he revealed Pelagia's great wealth, explaining that she had ridden about town in an elegant carriage surrounded by her followers and worshipers. Robert paused for a breath, and the twins leaned into each other, whispering in such tones that he could not hear a word. For all he knew, they could have been humming words to the devil. "But Pelagia was no fool," Robert told them. She knew her beauty would not last forever, so she did something unexpected. She entered the basilica of Antioch and confessed her sins to the Bishop Nonnus, a man well known for his sanctity and kindness. "Bishop Nonnus told her that if she truly repented her past existence, Christ would forgive her and make her his bride. Pelagia, overcome with hope, fell to the pavement and held the feet of the good Nonnus in her arms, washing his feet with her tears and wiping them with her hair. Bishop Nonnus, though tempted by Pelagia's touch, focused on her soul. 'You must declare with certainty that you will not fall back into your sinful way,' he said to her. 'Then you may be baptized.'"

Quite suddenly, Agnes dropped Arsen's hand and together

the twins stroked Robert's thighs, the identical pressure of their fingers increasing his torment two fold. Had Arsen not been distracted by a man's hoarse gasp, they might have succeeded in their seduction. But her fingers stuttered and Robert, released from their spell, began praying silently the words that the Bishop Nonnus had spoken aloud to Pelagia—*Do not entice me, for I am but a weak and sinful man intent on serving God.* As if in answer to his prayer, Robert felt a falling off of desire, a settling in of divine direction that allowed him to continue. "Pelagia readily confessed to all her wrongdoings. And as the reformed harlot aged, instead of growing ugly and decrepit, she grew more beautiful with an inner light, God's sign of sanctity."

Robert felt a sudden peace fill the room, a radiant presence that washed a warm light through his body. The twins gasped, withdrew their hands from his leg, and began sucking on their fingertips, as though they had been blistered by fire.

"Repent," Robert said. "Offer up your blemished souls to Christ and you, too, shall be saved."

"And if we do," Agnes said, "Will we remain forever beautiful?"

He hesitated. "Your souls will glow with a brilliance that surpasses physical beauty."

Downstairs a door closed with a whoosh of air that climbed the stairs, flickered candles and danced their shadows—a hideous beast with three backs—against the wall.

"But who will know?" Arsen asked. "Who will know the brilliance of our souls if our bodies are ugly?"

Descending the stairs that morning, Robert could think of little else but his failure. Down below, one of the children fussed and a cock crowed in the distance. *Preaching is like fishing with a net that catches every kind of fish,* he thought. *Put the good ones into a basket and cast the bad ones aside.* But the thought did not comfort him.

A dim light lit the room. The fire ebbed to a dull glow. Some of the girls prepared for bed while others tended to the children.

Marie occupied her familiar seat before the fireplace, her head lying against the back of her throne as she rested. Robert quietly took a place on a bench before the fireplace and, listening to Marie's labored breathing, remained silent while she examined him through the slit of her eyelids.

Finally she shifted in her chair. Without a word to Robert she plunged her poker into the banked fire, scattering gray ash in search of a hot spot.

Madeleine appeared with an armful of wood. Dropping to her knees to release her load, she cast a troubled look at Marie.

"I'm feeling the chill this morn," Marie said. She grabbed a pinecone from a basket near the hearth and tossed it onto the coals. The sap sparked a flame and she grunted her approval, indicating with a wave of her hand that Madeleine should lay the fire.

Madeleine nodded. She looked like a simple peasant girl, barefoot, wearing a plain wool chemise extending to her calves. She gingerly balanced a log between the andirons.

"Maddy tells me you've promised my girls a better life." Shaking her head, she sucked her teeth. "It's my experience that men are big on making promises but not so keen on keeping them."

"My promise is God's promise, for I have a holy vision," Robert said.

"Maddy told me of your…vision," Marie said, waving her hand dismissively. "I'm not interested in your prophecies or dreams. My concerns are practical. You say you want to help women, and perhaps you do. But why? I wonder."

Robert chose his words carefully. "It all began in Toulouse," he said. "After Pope Urban heard me deliver a sermon, he gave me free license to preach anywhere in France." Robert paused to adjust his robe, warm his hands by the fire and clear his throat, noting with satisfaction that his silence did not disturb Marie. "After a while I gained a reputation for eloquence among the people of Northern France."

"Bah," she said. "People will listen to anyone as long as the words sound pleasant to their ears." She blew air through her nose. Madeleine finished with the fire and made to leave, but Marie took her hand and kissed her palm. "Stay," she said. "Listen to what your prophet has to say."

Robert studied the fire, watching a single flame fork into a half dozen tongues that licked the darkened firebox.

"Go on then," Marie said to Robert. "We're listening."

"I prayed for direction. I asked God for the strength to resist the devil. I implored him to provide the answers to my questions: Why am I drawn to sin? What is the purpose of my gift? How may I serve thee?"

Marie adjusted her great bulk, settling more comfortably into her chair. She did not bother hiding her yawn. "And then what?" she asked. "The good Lord told you to visit whorehouses?"

"He told me nothing at first." Robert paused to study the two women. Marie seemed caught up in his story, suspended between mistrust and curiosity. Madeleine's lips parted and she touched her braid.

"The answer came to me in the form of a vision. A beautiful woman who reminded me of a certain Parisian whore." He said nothing of the resemblance to Madeleine.

Marie no longer tried to disguise her interest. "I've sinned often in my life and struggle daily with the sin of lust," Robert said. She leaned forward in her chair, her labored breathing growing more rapid. Madeleine's brow creased with concern.

"I'm fine, child," Marie said. "Continue with your story," she directed Robert.

"I think in helping women I will also help myself."

Marie twisted the poker into the embers. "And how do I know you're speaking the truth? You're not the first man to enter this house with a handful of change and a mouth spouting empty promises."

"My message comes from the Lord, Mother Marie. Our new home will be a slice of paradise in this dark world. We will build a great church, dedicated to the Virgin Mary, and next to it a convent for you and your girls, consecrated to Saint Mary Magdalene. And your every need will be met, by me and by brothers dedicated to serving you."

Marie laughed raucously. "Men serving women? Are you mad? Have you lived so long as a priest that you do not see the world for what it is?" Turning suddenly serious, she pointed her finger at Robert. "Do not mock me, Master Robert," she said in a commanding voice. "I am no fool!" A burst of blue and red flames curled against the logs. Marie leaned back into her chair and released a drawn out sigh.

"I am sincere in my proposal. I am offering you a safe haven."

"Do you have a plan," Marie demanded, "some practical way of realizing your dream? Did this beautiful woman from your vision also provide you with monies for this…place of light?"

"I have a good friend and mentor at the monastery of Vendôme. He will help us."

Marie sighed, a deep and troubled sound. "I do not entirely trust you, Master Robert," she said. "I hear a keen desire in your magnificent voice, but a desire for what? You say your desire is to help women, that in doing so you hope to redeem them and yourself as well. But that desire does not account for the pride I hear in your powerful voice. Why is it, Master Robert, that while you freely confess your lust for Parisian whores, you are hesitant to confess your arrogance?" She shook her head. "The whole of your intent is not clear to me. Perhaps it is not yet clear to you. What is certain is that you have charmed my girls and they are bent on following you."

Marie placed her thumb and index fingers against her eyes and rubbed them with drowsy deliberation. "I am old and my lungs are full of phlegm." Her words were barely audible above the rattle of the tabby's purr and the pop of the fire. "Soon I won't have the energy to run this place. Then what? The girls are young and inexperienced. Not a one, not even my Maddy, knows enough about the business to take over." She chuckled. "You think me proud? You would be right. That's how I can so easily recognize the sin in others!" She laughed again, a rueful sound that sputtered into a wheeze. Then, looking intently into Robert's eyes she asked,

"Will this place of light be warm? Will it have a well-stocked kitchen?" she asked, cupping her substantial belly in her hands.

"In my vision…"

Marie frowned and pursed her lips.

"Yes," Robert said. "You will be comfortable and your stomachs will be full."

"Hmmph," she said. "Then I'll go with you, but I go reluctantly."

"The Lord shall bless you, Mother. I will not fail you," Robert said.

"We shall see," Marie said. "We shall see."

In the hour before dawn, Marie commanded Madeleine to fetch a jar from under the floor where her bed had been. "Here," said Marie, "take Bodkins. I will carry the money."

"We will not want your coins. They are ill-gotten coins, the Devil's ransom," Robert said.

Marie reached for the jar. "We will need money to buy bread. I do not intend to starve." She poured the tinkling coins into a cloth bag that she fastened to her girdle. A few short days later, Marie and her girls removed the last of the furnishings from the little house and prepared to follow Robert. Even the twins, when they heard that the others had all agreed to go, shrugged and packed their things.

Fourteen-year-old Philippa found the first leg of the journey, three days gliding the Garonne River on a covered boat, most agreeable. The sounds of swallow and cuckoo punctuated the expansive quiet. Trailing her fingers through the water, she combed the banks in search of roe deer and the occasional wild boar. But the latter part of the journey, the slow trek over land from Bordeaux to Poitiers where her wedding would take place, tried her patience. For three weeks Philippa and her aunts Sibyl and Sophie bumped along the slick winter roads in a heavy four-wheeled wagon. Hampered by puddles and quagmires, their party, escorted by her brother Raymond and a score of vassals, progressed at an alarmingly slow rate.

On the twenty-fourth consecutive day of travel, Philippa complained of boredom. Sophie instructed Chaplain Berenger to open a crate of books, a gift from Philippa's indulgent father. After much deliberation, Philippa selected *The Aeneid*. Settling into a pile of fur-covered wraps stacked knee high in the wagon bed, she immersed herself in Virgil's tale.

A slim-figured young woman with green, almond-shaped eyes, lush lips and a mass of springy gold curls, Philippa loved a good story. The heroic exploits of Aeneas kept her occupied until sun set. "It's so cold," she said. "And I'm tired of riding in a wagon!"

Aunt Sibyl, a large compassionate woman who had been married and widowed so long ago that it must have seemed like a dim dream, swiveled in her seat and smiled sweetly at Philippa. "Think of the wonderful life that awaits you!" she said. "Your Duke is tall and handsome and valiant. They say William fought in Spain and proved his mettle against the Moors," Sibyl rambled breathlessly, her tongue whipping over her perpetually chapped lips while her thumbs brushed her fingertips in a mesmerizing dance of nerves. "Imagine being married to such a brave, noble man! Oh, I have heard such good things! Do you know he risked his life leading French troops in Cutanda?"

Talk of battles sparked Philippa's interest. Scooting forward in the wagon bed, she clutched *The Aeneid* in one hand and, gripping the back of her aunts' seat with the other, rose up on her knees. "How?" she asked, thrusting her head between Sibyl and Sophie. "How did William risk his life?" She recalled Virgil's Greek soldiers concealed in the hollow belly of a wooden horse and held her breath in anticipation.

"Yes, sister, why don't you tell Philippa more about her heroic knight?" said Sophie, a fleshy widow with flyaway hair knotted in a bun. A wispy gray strand of hair trailed her cheek.

"Even wounded William refused to go home, returning to the battle field and helping to retake the city," Sibyl explained.

"But how did he retake the city? What exactly did he do?" Philippa turned from one aunt to the other, her tight curls bouncing against her flushed cheeks.

Sibyl frowned, wagging her head back and forth. "Oh Philippa, you do ask the strangest questions! I know nothing of battlefields," she continued, "and there's no reason you should either. Suffice to say, you are betrothed to an heroic man of courage and strength of character." She patted Philippa's hand and smiled.

Despite her aunt's reassurance, Philippa remained anxious. How did one behave around an heroic husband? Or any husband for that matter! At twenty-three, William seemed decades older than Philippa, and her responsibilities as his wife vague and ill defined.

As if reading her mind, Sibyl abruptly shifted from battlefield to boudoir. "It is your duty as a wife to produce a male heir," she said. Speaking in an emphatic voice, Sibyl's words ticked with certainty. "Follow his lead and think of the children to follow," she instructed, blushing a most interesting raspberry.

"Lead?" Philippa asked, picturing a rider tugging on his horse's bridle.

Sibyl frowned and shook her head before launching into another story. "They say Duke William is a man of curiosity and inventiveness. Wishing to discover the best profession for a man, he disguised himself as various artisans and worked at their crafts. Imagine, first a tailor, then a cobbler . . . ."

"And what did he discover?" Philippa asked.

"That a merchant's life is best, for on every market day, he feasts at the local tavern and enjoys the good life."

"The good life?" Philippa asked, furrowing her brow.

"Good enough," Sophie said. "Until he has to pay the bill!"

"But," Philippa asked, "what's the good life?"

"Go on, sister, answer the girl's question. Tell her about the good life," Sophie said.

Sibyl frowned. For a while at least, they rode in silence. Only later, when Philippa's aunts assumed she had drifted off to sleep, did Sophie whisper *her* stories. "Fairy tales are no help."

Philippa imagined Sibyl's nervous fingers plucking at her bodice while Sophie rode stiffly with both her hands folded in her ample lap.

"The girl should at least be prepared for her wedding night," Sophie said.

Philippa held her breath and listened carefully, for despite Sophie's prickly, melancholic temperament, she was always sensible and decisive.

"Tell her how William once took up residence in a Niort whore house where he and his shameless companions christened the prostitutes with the names of holy women."

"Blasphemous! Enough, I say!"

"Is it? I think the child deserves to know that there are two sides to every man"—lifting her voice in a painfully accurate imitation of Sibyl's quivering falsetto, Sophie continued—"a bright side that shines with heroic virtue and," here she lowered her voice and spoke in her usual ominous rasp, "a dark side that is danger to women. This fine duke, so noble in battle, treats his women as he treats his horses—he rides them 'till he tames them, then he sets them to pasture, seeking new mounts."

"What is to be gained by such knowledge? Do you think our girl's life will be easier for knowing these stories? Let us pray and hope for the best."

A cold fear gripped Philippa as she sunk deeper into the wraps. Rather than dwell on the unknown, she thought of the long, lazy days before her betrothal. She forgot the tedious hours hemming napkins and arranging flowers, recalling instead the glory and warmth of sunlight streaming through stained glass windows in the Cathedral of St. Sernin, where less than a month ago, Sibyl and Sophie had escorted Philippa to mass.

Scores of clerics and nobles had attended Robert of Arbrissel's sermon. Philippa sat in the front pew between her two aunts, a veil covering her blond hair. A white-robed choir entered the nave chanting a slow rhythmic alternation of an Easter psalm. The choir split before the altar and took seats on either side of the chancel. Pope Urban, wearing his great miter and a golden samite alb, carried a gem-studded Bible to the pulpit. Two altar boys, holding candles and waving censors, followed in his wake. After placing the holy book on the lectern, the Pope blessed the congregation and announced that the day's sermon would focus on the Seven Deadly Sins. He nodded to the dark-haired, barefoot priest before taking his seat with the other prelates behind the altar.

Bracing his hands on either side of the lectern, Robert took a slow, measured breath and scanned the congregation. Perhaps Philippa only imagined that his glance lingered on her.

He spoke of the pride and anger of princes and prelates. He dwelt on the envy and avarice that led to the crime of simony, and blasted disobedient monks for their sloth and gluttony. And while the holy man's words had little to do with Philippa, the sound of his voice prompted her to contemplate her own sins. She judged herself headstrong and disobedient. Although she suspected that her father, who allowed his only daughter to be educated alongside his son, took secret pleasure in her quick mind and independence, she knew her aunts judged the same qualities not proper in a lady. As she listened to Robert's words, contrition swelled her throat. She wondered if her transgressions were evidence of a wicked nature.

Robert's sermon reached its crescendo when he approached the last of the deadly sins—that of lust. "The reward of lust is a loss of will," he said, "for when lust becomes custom, and custom necessity, we are trapped in a chain of desire that we cannot break."

Philippa, who knew nothing of lust, focused on the passion resonating from his voice and bearing. He spoke persuasively and, she could not help thinking, from experience. "Lust is a vain self-seeking, a perverted will bent on its own gratification and shunning true love, which comes from God, which is God."

Philippa leaned forward, her whole being tilting to meet his next words. His voice found a new cadence that echoed with divine conviction. "We choose whether our bodies will be vessels of lust or temples of God. We may wallow in filth and sacrifice our bodies to a prostitute, becoming one body with her, dying in spirit. Or we may keep our bodies pure, love them in God, and the Spirit of the Lord will glow within us." The Cathedral fell silent. Sunlight funneled through a clerestory window and illuminated the lectern, caressing the intricate fluting and bouncing beams of gold against the great ribbed arches. The Pope rose and nodded to the church leaders and clerics in the pews before addressing Robert.

"Robert of Arbrissel," he said, "you are a sower of God's words. I grant you the authority to preach anytime anywhere in the western provinces."

Without understanding why, Philippa felt relieved of some burden.

As she drifted off to sleep during the final night of the long journey to Poitiers, Philippa found herself hoping that her betrothed might move her as Robert had—by exciting her heart and amazing her mind.

Guiding an ass by a frayed rope, Robert led his pilgrims along the river Seine, keeping to the main roads, traveling from one town and village to another. On a damp winter afternoon, several months into their journey, the party paused for a brief rest outside of Paris. Two of his followers, a grey-haired widow and her grown daughter stood atop a rise of land thrusting up from the flooded meadow. What attracted Robert's attention was not their muddy feet or slumped shoulders but the passionate sound of the widow's voice.

"In converting prostitutes, the Master has performed a miracle!"

Robert's face flushed with pleasure and shame. Wrapping the ass's lead more firmly around his hand, he worried that pride, not piety, had occasioned his pilgrimage. Taking a deep breath, he judged himself a fool of little consequence. Yet even a fool had obligations, and as a man of the cloth, he felt compelled to speak the truth. Robert's feet made sucking sounds as he guided the ass to the widow's side. His bearing, if not his pace, projected urgency. "Believe me, I'm no saint. I'm only a man struggling to do God's work."

A light in the widow's eyes guttered out, as though his words had extinguished a flame inside of her. She grabbed the sleeve of his robes and, lifting her wind-chapped face to his, she whispered, "But you are also humble, and you are patient and kind."

Robert's blunt words had frightened her, for if he were not a miracle worker, what manner of man had she been following? While he collected his thoughts, Robert gazed at the caravan of pilgrims that stretched out beyond his line of sight. Over that first long autumn and early winter the number of converts had swelled from thirteen whores and a tomcat to three oxen, one ass, a half dozen mongrel pups, and well over a hundred pilgrims. The sight of Marie's cart at the end of the caravan settled him, even though he knew she would scoff at the widow's words.

The ass twitched its long ears and tail-flicked the damp air. Robert wrapped the animal's lead around a shrub and took the widow's hands in his. "We must rid our hearts and minds of distractions and walk the course mapped out for us with our eyes on Jesus. Tomorrow we should reach Paris." Though he had spoken the words to comfort the women, they soothed his frayed resolve as well.

The widow clasped her hands together. "Bless you, Master!" she said. "Oh, bless you!"

They spent a fortnight in Paris. Robert preached the Word in public squares and back street brothels before he and his pilgrims set out for the Loire River Valley. Among Robert's growing number of followers were a handful of young men, and some half dozen holy men—two monks from Jumièges, two lay clerics from Saint Denis, Peter, a musician from Saint Benoît sur Loire, and Moriuht, a former Viking slave. Dissatisfied with a vocation that had become fat and lazy, these religious men joined Robert's forces inspired by his promise of a truer spirituality.

The men accompanied scores of peasant women and prostitutes ranging in age from fourteen to fifty, some carrying babes or leading children by the hand. Everyone, except for the lame and the very small children, carried leather scrips slung over their shoulders. A few began the journey with precious yards of lace and silver teaspoons, but soon traded these finery with farm wives for more practical items—needles, thread, wooden bowls and medicinal herbs and spices. An Orléans seamstress contributed three bolts of pewter, gold and alabaster silk from which she fashioned cloth crosses that the young virgins sewed onto the pilgrim's robes and hats.

At night Robert sometimes found the group lodging at farmhouses or local inns, but often the pilgrims simply wrapped themselves in blankets and bedded down in an open field. Mindful of propriety, Robert settled the men on one side of the road and the women on the other while he himself moved freely from group to group—promising new life, praying aloud to God and the Virgin.

Inclement weather was their biggest challenge. Rain fell for six weeks straight. Brown slush sucked at their feet. Spelt, barley and rye molded in water-soaked burlap sacks and whole baskets of chickpeas split and sprouted before they could be boiled. The pilgrims were forced to beg for alms and forage fields for scallion and watercress.

His faith wavering, Robert worried that his vision in the Forest of Craon had been the work of his imagination, a febrile manifestation of his own desire to implement God's work and make amends for the life of sin he had lived in Paris. Plodding through dripping forests he strived to evoke the sacred power of that stormy day he had learned his destiny. But while he could recall with astonishing precision the figure and face of the beautiful woman, he could not always retrieve the passion she had awakened in him. Turning inward, he spoke less and less to those around him. On the worst days, he imagined the pilgrims all dead, victims of ravenous floods or pestilence. Robert's followers misread his silence as evidence of divine direction, and the rumors of his sainthood continued.

Just as he feared he could not go another step, one day in early spring Robert climbed a gentle slope and spotted the Loire Valley. Gnarled cabernet vines budded pale green beside densely tufted squirrel grass. Along the great expanse of scattered tributaries, rush and trailing periwinkle blossomed in profusion. A green island of hemlock bristled in a wide bend of the river, and on the other side of the valley, a line of bluffs grew woolly with vegetation.

Turning to the cluster of pilgrims, Robert announced in

a voice that lifted up and carried through the clear air, "Today we celebrate mass under clear skies. Afterwards, we rest. Then tomorrow, God willing, we'll reach Vendôme." Guiding the ass beneath the shade of a cypress, he dismounted and began dragging sack after sack from the animal's back. He placed the sack of holy implements on a patch of clover. On his knees, right arm buried deep in the burlap sack, he was searching for his silk amice when he heard someone approach.

"Master," Moriuht said, "Bernard and I have been hunting. Look what we bagged!" In one fist he clasped the ears of a hare, in the other he dangled two fat partridges by the legs. His smile revealed a scarcity of teeth, one chipped at an angle, a gift from the Vikings who had captured him in his youth and keep him in servitude for five years. His hair, which grew away from his face in great ragged snarls, was a shade or two lighter than his gold-streaked beard. "We have food. Let the women prepare a meal."

"And where did you hunt these animals?" Robert asked.

Moriuht looked down at his bare feet. "Over yonder, in that forest beyond the stream." He pointed to a lush expanse of trees covering the opposite slope of a valley.

"Is that ... open land?" Robert asked.

"Some of the trees bore noble arms." His right foot moved back and forth over new grass. "But our fare has dwindled so ..." he added.

Lean and hollow-eyed, the pilgrims looked to Robert for direction. If he were to lead them, he must tend to their physical needs as diligently as he ministered to their souls, fostering hope as freely as he dispensed blessings.

"My son, do you realize that theft is a sin?" Robert said. His compassionate tone took some of the sting out of his words.

Moriuht's shoulders slumped.

"Now my son," Robert said, placing a hand upon his shoulder, "do not despair. Each of us sins seven times a day. What is important is to recognize your sins, repent, and avoid repeating them."

"Yes, master." Moriuht said. "I shall pray for forgiveness and promise never to poach a Lord's land again!"

Robert marveled at how God could transform a mouth of rotten teeth into such a compelling smile. "What's done is done. Now give your ill-gotten gains to the women. The pilgrims need sustenance."

Moriuht hurried off to join a group sitting on a field of grass commanding a view of the valley below. He lifted the game above his head, laughing. The women rose to their feet and cheered. Immediately they began gathering peat and cow dung—fuel for a dozen fires.

Part of Robert took delight in their joy. More and more his mind felt muddled by contradiction. Theft was a sin. On the other hand, the people were hungry and deserved their share of God's plenty.

The pilgrims gathered for mass under a cloudless sky. Afterwards, Robert sat at the base of a tree and watched Marie prepare stew, adding radishes and carrots to the fresh rabbit and partridge. The sweet odor drew Robert and repelled him. He had not eaten meat for several years, nor even tasted warm food for months, since asceticism led him to eat mostly herbs and roots and drink only an occasional drop of wine.

"What is it you're thinking about with that far away look?" Marie asked. "Is this your place of light? Is this where you're taking us?"

"No, mother," he said in a soft voice. "Our journey is not over."

"I thought not," she said. As she stirred the stew, Marie looked off into the rolling landscape. Since they had left Rouen, her cough had worsened, her breathing grown shallow and labored.

"You know the story of Mary Magdalene?" Robert asked, sitting at the base of a tree.

"You mean the crazy woman who witnessed the Lord's Resurrection?"

He nodded, rolling his tense shoulders. He took strength in the scent of new growth and the solid feel of the bark against his back. "Mary Magdelene was a woman devoted to sin whom Christ saved, a great example of His love for even the lowliest of his creatures."

"I have heard she was a woman possessed." Marie brought a wooden spoon full of stew to her lips and slurped noisily before adding several pinches of salt.

"Yes, Christ expelled seven demons, and she became his follower."

"I guess the world has always been hard on whores," Marie said, shaking her head and frowning at Agnes and Arsen who were spinning great dizzy circles in a patch of clover.

Marie again brought the wooden spoon to her lips, blew away rising steam, and took another sip of the stew. This time she smiled and nodded with satisfaction.

Robert followed the twins' progress until he noticed Madeleine on a nearby knoll. She smiled at the flight of a starling before stepping into the shade of a broad-leaved oak and returning the call of a warbling turtledove. The twins' laughter rolled up from the valley floor where they stood in knee high clover, watching Robert watch Madeleine's every move.

"Beatrice, Flo," Marie called out, smoothing her serge cloak with the flat of one palm. "Tell Maddy to stop talking to those birds and the three of you come help me serve."

While the young women ran off to retrieve Madeleine, Robert went to stand beside Marie. "How are you feeling?" he asked.

"The coughing fits come and go," Marie said with a note of resignation.

"I, myself, am given to frequent fevers. So I guess we have something besides our pride in common, don't we?" Robert said.

Marie looked at him and a wry smile formed on her lips.

"Maybe we do," she said.

In Toulouse, the city of Philippa's birth, the buildings flushed strawberry at sunrise. La Rose, the residents called it. The bricks, molded from Garonne river mud, were flecked with quartz. Sunlight fondling crystal gave the buildings their astonishing color although old timers attributed it to a miracle.

Philippa was a young girl sitting on her father's knee the first time she heard the story of the miracle of Toulouse.

"An old nun seeking shelter for a band of weary pilgrims became hopelessly lost in the brambled forest of Espinasse," he began.

"What's brambled?" she asked, for Philippa never hesitated to interrupt her father. She knew that, unlike most grownups, her questions delighted him.

"Brambles are prickly shrubs, like rose bushes or raspberry canes," he explained, tousling her hair. "The nun and her followers would surely have perished had the Virgin not looked down from heaven and, seeing their plight, warmed the cool night with her rose-scented breath. Then, guiding the pilgrims to a clearing, she instructed them to build a city on the hill. For many months the pilgrims quarried and cut stone, working long hours in the warmth of the Virgin's command. Even after the task was completed, her holy presence lingered in the quartz-flecked Garonne river bricks," he said, kissing Philippa's crown. Her father's kisses felt like warm tickles, but before she could share this discovery with him, he lifted her off his lap. "Now run along my gold-haired darling," he said, "but never forget that you come from a place of miraculous beauty."

✦

The day Philippa's party arrived at Poitiers, puddles froze and fog dripped beads of moisture that clung to Philippa's curls. What struck her first, however, was not the inclement weather but the starkness of the buildings; even William's stone palace, situated on a large hill in the center of the city, lacked color. Massive crenellated towers with narrow loopholes flanked the entrance. William's coat of arms, engraved above the doorway, provided the only ornamentation. Philippa pulled her cloak tight against her shoulders and wondered what manner of man could live in such forbidding bareness.

The Duke's steward, a tall man with an officious voice, greeted the travelers and explained that William had been called by the King to engage in battle against the northmen. He led them through an arched doorway into the Great Hall. The enormous rectangular room, cluttered with tapestries depicting battle scenes and hunts, smelled of mildew and yesterday's repast. A raised dais lit by a double row of windows dominated the wall opposite the entrance.

"A most imposing size," Sophie said, lifting her head to the towering ceiling.

"Careful with that trunk!" Sibyl chastised a servant, her fingertips nervously brushing her thumbs. The hollow echo of footfalls reverberated as she hurried across the tile.

Philippa surveyed the cold expanse of her new home and her throat tightened. No vase of flowers brightened the enormous trestle table that ran the length of the platform. No bundles of dried lilac or bowls of rose petals sweetened the stale air. The thick walls reminded her of a dungeon.

And indeed, after her brother returned to Toulouse, she and her aunts spent several days sequestered in a dank chamber on the upper floor of the palace waiting for William's return.

"I shall go mad with boredom," Philippa said, rising up on

tiptoes and peering through a high window to the empty keep below.

"Let's put our idle minds to work reading biblical passages aloud. Here," Sibyl said, passing Philippa the leather-bound book. "You first."

Initially the familiar passages provided distraction. But after an hour Philippa closed the Bible, placed it on an end table and began pacing. "How much longer will he keep us waiting? I can't stand it!" she said, pausing to stomp her foot.

Sophie frowned.

"Oh, dear," Sibyl said, plucking at the cloth of her skirt, "I'm sure your Duke will arrive soon enough."

Before dawn the following morning, the sounds of shouts, clinking bridles, and slamming doors woke Philippa. The scent of cooking and the sound of loud, raucous laughter thrilled Philippa and reminded her of the time a spooked gelding had carried her wagon to the pebbled edge of a ravine. The fatigued tread of a booted man mounting the stone stairs ended Philippa's reverie. She held her breath at the sound of a key slipping into the chamber door.

"I am William," the intruder announced, in a voice burnished with power. Philippa could not see his face, just his shadowed bulk in the doorway. And while she felt certain that the words were directed at her, they seemed to exclude her as well. The Philippa Lord William addressed was the daughter of a wealthy man. The one who listened was the secret climber of elm trees, the one with the courage to scale wobbly ladders and straddle fences. *That* Philippa could coax a laugh from gruff Uncle Bernard, knock almonds from the highest branches, sew French seams and flatter chrysanthemums into blooming long past their season.

"Gold hair," he mumbled. "Your father said you had gold hair."

Sibyl and Sophie buried their faces in blankets. Their gray hair, lit by the glow of a full moon, fanned against their pillows.

Slowly Sophie slid both arms beneath her coverlet, a silent stealth that frightened Philippa more than William's presence.

His heavy boots scraping the floorboards, his scabbard dragging, he approached her bed.

"Gold!" he said, winding a strand of her hair around his finger.

A bolt of fear surged through Philippa's body. Her breath puffed white in the icy room.

Without another word, William removed his poppy-colored cloak, and climbed on top of her.

Philippa wrapped her hands around William's biceps. "Stop!" she said, dragging her nails the length of his forearms.

With drunken urgency, he gathered a fist full of Philippa's gown and yanked it up over her knees, belly, and breasts until the gown noosed her neck like a tourniquet. Hands shaking, Philippa reached up and pulled the gown over her head.

His hard body—wooled over and muscled hard as a bull's flank—bore down on hers with dumb animal insistence, prodding her insides and tearing her open. Her womb clinched like a fist and her stomach surged. Light splintered and exploded into pain that settled behind her eyes. She felt a brief flutter of William's heartbeat before he gasped and rolled off of her.

The musky smell of the barn filled the air. Standing beside the bed, William used a corner of the sheet to wipe a smear of her blood from his sex. And then, turning his head, he seemed to notice for the first time the scratches on his arms.

"She devil!" he mumbled. "Golden-haired she devil!" Swabbing at his scratches with the soiled sheet, he mingled his blood with hers.

Before he tugged up his breeches, Philippa studied his privates hanging soft between his thighs, the blond tuft of public hair that climbed and thinned below his navel. Wanting to see and not wanting to see, she looked until she realized that her curiosity delighted him. His smile turned into a smirk, and quite suddenly she was aware of her own nakedness. Blushing, she covered herself as best she could.

"Now we're married," he said, and made to leave the room. At the door he hesitated. Palm flattened against jamb, he turned and walked back to her bedside. Time slowed as William lifted Philippa's wrist to his mouth. Even as she struggled to pull free, she felt her pulse flutter.

William shrugged off his tunic, unbuttoned his pants and took her again, slowly. His hands brushed her thighs and glided the length of her torso. His breath glossed her lips when he called out her name. Afterwards, he kissed her, dressed and left the room.

Philippa huddled in silence, not wanting to wake the others (although surely they only pretended to sleep!). Sophie turned in her cot and sighed, as though relieved to have it over and done with. William's smell—smoke-spattered and musk scented—lingered in the room. In the place where he had been Philppa felt cold sticky dampness. Clamping her thighs together, she willed herself to remember Toulouse—sunlight fondling quartz, the rose-scented breath of the Virgin.

W rapped in a wool blanket, Madeleine lay curled on the warm edge of sleep.

"Madeleine," Robert said in a hushed voice that reminded her of Bodkin's raspy purr. "Wake up, Madeleine. I need your help preparing simples."

During the long fall and winter of their pilgrimage, Robert had often singled her out, spoke, without pride, of the years of penance he had undergone: the fasting, the vigils, the wearing of hair shirts. All this he revealed in whispers, as though forcing words through the grate of a confession. Therefore, although she did not understand his special trust in her, Madeleine felt no surprise when one cool spring day Robert woke her before dawn and asked for her assistance.

"Simples?" Madeleine asked, rising up on one elbow.

"Come," he said, "I'll show you." He carried a folded blanket and leather satchel.

Shivering in the morning chill, Madeleine braided her hair as they wove their silent way between sleeping pilgrims. The doves cooed their morning greetings as the edge of the sky turned from hyacinth to rose. Once the others woke and lit the turf fires, smoke and ash would foul the air, but for now a clean breeze blew fragrant with the honeyed scent of jasmine.

Robert spread the blanket beneath an ash tree near the three sleeping oxen. "Please sit," he said, dropping to his knees beside her. "My father learned the properties of herbs and passed on this knowledge to me. Herbal remedies are called simples because each herb possesses its own particular virtue and the brewing of each produces a simple remedy for a specific ailment." As he spoke Robert removed a half dozen linen pouches from his satchels and sprinkled medicinal herbs onto the blanket. His fingers fanned and caressed the drying leaves. The flickering rim of his nimbus reached out and tangled with hers. The tug and pull of their separate colors produced an aching tension in Madeleine and her heart beat far too rapidly for a mere discussion of herbs.

"Nettle strengthens the blood and violet fortifies the lungs," he whispered or seemed to whisper. His dark hair looked glossy as a blackbird's feathers in the light of dawn. "These green fennel seeds are fine for treating coughs, and this one, chervil, stops bleeding. These two, worm wood and absinthe, diminish fevers." He fingered the appropriate bundles as he spoke. A breeze rustled leaves and carried the tangy, but not unpleasant, odor of cattle and manure.

"Robert," Madeleine said, "how much longer?"

"Not much," he said. "We are very near Vendôme." Then, look-ing into her eyes he assumed a humble tone. "Please Madeleine, you must have faith."

Madeleine heard the fear and doubt beneath the humility and wondered why a holy man would seek reassurance from her.

"Please," he whispered.

Madeleine dropped her eyes before answering. "Of course, Master," she said.

That day the pilgrims walked five grueling miles before pausing for a rest. Madeleine lowered herself onto a patch of grass and was admiring the beauty of a passing cloud when the twins joined her. The vertical bar of Arson's silk cross had separated from her robe, and now it curled like a beckoning finger. She touched the frayed edge absentmindedly and mumbled to her sister in a voice just loud enough for Madeleine to hear, "Why did we follow this mad man? We've been walking forever in this god forsaken forest and there's no end in sight."

Arsen's indirect accusation was clear enough. Had Madeleine not persuaded Marie to join Robert's pilgrimage, the twins would not be wandering the countryside hungry and tired.

The twins removed their sandals, wriggled their toes and asked Madeleine to rub their feet. "Please, Madeleine," they begged. "Just this once?"

Madeleine sighed. Rising to her knees, she dug her thumbs into the arches of their calloused feet, first Agnes and then Arsen. Nearby a Jumièges pup with brindled fur and a freckled belly worried a hickory stick. Tossing it into the air, the mongrel jostled Madeleine's elbow with his body and together they toppled into the ankle-high spring grass. The three women laughed for the first time in months.

Agnes winced but did not complain when Madeleine resumed working her feet. Madeleine hardly noticed, so intent was she on contemplating her good luck. The freedom to ponder a sky marbled with turquoise, ruby and apricot clouds filled her with joy.

"We're nothing but bones," Arsen said, stroking her lean ribs.

"And our hair has grown dry as straw," Agnes said. Before they left Rouen, one of their regular customers had given the twins a set of ivory combs carved in the shape of fanned peacock tails. Now Agnes adjusted one of these combs in her hair, studying Arsen as though assessing her own reflection. Arsen pushed Madeleine's hands away with an exasperated sigh. "We're ugly and I'm hot, hot, hot!" she said, pulling her robe over her head and wriggling free of the heavy serge. She leaned back on her bent elbows. Her linen gown pulled tight against her unbound breasts and raised her nipples. "For sure we were fools to follow this crazy barefoot wanderer!"

Madeleine watched Arsen straighten her girdle and recalled Robert's fingers fanning simples. "We will soon reach our destination," she said. "The Master is an honest and admirable man."

"Is it admirable that he so often seeks your company?" Arsen asked. She tilted her head and assumed the guileless gaze of a child.

"Robert is mindful of all of his followers," she said, thinking the twins jealous. "He seeks out the two of you on occasion and many others as well."

The twins met Madeleine's response with blank stares. "We're tired," Agnes said, and together the sisters laid back into the grass. Turning onto their left sides, Agnes coiled into the scoop of Arsen's embrace and the two drifted off to sleep while Madeleine went in search of Robert's company, the mongrel pup cavorting at her heels.

She found Robert addressing the lepers, who, despite their disease, proved resilient during the journey. Some suffered horribly from their affliction, their faces swollen red and ravaged by blisters, their eyes lidless and fixed, while others seemed almost normal, only a few blemishes hinting at disease. Settling on the edge of the group, she studied Robert's composure and felt a pleasant heave of relief, for she could not detect the uncertainty he had revealed to her earlier that morning.

The puppy zigzagged between the lepers before rolling onto his back and offering his belly to their outstretched hands.

Madeleine, who often felt the need to keep her own hands busy in Robert's presence, turned to the daisy shrub on her right. She plucked one yellow flower after another until a heap of flowers filled her lap. Using her thumbnail, she opened a buttonhole in each stem, threading one through the next until she had formed a chain. Linking beginning to end, she closed the circle. She was dropping the necklace over her head when Marie entered the group.

Robert nodded to Marie and continued his sermon. "'Now,' the Lord said, 'I have come down to bring my people to a land flowing with milk and honey.'"

"Do you liken yourself to Moses, Master Robert?" Marie asked, leaning into her cane and moving nearer Robert with difficulty. "Has God spoken to you from a burning bush? Has he turned your staff into a snake?" she demanded.

"Mother Marie," Robert said, "I would never compare myself to Moses."

"Yet you imply that you are leading us to a land of milk and honey. Bah! Better a little mutton and a carafe of wine! Better a fat partridge and a draft of ale!" Her hair had thinned during the journey, a shine of pink scalp visible at the center part. "We are hungry, Master Robert. What," she bellowed, "do you intend to do about it?"

"We will find assistance in Vendôme," Robert said. "Have faith a bit longer, Mother Marie."

Shaking her head, she reached into her bodice and retrieved the sack of coins she had carried with her from Rouen. "Faith will not feed my belly," she said. "Consider this my oblation." Tossing the sack at Robert's feet, she turned and made her way back to the wagons.

Madeleine rose and retrieved the coins. "If the Lord provides herbs to ease our afflictions, might he not also provide money to sate our hunger?" she asked, placing the sack in Robert's hands.

rother Girard entered the oratory pew, dropped to the kneeler with a heavy thud and began whispering his rosary, enjoying the sensuous slide of wooden beads between the strong fingers of his right hand. But instead of focusing on the Holy Mother, Girard contemplated the taste of beef simmering in a peppery broth of summer leeks and cabbage.

Brother Rainald's footfalls interrupted Girard's reflections and he returned to prayer most fervently. As he did every day he prayed that today would be the day he was released from his incessant thoughts of food. Even when his belly sagged and obscured his sex, even then, he could not stop eating. Not when his heavy thighs blistered with rash, not when his joints ached with contrition.

"I accuse myself of gluttony," he said so loudly that shy and timid Brother Rainald, stumbled in his genuflection. Girard buried his face in his hands, but not before coveting Rainald's lean visage and adding envy to his sins.

"My Brother," Rainald whispered, lightly touching Girard's shoulder. "Pilgrims are approaching the monastery. Abbot Geoffrey asked that we finish our prayers and then greet them."

Girard nodded. "Hail Mary, full of grace … " he recited. And though he tried to join the Holy Mother in her infinite devotion, he could not. Between the polished words of the prayer slipped a memory of his own mother trilling her fingers through a basket of dried lentils as she prepared his father's funeral banquet.

On the day of the funeral, the family had slaughtered a goat and four chickens before Girard's brother added a gray partridge to the fare. "Here," Bernard said, returning from his early morning hunt. "Ma wants you to pluck this. And be quick about it." His eyes, hooded in grief, hardened into arrogance at the sight of Girard.

Sixteen-year-old-Girard did not need Bernard's contempt to remind him of his inferior position in the family. Because of his defect—a flaccid left arm that stopped six inches short of his right—Girard could not hunt. Instead, he tended the family garden and combed the nearby meadow scavenging for asparagus and watercress. His mother had promised Girard that her eldest brother would secure a place for him at the Benedictine seminary, and so Girard tolerated his role as kitchen helpmate until Bernard, two years younger than he and not nearly as bright, learned to hunt. Bernard roamed the countryside with such freedom that Girard grew jealous. And though he tried to deny his feelings, they played out in brooding silence and unexplained rashes made worse by his father's disregard.

Bernard Senior valued physical stamina and valor, not intellect. A practical man who thrived in the here and now, he gave barely a thought to the uncertainty of some ethereal afterlife. And while Girard found the words of the Bible lyrical and compelling, his father judged all spiritual matters womanish, distracting, and entirely too complicated. Girard's mother strived to make up for her husband's distance with a fawning concern Girard found claustrophobic and self-serving. "My poor baby," she whispered, tucking him in at night. "My poor, poor little boy."

Shortly before his birth, she had come across a rabbit snared in a bear trap, its left foreleg mangled between the wooden teeth and the trigger pan. Convinced that the sight had upset the careful balance of sanguine and melancholic humors in her womb, she blamed herself for her son's deformity. Oddly, and to Girard's dismay, her guilt often took the form of impatience. "Go get me some fennel from the garden, and be quick about it," she had demand. Girard complied not because he was humble but because he was ambitious. He knew that if he performed the duties of a devoted son his mother would keep her promise and send him to study at seminary.

"Are you listening?" Bernard asked, giving his brother a kick. At fourteen Bernard stood six feet tall and possessed the proud bearing of a man. After throwing the partridge at his brother's kneeling form, Bernard headed for the house in long, sure-footed strides.

Girard glared at Bernard, his lips caught between a smile and a grimace, as he mumbled Christ's words to John. *If the world hates you, you know that it hated me first.* Picking up the game, he walked to the barn.

Seated on a bag of grain, he positioned the partridge between his knees and fingered the throat feathers. "My poor little bird," he said. Following the shaft of a gray capular feather, his fingers found the buried tip of the quill and tugged. "My poor, poor little bird."

That evening at the funeral feast Girard ate until his stomach bloated and stretched tight as a wine bladder, gorging himself on tare-flavored bouillon, roasted game marinated in wine and marjoram, chicken boiled in an aromatic broth of sage, mushroom fried in olive oil and garlic, brain flavored with vinegar, pepper, ginger, and parsley, and finally, for dessert, pears saturated in wine sauce spiced with cinnamon and cloves and topped with soft cheese. He washed his meal down with a carafe of burgundy and barely made it to the garden before his stomach erupted and nothing remained but black bile. Returning to the banquet, he refilled his platter again and yet again.

The following week he left for seminary.

Five years later, Brother Girard stepped through the south door of the transept of Trinity church and watched a flock of pilgrims ascend a hill and make their way towards Vendôme. A single file of pilgrims—a hundred people at least!—beaded through the horizontal spread of a cypress grove. The stunning display of silk crosses patched onto the shoulders of their cloaks took Girard's breath away. With Brother Rainald at his side, Girard stepped into the shade of a maple where he watched a slumped figure astride a mule take the rise of a knoll.

"More souls come to venerate the Holy Tear," Rainald said, ignoring altogether the splendor and enormity of the group.

"I hope there are no lepers among them," Girard said, rubbing his tonsured skull, and contemplating his old fear. The young Girard and his mother had once stumbled across an encampment of lepers in a forested area just outside their village. His mother grabbed his hand and led him quickly away, but not before he smelled their rotting flesh and saw their blistered lesions. His mother crossed herself and muttered, "What could be worse than dying by degrees?" Girard felt her shudder to the tips of his toes.

"But brother," Rainald said, calling Girard back to the present. "We are all children of God! If you show partiality, then you are practicing sin." He crossed himself and looked hopefully at his brother.

Girard heard the shrill, high-pitched scream of a swift and lifted his head to the sound. "Yes, only some children are deformed by disease or providence," Girard said, watching the sooty blur of the swift's flickering ascent, "and some are not." Lowering his head, he looked into Rainald's startled eyes.

"Surely one may enter the kingdom of God by the way of many afflictions," Rainald said. He fingered the rosary belted to his waist, his lips moving in silent prayer.

Girard sighed. Only his brother's innocence spared him the awful knowledge that the human soul was a flawed and fragile thing. "Forgive me," Girard said. "Of course, you are right. You should love your neighbor as yourself."

"It is not for me to forgive," Rainald said, even as his face lit with gratitude.

Girard wondered if Rainald's cloying devotion was yet another test of his faith. Girard found the Lenten season particularly trying. At nones, the brothers received a meager ration of vegetables, black bread and Cabernet, a meal that merely whetted Girard's appetite. Rainald, on the other hand, picked at his portion before lowering his head in prayer. The man's self control sparked in

Girard a voracious cruelty that, much like his craving for food, seemed never to be sated.

Not that he did not strive to follow the Lord's commandments. More than anything, he longed for absolution and redemption. Eight weeks running he had asked, in the name of the healing virtues to better serve his holy community by assuming Brother André's kitchen duties. With the best of intentions he carried out his penance, a labor made awkward by his withered arm. A wooden platter carefully balanced on the fingers of his good right hand, he walked the narrow hall that joined the refectory to the kitchen and felt a slow simmering of faith.

And perhaps Girard would have found salvation in the sudsy water and kitchen grease if Brother Jerome had acknowledged his tentative smile. Later, it occurred to him that Jerome, a popular and passionate disciple with an imposing muscular profile, had simply not seen him in the dimly lit passageway. But his realization came too late.

The day of Jerome's real or imagined slight, Girard hurried to the kitchen, replaying over and over in his mind the cruelty of Jerome's insult. With an urgency that recalled his father's funeral feast, he gorged on the discards of his brethren—dark crusty hunks of barley bread and bowls of vegetable soup. His face smeared with cabbage and squash seed, Girard prayed to the Almighty— *Forgive us our sins ... And bring us not into temptation.* He wept for his innumerable weaknesses of body and spirit, but still he could not stop until he had eaten every morsel of food on every plate, scraped the cooking pots, licked the great spoons, and even picked through the kitchen refuse.

So while the other brothers grew gaunt in their Lenten abstinence, Girard grew more obese. Suffering from heartburn and nausea, he spent his nights in fitful erratic sleep.

"Here they are," Rainald said to Girard before mumbling to himself, "I must remind them to take no relics with them."

Watching the pilgrims sit down beneath the cypress, Girard was both hungry and tired. But then the cowled figure dismounted his mule and spoke—"I am Robert of Arbrissel. These pilgrims have nothing to eat"—and Girard was quite suddenly neither. The stranger's voice, the first sound of his life that made complete sense, filled him joy.

Girard stepped from the shade of the maple into the afternoon sun and did not notice the difference. Looking into the eyes of the haggard pilgrim, Girard's withered arm seemed to grow and flex.

"The Lord be with you, Father," Girard whispered. At seminary he had adopted a commanding, some would say arrogant, manner of speaking. Pausing dramatically between words, he had crafted an emphatic delivery. But this time, his tone was gentle and unassuming.

An alarmed Rainald rested his hand on his brother's shoulder. Girard shrugged off his touch.

"And with you, my brother," Robert said.

Rainald opened his mouth to welcome the guest, but Girard cut him off. How many times had he listened to his brother recite the history of Trinity of Vendôme with the same annoying exhilaration?

"Welcome to the Holy Trinity, Father," Girard said. "I am Brother Girard and this is Brother Rainald. Please come in out of the sun, and I'll share our history with you."

After Robert guided his mule into the shade, Girard cleared his throat and repeated Rainald's lecture word for word. "In the year 1044, Geoffrey Martel, Count of Anjou, founded the church and abbey to house a sacred relic he had brought back from the Holy Land—the Holy Tear Christ shed at Lazarus's tomb." Girard felt his brother's body tense, but he did not stop, for he desired all of Robert's attention. In Robert's presence, Girard felt a flood of love and respect that knew no bounds. "Would you like to worship and sing praise for the Tear?" Girard asked.

A young woman stepped forward. Freckled and lean with reddish-blonde hair and sun-parched lips, she looked directly into Girard's eyes. Girard had little experience with women, but those he had known while growing up had all deferred to men, particularly clergy. This one's behavior startled and intrigued him.

"I am Madeleine. This man is ill with quartan fever," she said, lifting an impossibly small hand in Robert's direction. Girard noted the birthmark spreading her neck like a swallow of sweet rosé and felt inexplicably drawn to her. He fingered his cincture, the belted cord symbolizing his vow of chastity, and prayed for strength and guidance. Looking into her exhausted eyes, he discovered sorrow and a hesitancy of spirit that mirrored his own.

"Please," the woman said, "can you help him?"

Girard thought that if he could remain forever in this place with this godly man and this sorrowful woman he would be happy. If he were never again to rise at four, never to kneel on pained knees, never to lie awake in his narrow pallet shaken by dreams of gluttony and lust, he would be happy.

"We have an infirmary," Rainald said. "I could take Father there myself."

Girard glared. "I will handle this, Brother Rainald."

"But ... "

"All in good time, my sons," the man said in a voice that lifted words beyond their meaning. "First, I must see the Abbot."

Girard saw beyond the enormous power of his presence to his yellow-tinged skin and sunken cheeks.

"Father ... " Rainald began, but before he could complete his thought, Girard pointed to the pilgrims clustered in the shade of the cypress trees. "How many are there?" he asked.

"A hundred. Maybe more," Robert said.

"Brother Girard wondered if there might be lepers among you?" Rainald asked in a sweetly insinuating voice.

If Robert heard, he gave no indication. Pale and fatigued, he seemed lost in prayer. "Rainald," Girard said, in a commanding tone. "Move the pilgrims to the cloisters."

P hilippa slouched in a brocade armchair before the fire. Brow furrowed, she took a sip of tea before issuing a long sigh.

"You can't expect a husband to be a father, a brother, or a friend," Aunt Sophie cautioned, as though reading Philippa's mind.

"I don't!" she lied.

Philippa could tell by her aunt's pursed lips that she knew otherwise. "I'll leave you to conduct your affairs."

Alone in her chambers, Philippa pondered the mystery of her husband. Accustomed to her brother's verbosity and her father's affable good will, she could not make sense of William's reticence. She wondered if his phlegmatic temperament might be a deliberate composure assumed in response to the dictates of battle. Or perhaps his silence was the secretive behavior of a man with something to hide. Occasionally William tilted his head or wrinkled his brow while she spoke, but whether her conversation annoyed or engaged him, she could not tell, and pride prevented her from asking. Her marriage, after all, had but two purposes—to produce heirs for the house of Aquitaine and to consolidate William's control over her native land, Toulouse. Whether or not William found her entertaining was, she understood, entirely irrelevant.

William did talk, however, in the privacy of their bed, a four-posted canopy draped with ruby-colored damask curtains. One evening, flat on his back, his fingers laced behind his head, he spoke eloquently of his heroism against warring rival barons. "My men and I invaded Parthany and conquered the fortress of Germond," he explained to Philippa who sat cross-legged on the bed beside him.

Philippa, who had heard tales of innocent young girls forced into marriages with ugly old men and tyrants, felt lucky to have married a young, handsome man. "How many men?" she asked. "Did all of them survive?"

William's face hardened into a mask. "The details are . . . un-important. The point is we won." He snuffed the candle, pulled the covers up under his chin, and turned onto his side. "I have some business to attend to in the morning," he said, leaving her to toss and turn in the dark.

This was what Sophie meant—that what a father tells a much loved and cherished only daughter differs greatly from what the same man tells his wife.

But the following night, William surprised Philippa by asking questions about her family. "What was your mother like?" he said.

Philippa responded in a tentative whisper, as though the most ordinary utterances were secrets too frail to be shared. William's breathing slowed until it matched her own. "I was so young when my mother died that I hardly remember her." Then, because she had not completely forgiven him for hurting her feelings the previous evening, she added, "But I adore my father, for he is a godly, modest man."

William lifted an eyebrow. Philippa blushed, turning her head away and fiddling with the bed curtain. William intrigued her. Behind his bluster lurked a man sharp enough to detect criticism caged as compliment.

"My brother, on the other hand, is a trickster and a clown," Philippa said, maneuvering conversation to safer ground. "Once he put a whole bottle of caterpillars into the cot of our bossy nursemaid."

The sound of William's laughter opened her heart and she saw her husband's crowing in a different light, a way to feel less awkward in a woman's delicate world of tapestry and lace. When he touched her thigh, she closed her eyes and listened with her skin, judging William's meaning by the pressure of his hand. Positioning his body above hers, the weight of him poised on palms and bended knees, he whispered, "At the siege of Cutanda I gave the order to mine the towers."

His breath warmed her forehead, reminding her of bright afternoons spent drowsy in clover, the iridescent play of color behind closed eyelids, the taste of berries and the scent of jasmine and honeysuckle.

"My men and I dug beneath them," William said, "stuffed timber and wood into the hollowed out holes, and lit them. Poof! The first tower went up in a ball of fire."

He parted her lips with his tongue, slipped his knees between her thighs and nudged open her legs. Arching her back, she pressed her body the length of his.

"I was the first to breach the opening," he whispered. "I rode my courser directly into the armed Saracens ... "

The sound he made entering her reached for and tangled with her own.

Afterwards, while she lay sprawled on her back, he propped himself up on one elbow and brought his face so near to hers she felt the brush of his long russet lashes against her cheek. Falling back onto the bed, he draped her hair (*the gold*, he called it) across his face and sang a love song that would have sounded ridiculous in daylight but which resonated with sincerity inside their draped sanctuary. "Our kingdom of the curtains," he called it.

During the day Philippa continued to endure protracted official ceremonies—the confirmation of the rights of Montierneuf, where William's father was buried, the restoration of mills to the monks of Noaillé. But at night, she lost herself in William's touch, the yeasty taste and musky scent of him. Because Philippa's aunts had told her that women took no joy in sex, that the act of procreation was messy, necessary and otherwise unmentionable, she thought the fierce surge of desire she felt as William entered her, the fluttery sensation that started in her middle and pulsed to the tips of her fingers and toes, must be unique to their coupling, that the singular and special joy that together their bodies created belonged to them alone.

⊰⊱

"Welcome to the Holy Trinity of Vendôme," fat Brother Girard said, his halo clenching into a fist of light.

Madeleine studied Girard and wondered, not for the first time, if the colors she saw might be something other than haloes.

"Please come in out of the sun, and I'll share our history with you," he said.

Madeleine only half-listened to his memorized speech involving a Count and a sacred relic. When Robert refused treatment at the infirmary, Madeleine frowned but remained silent, for she understood that a woman must not contradict a man and a holy one at that.

After Girard left to notify the Abbot of Robert's arrival, Rainald escorted the pilgrims to an enormous garden where purple endive thrived along side sprays of carrots and parsnip, and an arched lattice bowed beneath the weight of flowering sweet pea vines. Madeleine stood beside Marie who waited until all of her girls had their fill of water from the well before taking a drink of her own. Afterwards Marie lay down under the shadowy spread of an olive tree and immediately fell into a deep sleep.

Madeleine lowered herself onto a nearby patch of chamomile. The little daisy flowers emitted a sweet creamy scent. A few stubborn clouds spotted the sky. Robert refused Rainald's offer of wine and bread, but the rest accepted with gratitude. Perhaps a half hour passed before Girard returned. "Come this way, father," he said to Robert. "I will take you to Abbot Geoffrey."

Robert's step faltered and Madeleine rose up from the chamomile and took his arm. Girard studied the exchange with a scowl. The twins ceased their incessant whispering, reached for each other's hands and stood as if to follow. Their tilted heads and tensed bodies reminded Madeleine of animals, all instinct and curiosity.

"Watch over Marie," Robert said to the twins, gesturing to where she slept. "Madeleine, please come with me." The two of them followed Girard to a large door framed in stone blocks.

Girard glanced back and forth between Robert and Madeleine. "Abbot Geoffrey prohibits women from entering the sanctuary." He took a great gulp of air and then exhaled as though relieved of an obligation. Madeleine discerned arrogance in the thrust of his chin and a keen desire to be loved in the slump of his shoulders and determined that the fat monk was both complicated and dangerous.

Robert frowned. "Brother," he said, having regained his composure and calm, "does God deny His grace to women?"

Girard ran his hand over the skin of his tonsure. "Abbot Geoffrey will be angry if he learns his orders have been disobeyed. He will think I've been derelict..." His voice wobbled to a stop.

Robert placed his hand on the monk's shoulder. "Don't worry, Brother Girard," he said. "You need not fear the abbot. We are old friends, and I will make it clear to him that you dutifully warned me."

Girard's nodded in gratitude. Glancing once again at Madeleine, he held open the church door, "You may enter," he said.

Madeleine held her breath in awe at the expansive beauty of the sanctuary. The rising of the columns was like a lifting of the soul, the bright clerestory windows and the arched ceiling like the bright ache of a gorgeous day. A calm washed over her.

Girard led them to the other side of the transept then down a dimly lit passageway to a dark alcove smelling of beeswax, incense and damp stone.

"Please, be seated," Girard said, gesturing toward a bench lining the wall. His halo—surely the most changeable Madeleine had ever seen—whittled color into an olive green cord.

Girard disappeared through a door. Robert fell onto the bench with a sigh of relief, and Madeleine sat beside him. As always his closeness confused her and sent a rush of heat through her body. By way of distraction, she studied the room. A small lattice window let in feeble light, and as her sight adjusted, burnished cabinets and dark stained walls emerged from the shadows. It was so quiet she could hear Robert's breathing, the thrum of her own heartbeat, and then muffled voices coming from the rectory.

The door opened and Girard's tonsured head appeared bright and round in the dusky light. Madeleine glimpsed shame in his nimbus, a purple black that bled through the other hues like a bruise. "The abbot will see you now," he said, holding open the door with his right shoulder. He kept his withered left arm hidden in his robe. They entered the rectory, a large room with filigree windows nearly stretching to a high ceiling, paneled in dark rosewood. The room was dim in the twilight and smelled musty from books scattered atop cabinets and benches.

"Master Robert, welcome to Vendôme. It has been a long time, my dear friend."

Abbot Geoffrey, a thin, older man with scant gray hair surrounding his tonsure, embraced Robert. Madeleine knew that during the time the two men had attended lectures together at Angiers, Geoffrey had been a vigorous man in his middle years. But clearly the prelate had aged. His eyes milky and his gait arthritic, he moved slowly and painfully.

"But Robert, you are not well," he said. "We must take you to our infirmary right away." He glanced at Girard, as though he would immediately act on his orders.

"It's only a bout of quartan fever, my dear Geoffrey," Robert replied, his cheeks glistening with sweat in the reflected light. "It will be gone tomorrow."

Geoffrey's furrowed brow suggested concern. But when he glimpsed Madeleine in the dark recesses of the room, he stiffened with anger.

"Robert," he said, "hasn't Brother Girard informed you that

we do not allow women in the monastery?"

"Yes, he has," Robert said.

"Surely I don't need to explain the reason for the rule. You, as much as any man, understand the danger women pose."

Madeleine stepped back into the shadowed corner. A simmering anger welled up inside of her. Robert's halo swelled and bumped Madeleine's colors. Remembering her position, she turned her anger into a sneeze and focused her attention on a vase of iris.

"My lord Geoffrey," Robert said. Madeleine recognized the gravely sound of restraint in his voice and wondered if Geoffrey heard it as well. "Surely women are God's creatures too, worthy of salvation. If we prohibit them from entering God's house, where shall they implore him for his grace?"

"There are other churches they can enter, Master Robert," Geoffrey said. "This is a monastery, open only to men." His clipped words came to an abrupt halt. The muscles beneath his flushed face tightened.

"Brother Geoffrey," Robert said, "I have not come here to argue, but to seek your help. I have led these hundred pilgrims, sinners who have converted to God, for many months. We are homeless, hungry and exhausted. I ask only for temporary respite, a safe haven until we can move on and find a permanent place we can call home."

With a sigh, Geoffrey's gruff voice turned soft. "Sit down, Robert," he said, motioning to Girard, who moved a heavy chair before the trestle table. Geoffrey took a seat across from him, his back to the windows, his dark form framed in light. On the table before him there were writing utensils, a wax tablet and stylus.

Girard removed books from a chair to create a space for Madeleine to sit. Back turned to the others, his eyes crawled her breasts with the languid creep of a drowsy fly. She tried to hide her aversion, for she knew that some men were excited by a women's disgust. Girard nodded that Madeleine should sit. His good hand grasped the back of the chair as though he hoped to brush against her back or shoulder, and his halo sparked lusty red. But when he stepped away from the chair without making any attempt to touch her, Madeleine wondered if she had, perhaps, misjudged him, for anger sometimes clouded her vision and interfered with her ability to read others.

"Very well, Robert, I will help you," Geoffrey said, as he leaned back in his chair, bringing his hands together so his fingertips touched. "But I would feel remiss if I did not warn you about the dangers you place yourself in by this proximity with women." He glanced in Madeleine's direction. She pretended not to see his gaze and ran her fingers across the surface of a leather-bound tome. "Only a fool places tow next to fire."

"There are many ways to follow our Savior," Robert replied. "I dedicate my life to saving the less fortunate, even if that means approaching fire."

Madeleine took a deep breath and studied the stone floor. She tried to leave her body behind and enter Robert's promise, that place of comfort where every woman's needs would be met by the brothers who served them, but she succeeded only in conjuring up the scent of lilacs before the sound of the abbot's voice split the seams of her fancy wide open.

"Women are the root of all evil, Robert," Geoffrey said darkly.

"And women are God's vessels, the brides of Christ."

"Just be careful, Robert. The higher you climb a mountain, the greater the fall should you slip." Brother Girard carried a candle to the table, walking slowly so its flickering flame would not extinguish, and placed it next to Geoffrey. The candle's light cast a circle on the gleaming black surface, making the room seem even darker.

"While I do not approve of your scandalous familiarity with women, my concern for your health is great. I will allow your followers to occupy the cloisters, which lie outside the monastery. You will be exposed to the elements, but we can provide food and provisions for you."

"Thank you, Brother Geoffrey. You are merciful and blessed."

"But mind you," he quickly added, "the arrangement must be

temporary. You will have to find a permanent place elsewhere for your congregation."

"Yes, I am aware of that," Robert said.

Madeleine knew from the settled sound of Robert's voice and the compassionate glow of his halo that he was remembering his vision.

The Abbot pulled himself up in his chair and touched his tonsure with a soft, well-manicured hand. "I believe I can be of some help in securing monies for your venture. I am second cousin to the Duchess of Aquitaine, whose father recently died. She is a pious woman who has in the past contributed generous funds to the reform of prostitutes by supporting Magdalene houses." He directed a smoldering look at Madeleine before continuing. "Lady Philippa might be interested in assisting your congregation. I will compose a missive asking her if she would be willing to donate land to you and your followers, perhaps a gift in her father's name. You may hand deliver it to her yourself, for your words are far more persuasive than any I could pen."

"I thank you in advance for your assistance, Geoffrey," Robert said. "I knew you would help me realize my dream."

Geoffrey looked over at Girard, who was tending the fireplace. "Brother Girard," he said, "bring Robert to our infirmary, and tell Rainald to let the pilgrims enter the cloister."

"No," Robert said, raising his hand. "I will stay with my people."

"Very well," the Abbot said.

Madeleine took one final glance at Geoffrey. He was carving figures into the wax tablet before him on the table, perhaps already composing his letter to the Duchess of Aquitaine. "Brother Girard," he said without looking up from his work. "Take Robert and his pilgrims to the cloister."

A short while later the women passed though the great portals of Trinity. Madeleine watched how, hungry and tired, they composed themselves with quiet dignity and stood tall beside the men.

Philippa's first pregnancy ended in miscarriage—a painful, bloody affair that left her weak and sorrowful. Mere weeks later, she conceived a second time. This time she felt vigorous, healthy, and full of a new and tingly knowledge. Every morning before she rose from bed, William's mother, Mathilde, brought her a vegetable broth infused with fortifying herbs.

Mathilde, whose own childbirths had involved an impatient barber surgeon who induced her to labor with whips, insisted that William retain Wallada, a lean, copper-skinned Spanish Moor with a head of woolly black hair and long muscular fingers, to assist with the birth. William hesitated until Mathilde quoted from the Bible. "The book of Exodus clearly states 'God dealt well with the midwives: and the people multiplied, and waxed very mighty.'" Wallada examined Philippa and pronounced her fit. A delighted William postponed his trip south to stay by her side.

Sibyl and Sophie, who returned to Poitiers to attend the birth, warned Philippa that William's attentiveness was transitory.

"Men have fun putting their babies in," Sophie said, pointing to Philippa's expanding middle, "but few want anything to do with getting them out." A wisp of flyaway hair eclipsed Sophie's right eye.

Sibyl shook her head and pursed her lips. "If men grow timid when their wives' time arrives," she said, "it's because they are frightened by the pain of labor and helpless in the face of it."

"William has fought great battles. He is not likely to cower at the birth of a babe," Philippa said.

Sibyl rocked slightly in her chair. "Phillipa, sweetheart, William is, indeed, a brave man. But childbirth is beyond his experience. Because men are accustomed to being in control, they fear loss of power." Her fingers plucked at her smock and she smiled a small conciliatory smile.

"You are wrong," Philippa said. "My husband fears nothing and no one."

"I know little of men's private fears," Sophie scoffed, "only what I have witnessed. Most husbands spend their wives' labors in drunken, premature celebrations. And afterwards," she paused, "they are often jealous of their offspring. Bah," she said, waving her hand in dismissal, "most men are vain and self centered, and even the best are obsessed with leaving an heir. Do not expect much from your William and you will not be disappointed."

On a balmy spring afternoon, the mild backache that had plagued Philippa most of her pregnancy began to throb. The child was not due for another month, so she did not suppose her discomfort to be the onset of labor. Rather, she assumed her morning walk had tightened her muscles and produced spasms. Over the proceeding weeks, she had grown awkward in her gait, the smallest gesture an onerous task. Reaching for a dropped napkin had become an agony. Philippa told no one about her aching back, but her aunts must have guessed her discomfort, for they insisted that the three of them suspend chores and squander the remainder of the day sharing fables and fairy tales. One of the maids laid a fire and the women formed a crescent of chairs. Sibyl and Philippa sat in rockers. Sophie settled into her favorite ladder-back, crossing her hands over her girdle, a broad band of silk that looped once around her waist, crisscrossed behind her back and knotted in front.

For two months Philippa had worn nothing but loose chemises and linen gowns. That morning, she had added a fur-trimmed, richly embroidered pelisse, well open in the front and reaching to her knees. Playing the fingers of her right hand the length of one silky bell sleeve, she imagined herself with a waist small enough to girdle. A scullery maid served mugs of hot cider. The scent of clove and cinnamon soothed Philippa's backache as surely as the warmth of the fire and the distraction of story telling. One tale in particular riveted her attention—the tale of Mélusine, cursed to assume, on every Saturday, the body of a fish from the waist down.

"The fish tail was not unbeautiful," Sibyl explained, her tongue sliding over chapped lips. That morning she had wound a dark wimple about her head, and only a few curls showed at her forehead. "The scales shimmered turquoise. The fin, a pearly translucent fan, sparked silver in sunlight and moon glow." She smiled at her niece's obvious delight.

"One day by the Fountain of Fays in the forest of Combiers in Poitou," she continued, "Mélusine came upon Count Raymond who, struck by her enormous beauty, fell instantly in love with her. They sat by the fountain and talked all night. Raymond was charmed by her tenderness and wit. Before dawn, he asked for her hand in marriage.

"Mélusine, no less enchanted than he, accepted immediately, but only if he first agreed to build her a castle where she might keep her secret hidden. 'You must never intrude on my private Saturdays,' she explained, 'for if you do, we will be forever separated.'

"Count Raymond agreed. He built Mélusine a great castle at Lusignan on the very spot where they had met."

"And were they happy?" Philippa asked, holding out her mug for the scullery maid to refill.

"For a while they were very happy," Sibyl said. An owl screeched in the distance. The fire popped and the logs sputtered sap.

"Until," Sophie interrupted with her raspy whisper, "Raymond was prodded by malicious gossip to discover how his wife spent her days apart from him. Some said that every Saturday she visited with a coven of witches. Others hinted at a mysterious lover."

A log split in half and thumped against the grate, tossing live embers onto the hearth. Waving aside the maid, Sibyl grabbed the poker and jabbed the two pieces between the andirons. Philippa's rocker creaked and groaned.

"Finally," Sibyl said, setting aside the poker, "Raymond could not stand it any longer. He had to know Mélusine's secret or he could not survive another day. On a Saturday morning, he slipped into the castle. After searching for his wife in the bedroom chambers and the spinning room, he approached her dressing chamber. Discovering the door locked, he peered through the keyhole. Mélusine laid sprawled in the tub, head thrown back in abandon. Her long hair, flaming red against the copper tub, curled in the damp air. Raymond felt shamed at having violated his wife's trust and was about to leave when some strange compulsion bid him take another look. One quick glance, he told himself, and then he would go and no one would ever know of his indiscretion. Raymond held his breath, tilted his head and adjusted his eye." Sibyl leaned forward in her rocker, tilted her head and squinted through an imaginary keyhole. "Anticipating the slender length of Mélusine's legs," she whispered, "Raymond was shocked to see a blue-scaled tail splashing the water."

"And?" Philippa said leaning forward in her rocker, having all but forgotten her back pain.

"At first Count Raymond said nothing to his wife or anyone else. But he could not forget what he had seen. He thought he knew her fully, completely, that together they made one whole. And now he wondered what other secrets she had withheld, and he began to question the integrity of their life together. Several weeks later, in the midst of a fearsome argument, he lashed out at her in anger. 'Get away from me you loathsome mermaid.' he bellowed."

"But why?" Philippa gasped. "Aunt Sibyl said Mélusine's tail was not unbeautiful. Why did the Count call her loathsome?"

"Women best keep their private business to themselves," Sophie spat. "Men claim they want to know the truth, but they are deluded. Men prefer to remain behind a veil of ignorance and are too often made queasy by the secrets of a woman's body."

Philippa's considered her blue-veined breasts and bulging belly. Was it possible that William found her loathsome?

Sibyl frowned at her sister's words and rushed to conclude the tale. "Once Mélusine understood that her privacy had been violated, that her deepest secret had been stolen, she had no choice but to leave her young count."

"Did Mélusine ever return?" Philippa asked. Her back throbbed. She shifted uncomfortably in her rocker. Her pelisse gaped open, revealing the knobbed thrust of her navel pressing against her gown. "Was their love ever as it had been?" she asked.

Sibyl reached out to pat Philippa's leg. "It's nothing but a fairy tale, my little one," she said in a soothing voice, "a story to amuse."

Ignoring her sister's words, Sophie tucked a strand of hair behind her ear and leaned forward. "Never," she whispered ominously. "She never ever returned. The castle of Lusignan has stood empty thereafter, haunted by the ghost of the vanished countess mermaid."

That night Philippa dreamed of a roiling sea. A scaly creature wrapped its tentacles around her middle and squeezed as she struggled to break free of its oily embrace. Around midnight, her water broke and she called out in fear. Sophie appeared at Philippa's side in seconds, her hair a tangle of gray in the moonlight.

"What is it little one?" she whispered. "Is it time?"

Sibyl woke Wallada who entered the chamber humming a melodious tune that reminded Philippa of the sound of rain splashing a pond.

Sophie sat stiffly composed by the door. No one mentioned William.

As labor progressed, Wallada massaged Philippa's opening with olive oil and the bedroom took on the pleasing scent of the kitchen. At dawn, the baby's head crowned and then, inexplicably, the birth stalled. Philippa bore down with all her strength, but the child would not budge. Between contractions Wallada slipped a hand inside Philippa. "So, that's what's holding things up," Wallada mumbled, withdrawing her hand. She rolled her shoulders and wiped her brow with her forearm before repositioning her hands. Palm facing palm, she straightened her fingers as though she were preparing to receive a skein of yarn. Taking a deep breath, Wallada slid all ten fingers inside Philippa. "There!" she whispered. And then, with one seamless gesture she slipped the cord that looped the baby's neck over his head. "Alright, my lady! Help me get this little one born!" Pain gripped Philippa's back and spread to her belly. Rising up on her elbows, she bore down. And when the babe burst from her into the midwife's competent waiting hands, the relief was numbing.

"It's a boy, my lady," Wallada said, lifting the howling babe into the air.

"Will," Philippa said. "After his father."

If only William had waited until the babe had been swaddled and Philippa sponged with lavender water their lives might have taken a different turn. But Wallada had only just delivered the afterbirth when William stumbled into Philippa's chambers, disheveled, unshaven, and reeking of mead. "Your lady did a fine job, my lord," Wallada said, nodding to the corner table where Sophie and Sibyl watched a maid bind the babe's navel with a band of linen. "God has granted you a healthy child." She dropped the afterbirth into a copper bowl and carried it from the room, but the metallic scent of blood lingered.

William blanched and cleared his throat. "Do I have an heir? Is the child a son?" he demanded, his voice too loud for the tiny chambers.

Sorrow replaced Philippa's great joy. Had he no words of love for her? Then Sibyl placed Will in Philippa's arms and she forgot all about her husband. Sunlight flamed her child's hair a rosy auburn that reminded her of Toulose. She placed her lips against the soft spot on her child's crown and found the pulse of her own desire—to love completely, possessively, and without reservation.

"William," she said, "here is your son."

Baby Will puckered his face and whimpered. Philippa's breasts tingled. Sibyl placed one pinkie into Will's curling fingers. "He is strong, your son," she said to William. "Look here." She touched Will's tiny dimpled chin. "Here is your cleft. And his eyes are the same blue that greet you in the looking glass."

Wallada returned to Philippa's bedside with a mug of boiled water and honey. "Drink this, my lady," she said. "After you've finished, it's time to put the babe to breast. The child is fit but early. It is best that he be suckled by his own mother." She spoke to Philippa, but all present knew her words were meant for William. He would not happily accept Wallada's recommendation, but for now he remained silent, momentarily distracted by the sight of his son.

"He's smaller than I thought he would be," William said. The look on his face was not one of wonder but one of evaluation.

"He is not so very small," Philippa said, and for the first time in their married life she contradicted her husband in the presence of others. "And soon he will grow as tall as his father. Or perhaps," she added, "the child will grow even taller."

Aunt Sibyl made a breathy, hissing sound and shook her head. William stiffened, his lips tightened and his eyes marbled over.

Distracted by her son's reedy howl, she did not apologize. Already the rhythm of their lives together, a deep intimacy that blurred the boundaries between where she left off and the child began, had started.

Girard felt reborn when Abbot Geoffrey asked him to accompany Robert to Poitiers as a representative of Trinity. Placing the missive he had penned to Duchess Philippa into Girard's hand, the abbot added, "The woman Madeleine and Brothers Peter and Moriuht will undertake the journey as well."

Clenching his jaw, Girard struggled to replace his disappointment with obedience.

The candles on the desk cast a ruddy glow onto the Abbot's tonsured skull and elongated his purple nose. "Robert is stubborn," he said, examining his fingernails. "He would prefer to travel alone, but his poor health simply will not permit it."

"And the other pilgrims?" Girard asked.

"They'll remain at Vendôme until your party returns," the Abbot said, dismissing Girard without another word.

The first night they camped along the side of the path in a clearing of chamomile and, Girard discovered as soon as he lowered himself to the ground, a scatter of sharp pebbles.

"We must eat sparingly on our journey in order to conserve our supplies," Robert explained, offering each pilgrim a few dry tubers for dinner. Madeleine, Peter and Moriuht seemed satisfied, or at least resigned to their bitter fare. Girard, however, winced at the tiny white bulbs in his hand.

"Brother Girard," Robert said in a soft voice only Girard could hear, "every man carries a cross. Believe me, if you have faith that

God will deliver you, you will be able to master your appetite and find glory in your affliction."

Girard placed one of the tubers in his mouth. Chewing slowly, he concentrated on how the bitter pulp yielded a sharp peppery pleasure.

"You see?" Robert said. "The Lord helps those who turn to him."

But he had not seen, not at all. That night, hungry and cold, Girard lay awake wrapped in a rough wool blanket that tickled his shoulders and did little to cushion the jab of pebbles. Even after falling into a restless slumber, he dreamed of sweetened pears larded with cinnamon and cloves. The dream titillated his palate, waking him hours before anyone else. Readjusting his body, he occupied his mind by constructing an astonishing and fanciful banquet—tables laden with roasted pheasants, mutton, and venison tenderized in delicate wine sauces flavored with garlic and saffron pepper. Food fantasies pushed aside prayer and left him light-headed and vaguely nauseous.

The other pilgrims woke before dawn and sipped water from a shared pig bladder. No one mentioned food. After two arduous days of walking bramble-choked paths, they arrived at Blois and took shelter in a small inn. *Praise the Lord!* Girard thought. At last they would eat a real meal and be spared the misery of sleeping in dirt. The pudgy Blois innkeeper announced the menu before the five pilgrims were even through the door. "We offer onion soup and capons," he said in a loud, exuberant voice. Around his neck hung a whittled cross fastened together with strands of scarlet thread. "Or, if you prefer, we have this hour finished roasting a suckling pig."

Girard fantasized biting into pork shank, the warm fat trickling down his chin.

The innkeeper drummed thick fingers against a belly girdled snug by a grease-splattered apron. "What will it be, my good people?"

"Plain broth and bread," Peter said. "And perhaps," he added, glancing at Robert, "a bit of red wine." Peter, a tall thin man with a blond thatch ringing his tonsured crown, had been a musician at

Sully-sur-Loire where he recorded liturgical chants and hymns on parchment. Though a man of few words, he often hummed sad, lugubrious melodies.

How can he settle for plain broth and bread! Girard thought, *when there's onion soup, capons and, my God suckling pig! That Peter eats nothing but notes!*

Girard glanced at Madeleine who appeared absorbed by a vase of gold snapdragons languishing on a deal table. He entertained a fantasy of Madeleine's fingers brushing his withered arm and felt an unsettling surge of pleasure and shame. But even lecherous daydreams did not disturb him as much as the thought of eating plain broth and bread for dinner.

Moriuht, a sinewy compact man who wore nothing but animal hide against his bare skin, claimed a stool near the fireplace, seemingly oblivious to the repellent sight he offered Girard each time he opened his legs. Filthy and unkempt, the man reeked of sweat as pungent as a field of wild onions. Even the clove oil Moriuht used to treat his diseased gums did not mask his powerful stench. During the journey, he exhibited the energy of a half dozen men. Instead of walking he bounced. Sidestepping nettle and foxtail he disappeared into thickets, sometimes reappearing with a smile, holding a robin's nest or a tangle of translucent snakeskin. "Master Robert," Moriuht said, scratching his back with such sensual abandon that Girard flushed in embarrassment, "we'll not be eating tubers tonight!"

Robert smiled, his fondness for Moriuht apparent in the softening of his features.

Moriuht scratched his jaw and muttered, "Blasted chiggers and lice!" Girard wished that, in addition to Moriuht's beard, vermin might inhabit the wiry snarls of his nether regions. But even as Girard framed the thought, he felt remorse.

"Yes, my friend," Robert said, "Tonight we dine on broth and bread."

But Robert remained in his room long after the group assembled for supper in the common room.

✸

The innkeeper served the thin broth in simple bread trenchers. "The bread is made from a recent harvest of rye," he assured them. "Of excellent quality and taste. Can't be too careful these days. A fortnight past Vital from Bourges served bread made from grain milled the previous spring, and his guests fell grievously ill."

"Ill?" Peter asked, his brow furrowing.

"With fevers and powerful visions," the innkeeper said. "A doctor was called who claimed the sickness was most likely caused by the old flour used in preparing the bread. But the stable boy and scullery maid felt certain the afflicted were victims of the devil, for why else would their visions be so violent and obscene?" The innkeeper pursed his lips and frowned.

Girard wanted more details concerning the specific nature of the "obscene" visions, but kept his silence.

A look of fear pinched the innkeeper's features, and he caressed his whittled cross until he regained his composure. "The parish curate agreed with the servants. But whether it was bad faith or bad grain that caused the trouble, you fine folks needn't worry," he said with false cheerfulness. "I have heard of Robert of Arbrissel's sanctity and of the good Christian souls accompanying him on his pilgrimage and, of course, at this Inn we are careful with the preparations of all our meals, serving nothing but the best! Besides, only a fool would fail to recognize the bitter sting of tainted grain. Now then," he said, wiping his hands on his apron, "if anyone has a change of heart, the suckling is crisp and tender."

"This," Peter said, passing his hand over the plank table, "will suffice."

The innkeeper nodded, poured the wine, and retreated with the empty trays.

Bowing his head, Peter began to sing a sorrowful chant, his deep mournful voice rising to quivering perfection, "captivatis morti datis mater natis dedit gratis vitae bravium…"

Girard quickly translated the Latin in his head: *Exiled, captive, given to death, the mother gave the gift of life to the sons …* The sorrowful lament about Mary and Jesus seemed an odd choice to sing at table.

Even without knowing the meaning of the Latin verse, Madeleine's eyes filled with tears at the power and the purity of Peter's song. After Peter had sung the last note, Moriuht, his parted lips revealing inflamed gums and a scarcity of teeth, slammed his palms against the tabletop with an exuberance that caused the wine to climb the sides of the goblets. "Oh, but you have a fine voice, Brother Peter! Fine as any troubadour!"

Peter's mouth pinched into a small ascetic smile. "Now let us pray."

The four bowed their heads and offered up thanks for God's bounty. Girard swallowed a small draught of wine, the hearty cabernet spreading through his body and filling him with warm resolve. He, like Master Robert, would offer up his hunger as an act of devotion, starving his body and feeding his soul. Robert, recognizing Girard as a man of unusual sanctity, would hail him as a valiant soldier of Christ and together the two men would found the abbey of Robert's vision!

But, sadly, the needs of the flesh prevailed. His appetite ignited by the first sip, Girard gulped the whole of the tasteless soup, greedily consuming the trencher with such haste that he barely noticed the spicy tang of caraway seeds. His hunger blunted, he wiped his mouth and recited a silent prayer of contrition that was interrupted by a casual glance from Madeleine. She just as quickly looked away.

How dare she judge me! Girard thought. Robert had spoiled her and all the other women in treating them with the same respect afforded men. Righteous anger knotting his belly, Girard turned his hatred to the one who had born witness to his shame. He would hate her long and hard.

"I shall never fit into my wedding gown," Philippa told her maid, "no matter how tightly wound the binding cloth."

"Oh, but you must!" Emma said. "Ladies always wear wedding gowns to their post confinement ceremonies! Don't you worry, my lady. I've eased the seams a bit. Here we go," she said, sliding the gown over Philippa's head and fastening the plackets. "Perfect! Now all that's left is the veil." Emma said, securing the simple but costly netting with a half dozen hairpins and a silver comb. "You look lovely!" she declared, just as the first guests arrived.

Accompanied by William, her aunts, and a handful of family friends, Philippa descended the hill from the palace and walked in silent procession to Saint Radegund Church. The snug gown forced her to take shallow breaths while the veil blurred her view of William's face. The previous evening, as they sat before the fire, William had scolded Philippa, telling her she spent too much time coddling her child at the expense of her supervision of the household.

Philippa had apologized for her negligence and promised that she would be more attentive to her duties, but she suspected the real source of her husband's anger lay elsewhere. William wanted many sons to carry on his lineage and assure the continuation of the House of Aquitaine, and the prohibition against having sex with a nursing woman disrupted his plans. Even when Philippa's mother-in-law's offered to procure the services of a wet nurse so that Philippa might be more available to her husband, Philippa stood by her decision to nurse her son, at first because Wallada insisted and later because she had grown to love the drowsy intimacy of baby Will against her breast. She reassured herself that a good mother considers what's best for her child before conceiving another.

A priest handed Philippa a lit candle on the steps of the church. Entering the vestibule, she knelt just as Abbot Raynaud arrived. Sprinkling her with holy water in the form of a cross, he prayed, "The earth is the Lord's and the fullness thereof." Offering Philippa the left extremity of his stole, he led her into the church. "Enter thou into the temple of God," he said. "Adore the Son of the Blessed Virgin Mary who has given thee fruitfulness of offspring."

Philippa and her party followed Raynaud down the nave to a set of narrow stairs descending into the dark crypt. While the others fanned out against the walls, Raynaud directed Philippa to an austere stone sarcophagus set atop a raised foliated platform in the center of the room.

The casket bore the ragged edge of the stone mason's chisel. Philippa trailed her hand across the granite, admiring the splinters of feldspar, mica flecks and forking veins of quartz. Six monks entered the crypt, surrounded the tomb and, in response to the Abbot's nod, lifted the stone lid.

"Pray to the holy Saint Radegund," Raynaud said, "ask her to intercede for you and your child's benefit."

Philippa knelt before the Saint, lifted her veil and looked at Radegund's uncorrupted body, seeing beyond the sunken nose and drawn cheeks of the leathery face to the beauty that had once led holy Fortunatus to sing hymns of praise. "Oh Lady," she prayed, "thou who hast lived in this world, brought a piece of the Holy Cross to this monastery, pray on my behalf to Christ and Our Father, to the Holy Spirit and the Virgin, for my benefit and my son's. May he grow to be a good Christian," she said in the passionate voice of a true believer. Since giving birth, Philippa had grown more calm and reflective. Now that William seldom visited her chambers, she often read the Bible at night. Lulled to sleep by the glory of the Word, she awoke each day feeling renewed and prepared to meet the challenges inherent in raising a son.

At the close of the ceremony, Philippa lowered her veil and exited the church with her eyes focused on her feet, for Sibyl had warned her that should Philippa see anyone of evil character or physical defect, dear Will might thus be afflicted. Climbing the hill to the palace, she recalled Saint Radegund's exquisite beauty and realized that even a nun could be both fair and powerful.

The following week, a mere seven weeks after Philippa had given birth to his son, William prepared to lead a band of knights and a sea of pilgrims to the Holy Land. Now that he had a male heir, he was eager to travel. Before embarking on his crusade, William requested that Philippa oversee a mid-day banquet, a grand affair attended by two score guests. Six trestle tables set with gilded plates, silver cutlery, and voluptuous bouquets lined the walls of the great hall. Servants poured water from pewter ewers shaped like knights on horseback. The butler carried in carafes of wine and the Duke's musician plucked his viol and strolled around the tables singling. Boson, Count of Marche, sat across from his enemy Guillaume Taillefer, a mighty man whose powerful arms were legendary. He would later kill Boson during the siege of Confolens. Aimery of Thouars, an effete gourmand, fed candied pork to his pretty wife, of whom he was overly fond. He would one day be murdered under suspicious circumstances. Also present were a smattering of prelates.

While most clergy wore simple black robes, the laymen arrayed themselves in narrow tunics fashioned from sumptuous materials dyed blue, yellow, crimson, and purple. Wide sleeves covered their wrists and exaggerated trains trailed the floor behind feet shod in fashionable *pigaches*, pointy shoes that curved at the toes. Many of the men were clean-shaven—in the latest Parisian style—and the women wore their long hair twisted and crimped into elaborated styles.

A crisp roast goose, well-seasoned mutton, partridge powdered with rose sugar, and a white wine of exquisite taste and unusual transparency were served. The centerpiece of the feast, a whole glazed boar's head garnished with purple banners and white day lilies, rested on a gold-rimmed maple platter surrounded by fruit jellies molded into the shapes of lions and eagles.

William stood and proclaimed, "My brother Hugh has agreed to conduct my affairs while I am away." The guests, many of them Hugh's comrades, nodded their approval, some clanking tankards as they shouted, "Here! Here!" in thunderous discord.

Hugh and Philippa were seated on the high dais on either side of William. Behind and above them hung a tapestry depicting the New Jerusalem, which bore an uncanny resemblance to King Philip's royal residence in the heart of Paris. Crenellated walls, rising towers and steepled turrets surrounded the small golden city. At its center rose a church, hardly larger than a chapel. Below it swirled a turquoise, saffron-striped river. Hugh stood to salute his friends. From the floor it must have appeared as if he were part of the tapestry's indigo landscape.

Hugh's face was drawn and coarse-skinned, and he suffered from gout. His dissolute life had aged him prematurely. He devoted his nights to drink, debauchery, and dice, and slept most days until late afternoon. And yet, he captivated men and women alike with his hearty laugh and boyish charm. After Philippa gave birth to Will, he presented Philippa with a single rose and Will with a silver cup inscribed with the family coat of arms. She recalled these kindnesses when, tipsy with wine, Hugh addressed those sitting below.

"It is my honor to rule my brother's provinces while he follows the cross to the Holy Land. I promise to fulfill my pledge to protect all his possession, including this fine palace and his pretty wife." Hugh raised his tankard as though prepared to make a toast, then clumsily brought it to his lips and drank deep. His companions followed his lead, rising to their feet and bringing their drinks to their mouths.

From the beginning the arrangement left Philippa uneasy. Hugh had no experience managing practical matters and none of the personal assets necessary to conduct William's affairs or protect his holdings. Although to even think it was absurd, she felt in her heart that she would make a better regent than Hugh. She knew much more about William's concerns than Hugh did. She had sat beside him during tedious official functions and witnessed many an agreement of reconciliation. But as a woman, a nursing mother at that, her knowledge of William's estate and her ability to manage his affairs were not relevant. In deference to expectations and in the interest of matrimonial harmony, she listened silently to her husband's words, a mask of obedient concern affixed her face.

After the guests departed, William pulled two chairs before the fire and indicated that he would like to speak with her. While she waited for William to pour himself another glass of wine, Philippa thought about a young prelate she had spoken to at the banquet. After complimenting her on the delicacy of the meal and quality of the wine, he had spoken in glowing terms of Robert of Arbrissel, the very man she had heard preach at the Cathedral of St. Sernin the month of her betrothal. She recalled how the priest's voice—a magnificent instrument of God—had moved her, and she wondered if William might consent to Robert performing their son's baptism.

Wine goblet in hand, William took the chair beside Philippa, interrupting her musings by explaining that Herbert of Lusignan and Fulk of Angers would come to Hugh's aid should he need them. "And, of course, Hugh can always call upon Ponce and Gautier should any emergency arise," William added.

Philippa bit her tongue and did not say what he must already know, that while Ponce and Gautier were strong, reliable men, well trained and eager to serve, household guards needed the direction of a self-assured Lord. Dear, sweet Hugh was ineffectual. He could not organize a hunting party on his own let along command the attention of soldiers.

"I doubt either of these contingencies is necessary," William continued, in a hearty voice meant to reassure the both of them. "Most of the troublemakers have left Aquitaine for the Holy land. Why do you think Urban called for this crusade to begin with?"

It did not surprise her that William suddenly shifted his talk to a consideration of papal motivation. He was more comfortable expressing political opinions than he was pondering the messy vagaries of family dynamics.

Their son, abed in the nursery, cried out in hunger, his voice rising and falling in visceral, howling impatience.

Most mornings she loosely bound her breasts, placing linen squares over each nipple before wrapping her chest in a length of thick flannel, but this morning she had foregone such precautions. Now she watched in dismay as her milk let down and stained her bodice.

"The babe is hungry," she said, quietly interrupting her husband's discussion of the pope. But William ignored her implicit request and continued speaking. She sensed a nervous energy that had not been present during the banquet.

"Urban," he said, answering his own question, "encouraged the holy crusades because he wanted to rid the West of landless knights with too much time on their hands." He lifted his wine glass, as though toasting his own insight. "I," William said, in a boastful voice, "have been asked by several such knights to act as their leader." After he drained the goblet, he noticed Philippa's wet bodice.

"Take care of yourself," William said. His face registered the same distaste as when he instructed a servant to clean up dog vomit.

Philippa rose from her chair and walked demurely past William. Once she cleared his sight, she took the nursery stairs two at a time. As she hurried towards her son, she prayed that her fears were unfounded and Hugh would prove worthy of his brother's trust.

After spending the night slumbering on straw pallets, the five travelers took a skiff down the Loire as far as Candes-St-Martin. They sat closely together—Madeleine, Robert and Peter on the windward side, Girard and Moriuht on the leeward. The boatman steered from the stern using his oar as a rudder. Almost immediately Girard grew nauseous. Holding tight to the gunnel, he looked up at a milky blue sky swimming to and fro.

"I feel a change in the weather," Moriuht said to no one in particular. He rubbed clove oil onto his gums and placed the medicinal vial into a deep pocket sewn into his animal skin robe. "Enjoy the sunshine while you may."

"Are you a prophet then?" Girard hissed. Queasy in both body and soul, he felt an unholy desire to offend.

"I see no clouds or other signs of inclemency," Peter said.

"Oh well, perhaps you are right," Moriuht conceded in a cheerful voice. Leaning precariously over the side, he cupped his hands and scooped up river water. The man drinks, Girard thought, with the snuffling sounds of a rooting boar.

After a while, Moriuht and Peter fell asleep, lulled by the gentle rhythm of the skiff, and Girard turned his attention to Robert and Madeleine.

"The Loire is as clear and calm as a font of holy water," Robert said to Madeleine.

Girard marveled at Robert's ability to see the best in all things, for while the water was clear and calm, it also carried the bracken stench of dying willows and dead fish.

The slumbering Moriuht's shoulder brushed Girard's. He winced and slid sideways on the seat. Moriuht sighed and immediately took ownership of the newly created space, his muscled thigh settling snugly against Girard's. Attempting to distract himself from the loathsome creature's touch, Girard focused on the deep echoing croak of a distant chough, the whoop of a shorebird, the whisper of wind rustling the hollow-stemmed rush lining the riverbank. Knowing that Robert must hear this same music filled him with the bliss of shared intimacy. His breathing slowed, the warmth of the sun settled against his shoulders and he grew suddenly calm. Just before drifting off to sleep, Girard blessed Robert and struggled to relinquish all jealousy.

They reached Candes-St-Martin in the late afternoon. The land rocked like the river as the five tried to walk. Having received news that Robert of Arbrissel was passing through their territory on his way to see the Duchess of Aquitaine, a group of men and women awaited their arrival. As Madeleine and the three men gathered their belongings from the boat, Robert approached the crowd.

One of them, a pockmarked woman with berry-tinted lips, stepped forward with a sway of her hips. "Please, Master Robert, won't you spend the night at my house?" She smiled, and a dimple appeared on her right cheek.

"I would be honored," he replied.

The mayor, a portly man of rigid bearing, moved toward Robert. "Master Robert, you do not wish to stay with this woman. She is … not fit for the company of a man such as yourself. Come now, you and your friends must stay at my quarters in the town hall, where there is plenty of room and good food."

Girard prayed that Master would accept the man's generous offer.

"But the young woman offered me lodgings first," Robert replied kindly to the man, "and I have accepted."

A cleric with a sputtering lisp and hunched shoulders, spoke up. "Surely a holy man should not sleep under the same roof as a whore. Think of the danger to your soul."

"She is in greater danger than I," Robert said, "for she will suffer eternal damnation unless she repents and is saved."

Robert turned to the town mayor. "But my companions here would be most grateful, I am sure, of your hospitality."

Girard felt a wave of gratitude, not toward the pompous mayor, but toward Robert for allowing them to spend the night in the comforts of the town hall.

The magnificent town hall, a spacious building with high ceilings and large windows, offered a grand view of the river. A female servant took Madeleine to her room and a valet ushered the men to their quarters. Girard collapsed onto one of the down beds, still feeling, but only faintly now, the sway of the boat. As soon as his nausea passed, hunger began gnawing at his stomach. Robert, he knew, faced more than hunger. The woman, no doubt, intended to seduce him. Perhaps she hoped to catch him off guard by slipping into his bed while he slept.

"Dinner is served," the servant announced at the door of the men's room.

Peter, who had been reading a small quarto as he sat on his bed, looked up at the man. "Thank your lord for his generosity," he said to the young man, "but we have our own food. If you could just bring us plates and a little water or wine, we'll be fine here."

Moriuht turned from his place by the window. "Surely today we shall have something more to eat beyond roots and herbs, won't we Brother Peter?"

Suddenly Moriuht seemed a paragon of common sense to Girard.

"Suit yourself, Brother," Peter replied, looking back at his book. "I'm satisfied with what we have."

"Very well, we will have water and wine," Moriuht said, rubbing his palms.

"If you change your mind," the servant said, "there is food in the kitchen—veal pot pies and wastel bread."

Girard's heart dropped. He imagined breaking the crust of the pie open and releasing tender morsels of veal coated in gravy. Yet even as he trembled in anticipation of that first bite, he felt depleted, powerless against his own enormous appetite.

The servant returned with a carafe of wine, a pitcher of water, and three goblets. Peter poured merlot into three cups, diluting each with an equal amount of water. Girard watched with dismay as the hearty red wine blanched an unsubstantial pink. "Ah, I almost forgot!" Peter said. Taking two small pouches form his robe, Peter flavored his portion with dried fennel and a sprinkle of breadcrumbs before passing the pouches to Moriuht, who did the same. When Moriuht passed them to Girard, only tiny fragments of fennel and a dusting of breadcrumbs remained.

"You don't need as much as we do," Moriuht said as Girard reached for the goblet. "You have more in reserve." Moriuht feigned lifting a heavy belly and laughed. Peter, having already downed his dinner, glanced up from his book and frowned.

That night Girard lay in bed consumed by thoughts of the nearby kitchen. Finally, the demons of gluttony took him over, and he rose from his bed.

"Where are you going, brother?" Moriuht whispered in the darkness.

"I . . . I must relieve myself," he lied, wondering if Moriuht's diseased gums kept him awake or if he just naturally slept the light sleep of a wild animal.

Moriuht grunted and rolled onto his side. Girard moved out of the room on tiptoes, trying not to waken Brother Peter, and sought the kitchen. He found the main room, which was bathed in moonlight, and began a methodical search, entering one doorway after another. Finally a swinging door opened unmistakably to his goal. Above a central cutting table, ghostly pots and pans hung in faint moonlight. Girard felt his way around the kitchen, sliding his hand along immaculate sinks and counter tops, until he came to a large pantry. He opened the door slowly, in deference to the squeaking hinges and because he wanted to prolong the exquisite pleasure of anticipation. The sight of four potpies sitting on a shelf filled Girard with contemptible desire. He reached towards one of them, held his arm in mid air and hesitated. But the scent of veal was irresistible. Not bothering to look for a knife or spoon, he tore into the pie with ravenous teeth, immersing his face in its entrails, sucking at the faintly warm veal. He finished one and took another. Looking for the wastel bread, he came upon custard tarts, tiny and tempting with raspberries nestled in their centers. He placed an entire tart in his mouth. Flaky, butter crisp gave way to creamy sweetness. He grabbed another and swallowed it whole, then another, and then one more.

Now, Girard thought, *now I am satisfied*. Even as he framed the lie, a surge of self-loathing dropped him to his knees on the cold marble. Amidst the dirty dishes, the crumbs of his feast, the smell of berries, veal and grain, Girard bowed his head and mumbled the comforting automatic words of confession: "Bless me Father, for I have sinned ... " Before he left the kitchen, he destroyed all evidence of his presence, swept the floor of crumbs and cleaned the pie tins. Turning to leave, he slipped a palm-size custard tart into the pocket of his robe.

No sooner had William departed for the Holy Land than a messenger from the west arrived to inform Philippa that Eblo of Châtelaillon, against the express orders of the Pope, had seized the Mouillepié marsh and half the isle of Oléron, both of which belonged to the monks of Saint Maixent.

"Please wait," she instructed the messenger, hastily composing a note to her brother-in-law.

Several hours later, the messenger returned to the palace. "Sir Hugh is absent on a hunt," he announced. "None of his servants know how to locate him."

Anger welled up inside of Philippa. At the very least Hugh could have told his servants where his party planned to hunt! She frowned and her breath quickened. Will began to cry. As she considered her next move, she crossed her arms and pressed them against her chest to keep her milk from spilling. "Wait here," she told the messenger. After ringing for a scribe, Philippa instructed him to prepare two missives, one to Herbert of Lusignan and one to Fulk of Angers. They will know what to do, she reassured herself before hurrying to her son. Upstairs she untied her gown and took the squalling Will from the nursemaid's arms. Sensing his mother's tension, Will fussed at Philippa's breast, turning his head from side to side before clamping down hard on nipple.

"Ouch!" Philippa cried.

Startled, Will opened his mouth and howled.

"Shh, my sweet," she whispered, but some time passed before he calmed enough to nurse.

The following morning, Philippa received word that both Herbert and Fulk were away from their palaces, Herbert in the south preparing to cross into Spain, Fulk in Paris negotiating with the king.

In desperation, she ordered Ponce and Gautier to gather what men they could. Then, Philippa turned her son over to a wet nurse and, in an audacious move that shocked her aunts, announced that she would lead an army to the coast.

Over the next few days twenty knights and dozens of foot soldiers gathered at Pré-le-Roi, a vast plain stretching below the city walls. From the palace window Philippa surveyed their colorful banners. Astounded by their beauty and terrified by the task before her, she laid one hand across her queasy stomach and whispered, "What have I gotten myself in to?"

Sibyl, who had risen early to supervise packing, joined Philippa at the window. "Did you say something, dear?"

Determined to hide her trepidation, Philippa straightened her shoulders and smiled. "See the blue flag with dark horizontal bars? It identifies Aimery of Thouars' followers."

"Why there are scores of foot soldiers!" Sibyl said.

Philippa nodded. "The red shield belongs to Hubert the Devil," she said, pointing to the middle of a sea of shields bearing chevrons, crosses, gauntlets and lions.

"What's in the two wagons?" Sibyl asked.

"Food, equipment and armament."

At the mention of armament, Sibyl's thumbs began nervously brushing her fingertips. "Oh dear! I do hope you're making the right decision."

The whinnies of the knight's horses and the loud banter of the foot soldiers climbed the small mountain and echoed off the walls of the palace. Philippa's heart pounded with nervous excitement. "It's time," she declared. Having said her goodbyes the previous evening, she had only to kiss her aunt's cheek before descending the palace stairs and stepping aboard her waiting wagon, a covered conveyance similar to the one that transported her from Toulouse to Poiters.

After Philippa reached the plains, the driver reined the horses while the assembled knights and foot soldiers fell into ranks. The clank of armor and the buffet of wind-whipped banners underscored the contingent's silence. Rising to her feet, Philippa addressed her soldiers. "I commend you for your prompt response to this crisis and thank you for your loyalty and service to Duke William," she declared, in a commanding voice pitched loud for the rearguard to hear. The soldiers cheered, lifting their banners and brandishing their shields. Hubert the Devil's horse reared up on hind legs, pawing the air and agitating the other horses that pulled at their reins. "Onward!" Philippa yelled, her heart pounding. Taking her seat beside the driver, she said a quick prayer for the safety of her troops before telling the driver to proceed.

More men joined the small band in Niort, and by the time they reached the coast a fortnight later, Philippa's army had swelled to one hundred knights and over a thousand foot soldiers.

Eblo's main force occupied the island while a smaller contingent remained in the marshes to the north. She knew her own men could not take Oléron without suffering heavy casualties crossing the channel, and the marsh of Mouillepié was equally dangerous, especially for the knights weighed down with heavy armor. So she made a decision that was later considered ingenious: She struck at Eblo's home, Châtelaillon itself, whose castle lay between the marsh and the island. Thinking Philippa would attempt to retake the island, Eblo had foolishly left it unguarded—only a few ill-equipped household servants put up a feeble struggle. After taking the stronghold, Philippa and her army took Eblo's wife and small children hostage, leading them back to Poitiers.

Eblo immediately agreed to terms: he would return the island and the marsh to Saint Maixent, and he would make annual donations of 500 sous in reparation for his destruction of the church of Saint George, located on Oléron. Once the compact was signed, Philippa returned his family to him.

Having heard news of his sister-in-law's success at Oléron, Hugh returned to Poitiers. He was not angry at her preemptive move but, rather, childishly relieved that he had not been called upon to make a decision or issue a command.

Philippa, on the other hand, was exhilarated with her success. Lords and ladies praised her exploits, especially since she had brought the proud Eblo to his knees without sacrificing the life of a single man.

But her joy was short lived, for soon after she was called upon to settle another dispute, this time between two brothers, Ebbon and Gelduin of Parthenay. Before William left for the Holy Land, he had helped Gelduin take the fortress of Germond from his brother, but Ebbon now was threatening to retake the citadel. So again, with the assistance of Ponce and Gautier, Philippa mustered an army and marched west. Some of her men managed to enter the castle and fortify it against Ebbon, who had laid siege to it, but when Ebbon grew weary with the prolonged standoff, he ordered his men to mine the towers and set them on fire. After the towers fell, Ebbon's army stormed the citadel, and many men were killed, including Ebbon's brother. Fearing more carnage, Philippa commanded her men to retreat.

This defeat was sobering. She now understood more fully the meaning of power, the ability to shed blood, inflict pain, and end life. Gelduin's wife was now a widow, his children orphans. If she had managed the situation differently, might Gelduin still be alive? William, she realized, did not simply revel in power. He also faced hard decisions, life-and-death choices, with consequences that affected an entire province and the men and women in it, from serfs to aristocrats.

Whereas previously she had envied her husband's position, now she respected and admired his skills. She continued to rule, but cautiously, striving to emulate William's grave and officious manner whenever she was called upon to ratify a contract or confirm a donation.

Philippa and her small son and aunts often spent weeks traveling from one dependency to another, moving their entire household, tapestries, tables, even William's favorite bloodhound, for lengthy stays at the residences of various vassals, who were obliged to feed, house, and entertain the lady and her party. That first winter, Philippa successfully managed both household and estate.

Of course, sometimes Philippa's heart would not cooperate with her mind. In the midst of business she would get waylaid by a desire to hold Will. Many a day ended with a headache and a queasy stomach. And yet, she persisted, for she saw no other choice.

Then, following a small success in quelling a rebellion in Saint Macaire, she grew more confident of her ability to rule. Instead of destroying the city and its castle, as she may have easily done with her superior forces, she offered the rebel barons generous terms, which they accepted. She discovered that whereas William ruled by fear, she could be just as effective by using subtle negotiation. This skill, she realized, she had gleaned from watching her father, who always preferred conciliation over confrontation, and to this style she added a feminine touch, cajoling men into harmonious interaction which, more often than not, resulted in a settlement of interests and restoration of trust and goodwill.

Sibyl and Sophie, however proud they may have been of their niece's successes, cautioned Philippa to rein in her masculine tendencies.

"You may be mistaken for a witch, or worse," Sibyl admonished in her high stilted voice.

"What could be worse?" Philippa laughed, for she had learned that Sibyl's alarmist comments were best handled with humor. "Except perhaps to lose my husband's estate."

She did not intend to be rude. Her aunts were kind, compassionate women she loved dearly but not beyond reason. She had begun to suspect that wealth of experience and not age alone contributed to wisdom, and because her aunts led constricted, parochial lives dependent upon male relatives and parish law, Philippa questioned whether or not their opinions were any more valuable than her own. For while Sophie and Sibyl were loyal and loving companions, neither had given birth or known the exquisite intimacy and daily challenges of raising a child. Nor had they managed a household as large as Philippa's.

Sophie, her fierce composure as compelling as ever, cautioned, "Power is addictive."

"But," Philippa explained, "I have no interest in attaining power! I am only acting as William's regent in his absence."

Sophie frowned, a lock of runaway hair crossing her forehead.

"Women are held to a higher standard than men. To pretend otherwise is to dabble in self deception," she admonished. Then, looking looked deep into Philippa's eyes, she stated flatly, "Do not forget, little one, that pride goeth before a fall."

Despite the distraction of a growling belly, Girard felt drawn to the stark beauty of Poitiers. The towers and steeples of the white city rising on a hill formed a perfect backdrop for the flock of skylarks darting the pale sky. The narrow cobble streets were immaculate and empty except for the occasional shopkeeper raising shutters or maidservant heaving slop into the central gutter. Philippa's palace, a stone structure with four powerful towers, was situated on a hill in the center of the city.

Girard surprised himself by keeping pace with the others in the party of five as they trudged up the steep incline. Although breathless, hungry, and limping in pain, he ignored his physical discomfort, focusing his attention on the stunning grandeur of the building. Atop the east tower a flag bore William's coat of arms, a gold lion rampant on a sea of red. A porter appeared to direct them to a warm parlor next to the foyer.

A great tapestry of horsemen riding to battle, spears and banners erect, covered the wall above the hearth. The horses had the faces of strange beasts, and riding behind was an ecclesiast, a bishop perhaps, wearing a precious miter and carrying a crosier in his hand. A slender young woman with hair the color of churned butter entered the room and greeted the exhausted pilgrims with gracious, if reserved, hospitality. She wore an amber-colored silk gown and an embroidered pelisse fastened at the neck with a broach.

"Lady Philippa," Robert said, "Your cousin Geoffry has told us of your loss. Please accept our condolences on the death of your father." He cupped her delicate hands in his own. "Remember that our help comes from the Lord," he said. "He will deliver you on your day of trouble if you only call on him."

Moriuht, reeking of clove oil and wrestling to keep his enormous energy in check, shifted his weight from foot to foot. Peter, an ascetic's inward glance smoothing his face, swayed slightly in silent, self-contained prayer while the perpetually distracted Madeleine lifted her hand to a scatter of dust motes riding a beam of light.

"Thank you, Master," she said. Her eyes teared, but she remained composed and cordial. "Some time ago I heard you preach a sermon at the Cathedral of St. Sernin, and have wanted to meet you ever since," she said. And though she smiled, she appeared stunned with grief.

For the first time in his life, Girard felt compelled to console another. He examined the other pilgrims and found them oddly unmoved. "I'm humbled by your kind words," Robert said.

"My maid tells me you have brought a missive with you from my cousin," Philippa said.

Girard's joints ached and his right heel throbbed painfully. He longed to sit somewhere quietly with his feet up, and yet he needed even more to hear the lady's words.

"Yes, my lady," Robert said, withdrawing the letter from his pocket and placing it in Philippa's hand.

"Thank you. I shall read this after I attend to your needs," Philippa said. "You must be tired from your journey. Please sit," she said, indicating an arrangement of chairs and stools before the fireplace. "Are you hungry? Would you like something to eat and drink?"

Girard's stomach growled in response. He cleared his throat and shushed his feet against the tile, a move that sent a stab of pain from his heel to his groin.

"We thank you for your hospitality, but I would first like to offer my prayers for the soul of your father," Robert said.

A sad, sweet expression lit Philippa's face. "How very kind you are, Master Robert. But wouldn't you rather rest a bit first? You've been traveling for days. You must be very tired."

"Brother Girard suffers from a stone bruise. I'm sure he would be grateful for a chair. As for the rest of us, let us pay homage to your father first. Then we'll relax in your hospitality."

Accompanied by Peter, Madeleine, and Moriuht, Robert descended the hill to Montierneuf monastery to pray for the soul of Philippa's father. But at Robert's insistence, Girard stayed behind in the care of the kind lady.

Philippa indicated that Girard should rest by the fire. Settling into the satin cushions, he sighed with gratitude.

Philippa rang for a maid. "Bring our guest sweet bread and honey. And if there's any soup left from last night's meal, bring a bowl of soup as well."

The soup looked exquisite. Sops of bread bobbed deliciously amidst cumin and clove seasoned chicken broth thick with chickpeas, carrots and potatoes. Girard mumbled a prayer of thanks and consumed the lot without hesitancy or embarrassment before devouring a loaf of bread. Only after he was sated did he speak.

"I cannot control my hunger," he said, glancing with distaste at his protruding belly.

Philippa did not respond, except to look into his eyes and nod encouragement.

"The night of my father's funeral feast was the first time I ate to excess," he said and rested his short arm on his belly, reasoning that if she were to *hear* it all, she might as well *see* it all. He had never spoken so freely, never revealed his own fears and frailties, and yet with this woman he could. "That night," he explained, "I knew for the first time the enormous hunger that would control my life."

Girard did not discuss his father's disgust or his mother's guilty love or what either had to do with hunger. But even without the messy details, he felt that Philippa understood the emotional truth of his life. Whereas Madeleine agitated his body, Philippa settled his soul and focused his mind on a comfortable place between insight and resolve. Girard felt as though a unity of purpose bound him to her in some inexplicable but permanent way.

"Your words touch me deeply, Brother Girard," Philippa said, running her hands the length of her sleeves and leaning closer to the fire. Sighing, she reached out and touched Girard's crippled arm. He did not flinch or pull away. "To live is a constant struggle, but it helps to know someone else has sorrowed as I have," she said in hushed tones. Removing her hand, she leaned back into the chair and took a deep breath. "My father was mortally wounded in battle and died before last rites could be administered. In addition to mourning his death," she said, grasping the arms of the chair, "I mourn the deaths of the men that I, myself, led in battle." She paused and brought her fingers to play against her throat.

Girard shifted in his seat. "Even as we speak, Madame, Robert and the others pray for your father's soul. Rest assured I will pray for all the good men lost in battle. Prayer," he added, "has saved many an anguished soul. Were it not for my own heartache, I doubt I would have discovered my calling." As soon as he spoke the words he knew them to be true, for only after his father died did Girard fully realize how much he longed to be part of a religious community. "Perhaps my lady would find a similar comfort in prayerful contemplation of our Lord?"

Philippa relaxed her grip on the arms of the chair. "I have often taken comfort in the Lord's words," she said. "Only lately, I can't seem to focus on their meaning."

"In the midst of mourning, we all feel the same," he said. "But if the Spirit of God is at home in you, you will once again know peace." Girard, who had never spoken with such heart-felt fluency, was surprised to discover that in offering comfort he had received some of his own.

Philippa stood and approached the hearth. Massive andirons smelted to resemble the paired silhouettes of two fierce-looking lions thrust their open-mouthed heads upward as though prepared to pounce into the throat of the smoke chamber. A firebrand split, releasing great fingers of flames that clawed the blackened stone. "Thank you, Brother Girard. You have been most helpful. Sometimes one needs the kind words of another to remember what's most important to one's self," the duchess said, her tall, slim figure dark against the glowing fire.

Girard, completely at peace in her silent company, felt no need to speak.

"Would you mind reading aloud the epistle from Abbot Geoffrey?"

"Of course, my lady," he said, grateful to be of service.

Philippa withdrew a rolled parchment from her robe and handed it to Girard, who broke the seal. "'A most worthy holy man has come to our monastery with a great following of converts who lack a permanent residence. I have told this man that I would intercede on his behalf and ask you who have long been a strong supporter of religious institutions to grant him a tract of land where he and his followers establish a home. Such a donation would be a memorable act, befitting the daughter of the great lord of Toulouse. You may have heard of the man's name, for his fame has spread wide: Robert of Arbrissel.'" Girard lowered the letter to his lap and looked up at the duchess.

Staring into the fire, Philippa took a moment to compose her self. "An abbey," she said in a thoughtful voice, "needs privacy, yet it must also be accessible by water and by land." She frowned, deep in concentration.

Girard, completely comfortable for the first time in days, basked in the warmth of the fire and waited patiently.

"I know such a tract of land," she said at last, "just south of the Loire, good valley land that is uninhabited!" A smile lit her face. "Would you mind helping me draw up a charter documenting my donation?"

"Indeed, Madame, I would be most honored to assist you in whatever way I can."

"Let me call my maid. She will bring necessary instruments to make this contract."

Philippa raised a small silver bell resting on the fireplace mantel and shook it. As they waited, she walked to a small table next to the hearth that held a marble chessboard mounted on golden trestles. Carved ivory pieces stood scattered mid-game. She placed her hand on a white bishop's miter before settling on the intricately carved crown of the king.

The parchment and writing tools were brought and laid out on a table beneath a window. Girard lifted his bulk from his comfortable chair before the fire and took a seat on the small stool. The countess paced to and fro as she spoke.

"And how shall we begin, my new friend?" Philippa asked. Girard saw the pallor beneath the blush of her cheeks, and he sensed a steely strength of will tempered with kindness and grace.

Unashamed of his withered limb, Girard smoothed the soft lambskin vellum with his crippled hand. "Let's say that you shall grant this land to Robert and his followers in honor of your father, for whose soul the nuns shall sing perpetual benedictions."

Philippa smiled and drew herself up. "Yes!" she said, "what a wonderful suggestion! I, Philippa, Countess of Poitiers, stirred by heavenly love…"

Taking the quill in his right hand, he dipped the nib into the ink well.

"Good, my Lady," Girard mumbled, and then spoke the Latin aloud as he dutifully transcribed her words on the page, *Ego, Philippia, comitissa Pictavensis, divini amoris devotione compuncta…* His penmanship was precise and swiftly executed, each letter rounded to perfection without ostentation or undue ornamentation.

"…do hereby bequeath Fontevraud, the tract of land where three diocese, Poitou, Anjou, and Tours, meet…"

…concedo et dono terram quae Frontem Evraldi vulgare nominatur quaeque in conjunctio tres diocesiarum est, Pictavensii, Angevensii, Torrensi…

"To Robert of Arbrissel, in honor of my father, Count of Toulouse…"

Ad Robertum de Arbrisello, in honore patri mei, comiti Tolosani…

"For whose soul he and his followers will sing perpetual benedictions."

Quoram per animam perpetuam benedictionem supradictus Robertus et religiosi sui cantabunt.

Girard repeatedly dipped his pen in the ink well and drew characters on parchment, moving his tongue along his upper lip as he did so. Then he turned to Philippa and handed her the quill. "Please make your mark here," he said, pointing to the bottom of the vellum. She drew an ornate *P* and crossed it at the stem.

"Lady Philippa, who is the land named for?" Girard asked.

"For Evraud, a robber who made his home in the forested area that surrounds the fresh water spring. But you've nothing to fear. Rumor has it that he and his brigands moved south last winter, and I've heard no mention of their exploits in a long time."

Girard nodded. "I will make sure that Master Robert signs as soon as he returns from church."

True to his word, the moment Robert returned from mass Girard rushed to meet him, his limp transformed into a self-important shuffle. "Master Robert," Girard said, "the Duchess Philippa has granted a tract of land where you and your followers can establish a permanent home. You have only to sign here…."

Robert's broad smile fell upon Girard like a blessing.

To be blessed twice in one day, first by the duchess's kindness and now by this man's joyful approval! He vowed to himself to fast that night in recognition of His glory.

"You and Peter take the vanguard," Robert told Girard on their second day's journey from Poitiers. "Moriuht and Madeleine will follow behind with me."

Without a word to anyone, Madeleine grabbed hold of the reins of Robert's roan stallion, a generous gift from Lady Philippa. Robert, looking feverish and fatigued, made no move to stop her. Girard sighed and accepted his fate. Madeleine held the reins, but at least he was in the lead, even if he did have to share the glory with Peter.

Mid-day they paused for rest beneath a densely shaded stand of chestnut trees. Robert mounted his steed and announced that he would climb a nearby rise to see if he could spot the land Philippa had granted him and his followers.

"Master," Girard said, "let me accompany you."

"Peter will accompany me," Robert said. Then, as though an afterthought, he untied his heavy satchel from his saddle horn and handed it to Girard. "Please guard this in my absence."

"And what of me, Master? What would you have me do?" Moriuht asked.

"Stay nearby," he said. "We'll not be gone for very long."

Madeleine handed the reins to Peter. She appeared unperturbed when Robert disappeared into the underbrush. Moriuht, with a grin of expectation, nodded at Girard before bounding off into the nearby bush. Girard assumed he went in search of another of his filthy treasures—a speckled bird's egg, perhaps, or the plume of a pheasant. Attracted to bright colors and smooth shapes, Moriuht

was child-like, energetic and more than a little strange. Yesterday
he had presented Robert with the alabaster skull of a decomposing
rabbit, behaving as though animal bones were valuable relics!

Propping Robert's satchel against the base of a lone fig tree,
Girard noted the unripe fruit and sighed. All morning long he
had fantasized an escape into the bush where he might enjoy the
remainder of the gift Philippa bestowed upon him before the five
departed Poitiers. "I arranged for the cook to prepare a package
for your journey," Philippa explained. "It isn't much, just a little
salted herring and wastel bread." She pressed the bag into his
good right hand and squeezed the other. "Thank you for your
kindness," she whispered. Her touch had filled Girard with hope.

But when Robert chose Peter instead of Girard to accompany
him to the rise, Girard sat down beneath the fig tree. He recalled
the many glances of pity and judgment leveled against him over
the years. He did not understand why Peter should accompany
Robert while he stayed behind to protect a satchel—and from
what? Marauding rabbits and squirrels? He longed to take a bite
of the herring but he did not want to eat in front of Madeleine
who, standing a bit to the side, appeared to be studying the
bark of a chestnut tree. Hungry and out of sorts he attempted
to distract himself from his various grievances by focusing on
his brief encounter with Philippa, the kind and lovely Duchess
of Aquitaine. Reconstructing their brief meeting, he assessed
and assigned meaning to each of her gestures and words. For
he believed that except for faith in God's goodness and grace,
everything else in life demanded a sensible explanation.

A nearby rustling startled Girard out of his revelries. Perhaps a
family of quail, or maybe a pair of cottontails. He was wondering
if he would ever again taste the meat of either animal when, quick
as sparrow hawks, three men leapt out of the brush and struck him
with cudgels, knocking him to the ground with bellowing shouts.

Girard opened his mouth to cry out, producing no more
than a mousy squeak. Curled on his side, gasping for breath, he
cowered beneath the blur of angry faces and rising clubs. They

would have beaten him senseless had not Moriuht burst through the underbrush. With the growl of an enraged animal, Moriuht wrested one of the clubs away from the attackers and madly struck at them, turning in circles, driving them back.

Girard raised himself up on his good arm and watched. He felt oddly detached. He knew that he should do something, but what?

"Give me your best, you demons!" Moriuht roared, weathering blows to his arms and head.

One of the brigands, a large muscular man with snarls of dark hair and an angry pink scar that cleft his lower lip and slashed his jaw, laughed and lifted his cudgel. With one swift blow to the head, he knocked Moriuht to the ground.

The hollow thump of Moriuht's body brought Girard to his senses. Grasping his cross in his hand, Girard called out. "Wait! We are followers of Robert of Arbrissel!"

The scarred one laughed. "What do we care?" he bellowed. The man's shiny black tunic and scarlet leggings reminded Girard of the glossy plumage and red feet of a chough.

"Unless," the brigand added, fingering the sheath belted to his waist, "this pilgrim has a stash of offerings." As the beast strode towards him, Girard released his cross and lifted his withered arm. "Move aside, cripple," the man said, kicking Girard's thigh before setting down his cudgel and riffling through Robert's satchel.

"O God, to my rescue, "Girard prayed, "O Lord, to my help make haste."

The robber tossed Robert's Bible and ceremonial vestments into a pile near the stricken Girard, but he placed the gilded chalice into his own satchel. Then he loosed the twine that bound a heavy linen sack and plunged his hand into the treasure of coins. Smiling at his good luck, he retied the sack and slid it into the leather scrip strapped across his chest. "The Lord helps those who help themselves," he declared, laughing and patting the bulging scrip. Girard cringed. The heathen sniffed a bundle of absinthe and rubbed a small amount of holy oil between his thumb and forefinger before slipping both the medicinal herb and the vial of oil into a pocket of his tunic.

Moriuht stirred and came to with a roar. Three men tied him to a tree. "This one's a good fighter, Evraud," a squat, hungry-looking man yelled to the one with the scar.

Evraud? My God, it's the very robber for whom Fontevraud is named! Girard thought.

The squat one's grizzled beard, snarled with bits of grass and filth, reached to his lean belly. His short legs bowed like a dwarf's, but his arms were well formed and the length of a much larger man. "Perhaps he will join us, eh?" he said, nodding his head at the struggling Moriuht who, wriggling free of the ropes that bound his legs, kneed the bearded one in the groin.

"He doesn't seem interested in joining us, Thomas!" Evraud said, laughing aloud as Thomas bent at the waist and swayed in breathless agony.

Groaning, Thomas straightened, slapped Moriuht with the back of his hand and retied the rope, binding him more securely to the tree before turning his attention to Madeleine, who stood in an unexpected shaft of sunlight. Only when Thomas approached her with a lecherous grin did she turn to flee.

But she merely ran into the open arms of another thug, a coarse lumbering man with matted hair, who lifted her and pressed her back against a chestnut tree, laughing as her slender arms and legs began churning the air. When her bare foot connected with her captor's shin, he slapped her face with the flat of his palm. "Kick me again, bitch, and you'll wish you hadn't!" He clasped her wrist with one hand, wrenched her arms above her head and tied her to the tree. Girard heaved himself to a sitting position, bowing his head, he muttered a prayer of courage: *The Lord is my helper, I will not fear.*

"This one's a pretty little thing," Madeleine's captor said. "Do you fancy her, Evraud?"

Girard sat, his fat thighs splayed wide as any whore, his enormous belly resting on the earth between his bent knees until, with a jolt of horror he realized that he too would like to touch Madeleine, or barring that, he would like to watch the robbers touch her. Certain that the furious thrumming in his ears was the sound of his soul unraveling, Girard heaved himself up onto his knees, closed his eyes and resumed praying. *The longings of the flesh are contrary to the spirit; those of the spirit are contrary to the flesh.*

Ignoring Girard, Evraud strode deliberately to Madeleine. Setting aside his satchel of stolen goods, he took her chin between his thumb and forefinger and, turning her head from side to side, studied her features. Without a word, he leaned forward and lapped the wine stain on her neck with his tongue. "A freckled beauty, sure enough," he said, dropping his hand. "Hold her down, men. You will have your turns soon enough." The matted-haired wild one threw Madeleine to the packed earth strewn with shale and bristling chestnut pods. He pinioned her wrists above her head while another brigand held her ankles.

Girard watched transfixed, his mouth opening and closing, as Evraud, dropping to his knees, tore away Madeleine's robe and linen chemise to reveal her small breasts, the sparse copper hair of her triangle and the delicious cleft of her sex.

Madeleine twisted her body from side to side, angling her hips away from Evraud without a sound escaping her pursed lips. Girard marveled at her fierce resistance and the eloquence of her silence, guessing that she did not cry out because she did not want to offer up the pleasure of her voice. The thug with the matted hair leered in anticipation of his own turn and laughed maliciously, a cruel sound that emanated from deep in his chest. "The bigger the fight, the better the fuck," he said, dragging his palm across his mouth. "She is wanting it, for sure."

Evraud lifted his tunic and tugged down his undergarments. Girard glimpsed the length and girth of his arousal and felt a sympathetic quiver in his own loins. Straddling Madeleine, bearing the weight of his body on his palms, Evraud separated her legs with one knee and entered her with a powerful thrust of his hips. Madeleine cried out in pain. Girard's member pressed against the rough serge of his robe.

"No!" Moriuht roared, writhing against the ropes that bound

him to the tree.

Only then did Girard grab up a jagged piece of shale and rise to his feet. He did not want to bear witness to rape, yet he did not throw the rock or look away. The high-pitched scream of a bird circled the treetops. Breathless in the penetrating heat, flush with disgust and yearning, Girard watched Evraud thrust, shudder and pull free of the motionless Madeleine.

Too late Girard hoisted the rock above his head and took aim at Evraud's skull. A brigand knocked him to the ground with a sweeping blow to the belly. Clutching the rock and struggling to breathe, Girard lifted eyes to the sight of Robert riding high on his red roan.

"I command you," Robert said, "in the name of God Almighty, stop!"

Peter, emerging from the brush a step behind Robert, charged fearlessly into the foray.

Evraud leaped to his feet and drew his knife. Robert threw back his head and opened his arms to the heavens. Then, as Girard would recount again and again until he had memorized the words and the telling took on a truth separate from the details, the sun turned brown as sackcloth and the hillocks shuddered. A funnel of wind lifted pebbles and chestnuts, swirling them into the air.

The shocked robbers released Madeleine just as Peter reached her side. Blinded by air-born debris, Girard rose to his feet, stumbled and dropped the rock. The winds ceased and a fetid miasma of low-slung clouds blanketed the forest. Gasping for breath, the two thugs bolted, their dark figures sliding through mist.

Madeleine whimpered and clutched her belly, crying out as though agonized in the pangs of delivery.

Robert stood in swirling vapor. He pointed his finger at the chestnut tree arching above Madeleine and Peter just as a thunder-bolt struck into the very heartwood, splitting the trunk from roots to crown. The tree remained upright long enough for Peter to whisk Madeleine to safety and for four more brigands to flee. Only then did it crash with a force that rocked the ground beneath their feet.

Evraud and the matted-haired one looked from the felled tree to Robert astride his roan. "We have witnessed a miracle!" Evraud whispered, dropping his knife. "This man," he said, pointing at Robert, "is a saint!" The two robbers fell to their knees and prayed.

Robert dismounted, grabbed his discarded alb and strode to Madeleine. Dropping to his haunches, he handed her his alb. "Put this on," he said in a soothing voice that silenced the rustling leaves.

Madeleine slipped the silk robe over her head. Girard fingered his beads, disturbed at the sight of a woman wearing the robes of a priest.

"Now your arms," Robert instructed. She obeyed, as though the softness of his words induced in her a lazy, hypnotic compliance. "Good," Robert said, nodding as the bell-shaped sleeves slid the length of her arms and extended past her fingertips.

"Now see if you can stand," Robert said. Even with Peter's assistance, Madeleine rose with great difficulty, the hem of the alb puddling at her feet. Robert removed his cincture and looped the belt around Madeleine's waist, gathering the excess material beneath the cord before knotting it. Blood blossomed red against the back of the white vestment. Girard felt a surge of compassion.

"There," Robert said, in a reassuring voice, "now you can walk without tripping." He took her arm.

"Can't you hear, man?" Moriuht bellowed at Girard. "I said, untie me! Over there," he motioned with a toss of his head, "the knife!"

Girard stepped clear of the robbers, retrieved Evraud's bone-handled knife cut the knotted rope that bound Moriuht. Grabbing the knife, Moriuht wiped his bloody head wounds with the hem of his leather tunic and approached the prostrate brigands.

"Moriuht," Robert said, "the Lord takes no pleasure in the deaths of the wicked; let them transform their ways and live."

Moriuht held fast to the knife, pacing in fury and indecisiveness.

"My good man," Robert implored, "Do not repay one bad turn with another. Love your enemies."

Nudging each of the brigands with his foot, Moriuht spat on

the ground between them. "You have been saved by my Master's grace, not your own," he said, his obedience to Robert eclipsing his desire for revenge.

"Settle down," Moriuht said, approaching Robert's horse, which had been nervously pawing the ground. Securing Evraud's knife beneath the cord of his tunic, Moriuht took the reins in his left fist and stroked the roan's mane with his right palm. "There now, there."

"Moriuht, lead the animal to me," Robert said. "Peter, help me lift Madeleine onto the saddle."

"Master, may I do something?" Girard asked.

"Repack my satchel."

Girard felt intolerably shamed. He moved quickly to transfer the plunder from Evraud's satchel, abandoned near the felled tree, to Robert's, turned inside out and tossed some distance away.

Rising to his feet, Evraud reached into his leather scrip and retrieved the money sack. "Father," Evraud said, proffering the stolen goods with outstretched arms, "Please take this back."

Intent on hoisting Madeleine into the saddle, Robert did not respond.

Girard ripped the sack of coins from the brigand's hands and stuffed it into Robert's satchel.

"Hold onto the saddle horn," Robert instructed Madeleine. Grabbing hold with both hands, she swayed as though in a faint. "It's alright," he said, steadying her. "We shall ride tandem." He mounted and, encircling her waist with his left arm, took the reins from Moriuht.

"Father," Evraud said. Thomas rose up and stood beside him. "Please forgive us our sins."

"You must ask God for forgiveness," Robert said. A stern look creasing his brow, he prodded the stallion with the heel of his bare foot.

Peter walked by Robert's side while a subdued Moriuht, fingering the bone hilt of the confiscated knife, kept a careful eye on Evraud and Thomas, who followed at a distance.

Girard folded Robert's maniple and wedged it between the gilded ciborium and paten. With his good hand, he painstakingly tied the ends of Robert's satchel before scrambling to catch up. Staggering even with the roan, Girard wished that he were the one sheltering the wounded Madeleine in his arms even as he judged the act profane.

"Thank you, Brother Girard," Robert said, nodding to the satchel Girard clutched to his chest. Girard's heart pounded with joy, and he immediately regretted having questioned the priest's decision to wrap Madeleine in his robes. Madeleine was wounded and Robert was caring for her as he would care for any being—man, woman, or child.

Shortly before the original party of five and the two robbers reached the summit, Robert tugged at his horse's bridle and paused while the others caught up. Careful not to jostle Madeleine, he used a thumb and forefinger to massage his temples.

Peter stepped forward. "Are you ill, Master? Has the fever returned?"

"I will be fine, my brother," Robert said, his voice trailing off as he turned his attention to Madeleine, who stirred faintly but remained silent.

Peter cleared his throat. "You know best, Master," Peter said, "but if we are to reach Vendôme by evening, we will have to hurry."

"Of course," Robert said. Leaning forward in his mount, he urged the horse forward. In a matter of minutes he arrived at the summit. As he looked out over the valley below, his haggard expression transformed to one of wonder. "Praise be to the Lord," he whispered. Stretching out one arm he pointed to a spattering of grass near a bubbling spring. "There lays the fount of my vision."

A hush fell over the party. Peter and Moriuht walked quickly to the edge of the ridge while Girard, weighted down by the master's satchel, lagged a step or two behind. The robbers exchanged glances and followed. In an hour, twilight would obscure the view of the valley. But for now its lush expanse was clearly visible. Girard glanced from golden scrub to reedy hemlock, settling on the promised fountain.

"Oh, Master," Moriuht said, "the land is beautiful and the fountain a most welcome sight."

Robert nodded. "On the valley land bequeathed to us by Lady Philippa we will build our monastery," he proclaimed. "Thank you Jesus, Mary, and Joseph." He crossed himself, gently settled his arm again around Madeleine, and pointed the horse's head toward Vendôme.

Girard's heart lifted in exaltation even as he stumbled to keep up with the others. *We? We?* he repeated silently. Could it be that the Master wanted him to be a part of his plan!

PART TWO

✝

I will not even mention the young girls whom you place in separate cells as soon as they have professed their faith, changing their clothes without thought … The wretched results of this action should be cause for alarm: for some, about to give birth, have broken their flimsy prison walls; other have borne children in those very cells.

Marbod of Rennes, Archbishop of Rennes
Letter to Robert of Arbrissel
c. 1100

The evening before the pilgrims departed from Vendôme, Robert paced the grounds of Holy Trinity. Pausing beneath one of the silver maples that flanked the south door of the transept, he contemplated his next move. Now that the land for the monastery had been secured, the real work of building would begin. "Mother Mary," he prayed, "grant me patience and the fortitude to continue." A momentary peace calmed him, and he resumed walking until Girard's voice interrupted his solitude.

"Robert of Arbrissel cleaved a tree in half with the power of his faith, stunning two robbers into conversion!" the monk proclaimed to a group of women loitering near the entrance to the garden.

Appalled, Robert slipped behind a nearby tree, clinching his hands until his nails bit into the flesh of his palms. Despite his guilt, or maybe because of it, Robert said nothing to contradict Girard's blasphemy. God knew he was a weak, ineffectual man even if Girard did not.

After Girard and the group of women dispersed, Robert dropped to his knees and covered his face with both hands. If he could not keep Madeleine safe, how could he provide protection and guidance to a hundred more? Pounding his fist against his chest, he prayed for forgiveness. *Through my fault, through my fault, through my most grievous fault . . .*

While Robert did not question his love of God, a passion that eclipsed all else, he was less certain of his motivations in converting prostitutes than he had been in Rouen. Although he was bothered less and less by lustful thoughts of women in general, he could no longer deny his feelings for Madeleine. But he had never touched her except to bless or anoint her until that horrible day in the grove. Only after they arrived back in Vendôme did Robert acknowledge his far less noble feelings. He fought against these impure thoughts and desire with prayer and frequent penance. And, indeed, during the days, both proved adequate distractions.

But nights were a different matter entirely.

For Satan was clever. He assumed Madeleine's shape and followed Robert straight into his dreams with the smoldering allure of a Parisian whore. Night after night Robert mounted the same fiery horse, wrapped his arm around the sloe-eyed demon's middle and remembered the exquisite fit of Madeleine's body against his own, how nothing had separated their two heartbeats but a silk alb and a worn cassock. In his unholy dreams he called out Madeleine's name loud enough to wake himself and the men on the pallets beside him.

Now, once again kneeling in contrition, Robert fumbled for his beads and prayed for a way that would strengthen his resolve, help him overcome Satan's demons and renew his faith. He longed to be enveloped in God's unblemished grace and pledged to love Him with a love devoid of sexual confusion and full of pure light. Wind blew through the limbs of the trees, waking a pair of sleeping doves. Robert lifted his head to the cooing birds, and felt a warm flutter of fingers brushing his forehead. And though he could not see her, Robert knew the fingers belonged to the woman of his vision. "Have faith, Robert," she whispered in hushed, soothing tones. "You will be delivered."

Five days later the pilgrims arrived safely at the forested valley of Fontevraud where Robert led his one hundred followers to the bottom of a gentle declivity to a fresh water spring called Fons Ebraldi. Private without being isolated, Fontevraud was but a short distance from the bustling harbor of Candes and the fortresses of Saumur, Chinon, and Loudin. Climbing onto a flat rock, he spread his arms and proclaimed, "Here, at the junction of three diocese, Angers, Tours, and Poiters, we will build our abbey. Let us pray and give thanks to our generous benefactor and to our Lord Jesus Christ."

The fountain spilled over into a sun-lit pond. Those who lifted their eyes saw sooty shearwaters gliding the sky, dipping from side to side on powerful stiff wings. At the close of Robert's prayer, Moriuht charged through pussy willows and waded into the pond, scooping water into his hands and swallowing with great noisy gulps. "Sweet!" he announced, "and bitter cold!" He shook his head so that beads of water flew from his beard and sprayed the children lining the shore. Their giggles and squeals tangled with the yodeling high-pitched wail of the black-throated divers. Peter began a song of thanks that layered one note on top of another, climbed the branches of the trees, rose up past the canopy of leaves and nudged the clouds.

The next day Girard asked Robert for permission to permanently join his mission. The two of them worked beside the other pilgrims, tearing out briars by their roots, piercing their hands and stripping the shallow valley of its growth. At day's end, the men carried armfuls of prickly cane to a knoll on the lip of the valley and dropped them in a great sprawling mound, setting a communal fire on the spot where they would build the church. The flames leaped into the darkness and lit the faces of the exhausted pilgrims. Robert looked for Madeleine, but she was not among them.

Near the end of the first week, they began to run low on supplies. Marie, gruff, impatient and filled with purpose, approached Robert by the pond where he stood watching water bugs skitter the surface.

"Your followers are hungry," she said. "If they are not fed, they will not be able to continue the work." Hands on hips, Marie cut an imposing figure. "You cannot expect work from starving people," she said.

"Have patience, Mother Marie. Look what we have accomplished already." Robert said, pointing in the direction of the newly cleared land.

"Bah! The land is still littered with branches and stumps!"

"True," Robert said, smiling slightly, for there was something about her directness that delighted him. "But very soon we will level the earth and begin building."

"You think so?" Marie laughed, a mirthless sound scratchy with fatigue. A shearwater swooped the pond. Its wingtips kissed the surface and a shudder of ripples gilded the water. "The Lord has led us here," Robert said. And though he knew his knowledge of psalms would not persuade Marie of his holy intent, he hoped that the sound of the words might comfort her. "These waters will revive our bodies and souls," he said. Heartfelt passion imbued his words, for just looking at the restorative waters lifted his own flagging spirits.

"Hummph!" Marie said. "Our bodies will need more than dry tubers and water from your miraculous fount if you expect us to build a monastery."

"You must have faith, Marie. Just a bit longer."

"Will faith cure my aching belly?" Closing her eyes, she stood in silence. Her breathing grew even and relaxed, a soothing sound that gave Robert the courage to ask the question that had been gnawing at his soul. "Marie, how is Madeleine?"

"Her body is mending," Marie said. "As for her mind, I have no idea, for Maddy has not said a word since your … miracle … in the grove."

"Marie …"

"Save your confessions for God," she said and turned to begin her ascent to camp. "What's done is done," she called over her shoulder. "Now we deal with the consequences."

That night after the converts trailed out to sleep, Robert walked up the road they had traveled and, raising his robe, knelt bare kneed in the pebbly dirt. *Oh Lord*, he prayed, *be gracious to me and hear my cry. How long shall I keep planning in my soul and experiencing daily sorrow of heart?* He prayed until the evening fire burned to embers and the stars disappeared from the skies. He prayed until his knees ached and the muscles in his shoulders burned with the effort of touching palm to palm. He knew that despair was a failure of character, a cowardly surrender to Satan's powers, and prayed for a sign that the pilgrims would receive what they needed to survive. Only after he toppled in exhaustion to the ground did he make his way slowly to his pallet where he fell into a deep slumber.

Before Moriuht even touched his arm Robert smelled his presence, that peculiar blend of clove oil and unwashed skin. Opening his eyes to Moriuht's dancing feet, he knew that his prayers had been answered.

"We are saved, Master Robert! God has sent us provisions, bread and food and wine..." His joyful smile, full of nubbed teeth and inflamed gums, was exactly what they lacked. After the initial heady excitement, Robert and his pilgrims had grown grim in their work and their hunger. "Come," Moriuht said. "I have a surprise!"

Robert followed him to the spring where half a dozen peasants clustered beside a handful of congregants. The peasants carried straw baskets, wooden crates, and linen-wrapped bundles in their arms.

"A gift from Lady Philippa," a stout woman said, peeling back several layers of cheesecloth to reveal dark loaves of bread.

"Please thank the Duchess for her charity," Robert said. Dropping to his aching knees, he instructed his followers to do the same. "Let us also praise the Lord who has blessed us through this woman."

During the next fortnight, with full bellies and renewed hope, the congregants set about building wooden huts with thatched roofs and packed dirt floors. Only slightly larger than the cramped box of a confessional, the dwellings offered privacy and warmth at night when the winds blew through the valley. Separating the virgins from the reformed prostitutes, Robert placed two or three women in each hut. He and the other men slept outdoors.

In the middle of the encampment he helped construct a makeshift oratory where all could meet for worship at the canonical hours. Lady Philippa, who continued to donate food and clothing during these difficult times, persuaded other aristocratic women, Hersend of Montsoreau and Petronilla of Chemillé, to do the same.

Amidst all this activity, Madeleine never left the hut where she lived with Marie. Worried, Robert approached their dwelling. "I've come to offer counsel and comfort," he told Marie, who stood in the doorway, arms folded against her chest.

"Not yet." she declared with firm resolve.

"When?" he asked.

"When she's ready," Marie said. She had the scent of baking about her, a buttery yeasty smell that reminded Robert that he had not eaten all day.

"Has she spoken yet?"

Lips pursed, Marie responded with an abrupt shake of her head.

"And her health?"

"She looks better than you," Marie said. As Robert turned to leave, she called after him. "Master," she said, "you won't be helping any of us if you starve yourself sick. We need a leader strong of body as well as faith."

Master? He wondered if perhaps a full belly and a place to sleep had softened her attitude towards him, and the idea filled him with joy. "Tomorrow," he said, "I'll eat tomorrow."

The night air, thick with humidity and the peppery scent of vegetation, carried the high-pitch bark of a lone pup and the harsh clang of a leper's bell. Standing by the charred remains of that night's fire, Robert imagined the monastery he would build. The church unfolded in his mind's eye with the clarity of a holy vision.

Built of white stone, the exterior was simple, but within, the soul leaped: the central nave, massive and white, the flagstone floor, flecked with glittering mica, heavy columns and arches, established solid order, the only decorations small carvings in the capitals. At the end of the nave, bright light illuminates the chancel, its narrow pillars thrusting heavenward.

Flanking the church, he saw the huge quadrangle of the monastery. At its center, square lawns of the cloister were divided into smaller squares by hedges. Along one side of the cloister a large refectory terminated in an eight-sided kitchen. On another side stood the chapter house and common room.

Visualizing the buildings gave him a sense of purpose and direction. He realized that women need protecting, that caring for them was to be his life's true mission. He determined he would dedicate the oratory to John the Evangelist, and that the men—clerics, monks and laymen alike—would serve the women just as John served Mary. In this way he might partially amend for his sin with women.

Two winters after William left on crusade, the whinny of a horse startled Philippa awake. She assumed it was the early post to Toulouse and almost drifted back to sleep when she sensed a presence in the room. Heart pounding, she pushed up on one elbow. Her eyes had not adjusted to the muffled light of dawn before William swept aside the damask curtains on their bed and dropped an armful of bright-colored fruit onto the rumpled bed linen.

"They are called oranges," he said. "And I carried them all the way from Syria to surprise my wife. You remember that you are my wife, don't you, Philippa?" he teased. Sitting beside her on the bed, he lifted his eyebrows in a boyish way that reminded her of young Will playing hide-and-go-seek behind the wall hangings. Gathering the blankets around her shoulders, she looked at her husband and thought of their mischievous child, his pudgy baby feet peeking from beneath fringed tapestry, and her heart opened wide enough to hold them both. Perhaps they could begin their lives anew.

"I remember that I am your wife and the mother of your son." She picked up an orange and took a big bite, her mouth puckering at the taste of the acrid rind.

William laughed. "You eat the pulp inside."

Beneath his playfulness, William appeared preoccupied and sad. The limbs of the elm tree outside the window snagged the sanguine sun. William turned his head for a glimpse of the new day, and Philippa saw for the first time the keloid scar slashing the length of his left cheek. Kissing her fingertips, she placed them against the raised flesh.

"How?" she whispered, dropping the orange onto the bed.

"At Eregli," he said, his jaw tightening imperceptibly. "It's nothing." He dismissed her concern with a defensive shrug. "How is the young pup?" he said, changing the subject.

"Will is strong and brave like his father," she said, and understood that now was the time she should reveal the role she had played conducting his affairs. She hesitated, for she understood that while William might be grateful to her for having safeguarded his estate, he might also resent her ability to do so. Better he should hear from someone else.

Philippa watched as William began peeling the orange, separating the fruit from the peel with his thumb. "Taste," he said, placing a wedge into Philippa's mouth just as the elm branches released the morning sun. She bit into a new sweetness, aromatic with a trace of tart, a moan of pleasure rising up in her throat.

William was filthy, unshaven, and the weave of his clothing held the musky scent of sweat and smoky campfires, but his slow luxurious kiss was flavored with the sweetness of oranges. Philippa's breathing grew shallow and she lifted her hands to cup his scarred face.

"I have missed you, wife," he whispered, dropping the orange on the night table and kissing Philippa's neck, his breath a humid whisper against her shoulder. His sudden proximity, the way his body filled the bed with animal heat, unnerved her.

He moved his hands along her arms and hips. By the time he reached her thighs, Philippa felt split open and taken apart. Segment by segment she disappeared out the casement window. Even as her body gave in to an impulse that seemed beyond conscious control, a distant part of her wondered how her husband would react after he discovered that the woman in his arms was not the girl he had left behind.

⋇

Madeleine lay on a pallet in the hastily built hut she shared with Marie. The hut was dark and small, barely big enough to hold two pallets. Air blew under the door and squeezed through gaps between the rough-hewn planks. But she liked the clean scent of the new wood and the silver flash of starlight through scattered knotholes.

Marie's unicorn tapestry hung on the wall facing their pallets, and everyday Madeleine tried to focus her attention on the beauty of the animal's milky-white horn. But random impressions of that day in the grove leapt up at her with the persistence of a needy dog. Depleted by the long journey, weak from lack of food, she finally gave in and allowed the yapping mongrel to rest its wet muzzle in the palm of her hand.

She closed her eyes and the grove came to her in all its horror. Not with the graceful clarity of Robert's promises or the forward momentum of Marie's stories. But haltingly and in fragments, as though her heart could hold only one piece of misery at a time.

Red leggings and the call of a hawk.

A coil of unwashed hair wild with the scent of nervy exhilaration and lust.

The scrape and gouge of bark against her back.

Rough hands kneading her breasts, rolling her nipples between calloused fingers.

The sulfuric burn of spent lightening.

The creature's fixed, hazel-eyed stare.

A swirl of bark had distracted her from the scent of danger. Like a full moon or the silver overlay of fish scales, the bark contained a rippled symmetry her fingers itched to duplicate. She envisioned a garden of deep ambers and sunny yellows, and imagined planting asters and marigolds in tight concentric circles. Viewed from a hilltop, each bush would appear as a petal on a single gigantic flower. Convinced that beauty was hers to appreciate, lost in a world of her own design, she had let down her guard and missed the rustle of leaves and snap of twigs that announced the approach of robbers.

Over and over she relived the horrors of that afternoon. Near dusk, the beast backed off, curled at the foot of her pallet and drifted off, or pretended to. Madeleine felt its malevolent weight pulling the blanket taut against her legs. Then, she too must have slept. When she opened her eyes, Bodkins had replaced the beast and Marie had returned from her day of work. Cupping Madeleine's cheek in her palm, she kissed her forehead in greeting.

"Sometimes you have to settle into misery and let it have its way with you," Marie said, groaning and collapsing into the cot beside Madeleine. "My poor joints are stiff from kneading dough," she said, slowly flexing her fingers in front of her face, "and my back aches beyond words." She lay down on the straw-filled mattress and sighed. Bodkins, who had awakened at the sound of Marie's voice, leapt from his place at Madeleine's feet and settled on Marie's chest. "Oh well," Marie sighed, absent-mindedly scratching the cat's neck, "working the scullery sure beats hauling brush and boulders." Marie kissed the old tom's head before gently placing him onto the sage-sprinkled floor. "Robert's even got Agnes and Arsen clearing land."

"I hate them both," Madeleine said. She had not spoken to anyone in three months, not uttered a word since that day in the grove, an oddity of behavior that Marie neither condemned nor condoned. If Marie was shocked by Madeleine's sudden decision to speak or by the raspy grate of her words, she did not show it.

Marie settled on the edge of Madeleine's pallet and smoothed her flour-dusted skirt. The skin around her eyes pouched darkly. "The twins?" she asked. "You hate those two stupid girls?"

"Not them," Madeleine said, her breath coming fast and ragged. "I hate Robert for making me believe a better life was possible." For one whole year Madeleine's heart had beat with Robert's promise, fluttering against her chest like some crazy thing that had not known sorrow and disappointment in equal measure. For one whole year she had been stupid enough to believe her life would be different just because a wandering preacher with a kind voice and a rainbow arc of colors told her so. "And I hate …" she stopped, convinced that even to say his name would give him a new and frightening hold over her. "And to think this valley is named for the robber who defiled me!"

Marie pinched the bridge of her nose between her fingers and said simply, "Hate requires enormous energy. Better to do something more productive with your life."

Madeleine turned to look at Marie's tapestry, the one item of value Marie brought with her from Rouen. Safely transported throughout the journey, now it hung on the wall in the rustic hut. In the brothel Madeleine had learned to disappear into the strange beauty of the tapestry. But now everything about the beast appeared altered. The hooves seemed sharp-edged and lethal, the eyes malicious and wild. She could no longer envision leaping summer clouds on the back of a unicorn.

"How we miss the familiar, no matter if it's joyful or filled with pain and sorrow," Marie mused, a faraway look playing across her face.

"Is he here? Does he live among us?"

"If you mean Evraud, Robert has assigned him to build shelters for the lepers. You will not see Evraud unless you seek him out."

For a long time neither woman said a word. "I have not bled in three moons," Madeleine said. "I feel the monster's child growing," she said, resting her clenched fist against her belly. She closed her eyes, heard the throaty trill of a songbird outside their hut, imagined the graceful swoop and rise of flight and tried to hitch a ride. But she remained weighted to the ground.

"I know, Maddy," Marie whispered, settling on the edge of her pallet. "I know about the child." Slowly she massaged the back of Madeleine's hand until her fingers opened one by one and lay spread against her belly. Marie's touch, the only touch Madeleine could tolerate, calmed her and reminded her of how carefully Marie had bathed her useless hands and legs the day Robert carried her to the infirmary at Vendôme.

"It isn't mine," Madeleine whispered. "I had nothing to do with it."

"No," Marie said, "you didn't. But it's yours just the same." She shook her head. "But then there's little that women decide in this life except maybe how to deal with the problems handed them by men." Her words came to Madeleine smooth-edged and worn nearly transparent. "I know I wasn't consulted before your father left you and your sister on my doorstep."

Madeleine felt a familiar pain for the loss of her family and then a new sensation, a suffocating fear that tightened her throat and made it difficult to breathe. Had Marie not wanted her? Had no one wanted her? "Why didn't you refuse to take us, then? You could have told my father no," she said, petulantly sliding her hand free of Marie's.

"Yes, I suppose I could have. Don't think I didn't consider it. I knew at a glance that the two of you were too young to do me any good. But there you stood, all freckled and bold. And then you tugged at my skirt and I felt something like, well, like *need*. You needed looking after and I needed someone to love. Some choices in life really are that simple, Maddy girl." When Madeleine placed her palm against her stomach, Marie covered it with her own. Madeleine sighed, grateful for the warmth of their stacked hands. "If only we hadn't followed Robert," she said.

"If only I hadn't opened the door to your father. If only your father hadn't met your mother. How far back you want to take this?" Marie said, her look so distant and old that Madeleine knew she must have been thinking of some secret pain.

"Why me?" Madeleine said, in an aggrieved voice. Years of pain and disappointment snarled together and erupted into one long angry wail. "It isn't fair!"

"Fair?" Marie said, dropping Madeleine's hand and jutting out her chin. "And since when have you known fair?" Marie looked into her eyes. Madeleine wished that she could see the world through her direct and honest gaze. "Fair or not, the only thing you have to decide is what kind of mother you're going to be." She sighed. "Many a woman's birthed a child she didn't plan on having by a man she didn't know or couldn't stand. The only thing makes this time special is it's happening to you."

Madeleine's tears left her shuddering and gasping for breath. Marie scooped her up in her arms and held her close.

Madeleine heard an ominous rattling in Marie's chest that echoed the sound of her own sobs. She cried for her mother's wispy colors and her sister's giggle. She cried for the strong hands of the farmer or blacksmith or merchant she would never wed and for their children, conceived in love and loving them. And after she had mourned the life she had lost and the one denied her, she cried for the life she was living—bruised and unkempt, full of knobby edges and snarled hair.

"Life is never simple," Marie said. "Never. But for now it's what we have. You hear me?" Marie stroked Madeleine's hair with the same methodical calm she used to settle Bodkins. "And Maddy are you listening to me? Because this is important—all of us, each and every one, needs someone to love."

Madeleine's throat relaxed and she took a deep breath, inhaling the kitchen scents of vanilla and cinnamon on the palms of Marie's hands.

"Marie?" she whispered. "Every time I look into my child's face, will I see the monster's?"

Marie stiffened. "How do you know the babe won't have your freckles and your dreamy ways?" she asked.

Madeleine laughed. Her arms and legs tingled, and she felt a dim desire to rise up from her pallet.

"Maddy honey, there's no escaping what's growing inside you. The child belongs to you as surely as your arms or eyes do, and you'll need all four and more to raise it properly." She was quiet for a time, letting her words wash over Madeleine

Madeleine listened to the sounds of conversation carried on the breeze and, for the first time in a great while, she wondered what was happening beyond the four walls of her hut.

"I suspect you'll be wanting to contribute to this new community of ours," Marie said. "The old Jumieges nun who's in charge of the scullery is looking for someone to help her make bread. I could talk to her if you want. The work will do you good, and the sweet smells might remind you to eat. You're too thin for this hard life, Maddy. Too thin."

"We'll need a garden. I could help plant a garden."

"Well then, if that's what you want, I'll see what I can do." Marie loosed her arms and Madeleine settled back on the pallet.

"Marie," Madeleine said. Marie leaned forward to hear her words, "I want to want it, but I don't, and I don't know how to make myself."

"All in good time," Marie said and kissed Madeleine's forehead. "All in good time." Rising up from the pallet, she spoke in a voice that was everyday brisk. "Now get some sleep. Roll onto your left side. Right side's for growing boys."

Slipping beneath silk coverlets, Philippa waited patiently for William to finish undressing and climb into bed beside her. A day full of petty annoyances involving feuding servants and a tipsy cook had left her ill tempered and craving sleep. William, home from crusades for less than a week, contributed to her exhaustion. Having grown accustomed to the soft voices of her aunts and the deferential tones of servants, she found her husband's loud, commanding tone more than a little disquieting.

"Aquitaine thrived in my absence!" William declared, unbuckling his belt and letting his pants drop to the floor with a thud. The candle cast a bronze glow against his naked body. Tingling warmth climbed Philippa's thighs and settled between her legs.

"Hugh has done a fine job in my stead!" William said.

His words squelched Philippa's desire and filled her with apprehension. She must tell him the truth.

William climbed into bed and pulled the curtains around them. Gathering Philippa in his arms, he buried his face in her hair.

"Actually," she said, "Your brother was often… away… or… unavailable…when important decisions had to be made."

Releasing Philippa from his embrace, William rolled onto his back. "And Herbert of Lusignan? Fulk of Anjou?" he asked.

Philippa could tell by the clipped cadence of words that an angry, officious duke had displaced her playful, affectionate husband. "Herbert and Fulk were gone from their palaces for great stretches of time," she said.

William turned his head and glared at his wife. "Well then how…"

"It was up to me to conduct your affairs as regent of your state." She knew she had said enough, but the pride that Sophie cautioned against welled up and she continued, bragging of her stunning successes at Oleron and Saint Macaire. "I could act as your advisor," she said, balanced on one elbow and playing a tress of her hair against his cheek. "No one need know," she whispered.

"*I* would know," he bellowed. Throwing back the covers, he pushed the bed curtains aside with such force that one panel split at the seam. Without another word, he threw on his clothes and stormed out of the room.

Alone in the dark, Philippa hunched under the covers, and cursed her foolish pride.

The following morning William restricted Philippa's movements to the palace and surrounding grounds where her days grew monotonous as the blanched winter skies covering Poitiers. While her husband ruled his province and commanded his vassals, Philippa directed servants and, nine moons after William's return, gave birth to a daughter, Anne. She dearly loved their two children but treating colic and settling squabbles over toys was not as challenging as quelling battles between rebel barons. Though she continued to attend mass, care for William, order food and supplies, and receive guests, she grew more and more despondent. Sometimes she descended to the great hall only once a day for the mid-day meal, and more often than not William was absent, attending to official business.

During one such long and tedious afternoon Sibyl and Sophie asked if they might join Philippa in her chambers. She knew that she could easily dissuade the compassionate Sibyl by complaining of a headache, but Sophie was a different matter.

"You are bored," she said, studying Philippa's face before decisively tucking a strand of flyaway hair behind one ear. "We will entertain you with a story."

They sat in rockers by the hearth. Before taking a chair from near the mullioned window, Philippa placed a rock crystal vase on a table to act as prism to the harsh winter light, gratified when green, blue, and rose diamonds blinked, scattered and climbed the wall.

"In Brittany there was a brave knight named Eliduc," Sibyl said in her high stilted voice. She removed one of Anne's chemises from her sewing box and began cross-stitching the bodice. "This knight married Guildelüec, a fair woman descended from a line of high nobility," she said. "Eliduc served the King of Brittany—in those days a king ruled that region—and was the king's favorite, hunting at liberty in the royal forests, attending court whenever he wished." She paused to remove a loose stitch, her frantic fingers pulling at the thread while her tongue whipped across her chapped lips.

"Tell her of the backbiters and gossipers who grew envious of Eliduc," Sophie said, in her usual melancholic tone. "Tell her how they accused him of treachery to the king, who exiled Eliduc without explanation."

Sibyl frowned. "True, but first he bid his dear wife farewell. Promising to remain faithful to her, Eliduc left for England with a band of fellow knights."

Philippa wondered, not for the first time, if William had been faithful to her during the years he followed the cross to the holy land. It was not something she cared to dwell on. Better to recall his return, his hand drawing aside the damask curtains and dropping sweet oranges into her bed.

"In England, Eliduc learned that an old king was besieged in his castle because he would not allow his young daughter to marry another king's son. Eliduc put his valor to the test and ambushed the old king's enemies, causing them to flee. Then he swore allegiance to the king and promised to serve him.

"The king's daughter, Guilliadun, heard of Eliduc's bravery and his good looks and wished to meet him. The real story begins now," Sibyl said, looking up from her needlework and rocking so rapidly that Philippa feared she might tumble backward out of her chair, "for this is both a love story and a story of betrayal!" she said.

"Bah," Sophie said, waving her hands dismissively, "love, betrayal, they are one and the same, two sides to a single coin!"

Sibyl pursed her lips and shook her head, but otherwise said nothing in response to her sister's comments. "Eliduc goes to court and meets the princess," Sophie said, taking up the story in her raspy whisper. "He is polite and courteous and he sits next to her on a couch. She steals glances at him, admires his face, his body…"

"Really, sister!" Sibyl interrupted. "Why must you dwell on the unseemly?" she said, jabbing the needle in and out of the fabric with alarming speed.

"Because life is unseemly!" Sophie said. Removing her hands from the arms of the rocker, she folded them in her lap and directed her gaze at Philippa. "And love especially so!"

Sibyl let out a tiny gasp of exasperation but said nothing. Sophie continued with the story, taking her time, moving at a leisurely pace. "But no sooner do Eliduc and the princess fall wildly in love than the King of Brittany sends messengers asking his retainer back to court, as his lands are under siege. Eliduc tells Guilliadun he must leave. He asks her to accompany him. On the ship to Brittany a storm brews, tosses the ship, throwing men overboard. 'It's God's will!' some of them say, 'because Eliduc has a proper wife at home and now takes another woman.'"

"Righteous words!" Sibyl said. "The Lord punishes those who do not follow his law!"

Philippa focused on the diamonds cast against the wall and wondered why her aunts were telling her this story, for their stories always had a purpose beyond entertainment.

"When Guilliadun hears that Eliduc is married, she falls into a swoon. Eliduc takes the helm and guides the boat to shore. But Guilliadun does not awaken—she seems dead."

Since shortly after William's return, Philippa had been living in a trance, moving between her duties with little joy and now, hearing her aunt's story, her skin prickled as though a cold draft had whipped through the room.

"Eliduc places the body of his beloved in a chapel near his home in Brittany. His wife is joyous to see him, but he is cold to her touch. Everyday he visits the chapel, prays to God that He will bring Guilliadun back to the living.

"Now Eliduc's wife grows suspicious and orders a spy to follow her husband to the chapel. Her servant tells her everything, and while she feels anger towards her husband, she surprises herself by feeling pity for the dead girl. While Eliduc is away at court, she goes to the chapel with her servant and sees the girl lying inert on a bier.

"Suddenly a weasel enters the chapel, and the servant kills it. Then another weasel enters and circles the dead animal, as if in mourning. It leaves and returns with a red flower and places a petal in the mouth of the dead weasel, which miraculously comes back to life.

"After the weasels leave, Guildelüec picks up what remains of the flower and places a petal in the dead girl's mouth, and lo! She comes to life!

"Guilliadun, now revived, tells her story about Eliduc's deception. 'He was a wicked man,' she says, 'to deceive me.' And Guildelüec replies, 'Woman are foolish to trust in men.'"

"Amen to that!" Sophie chimed in.

Sibyl paused, looked up from her sewing and frowned at her sister. A cloud draped itself across the sun and obliterated the play of colors against the wall.

"And then what happened?" Philippa asked.

"Oh, my dear," Sibyl said, "the poor wife entered the nunnery!" Taking one final stitch in the hem of little Anne's chemise, she tied a knot and broke the thread with her teeth.

That evening, as Philippa descended the stairs to the stone keep to review provisions—they were preparing for many guests due to arrive in Poitiers for a great council—she heard Alice, the cook, speaking with the steward who supplied the household with fish. Guiscard mentioned Philippa's name, and she froze.

"They say he's abandoned her bed for the Viscountess of Châtellerault, Dangerosa."

"Ha! That is a fine name for a viscountess!" Alice replied.

"Especially one who has hooked the duke like a fish!"

Phillipa lifted a foot, intending to retreat up the stairs, then paused, to see if there was more.

"He has engraved her image on his shield," Guiscard said in a loud whisper, "and vows to carry her on the battlefield as she has carried him in bed!"

"Hush," Alice said. Her laugher was muffled, as though she had covered her mouth with the skirt of her apron, "someone may hear!"

Philippa tiptoed up the stairs to her chambers. Her heart raced with this terrible knowledge. Suddenly she understood the purpose of her aunts' story of Eliduc. They meant to warn her. Remembering Guildeluec's words—"Woman are foolish to trust in men"—she wondered at her own foolish nature. William was absent for long stretches of time—settling disputes, he told her, and tending to his estates. But might he be using his duties as subterfuge? Might he be in his mistress's bed this very moment? She imagined William trailing a lock of some other woman's hair across his cheek, recalled the throaty gasp of pleasure he made entering her (a sound as satisfying to her ears as any she had ever heard) and felt her stomach cramp in despair. Was some woman even now turning her head to catch the sweet urgency of William's sound?

Philippa moved from wretchedness to anger in what seemed a matter of breaths. He was, she understood, no different than any other man—a creature ruled by lust, incapable of lasting love. She would leave Poitiers, escape the cold white palace with her children and return home to Toulouse for an extended visit. Her mother and father were dead and her brother was absent, fighting Saracens in the Holy Land, but even an empty palace seemed preferable to her life with William.

She walked to the window, flung open the casement and looked to the heavens for answers. The only time Poitiers appealed to her was twilight when swallows soared the roseate sky, climbed until they could go no further, then plummeted towards earth, spent and exhausted. But that night as she watched the birds intertwine in their ascent and tumble down separately, she took no joy in their glorious flight.

The women came to Madeleine with flower seeds—poppies tucked into a cloak pocket, four o'clocks knotted in cheese cloth, sweet William hemmed into the skirt of a chemise. They came with garlic cloves, valerian, and aromatic sage. They handed over mother bulbs in burlap sacks, spilled seeds into her cupped palm, and offered up hope in the form of advice—

"Valerian makes a fine border, but take care it doesn't crowd the other plants."

"If you prune back salvia in the winter, come spring it'll blossom lavender spikes that'll take your breath away."

"Plant marigolds in full sun."

"… bearded iris and reticulata in well-drained soil."

Madeleine rolled the slippery seeds against her palm, fingering the fleshy scales of the root tubers and the grooved nodes of the bulbs before placing them carefully into a basket. Only then did Madeleine thank the women for their contributions to the abbey garden, whispering her gratitude while cupping each pair of hands in her own.

The following day, with Moriuht's help, Madeleine set about creating a garden what would be both beautiful and useful. Together they built raised flower boxes, a cone trellis, and an elaborate arbor. In her mind's eye Madeleine envisioned a mature garden. She imagined pansies separating herbs from root vegetables and sweet alyssum blossoming a fragrant line between trailing beans and scrambling vetch. Moriuht smiled and nodded so vigorously at her suggestion that they plant yarrow beside downy lamb ears that she felt certain he shared her vision, a deep desire to achieve the perfect balance of shape, color and texture.

"Next November," Madeleine said, "we'll plant hyacinth!" She smiled, imagining how they would stagger the planting, pressing some of the bulbs into shallow holes, burying others deep in the earth so that a colorful assortment of pink, purple, red, cream and salmon-colored flowers would bloom one after the other all through the month of March.

"And a dense mat of ground cover to comfort our feet," Moriuht said, wriggling his toes into the soil.

"Perhaps Scotch moss," Madeleine said, "since it is both soft and fragrant." The sun had bleached her hair platinum and scattered freckles the length of her arms. Work had calloused her hands and made her back strong. And while she did not welcome the birth of her child, she slowly came to accept the inevitability.

Girard passed by the garden, fingering his cincture and smiling a strained, thin-lipped affair that pinched his features. "The vegetables will be bountiful," he said.

Moriuht, who could hold anger for just so long, waved a friendly greeting and smiled broadly. Madeleine, who was on her knees thinning a mound of squash seedlings, remained silent.

"You do not like Girard?" Moriuht asked, the blade of his hoe uprooting cocklebur and crabgrass with swift incisive blows.

Madeleine lifted her head. "He saw what that monster did to me, and he did nothing," she said, remembering Girard's bloated incendiary colors scorching the air.

Moriuht frowned, shifting his weight from one soiled foot to the other. A faint whisper of wind rustled the hemlock leaves. The sun slipped behind a tangle of clouds and turned the drowsy sky murky green.

"The man's weak," Moriuht said, "but he's a man of God." He paused at the end of a row and turned his face to the fluting call of a plover, his body assuming a momentary stillness that reminded Madeleine of Robert.

Even as she avoided Robert, she missed his calm presence and his mesmerizing voice. Suddenly she felt hollowed out with longing she could not put a name to.

"Girard is not a wicked man," Moriuht said. "He constantly struggles against his demons, and when he falls, as we all fall, he is sincerely repentant." Leaning his hoe against the sturdy trellis, he looked deeply into Madeleine's eyes. "What else can a poor sinner do?" he asked. Reaching into a pocket of his robe, he removed a vial of clove oil, and used one dirt–smeared finger to rub the ointment onto his gums.

"He could have helped," she said. "You did."

Moriuht laughed, an embarrassed sound, and squatted to pull a weed. "Girard tried—he raised a rock—but remember he's fat and crippled."

"He *watched*," she said. "He *watched* what that man did to me."

Moriuht sprang to his feet, grabbed the hoe and resumed weeding—hacking and slashing so vigorously that he accidentally uprooted a fledgling pea vine. "You might as well hear it from me," he said, "Evraud intends to stay on after Saint Lazare is built."

The muscles in Madeleine's shoulders tightened and her stomach spun into knots. She stood and, looking down into the valley, spotted a ribbon of smoke rising from a tight copse of trees. Evraud was somewhere down there digging trenches or lifting stones. "Why?" she asked. "Why is he allowed to live his life as though nothing has happened, but I …" She cupped the thrust of her belly, a reflex that caused Moriuht to drop his eyes. Clutching the hoe in one hand, he worried his beard with the other.

"You should talk to Robert. He explains things better than I can."

She shook her head. Moriuht surprised her by dropping the

hoe and taking her hands in his own. "Madeleine, you must forgive for the sake of your soul."

"I cannot," she whispered.

"But the Master is not to blame for your . . . troubles. No," he said, vigorously shaking his head, "not anymore than Girard nor I." Moriuht's voice nudged the air between them, the tone as softly coaxing as when he spoke to wild animals.

Madeleine knew blame never healed anybody's pain, yet she could not temper the righteous anger that jabbed at her whenever she thought of that terrible day in the grove. "Robert promised that I would be safe," she said. "Then he left my safety in the hands of a cripple."

"And me!" Moriuht said. "I was there as well! Have you forgotten that the brigands outnumbered us? We would have needed a dozen more men to fend off their attack!" The pain in Moriuht's face was so bright, so personal that Madeleine looked away.

"All right," she said, her eyes settling on a skein of birds unraveling against the sky. "If it will make you happy, I'll speak with Robert."

Every evening before bed, Girard walked the perimeter of Fontevraud. Once the land was cleared and leveled, Lady Philippa had sent scores of men, including an architect and a sculptor, to assist the pilgrims with the construction of Robert's abbey. The building, however, progressed slowly. Weeks passed before the architect chalked the church's cross-shaped plan onto the bare soil, and longer still before the men dug foundations and drove pilings. Once the scaffolding was in place, the masons began the backbreaking work of cutting and hauling stone. At Philippa's prompting, a wealthy innkeeper from Limoges donated a surplus of blue-grey tile that would adorn the roof of the Abbey. The men's monastery, Girard knew, would not begin construction for quite some time, but at least the kitchen, an octagonal building studded with cupola-crowned smokestacks, was almost complete.

The workers set up camp in a forested area on the southeast corner of Fontevraud some distance from the leper camp, their fires clearly visible every night but Saturday when they rode their horses to Candes where they drank ale and bedded whores. The first Saturday, Girard assumed the men had defected having grown tired of the hard labor and their isolation. But they returned before dawn on Monday and did so without fail week after week, month after month. Such skillful and dedicated workers were not cheap.

One particularly damp night, Girard cut his stroll short and returned to the hastily built hut that housed the monks. Wrapping himself in a wool blanket, he lowered himself onto a pallet. His flaccid arm tucked fin-like against his growling belly, Girard courted sleep by cataloguing the rumors, nasty gossip that that spread like nettles in a rye patch. Some of the monks said Robert subjected the young virgins to the rigors of ascetic life, placing them naked in tiny cells. Others said he favored the widows and reformed prostitutes, counseling and comforting them far into the night. All but a few agreed that Madeleine had seduced the Master.

Using his good arm to heave his bulk onto his right side, Girard wondered how much longer he would have to reside in this hut sleeping with a dozen other brothers on a thin pallet and a dirt floor. Ignoring the burn in his chest and the relentless rumblings of his gut, he adjusted his coarse wool blanket, closed his eyes and attempted to rid his mind of the image of Madeleine and Robert. But while he succeeded in banishing the thought of the Master sharing a bed with a prostitute (for the godly man would not, *could not* do that!) the other image—the sight of Madeleine impaled on a chestnut tree—held his soul hostage.

Girard's change in position eased his heartburn, but did nothing to assuage the discomforts of his sour stomach. Gassy and bloated, he regretted the evening's cabbage even as he craved a bowl of soothing frumenty sweetened with almond milk and sprinkled with ginger. Who, he wondered, would settle for pease porridge if frumenty pudding was available? Following a cluster of loud, unseemly belches, Girard drifted off to sleep pondering the small self-contained delights of pasties and fritters.

In sleep, lust joined gluttony in a frightening duel of appetites that built on and amplified Girard's memories of that day of miracles and rape. Against a stormy backdrop of suffocating mist and lightening bolts, Girard dreamed that Evraud was force-feeding the naked Madeleine a meal of bread and fish. Holding a wastel-wrapped herring in his stiff fingers, Evraud thrust the morsel deep into Madeleine's mouth. Girard cried out "Stop!" Not because he wished to protect Madeleine, but because he recognized the meal as his own, the one packed for him by Philippa's cook.

Girard woke to a stiff prick and a growling belly. His lust and his craving for food had become one enormous appetite—painful, insatiable and never ending. *All are tested in faith,* Girard thought. *Your will, God, please let me know your will,* he repeated, over and over, until the repetition dulled his mind, softened his erection, and he drifted back into a shallow sleep.

The following afternoon Girard entered the sprawling garden. Ducking behind a cone trellis wrapped in the vines of a towering bean plant, he watched Madeleine glide between rows of herbs and stoop to pick a sprig of lemon balm. Her presence surprised and annoyed him. It was long past the morning hours, the usual time Madeleine, accompanied by that filthy animal Moriuht and a bevy of so-called *reformed* prostitutes, weeded, pruned and watered.

Girard had taken heart last spring when Moriuht began helping Madeleine plant the garden. Bounding between empty trellises and rows of seedlings, Moriuht had offered up his pitiable treasures—a fist full of leathery leaves or a pungent bouquet of lavender—with the same unbridled enthusiasm he lavished on Robert. With Moriuht's attention split between Madeleine and Robert, Girard hoped to replace him in the Master's affections.

Madeleine settled on a bench, and Girard recalled his purpose. He had come to pilfer a few green beans to hold him over until evening meal in the makeshift refectory, a mud-walled, thatched roofed room without windows. He abhorred his gluttony, his sinful failure to transcend his body's appetite, but hard as he tried he could not conquer his obsessive need for food. Every morning he pledged to fast as Robert fasted. By tierce he had modified his plan, determined that he would eat, but only a few scraps of bread and a mouthful of wine. Gradually he could ease himself into a more temperate lifestyle. But inevitably at the mid-day meal one bite led to another until Girard had gobbled every morsel on his plate. By dusk, he was newly ravenous and desperate enough to eat raw vegetables straight from the vine.

Hidden behind the dense foliage of the climbing bean plant, Girard studied Madeleine's expression. Expectant? Impatient? Certainly it looked nothing like the glance of pity she had given him in Blois. Just remembering *that* look caused Girard to bristle. For a brief moment anger swept aside hunger and made him bold. He would leave his hiding place and confront her, remind her that a man, not a woman, sat at the right hand of God! But before he could take a step in her direction, Madeleine, still holding the lemon balm, reached into a nearby bush with her free hand and fingered an amber flower. The shape and toasty color reminded Girard of fried fritters. In the time it took to draw one ragged breath his howling need for food returned twofold. Slowly, surreptitiously, he plucked a string bean from the vine and placed it into his mouth. Keeping his eyes on Madeleine, he tongued the length of the pod, luxuriating in the furred texture until anticipation gave way to necessity and he snapped the pod in half with his molars.

Reaching for another bean, Girard heard the familiar click of rosary beads. He held his breath and turned his head to see Robert entering the garden and walking purposefully to Madeleine's side.

She rose to her feet but did not greet him, frowning as she studied the lemon sprig in her hand.

By God, Girard thought, *their meeting is no accident!*

"Thank you for agreeing to see me." Robert said.

Madeleine nodded.

"Shall we sit down?" Robert's words were innocuous enough, but the tone was not the somber, nuanced sound of a holy man performing mass or granting absolution. His words to Madeleine resonated with a raspy timbre, a twilight sound that reminded Girard of his own shameful appetite. For the first time it occurred to Girard that the rumors he had heard about Robert and Madeleine might be true. Perhaps the child she carried was not Evraud's but the Master's. The thought aroused his body even as it crushed his spirit. He wondered if he had squandered his life following a common sinner. The muscles in his calves burned with the effort of supporting his great weight, a small price to pay for learning the truth.

Girard shifted his body and studied Robert, whose shoulders had broadened in the months spent splitting boards and hoisting beams. Indeed, he appeared a much larger, healthier man than the feverish ascetic Girard first laid eyes on in Vendôme. Watching Robert run his hand through his plentiful curls, Girard touched the sparse fringe ringing his tonsure and considered the possibility that he, like his father before him, would be completely bald before his thirtieth birthday.

"Your garden is beautiful," Robert said.

Surely the Master has not forgotten that beauty is devilish distraction! Girard thought.

"As a young man I was taught catechism by an old priest who thought nature's beauty a lure for the lesser beings," Robert said, as though he had heard Girard's thought. "I remember he used rabbits as an example, explaining that they are dim, soulless creatures that need the appeal of color—the orange carrot, the red berry—to guide them to their proper food."

Madeleine stroked the sprig of lemon balm in silence. "In a

similar manner, the old priest argued, bright fluted flowers attract insects and birds to the nectar that sustains them. For a long time I accepted his words as truth."

Tottering slightly on tired thighs, Girard feared that Robert and Madeleine might sense hear his strained breathing, but he need not have worried, for Madeleine appeared transfixed by the green-flash of a hummingbird hovering beside a periwinkle vine, and Robert could not take his eyes off of her.

"But on my journeys..." Robert paused then and started anew. "On the long road to Fontevraud I saw natural sights that inspired all that is good in me, and I've come to the realization that the old priest's definition of beauty is far too limiting. Your beautiful garden, for instance, nourishes both my soul and my body, for it is resplendent with flowers for the altar and bountiful with vegetables for the table."

His words strike a cord in her, Girard thought, studying Madeleine's face.

"Why, yes!" she said, "See the gold and yellow marigolds separating the rows of herbs? The flowers attract snails, drawing them away from the coriander and fennel."

"Mary's gold," Robert said. "Named in honor of the Virgin Mary. I've heard they lessen the pain of a bee's sting as well."

"And those violets," Madeleine said, growing more animated, "provide a colorful garnish for food while their oil soothes the skin."

"They too are associated with the Virgin," Robert added, "for they represent purity and innocence."

"But my favorite are the fragrant primroses," Madeleine said, waving a hand toward a bush hanging from a trellis, "for they are useful in so many ways, as preserves, garnishes, even sugar."

"And they are symbols of the Holy Spirit, and for this reason we spread them in churches during the movable feasts of Witsun and Corpus Christi," Robert said.

Girard shifted his weight slightly so that now he knelt in the dirt with his ass resting on his heels. The Master, it seemed to him, reveled in this celebration of worldliness.

"Beauty has a multiplicity of purposes," Robert said. Then, lowering his voice slightly he asked, "But has the beauty of your garden lifted you out of your despair?"

Madeleine twisted the lemon sprig in her hand and tossed it away.

"Madeleine…" Robert said and faltered. "So much pain we humans inflict on one another—sometimes with deliberate intent, sometimes not. Please do not let anger replace despair."

"Why shouldn't I be angry? What happened to me is not some passing violation. It lives on in this child." She looked down at her protruding belly then back at Robert. "Evraud should be punished," she continued, "He should pay for what he did!"

"We would scatter apart against the fierceness of our sins if we did not forgive each other our transgressions. I ask that you forgive Evraud his."

"You ask too much!" Madeleine said. "You cannot fail in your promise to protect me and then expect that I will happily carry the burden of your failure!"

Girard had two thoughts, the one slithering over the other—*So the child is Evraud's!* and simultaneously—*Her attitude is unusual in a woman!* Girard felt certain that no man would tolerate such insubordination, and was amazed when Robert assumed a posture of humility.

"Madeleine, we must not repay evil with evil, we must not take vengeance into our own hands, for vengeance belongs to the Lord. The Bible says we must feed our enemy, give him drink."

"How is that?" Madeleine asked. "How is feeding him and giving him drink going to make him pay for his crimes? His life grows better for his sin. Mine will never be the same!"

"He lives among the lepers," Robert said. "The Lord will give him what he deserves, either in this life or the hereafter."

Madeleine rose from the bench with her arms crossed and turned toward a patch of lavender. Robert also stood and watched her brush the purple flowers with a palm. He raised a hand but stopped short of placing it on her shoulder.

"We must forgive our enemies if we expect God to forgive us," he said.

Girard thought that perhaps Robert's glance lingered too long on the achingly sweet curve of Madeleine's neck.

"Is that what brought you here? You want me to forgive Evraud?"

The mood shifted, grew cloudy with old disappointment and something else Girard did not fully understand.

"Madeleine…" Robert said and faltered. The way he drew her name out, fondling the vowels and imbuing them with a swollen carnal sound, disgusted Girard.

Clearing his throat, Robert began again, this time he spoke with a windy sound that rustled leaves. "Madeleine," he said. "I have also come to ask you to forgive me for my failure to protect you."

Madeleine bushed back a lock of hair with her fingers, a feminine gesture Girard found almost as attractive as her sudden silence. "Please."

Quite suddenly Girard remembered a distant afternoon in his boyhood. Bored and curious, he had followed his brother deep into the woods where, instead of killing game, Bernard bedded the butcher's daughter. Hiding behind the trunk of a pine tree, Girard watched him cuddle the round-breasted beauty, seducing her with a playful barrage of kisses and deep-throated appeals—*please, my sweet, please*—until gradually, seamlessly he had lowered her to the mossy forest floor. When Bernard lifted the girl's skirt past her saffron-colored patch of public hair, Girard tugged down his own breeches and pulled at himself until he had reached a climax so intense he had had to bite his tongue in order to muffle his moan.

"No!" Madeleine's voice, quivering with rage, brought Girard back into the present moment.

Head bent, stance deflated, Robert continued. "Perhaps you're right, Madeleine. I am a prideful man for thinking that I might cover you with my cloak when it is only in God's arms you will find protection." Robert lifted his head and turned slightly away from

Madeleine, blinking against the sunlight. "But you must believe my intentions were sincere. The idea that you should be harmed in any way was and is abhorrent to me. More importantly, the anger you hold in your heart is not good for you or your child."

"What is good is not always possible," Madeleine said.

"Think of Christ," he whispered. "He endured crucifixion to save us. Each of us carries a cross, Madeleine. We all suffer a form of martyrdom that makes us worthy to enter heaven."

"I don't know if I have it in me to forgive," Madeleine said and rested her hand on her belly.

"Oh, but you do. Just as you've cultivated these flowers," he said, his hands stirring up the scent of hollyhocks and lavender, "so can you cultivate forgiveness. Plant the seed of compassion in your heart, Madeleine. Nurture it with prayer, and it will blossom into a thing of beauty."

Madeleine scanned the air around the master's body before lifting her hands to comb the empty space. Girard wondered if the experience in the grove had addled her mind. Whatever she discovered seemed to satisfy her, for she dropped her hands and acquiesced.

"All right," she said, "I'll try."

At that moment, a distracted Moriuht appeared at the edge of the garden and began warbling to a songbird sheltered in the branches of a chestnut tree. Girard feared that it was only a matter of time before the fool spotted him and called out his name. In his haste to depart, Girard tripped. He did not fall, but the scuffling sound his feet made attracted Madeleine's attention. Regaining his balance, Girard took a deep breath and, without a backward glance, fled the garden.

✳

Late in Madeleine's pregnancy, Mother Hersend sought her out in the garden to discuss the "miracle of birth." The widow of Lord Guillaume de Montsoreau, Hersend de Champagne had been among the noble women who had donated to the Abbey in the difficult early months. Not long after, she had taken orders following her husband's death. A non-judgmental, kind-hearted woman, she was tiny, barely five feet tall, with deep dimples and a rollicking laugh better suited to a milkmaid than a learned woman of authority. Even before she began speaking, Madeleine could see why Robert had appointed her Abbess. Something in her delicate but assertive manner simultaneously soothed and challenged. Hersend called out Madeleine's name just as she finished weeding a row of lima beans.

"Madeleine, you've worked wonders! And in such short time!"

"It's nothing," Madeleine said, blushing. "Gardening is my passion."

"When the Lord marries passion to need," Hersend said, "wonders may transpire. We'll have altar flowers and vegetables well into winter!"

"Brother Moriuht has been most helpful."

"I must remember to thank him," Hersend said. After a pause, she assumed a more purposeful tone. "You know, there are similarities between what you are doing here," she said, lifting her hand to take in the whole of the garden, "and here," she said, talking a step closer to Madeleine and touching her fingertips to the thrust of her belly. "Both germinate from seed and depend on warmth, fertile soil, and the goodness and grace of Our Lord to come into fruition." She examined Madeleine's face with a maternal scrutiny, and Madeleine wondered if Robert had prompted the abbess to speak with her. "Of course," Hersend said, "there are differences as well. The growth of a child is much more complicated. After the seed of the child is planted, it develops in stages."

Madeleine leaned on her hoe, eyes locked with Hersend's as she listened.

"At first, the child is like a vegetable feeding and growing…"

Madeleine thought of the lazy expansion of heavy orange pumpkins and plump red tomatoes.

A sudden breeze ruffled Hersend's habit. She spread her small hands (hardly bigger than a child's!) against her thighs, holding the robe in place until the gentle wind settled.

"And then?" Madeleine asked.

"Next it assumes the characteristics of an animal—feeling, moving, full of fledgling desire," Hersend said, rolling her tiny hands, one over the other.

The wild tumbling motion reminded Madeleine of Brother Benoît's young hound, whose devotion made his unbridled energy bearable.

"Finally," Hersend said, smiling a beatific smile and looking upward, "it acquires a rational mind and takes on human form." Her voice was turquoise, full of comfort and hope. "Only then does God endow the child with an immortal soul."

These last words struck Madeleine with pain, like deadly nightshade spreading its wild branches and sprouting poisonous berries deep inside her belly. She thought of Evraud, a soulless devil if ever there was one.

"You are thinking of the child's father," Hersend said, reaching out to smooth Madeleine's brow. "It might help you to think of the man's mother instead," she said, softly. Taking both of Madeleine's hands in her own, Hersend looked deeply into her eyes. "Consider the woman whose body nourished and cradled your child's father. She must have hoped, as all mothers do, that her son would grow into a man of kindness and worth. Perhaps you can feel compassion for this woman destined to become your child's grandmother?" Hersend squeezed Madeleine's hands, and for a brief moment, Madeleine felt sorrow that was not her own.

"Do not fear, my child. God will grant your child a holy soul." Rising up on tiptoes, Hersend kissed Madeleine's cheek just as the babe stretched and tumbled against her ribs.

By late Autumn Madeleine could no longer work comfortably in the garden. Whenever she stooped to sweet talk an ailing plant or uproot a pesky weed, the babe kicked and flailed about as though she intended it great harm. Bertrad and Florence took over her duties, and Madeleine spent her days sorting beans, soaking lentils, and measuring ingredients for Marie's breads and pastries.

Madeleine worried that Robert might imagine she had abandoned her work in the garden rather than chance another private conversation with him. In fact, after he asked for her forgiveness, she felt newly drawn to him and would have welcomed such an encounter. But Robert, consumed with abbey business, had no time for garden conversations.

Around this same time Mother Hersend arranged for Brother Girard, an efficient if reluctant scribe, to teach Madeleine and the twins their Latin letters so that they might read holy hymns prior to singing them. Though it would be years before the buildings were completed, Robert insisted that the work of the abbey begin immediately and that no one's spiritual life be put on hold.

The newly designated scriptorium, where Agnes, Arsen, and Madeleine met every day after prime for their lesson, was a rustic, temporary structure with pine walls and a thatch roof that smelled of newly hewed wood, honey, bees wax, and acacia gum. Two large cutouts served as windows, allowing natural light to fall on a half dozen small tables, each with a little bench, lining the walls.

Arriving early one morning, Madeleine and the twins interrupted Peter, who was sitting at one of the tables with his back to the three women, singing softly and writing musical notes on vellum pinned with knives to a triangular block of wood. His robe spilled over the bench and puddled onto the plank floor. While the twins lingered near the door, Madeleine, dizzy with anticipation, hurried to Peter's side.

"What is it you're working on?" she asked.

"Hymns," he said simply, without meeting her eyes. He held his brush politely aloft, but his tapping foot revealed he was impatient to return to his manuscript.

The twins, a step behind Madeleine, stretched their hands towards the gold paint, their fingers trailing the air as though poised to caress. They had grown plump on Philippa's rations. Their hair returned to its former luster and their skin assumed a pale radiance.

"Do not touch!" Peter said. "The notes are wet!" He shielded the unfinished page with the curve of an arm.

"We're only looking, Brother Peter," Agnes said. "It's alright to look, isn't it?" She arched one brow and slid her tongue across her upper lip.

Peter frowned, motioning that they might step closer.

The twins glided into place beside Peter who began a new song, placing his brush on the page and shading the bulbous tip of one spindly note.

Madeleine, intent on watching Peter's progress, did not realize Girard had entered the room until he spoke. "I am here to teach you," he said and walked to a small table across the room from Peter where he nudged aside the stool with one stout leg. Ignoring Agnes and Arsen, he tugged at the rope cincture girdling his waist and waved for Madeleine to join him. His halo, which waffled fitfully in Robert's presence, scorched fiery red.

"Shall we begin, then?" Girard said, brushing a crumb from his sloping belly. Madeleine recalled when she had last seen him, fleeing from the garden and wondered how much of her conversation with Robert the troubled monk had overheard. Abruptly, he turned to face her. She smelled bacon in the greasy folds of his

robe and garlic on his breath. A wave of nausea left her light headed. She grabbed the edge of the table to steady herself.

Girard, seemingly oblivious to Madeleine's discomfort, slid his
crippled hand into the drape of his robe. Leaning forward, he
placed his other hand onto the vellum. His body relaxed, and he
began to trace the letters with a sensuous slide. "Some are curved,
others capped, still others ornamented with fat bellies and big
feet," he said. "You must feel their variations in your fingertips
before you can hear them in your heart and know them in your
head." With a nod he indicated that Madeleine's hand should
replace his on the manuscript. She obliged, tracing the very same
letters his fingers had just touched. Girard's features softened
even as his breathing quickened. Madeleine ignored Girard and
focused on the letters.

What attracted her most in the beautifully ornate manuscript
were the large letters decorated with fantastic gilded figures.

"This is a b," Girard said pointing to a vegetable-green letter
collaring a blue dog's head. "And this one," he said, touching the
elongated neck of a rose-colored musician, "is a p."

"And this?" she asked, touching the curved tail of a majestic
yellow lion.

"The letter *y*," he said, placing his hand over hers and guiding
her fingers the length of the trailing loop again and again until his
colors blistered like the burnt edge of bacon and his breath puffed
ragged and foul against her cheek. She pulled her hand free and
stepped back, toppling the small stool in her haste.

The twins, sleek, voluptuous, and curious as crows, turned
their heads towards the sound of the stool thumping against the
plank floor. Holding hands, they crossed the room.

Before Girard uprighted the stool, he glanced the length of
Madeleine's body, his eyes lingering on the swell of her belly. His
expression was one she had seen on the faces of men who had
something to hide—a limp organ or a perverse desire. Often they
were angry afterwards, tossing down coins with violent, dismissive
gestures.

He motioned for the twins to move nearer the manuscript. "The letters are what's important," he said, his voice raspy and too loud. "The rest is for ornamentation. The dog, the musician, the lion are drawn for beauty's sake, for aesthetics."

"Aesthetics," Madeleine whispered, savoring the velvety roll of the word against her tongue. *How like a garden the page appears, with each flowery letter arranged to form a bouquet of meaning!*

The twins bumped hips and rolled their eyes. "Aesthetics," they said in high fluty voices.

Madeleine ignored their mimicry, for she had already determined that nothing would interfere with her learning to read.

"Do not act like children!" Girard scolded.

The twins muffled their giggles with the palms of their hands and backed away from the manuscript.

"Shall we resume?" he said to Madeleine.

He moved to her side. A great heat vapored off his body, and the air between them webbed with something ominous.

Each time William slighted Philippa, she recalled the servants' gossip and wondered if he had taken Dangerosa as his lover. The mere possibility put her in a leaden mood. On one such weighted morning, she bid Emma care for the children and declined a meeting with her aunts, claiming a sudden stitch had struck her in the night. Then, instead of tending to her duties, she lay in bed and studied the ivory carvings on the back of her hand mirror—a love story split in two by the gashed and dimpled trunk of a laurel tree. She seldom gave the familiar scene a second glance, but on this day the lovers demanded her attention and filled her with anxious dread.

On the left panel, a seated man, his eyes fixed on the eyes of a beautiful woman proffering a crown, held a cluster of grapes in one hand and lifted a chalice with the other. Both the man and the woman were smiling.

On the right panel, the woman now sat beside the man. Her knees were turned demurely away from his, but between her suddenly parted thighs the fabric of her gown bunched and pulled taut. The woman prepared to place the crown on the man's head. The man reached for the woman's breasts.

The closer she studied the carving the more she considered a different story than the one she had always read. For the first time she noticed that in the right panel the man no longer looked into the woman's eyes. Instead, he directed his gaze inward at his own separate desire. And in the woman's posture, Philippa sensed hesitancy as if she understood that while her lover knew her body, he did not know her soul. Tossing the mirror onto the bed, Philippa buried her face in her pillow and prayed for guidance. But none came.

Her mind passed randomly from one disappointment to another, created a dizzy momentum that spun her into a state of malaise. *Love and betrayal are one and the same*, she thought, recalling Sophie's words. A great pressure clamped tight against her ribs and made it difficult to breathe. For the sake of the children she could not surrender to despair.

Tossing aside the bed sheets, Philippa threw open the casement windows. The sun, a faint smear behind mountains of dark clouds, cast an eerie glow onto a spindly hedge of privet bushes half-submerged in fog. Grey puffs of chimney smoke filled the air with cinders. Head down, Philippa paced back and forth, opening and closing her hands, entirely unaware of the rattle of pans in the scullery or the chill of marble beneath her feet.

Saint Hillary's bells sparked a memory of Robert's sermon in

Toulouse. "Love," Robert had said, "comes from God, it gives without taking." Philippa's frantic breathing slowed. "That's it!" she said aloud. "I will write to the Master. He will tell me what to do!" She clamored for the maid's bell. The moment Giseld appeared at her door, Philippa grabbed the parchment and stylus from her hands and told her to fetch Ponce. "I need him to take a letter to Fountervaud," she explained.

"Yes, Madame," Giseld said, her fingers fretting the hem of her apron.

"Is there something else?"

Giseld blushed and took a deep breath. "The cook says to remind Madame that the duke and duchess of Anjou arrive today, and we must buy more poultry—hens and capons. They have a large entourage, and many others may come as well, lords and prelates," she said, a childish excitement infusing her words.

"Others? What others?" Philippa asked.

"The lords of Lusignan and Parthenay," she counted on her fingers. "And also the bishop of Angoulême …" Dropping her hands, Giseld began pleating the skirt of her apron.

Philippa's temple began to throb. Today was the Feast of All Souls. William had spoken of little else but his banquet for weeks. "Thank you," she said to Giseld. "That will be all."

The maid curtsied and backed out of the room.

By the time Philippa descended the stairs to the great hall that afternoon, most of the guests were already seated at the long trestle tables, listening to a performance by Eblo of Ventadorn. Guiscard and Alice had prepared enough food for a hundred people and arranged the great hall in grand fashion, setting the gilded plates, silver spoons, and maple mazers at each place and centering bronze ewers on the tables. The walls were festooned with colorful ribbons and flags, and an abundance of tapers lit up the room. A juggler wearing the rayed tunic of a court jester, tossed a half dozen balls into the air.

Philippa took her place on the dais, between William and his brother Hugh. As one course after another of fish, foul, and meat crossed the table, she scanned the room. On her right was Aime´, the Archbishop of Bordeaux, so old that he had to be carried to the table in a litter. Further down the table Count Fulk argued with his eldest son. Conspicuously absent was Count Fulk's wife, the lovely Bertrad, whose scandalous affair with King Philip had not ended even after Pope Pascal excommunicated Philip, instructing him to cease his adulterous behavior or face anathema. On her left sat Isabelle de Montfort, Count Fulk's sister-in-law, Agnes de Craon, Agnes de Aïs, and a tiresome group of William's comrades. Hugh, drunk on mead, and William, high on companionship, paid Philippa scant attention. She ate little but instead listened to Eblo's song, a strange mélange of fact and fiction, about Count Geoffrey defending the English queen against the slanders of a seneschal, then marrying the daughter of a merchant, but leaving her to defend his territories against the invasions of a Spanish king. Just as Eblo's song ended, Abbot Alexander of Talmond approached the dais.

"Lady Philippa," he said, bowing slightly, "you are married to a most generous man! Has Duke William told you how he wishes to make donations to the Abbey of Talmond so the monks may hold thirty masses for the souls of his father and mother and thirty more for the souls of Lady Philippa's father and mother? The duke has kindly offered one third of the domain of Scolis, including the rents," he said, wiping his brow with the back of his hand.

Surprised, Philippa turned to William. Was it possible he still loved her? "Don't forget the palfrey," William said, frowning slightly.

"Oh yes, we mustn't forget that," Abbot Alexander replied with a chuckle. Then, looking up at Philippa, he explained, "Duke William has taken a special liking to a fine dappled palfrey owned by the monks of Talmond. They are pleased to give the duke this horse in exchange for his generosity."

My dear God! Philippa thought. William had traded the souls of their parents for a horse! But before she could compose a word in response, William rose and escorted an ecclesiastic to a seat between the lords of Lusignan and Parthenay.

She heard the sound of carriage wheels and the play of hooves on cobblestones. Since it was William's habit to greet guests personally, she thought nothing of it when he left the great hall. Only later did it occur to her that he had all the while been listening for someone, his nervous expectation revealed in the clumsy stutter of his hand knocking over a goblet.

Curiosity and a wife's instinct compelled Philippa to turn her head towards the casement window just as a young woman alighted from her carriage. First the peak-a-boo thrust of a foot clad in a pointy-toed slipper secured at the ankle with a narrow band of ribbon, then the dainty, but not overly cautious, hop down onto cobblestone.

Philippa took note of the woman's red hair and expensive clothes. The silk cases that attached to and lengthened her thick braids were of variegated samite interwoven with gold and silver threads. Her gown, long, narrow, with wide bell sleeves and an exaggerated train, was the height of Parisian fashion. Philippa watched mesmerized as the woman's fingertips impatiently fondled the tassel of her girdle, a long rope of vermillion silk looped once and knotted loosely around her small waist.

Suddenly William arrived at the young woman's side. She turned with a voluptuous grace born of wealth and comely looks. Smiling, William reached for her bejeweled hand. Philippa knew instinctively that the lady placed great demands on servants, expected reverential treatment from men and, most likely, had not accomplished a single thing of import in her life—never guided a babe to breast, comforted an ailing parent or penned an important document. But so what? The way William's thumb lay claim to the back of the woman's hand said it all.

At that very moment, Philippa forgot the cold, calculating William who bartered the souls of their parents and recalled, instead, the warmth of him lying next to her in bed, the possessive way he pressed his knees against her legs before scooping her into the cradle of his embrace. Her heart relived the emotional truth of that experience even as her eyes took in the bare facts of the spectacle before her.

William entered the grand hall and passed before the dais with Dangerosa's hand tucked in the crook of his arm. Philippa smelled her scent—cloying attar of roses—before she heard Isabelle de Montfort's insipid voice. "Can you blame him?" she whispered. "What man would be attracted to a manly woman? Even if she does have gold hair." Her comment was greeted by the breathy titters of Agnes de Craon and Agnes de Aïsand—petty, narcissistic women disappointed with the shallowness of their own lives who were all too eager to take joy in someone else's pain. But worse than their laughter was the brittle glances of recognition from the ones who had been betrayed by wandering husbands and faithless lovers, those lonely, bitter woman who carved out niches of martyrdom and lived their lives huddled in the narrow space of their constricted dreams. Philippa felt humiliated and longed to be anywhere else. The room split apart into dizzy shards. She prayed that she would not faint.

At that moment she spotted her aunts making their way across the crowded hall. Sophie, walking three or four paces behind her sister, appeared serenely composed, her hands pressing the folds of her skirt. Sybil, breathless with frantic energy, moved awkwardly among the guests, her fingers fidgeting with a loose button on her gown. They had come to rescue her. "If your guests can spare a moment of your time," Sybil said, loud enough for those near the dais to hear, "you'll want to come quick and hear baby Anne's first giggles." Philippa wanted to kiss her aunt's freckled hands for having thought up a way for her to leave the hall with dignity.

"So soon?" Philippa said. It seemed like only yesterday that young Will learned to giggle and soon after that to talk. She recalled the sound of Will's voice—his words imperfect and clumsy, but passionately spoken and wholly his, and she felt buoyed by a deep maternal love.

Before Philippa rose from the table William introduced Dangerosa, the Viscountess of Châtellerault, to his comrades. The lust between William and his mistress was palpable. Philippa reeled with the insult. A great pain settled behind her eyes.

"Little Anne's delighted with the new sounds she can make," Sophie said, and glared, or seemed to glare, at William and Dangerosa. Philippa leaned forward to tuck a coil of her aunt's flyaway hair under the fold of her wimple. "Walk away with your head held high," Sophie whispered into her ear.

Girded by her aunts' love, Philippa descended from the dais and traversed the great hall with dignity.

Robert noted how pregnancy had softened Madeleine's features and streaked her blond hair russet. "Madeleine?" he said, his hand resting against the jam of the open door. She sat on the edge of her cot balancing a quarto on her lap. A candle placed on a table tossed a round of light upon her face. She appeared lost in concentration, one fingertip meticulously tracing the swirl and plunge of the manuscript's gilded letters. Robert's eyes settled on the butterfly fluttering the pulse of her neck and he knew the heady experience of a falcon plunging into a canyon. *Blessed is the man who stands up under trial,* he silently prayed.

"Madeleine," he repeated in a louder voice. He wondered what she saw when she looked at him. He knew that his hair and beard grew wiry and unkempt, and he suspected that in appearance he more closely resembled a madman than a priest. "What are you reading?"

"It's a passage from the Bible," she explained. "Brother Girard allowed me to take a small quarto back to my cell."

Madeleine placed the quarto on the cot and covered her shoulders with a shawl that lay tossed beside her. Since establishing Fontevraud, Robert had found women in general less distracting. But even pregnant with another man's child Madeleine drew him in. Guilty desire pained his heart and set his stomach roiling. He willed himself to remain dispassionate and focused on duty.

"Are you cold?" he asked. "I'll close the door."

"Marie will not be back for a while," she said, one hand modestly clasping the shawl at her throat. "Bertrad's son has come down with the croup, and she is helping to care for him."

"It's you I've come to see," he said. And then his mouth went dry and he could not think how to begin. He recalled the great crowds he had addressed in the cathedral of Saint Sernin on the day he realized that his voice could move people and he marveled anew at how often Madeleine rendered him speechless. Clearing his throat, he asked the first question that came to mind. "Have you found it in your heart to forgive Evraud?" he said, hoping his abruptness did not offend her.

"Forgive? My belly no longer heaves at the mention of his name," she said in a flat voice devoid of emotion. "Perhaps that is a step in the right direction." She shrugged.

Robert believed that with a few well-chosen words he could bring her to full and holy forgiveness. "Evraud is reformed. He is not the sinful man who attacked you in the grove."

"Don't," she said, raising her hand to stop his words. "There is nothing you can say that will change my mind regarding Evraud's nature. You forget, Robert, I have known many men. I can recognize evil, and that one is evil through and through. Still, I feel great potential in this child's kicks and lunges." Her hand stroked her belly. "And while I can not find it in me to forgive the father, I no longer hate him."

She had come so far since their talk in the garden. He had only to guide her that final step or two. But how? Looking around for clues, he noted a small shrine to the Virgin and Marie's unicorn tapestry hanging on the wall. Madeleine shifted slightly, rustling the vellum pages on the cot beside her. "What is that you're reading?" he asked.

"I cannot read," she said. "But I can recognize most of the letters in this passage." Handing him the quarto, her fingers brushed his palm. "I want so much to understand," she said and blushed though whether in response to touching him or because she was unaccustomed to voicing her desires, he could not tell.

"Shall I read the passage aloud, then?" he asked.

She nodded, sliding across the pallet so that he might have a seat nearer the candle. Usually he had no trouble gauging moods and interpreting feelings. Without even trying he could see the shape of a sinner's soul, feel her pain and know her misery. Sometimes entering the chapel, he felt the presence of a dozen spirits beseeching him for guidance or assistance. But Madeleine was different. He could not guess her feelings or her thought. He moved a finger across the vellum. "Osculatur me osculo oris sui," he read. "Oh that he would kiss me with the kisses of his lips."

Madeleine wet her lips with the tip of her tongue. Robert pressed his finger hard against the vellum, striving to feel the holy pulse of God's words.

"How odd that the brethren would read such a thing," she said, a frown furrowing the skin between her eyes. Leaning forward, Madeleine traced the letter O with the concentration of a scholar, unmindful of the shawl slipping from her shoulders. Robert took a deep breath, his first since entering the room. Placing one fingertip in the letter's void, she opened her mouth and blew the sound between puckered lips. He watched her fingers crawl the curve and bulb of each letter in *Osculatur.* And it was as though they were fluttering his insteps, caressing his ankles and climbing his legs. He closed his eyes and they were back in Rouen where the men and whores grunted on dirty mats and sweet Madeleine bathed his tired feet in a bowl of water that rained rivulets the length of her arms.

"Why are these words—*kiss me with the kisses of his lips*—in the Bible?" She asked.

Robert opened his eyes to the page before him. "It's from The Song of Songs," he said at last, "the Wisdom of Solomon. The language is spiritual. It has a deeper allegorical meaning."

"Allegorical," she repeated, caressing the syllables with her tongue. "What a beautiful word. But what does it mean?"

"An allegory is a story or a painting that has more than one purpose. For instance," he said, raising his hand and pointing, "the tapestry on the wall can be seen as allegorical. Because the unicorn is snowy white, it symbolizes virginity and purity, and for that reason it also signifies our Lord Jesus Christ."

Madeleine lips parted slightly. She studied the mythical beast as though she had only just laid eyes on it. Robert's body stirred and the beat of his heart throbbed against his skull. If he could harness his desire he could bring her all the way to Christ.

"But what of the lovers?" she asked, pointing to the miniature tucked in the hollow of the letter O. The woman's legs, pressed ankle to ankle, were splayed at the knees. Rich folds of scarlet fabric draped her lap and bunched a shadowed V between her thighs. Robert shivered. *Oh Lord, help me focus on Madeleine's soul,* he prayed. "The two lovers also have symbolic significance. The man is the bridegroom who represents Jesus," Robert said, indicating the bearded, white-robed figure. "And the woman, the bride, symbolizes the Holy Church or the human soul striving for the divine."

"I should like to do that."

Her words startled Robert. "Strive for the divine, do you mean?" She tilted her head and examined his face. He felt a rush of pleasure so intense that he had to remind himself to breathe.

"Paint figures, beautiful figures such as these," she said, her fingers fluttering above the page.

"It takes much work, much training before one can illustrate," he said.

But she was no longer listening to him. Her eyes were locked on a space above his head.

"What is it that holds your attention?"

"I see your halo," she said simply.

"Halo?"

"Your ... clouds of light. Your ... nimbus."

Having heard that pregnant women were often fanciful, he wondered if an imbalance of humors and an overactive imagination had caused hallucinations. He truly worried about her health and the health of her unborn child. And yet, running parallel to his concern was a more selfish consideration. Recalling the rumors that had followed him since Rouen, Robert briefly pondered the possibility that he had been singled out for sainthood before refocusing on the convert before him. "How long have you seen halos?" he asked.

"As a child I saw my mother's halo," she said. "Green, every shade of green."

He was considering the possibility that the Lord God had gifted Madeleine with special sight when she lowered her voice, "The sisters say you're humble, but humility is not what I see in your nimbus."

Her words unsettled him, made him forgetful of his purpose and also, to his dismay, defensive. "I strive for humility. I do not always succeed," he said and understood that pride, as much as lust, was leading him astray. "What else do you see in my nimbus?" he asked.

"Put down the quarto," she said, rising gracefully despite the bulge of her belly.

Robert laid the manuscript on the cot and stood. He felt weak and wondered if he were falling ill with the fever.

Madeleine raised her hands to either side of Robert's head and lowered them slowly, pivoting her wrists so that they glided past his shoulders and then down the length of his arms. Though her fingers remained a fluttering distance from his body, he felt the slide of flesh against flesh and experienced a great calm, like grace or fortitude.

"I think that you are tired, worn out in body and soul." She dropped her hands to her side and a chill entered the room.

Robert looked around to see if Marie or Bertrad had opened the door. But the door remained closed. "Have you told others of your ability?"

"Never," she said. "I have never told anyone but you."

Deeply gratified—because didn't this mean she trusted him above all others?—he prayed silently that he might be worthy of her confidence. Madeleine sighed and sat back down on the cot. Her belly, round as a gourd, reminded Robert of his purpose.

"Let us pray," he said, "for the health of your child and for the strength to forgive." But the only verse that came to him he could not speak aloud—*Your lips drop honey, my bride, honey and milk are under your tongue; and the fragrance of your garment is like the fragrance of Mount Lebanan.*

✠

On All Soul's day, Madeleine abandoned her studies to play with Bertrad's son, a rambunctious toddler.

"Don't overdo it, Madeleine!" Bertrad cautioned. But Madeleine paid her no heed, chasing the squealing boy around a clump of fennel stalks. "All that jostling can't be good for you!"

A sharp belly pain brought Madeleine to her knees. The boy, thinking her fall part of their game, squealed in delight and flopped in a giggling heap beside her.

Bertrad leaped to her feet, scattering the beans she had been sorting. Wiping her hands on her apron, she ran to Madeleine's side. "Oh, what have you gone and done? It's not your time for another moon! Lean on me. Let's get you inside. And you, little puppet," she said to her son, "follow your mama." Though Madeleine stood a head taller, Bertrad was stronger. Wrapping her arm around Madeleine's ribs, she half dragged her to her cell, all the while singing a nursery ditty to engage the attention of her son.

Lullay, mine liking, my dear son, mine sweeting,
Lullay, my dear heart, mine own dear darlin…

Obediently falling into step beside them, the son lifted his chubby legs to the beat of each syllable, joining his sweet baby voice to his mother's lilting soprano—"Lul laay, Lul laay, Lu laay…."

Once Madeleine was inside, Marie helped her out of her dress and into one of her own roomy chemises while Bertrad retrieved the *matrone*, a young countrywoman with broad shoulders and crooked teeth.

"It's a good day to give birth," the *matrone* said, arranging a hodgepodge of bowls, vials, and jars on a small table. Madeleine, who had felt no pains since the one in the garden, wondered if the hasty preparations were not a bit premature.

"This," the *matrone* explained, holding up a milky jar of ointment, "will bring things to a quicker conclusion!"

"How many babes have you birthed?" Marie asked the midwife as she sat down on a stool placed at the head of Madeleine's pallet.

"Oh, I have assisted at dozens of births!" the *matrone* said, flashing her crooked teeth.

"And on your own?" Marie asked, her voice stern, her forehead furrow with lines. "How many babes have you birthed on your own?"

The *matrone's* eyes flitted about the room in a feral way Madeleine found unnerving, but the woman's hands were gentle and her voice had a reassuring authority that reminded Madeleine of Hersend. "This will be my first," the *matrone* mumbled.

Madeleine had never been present at any of the births in Rouen, nor had she wondered overly much about what transpired behind the tapestry that screened the laboring girls from the rest of the brothel. Suddenly she felt woefully ignorant.

"Maddy!" Marie's voice and a sudden contraction startled Madeleine who groaned aloud. "Are you listening to me? You need to keep your mind on the business at hand. You need to concentrate on getting this baby out!" Marie rested her palm on Madeleine's belly and commanded her: "go with the pain. Don't try to fight it."

Madeleine took the wave of pain, slid down the face and barely caught her breath before another followed and then another. At the end of a particularly harrowing contraction, Bertrad pulled from her pocket a lump of iron ore and shook it. To Madeleine's surprise it rattled, as though it harbored a tiny stone within. "Like the babe in your belly," Bertrad said with a tense smile. "Hold this charm and your labor will be quick and easy."

Madeleine wrapped her fist around the rock and held tight, but her labor was neither quick nor easy. After what seemed like hours, the *matrone* made an announcement. "Her womb is wandering 'round her belly. It refuses to let the baby go."

She rummaged through the implements spread across the tabletop until she found what she was looking for—a foul-smelling potion rank as sulfur—which she placed near Madeleine's mouth and nose. Madeleine turned her head and gagged, but the *matrone* persisted. "This will force the wandering organ back to its proper place," she explained.

When that failed, she rubbed Madeleine's inner thighs with rose oil. A suffocating sweetness filled the air. "This oil is made from the finest hips," she said, her voice an insubstantial whisper. "The fragrance will draw the babe to where it belongs." Madeleine sensed the *matrone's* wavering conviction, and her own fear increased two-fold. "Hold tight to that eagle stone," the *matrone* said, motioning to the iron ore Madeleine clutched in her right hand.

Madeleine knew that Marie had always scoffed at amulets and charms—"ignorant poppycock, superstitious nonsense," she called them—but now, she pursed her lips and said, "I don't see how it can hurt."

Madeleine closed her eyes and tried to summon the strength to force the child out. She felt Marie's hand tighten around her own, and opened her eyes to the twins standing at the foot of the cot.

Arsen, looking steadily at Madeleine, twined a loose curl

around her finger. "We have heard that a piece of clothing …"

"… worn by the father of the baby at the time of conception …" Agnes said.

"…will hasten the birth if placed between the legs of the mother to be…"Arsen said.

There was a moment of pause punctuated by the sound of Madeleine's strenuous breathing.

"We would happily retrieve such a garment …" Agnes offered,

"… if only you tell us who the father is," they said in unison.

"Enough of this nonsense!" Marie thundered. "Both of you out!" She waved her arms as though she were herding a flock of honking geese. "This room is crowded and there are far too many distractions!" Marie's look turned malevolent.

The twins linked hands and backed to the doorway of the cell in silence.

"Let me take the pins from your hair," Bertrad said, loosening Madeleine's braid. "Then I'll untie all the knotted garments in the room and your babe will release his hold on you. Don't worry. The two of you will be fine." Her furrowed brow belied her encouraging works.

"Forget about untying knots," Marie said. "We need to get Maddy into a sitting position. Lying down is stalling things."

The *matrone*, whose darting eyes scrupulously avoided Marie's, nodded her head. "Yes, yes, just my thoughts exactly!"

"Bertrad, you take Maddy's right arm and I'll take her left. Once she's upright, I'll squeeze in behind her. I mean to hold her in my lap. Ready? Now lift!"

Madeleine tried to assist them, but a powerful contraction clenched her belly and left her breathless. But even without her help, Bertrad and Marie managed to prop her into a sitting position. Marie had eased herself onto the pallet and scooped Madeleine into her ample lap, wrapping her arms around her rib cage and whispering into her ear. "We're going to do this together, Maddy girl."

Madeleine nodded. The smell of birthing—earthy as root vegetables—filled the cell. Outside the dogs barked and oxen lowed. The *matrone* held a cold rag to Madeleine's forehead, and Bertrad hummed softly.

Madeleine folded into the soft contours of Marie's breasts and belly and listened to the soothing thrum of her big heart. Madeleine's womb clenched with the next contraction and Marie tightened her hold, pressing her arms down hard against Madeleine's belly until she cried out in agony.

"Work with it, Maddy girl. Work with it."

Madeleine bore down. The child turned and dropped into place. The *matrone* lifted the drape of Madeleine's chemise. "By the blessed Gabriel," she said, "the babe's crown is visible."

"One more time, Maddy, give it everything you've got," Marie said.

And so she did, calling upon strength she did not know she possessed.

"It's a girl!" The *matrone* announced, lifting the squalling infant from between Madeleine's legs.

Marie's colors—exhausted grays and sickly yellows—flickered and dimmed beside the rainbow wail of a new soul. The child's face was squeezed into a howl that obscured her features, but she appeared whole and healthy.

"The child is small but fit," the *matrone* announced before cutting the cord and tying it with linen thread. "This will dry and comfort her limbs and members," she explained, smearing the child with a mixture of salt and honey.

"Oh, Maddy, your daughter has a fine set of lungs! And look at her hair," Bertrad said, laughing and combing the tips of her fingers through thick, dark hair that was long enough to mat at the crown.

"Let's get you settled," the *matrone* said, turning her attention to Madeleine. "Lean forward so Marie can slide free."

While Bertrad swaddled the child, the twins silently reentered the hut, careful to stay clear of Marie, who placed her finger in the baby's hand and laughed as she grabbed hold. "It's good she's strong," she said. "A woman needs to be strong in this world."

"Oh, but she's a beauty!" Bertrad said, holding up the child for Madeleine to see.

Perhaps too pretty, Madeleine thought, noting the arched brows and plumb lips. The child blinked and Madeleine covered her mouth with her hand.

"Why, look at her eyes!" Arsen whispered, nudging her sister. "One is blue, and the other is hazel!"

"The babe has two fathers!" Agnes said.

Madeleine turned to Marie, but before she could say a word, she felt a warm rush of fluid between her legs.

"May the saints protect her," the *matrone* said in a trembling voice.

Madeleine saw the blood, clotted purple red and blossoming the length of the cot, and felt suddenly weak, as though the life were spilling out of her.

"Do something, fool!" Marie said to the *matrone* before bringing her face to Madeleine's. "Stay focused, Maddy. Don't go drifting off."

The *matrone* hastily splashed vinegar from a slender vial into a shallow bowl. The pungent aroma pickled the air and made it difficult to breath. "This," she said, soaking a square of linen, "will stop the flow of blood."But her trembling hands did not inspire confidence and her quivering voice no longer reminded Madeleine of Hersend. Using the full force of her fist, the *matrone* thrust the cloth deep inside Madeleine.

Narrow bands of winter light spilled through the turret windows of Lady Philippa's chamber, casting an underwater glow onto the whitewashed stone and wall hangings. Most of the tapestries, Robert noted, displayed coats of arms and battle scenes. Two, however, appeared designed to please children. In one, a colorful flurry of birds soared a purple sky. In the other, an ark of paired animals floated a turquoise sea. Two large standing candlesticks flickered an insubstantial light onto a pile of stacked ledgers and parchment.

The Duchess entered the room. Robert saw past her gracious façade to the sorrowful woman beneath. He thought immediately about the letter that had brought him there, a carefully word document that hinted at marital problems.

"Master Robert, thank you for coming. Please join me by the fire," she said, motioning to two armchairs angled before the hearth. Above the carved mantle hung a sculptured crucifix held aloft by three angels. "You are well? And the abbey is coming along?" she asked.

"I am quite well," he said. "And thanks to your generosity and the generosity of your friends the abbey is thriving."

"And how is Brother Girard?" she asked, settling into the armchair beside Robert. "He was kind to me after my father died, and I have thought of him often with gratitude in my heart."

"He is hard at work illuminating manuscripts," Robert said.

A maid entered with a tray holding two mazers, one carafe of water and another of wine. An old bloodhound with a white muzzle and labored gait followed behind. Loose hanging skin gave him a serious, preoccupied expression. Once he spotted Philippa, however, he danced about, hindquarters wriggling ecstatically, nails clicking against stone.

Leaning forward in her chair, Philippa cupped the old hound's muzzle in her hands, and whispered, "Hey Snout, hey boy," against the dome of his head. The animal responded with a resounding bark that made Philippa throw back her head and laugh aloud. At least for a moment the Lady's sorrow was held at bay.

Placing the tray on a round table between the two armchairs, the maid curtsied slightly before leaving the room.

"He was William's dog before he was mine," Philippa said. "A good tracker in his day. The best. He could locate a deer or boar before the other noblemen mounted their steeds and let loose their hounds." Tilting her head, she spoke in a hushed voice. "Couldn't you, boy? Couldn't you?" The animal's tail thumped against the floor. Philippa gathered his long velvet ears in her palms. "After William left for the crusades Snout accompanied me on my journeys."

Philippa dropped her hands, and the hound settled with a sigh at her feet. Philippa indicated that Robert should take one of the mazers from the serving tray. He mixed a little wine with water and then sipped sparingly from his drink, for he had not eaten all day and feared that the wine would muddle his mind.

"On the day of William's return, Snout greeted him half-heartedly and then quickly bounded to my side where he remained. William said it looked to him like the old hound had switched his allegiance. I felt guilty . . . but also pleased." She frowned and poured a full and undiluted mazer of wine for herself. "You see, William thought he could be absent for two years and everything would be the same. Well, it wasn't. It just wasn't," she said.

Robert knew that Philippa had not asked him here to discuss her old hound, so he waited patiently for her to put words to her distress.

"My husband, Duke of Aquitaine, has forsaken me for another woman," Philippa said. "The Viscountess of Châtellerault has taken my place in his bed." She lifted her glass and drank deeply.

Robert never grew accustomed to these moments of sudden intimacy. He understood it was the priest with the honeyed voice to whom she spoke and not the flesh-and-blood man who knew temptation and self doubt every day of his life, and he prayed that his own spiritual fatigue would not interfere with his obligation to comfort and direct her, for as soon as he had taken his first sip of watery wine, he had relaxed enough to feel his exhaustion.

Placing his mazer on the end table, he harnessed his remaining energy and offered up his full attention. William's infidelity did not surprise him. Men, even those married to beautiful women, were weak of flesh.

Robert considered the proud, practical woman before him. She likely knew which herbs to use for colic and how to trade two stallions for a parcel of fertile valley land, and he did not think that she would be find solace in his sympathetic words. She would want to understand both the reason for and the solution to her husband's infidelity. Yet Robert felt that some words of understanding and compassion were appropriate and perhaps even necessary for establishing trust between the two of them.

"I am sorry, Lady Philippa," he said. "These must be painful times for you."

Gazing at the tapestry of paired animals, she whispered, "Why? Why did he do this to me?"

The old hound whimpered in his sleep. Philippa leaned forward and stroked his belly until his breathing calmed and he settled back into a husky snore.

"Men are more susceptible to the sins of the flesh than women," Robert said, and just like that, an image of Madeleine's fingers brushing her hair away from her face sent a surge of heat through Robert's body.

"I'm not so sure," Philippa said. "I myself…" Pursing her lips, she grabbed tight the arms of her chair, drew herself up and stared into the fire. "When I was betrothed, my aunts explained that my duty as a wife was to satisfy my husband's needs. They told me that ladies did not feel the same desire as men. Children, they said, were the pleasant result of an unpleasant situation. This," Philippa said, dropping her voice slightly, "was not my experience." She refilled her mazer and took several sips while studying the crucifix above the mantel. "William's lovemaking was a secret pleasure that filled me with joy."

Robert recalled his first meeting with Madeleine, how she had loosened her braid, bathed his feet, and pressed her lips against his ankle. "Perhaps God has sent this woman as penance for my sinful ways," Philippa said.

Robert chastised himself for pursuing his own thoughts while Philippa anxiously waited for a priest's direction. "Lady Philippa," he said, "there is no sin in the love exchanged between a married man and a woman. It has purposes beyond generation: it preserves… and intensifies the love between husband and wife."

"If the pleasure of love is no sin, then the question remains— Why did William leave my bed for the bed of another woman? What did I do to deserve such shame?" Philippa said, looking at Robert with beseeching eyes.

"Do not blame yourself for your husband's indiscretions. There are pressures in a man's life, enormous obligations…" Robert faltered, unsure of his words, fearful that it was his own transgressions he was fumbling to defend.

"I am not a man, but I have known a man's responsibilities," Philippa said, her voice deep and brash with authority. "I have managed an estate and made decisions that affect hundreds. Yes, a man's responsibilities are daunting, but no less so than a woman's. Motherhood, above all else, requires constant vigilance and allows no time for hunting parties and mistresses."

"I did not mean to denigrate a woman's role nor to excuse William's behavior," Robert said. "I meant only to explain that your husband, like all men, is weak, unable to resist the smooth tongue of an unfamiliar woman." Robert laid his hand on Philippa's forearm. "Lady Philippa," he said, "consider your husband's mistreatment as your martyrdom and penance. Your pain will only make you strong and worthy of a place in heaven." He leaned back into his chair. Her hands, palms down against the arms of the chair, moved absentmindedly against the woven brocade. "I know you are right, Father," she said, one finger worrying a loose metallic thread. "But I am angry and hurt . . ." Crossing her arms, she sunk into the chair, her voice suddenly tired.

The cry of a child rose from the nearby nursery. Philippa tensed, turned her head, and waited for the wail to hush before continuing.

"Lady Philippa, is it possible for you to find forgiveness in your heart?"

The maid entered the room, added several logs to the fire and left again. "Forgiveness?" Philippa said. "I have birthed William's children and managed his estate. And while I long to do the right thing, I find it difficult to forgive a man who's admitted no wrongdoing. I'm ashamed to admit that part of me wants to hurt him as much as he has hurt me."

She shook her head in exasperation, and Robert struggled to think how to direct her energy into something more productive than revenge.

"I have been a good wife, and I do not deserve this abuse!" Philippa stood and walked to the window. "I shall not be mistreated!" she declared.

"No," Robert said. "You should not tolerate mistreatment. But, perhaps, you could be . . . gentler, more compassionate? Remember, Philippa, none of us is perfect. We have all sinned and fallen short of God's glory. Keep in mind the words of Blessed Augustine, 'Through a faithful wife an unfaithful man is saved.'"

One of the servants called out and another sang a lullaby in a quivering falsetto. Philippa returned to her chair and seemed to consider Robert's words.

"It's possible," she said, "that I am more—" she paused, searching for the word, "*spirited* than most women. My father saw to it that I was educated and encouraged me to speak my mind. Is it possible these qualities have rendered me flawed and unattractive in William's eyes? And yet," Philippa continued, her hand clutching the armrest of the chair, "William did not hesitate to take advantage of my so called *manly* qualities when he left me in charge of his estate." She drew a deep breath and slowly exhaled. "I am rambling," she said. "You will forgive me. I am not myself."

Once he saw that Philippa's bitterness ran deep and was based on far more than her husband's relationship with the viscountess, Robert proceeded cautiously. "Philippa," he said, "you must fight against your anger, if not for William's sake than for your own, for the Lord forbids us to become angry, commands us to present the other cheek to the person who strikes us."

"Controlling my anger feels like one more responsibility heaped upon my shoulders," she said, then turned her head and stared, mute and desolate, into the raging fire.

The sound of noisy bartering between a servant and a fishmonger could be heard through the window, the servant's shrill offer—"Two deniers!"—eclipsed by the booming response of the fishmonger.

"The haddock was fresh-caught this morning! Four! Take it or leave it!"

"I will take it, but someday you will pay a steep price for your thievery!" The exchange concluded with the bang of a door.

"Philippa?"

She blinked, as though blinded by a sudden and vivid realization. "I'm sorry, Master," she said, "but I do not wish to save my husband." Rising Philippa grabbed a fire iron and stabbed at a log. "I wish to punish him as the Pope has punished the King."

"Surely you don't want William excommunicated?!" Robert asked, stunned by the depth of her rage. If he did not intervene, he feared that her actions would humiliate her entire family. Perhaps if she were to witness first hand the spectacle of excommunication, she would see with her own eyes that revenge would not be satisfying. He waited for her to compose herself and return to her armchair before speaking.

"Lady Philippa, I must go now, for I must meet with a number of prelates before the council next month. But if you would like, we could talk after the council. You will be at the council?"

"I hadn't thought…" She glanced at the stack of ledgers on her desk and then back at Robert, her brow furrowed, a look of confusion on her face.

"I think you should attend," he said, his voice firm with resolve. "Afterwards we will talk. Until then, I would like you to consider your duty to William." Then because he wanted his words to inspire rather than admonish, he spoke in a gentler tone, "Remember, Philippa, a wife with strength of character does her husband good and not harm all the days of her life."

"Very well, Master Robert," she said, rising from her chair and taking his hand in hers. "You are kind and thoughtful. I will reflect upon your words."

A servant escorted Robert to the door. Outside, a bank of clouds stuttered across the sun, turning the stark winter sky a muddy-red.

⁂

The *matrone* stopped the hemorrhaging, but it was weeks before Madeleine regained her strength. Then her milk failed. Marie fed her beans, peas, and gruel boiled in cream, while Bertrad suggested more frequent nursing to increase her milk supply. Madeleine nursed Little Marie every two hours, but produced only a few swallows of milk. After Madeleine's nipples cracked and bled, Bertrad threw up her arms in exasperation. "Enough of this!" she declared. "It's hopeless!" Madeleine winced and Bertrad dropped her voice to a whisper of comfort. "It's not your fault. It's your illness that's to blame. Oh, but we came close to losing you!" she said, crossing herself. "Never you worry. I've milk for two little puppets." She patted her generous breasts and took the child from Madeleine's arms.

Madeleine felt both guilty and relieved. Even if her milk had been as plentiful as Bertrad's, she was too tired to take on any responsibilities beyond her own recovery. She did not share her feelings with anyone but, of course, Marie discerned them all on her own.

Marie spent most of her day in a rustic but serviceable rocking chair that Moriuht had fashioned from green pine. Wrapped in a ragged shawl, she sat holding her namesake, rocking comfortably a foot from Madeleine's pallet. "When a birthing is particularly difficult," she explained, her voice rising and falling in cadence with the slight groan of the rocker's wooden spindles, "the bond between mother and child is sometimes strained." She looked up from Little Marie's face to study Madeleine's. "But love is resilient, Maddy."

Madeleine suspected that in this, as in most other matters, Marie was right. Still, she worried that she did not feel that exuberant rush of tender affection she saw reflected in the faces of other mothers. Sometimes she blamed her detachment on Little's anxious nature. Other times she wondered if the mothering part of her had been irrevocably damaged by the life she had led in Rouen. Only when Little's body was molded against Marie's diminished but still substantial curves, did Madeleine experience a drowsy peace that might be called love.

Even as a babe in arms Little possessed an indomitable will. Every time she combed her tiny fists through the air, it seemed entirely possible that she might snag a beam of sunlight. In the child's concentration, Madeleine saw a resemblance to prayer. Perhaps for this reason (and because the child's hair was so dark and wavy), Little often reminded Madeleine of Robert. Except for the shape of her brows, Madeleine saw little of herself in her daughter, and she would not allow herself to see anything of Evraud.

Giving birth had nudged Madeleine towards a consideration of others. She noticed Bertrad's eyes closed in exquisite relief when her milk let down and that Marie's raspy breathing slowed to a purr whenever she cradled Little in her arms. She knew Bertrad to be a keen and attentive mother, but Marie's behavior surprised her. She, who had never shown any interest in children, held Madeleine's daughter for hours on end, inhaling Little's scent, kissing her plump cheeks and dark head, seldom putting her down except at night when Bertrad took the babe back to her hut. Amidst the somnolent routine of caretaking and recovery, Madeleine began to miss her dead mother and sister. In her loneliness, she felt even more drawn to Marie.

"Marie," she asked, "did you ever have a child of your own?" Marie rocked for such a long time without responding that Madeleine worried her question was inappropriate, offensive in some way. When Marie finally spoke, her voice had the wispy quality of distance and regret.

"I was very young, younger than you are now," she said.

Madeleine wondered why Marie had never spoken of the child before. But even more startling than Marie's silence was her own lack of curiosity. Why had she never asked Marie about her life before?

"But where is the child now?"

"The boy was raised by my older sister. She had a husband and no babe. I had a babe and no husband. An hour after my son's birth, I handed him to the wet nurse my sister had hired and never looked back."

Madeleine's breath quicken with fear. What if she were never to see Little again? But then before the fear could gather momentum, Little sighed in her sleep, a breathy coo as beautifully arresting as a dove's call. The cell, dimly lit by a single candle, pulsed purple and magenta, soothing colors that invited confidences.

"You've never seen the child since?" Madeleine asked.

"Never. It was what my sister wanted. She insisted." Marie's voice sounded battered and bruised. Studying her profile, Madeleine tried to imagine the painful tumble of her life.

"And the father?"

"Men do what they will and then move on," Marie said. "But then you already know that." Marie's eyes had a dark and endless depth that frightened Madeleine. This private, thoughtful Marie was not *her* Marie, but someone different, someone separate and apart from her. Time slowed to the pace of Marie's gentle rocking. The world outside their hut ceased to exist beyond the soft rustle of wind through poplars. "Mine is not a pleasant story, but there are plenty who've lived worse lives," Marie said. "I'm not sure if it will help or hinder you to hear the details, but if you want, I'll tell them to you now."

"Please," Madeleine said, "tell me."

Marie adjusted Little against her chest. "Shortly after my older sister married and left home, my family was captured by northmen. My brother and father were murdered, my mother and I taken to Normandy and auctioned at a Rouen slave market where we imagined ourselves lucky to be sold to a missionary and his young handmaiden. Before and after," Marie said. "That's how I have come to think of my life—the time *before* the northmen and the time *after*.

"The missionary's handmaiden was a homely creature of few words, a woman so chastened by life that she covered her mouth to hide her infrequent smiles and treated each day as a burden to endure. Lighting the morning fire she barely noticed the blue flicker of flame or felt the sputter of warmth before her mind moved on to the next chore. The only lovely thing about her was her singing voice, a soaring soprano," Marie said, smiling faintly.

Madeleine imagined a voice that mingled russet-colored sunsets with the scent of lavender and hibiscus.

"Everything good and powerful was concentrated in that voice. If only her courage had matched the strength of her voice," Marie said, shaking her head, "her life would have been entirely different. Mine too.

"The voice, that creamy promise beneath the plain looks, was probably what caught the missionary's attention. Or maybe I'm wrong. Maybe he acquired her with the same stern indifference he showed purchasing my mother and me. Most of the other men at auction stepped forward to examine the slaves, pulling back lips to count teeth and examine gums, grabbing thighs to measure the strength of muscle. 'Is this one fertile?' they asked. 'Any history of violence here?' The missionary was different. He did not touch. He asked no questions. With barely a glance in our direction, he pointed to my mother and then me. 'Those two,' he said, and counted out his money."

Marie kissed Little's head, a drowsy, deliberate gesture that opened up an ache somewhere deep inside of Madeleine.

"I was naive and vain enough to be flattered that the missionary wanted me to accompany him and his handmaiden on his mission to convert pagan northmen," Marie said. "We traveled by boat to a country with deep fjords and gray skies, made our way to city gates on market days. The preacher explained to me that the handmaiden would sing while I walked through the crowds holding out a collection basket.

"Even at twelve I was tall and well formed. The handmaiden —and why give her a name?—Let her be the timid, homely handmaiden with the voice of a siren—went unnoticed until she opened her mouth. As soon as the first note escaped her lips the people in the marketplace froze in mid-gesture and listened, mesmerized by the warbling grace of her song. Only after the song ended would the listeners become suddenly aware of the songbird's plain brown feathers. At his point, the missionary would begin to sermonize about Christ's passion and mercy, the joys of a virtuous life, the power of the will to choose good over evil, the beauty of the soul. His words, so soon after the spectacle of song, made everyone think of some hidden potential in themselves, some kernel of splendor they all suspected they possessed."

Madeleine leaned forward in her chair, completely mesmerized by Marie's story.

"I came to understand that the homely handmaiden and I were just the warm up act. The minister was the real show. Even then, I thought myself lucky. Better to listen to a pretty voice than to spend my days scrubbing floors and churning butter or, worse yet, starving to death." Marie sighed, shaking her head from side to side. "So in my own way I was as much to blame as the handmaiden who took me to her master's pallet at night and bid me lay down beside him.

"I was barely twelve, with downy new pubic hair that still surprised me. The missionary, a scrawny man with a bristly beard and hot metallic breath, was neither gentle nor kind. The whole while he was doing it to me he recited biblical passages. The beautiful words sounded ugly in his mouth. I tried to shut them out, but they battered past the thoughts I constructed to protect myself and hammered away at my soul, pinning me to the pallet and churning up images of my father and brother bleeding beet-red and sprawled in the dirt like butchered animals."

Madeleine thought of her mother's death, the gradual waning of her colors. Her grief, Marie's rage, their combined sorrow floated the air between them.

"It was the homely handmaiden who taught me how to survive. In the dim light of a splinter moon, she grasped my arm and whispered the gift that at first made no sense. 'Memorize the psalms first,' she said. 'Use them to your advantage.' I was, as always, surprised by her speaking voice, a well-worn sound that reminded me of the smooth handle of a broom. *My advantage?* I thought, *what could she possibly mean?* But we were in his presence before I could ask a single question.

"Why is it I can still hear the handmaiden's voice so clearly when the voices that mattered most to me have all gone missing?" Marie shook her head at the random nature of memory. "In the end I took the handmaiden's advice because none other was offered."

Marie's face tightened into the mask she put on to greet the men who showed up at her door in Rouen. "At first I could not separate the meaning of the psalms from the missionary's prodding, but I persisted, learning whole passages by heart—'The Lord is my Shepherd; I shall not lack; He makes me to lie down in green pastures. Yes, though I walk through the valley of the shadow of death, I will fear no harm.' It was the act of concentration as much as the words themselves that lifted me past the moment and staunched the memory of my loved ones' bloody deaths. The blessed act of concentration."

Madeleine studied the tapestry on the wall. She recalled how she had learned to make herself small as a gnat and wing herself onto the back of the unicorn, and she was happy that Marie had also found a way to leave her body behind.

"After he was done with me," Marie said, "the missionary would fall to his knees and ask forgiveness. Not of me, but of God for having fallen victim to Satan's lure."

"What about your mother?" Madeleine asked. "Didn't she know what was going on? Didn't she try to stop him?"

"She knew. She didn't stop him." Marie shrugged a forlorn, dismissive gesture that spoke the pain of a child neglected by a grieving mother. "I've always imagined that whenever my mother considered confronting the missionary, she saw the edge of the blade that the northmen used to cut my father's and my brother's throats and told herself that rape was better than murder."

Madeleine felt small and insignificant beside Marie's impressive endurance.

"After we returned to Rouen, I began to show, and the homely handmaiden stopped coming for me at night. The missionary told a gossip who questioned him about my condition that I was too familiar with a boy we had converted in Gotland. 'Of course,' he added, knowing full well that his lie would be passed on to others, 'I cannot be certain, for she has lain with many men.' He managed to assume a tone of forgiveness even as he implied that I was a hopeless, weak-willed slut."

Marie laughed then, the old derisive laughter that came as a relief to Madeleine who thought she could not bear to hear more misery.

"I told the missionary I was leaving with my mother. He did not try to stop us. After I bore the child, I had no money, no occupation. I did not know what I was going to do with my life, but I was determined that no man would ever have power over me again. And none ever has."

There was a note of finality in her voice, so Madeleine was surprised when she continued.

"My experience has made me wary of all religious. But Robert, I think, is different." A cock crowed outside the door of their hut. Marie startled, but Little slept on, secure in the safety of her arms. "Robert does not use biblical words as weapons or to satisfy his own perverse pleasures. He's no saint—don't get caught up in that confusion—but he's a caring man with a dream and the courage to pursue it."

Madeleine understood where Marie had been leading her. It was not her life or the lives of other women she wanted Madeleine to understand but her own.

A knock at the door jolted Little awake. Bertrad entered the hut out of breath and in a hurry. "How's my little puppet?" she asked, laying a forefinger on Little's plump cheek. "Are you hungry, my sweet?" Before Bertrad could take her stool or untie her chemise, Little was wailing with hunger.

"You and Little could do worse than to let Robert into your life," Marie said, placing the screaming baby into Bertrad's arms. Little latched on to Bertrad's breast with a great sigh that ended in a gulping swallow.

"Just give it some thought," Marie said.

Madeleine felt it before she saw it—the milky-blue color of possibility suffusing the room, lighting it up and encompassing them all.

The day of the council meeting, Saint Hilary was packed with onlookers, many occupying seats in the pews, tribune and choir stalls, others standing in the central aisle, all craning their necks to witness the proceedings near the altar. Philippa and her aunts followed their servants closely as they cut a path through a side aisle toward the altar. The rank odor of unwashed bodies commingled with the burn of incense and the singe of candles. Stone columns rose above their heads, supporting transverse arches and expansive clerestory window that flooded the cathedral with morning light. In a candle-lit alcove housing a statue of the Virgin, a fresh bouquet of red roses reminded Philippa of Dangerosa's cloying perfume.

When they reached the pew reserved for noblewomen, Philippa noted how they stood out like gems against the dark wood. Isabelle de Montfort's saffron dress highlighted her blond hair, which was pinned in cascading ringlets at the crown and lightly covered with a transparent veil. The Agneses, of Craon and Aïs, were artfully arrayed in summer pastels, their fingers and wrists heavily jeweled. Philippa's breath quickened when she noticed the arrangement of their hair, for both women had copied the Parisian style worn by William's mistress. Though their braid cases was not as luxurious as the samite one worn by Dangerosa, the effect was nonetheless startling. Philippa felt violated by their mimicry, as though in aping Dangerosa's fashion they had honored her.

To steady herself, Philippa focused her attention on the immense gathering. Hundreds of black-clad religious sat in the nave while laymen stood on the fringes. In the noblemen's pews across from Philippa and her aunts, lords and counts wore fine tunics in blue, red, and purple, and immediately behind them, a group of nuns, all in black.

Most eyes were on the holy pontiff seated behind the altar. Pope Pascal was an old man, sunk in his seat, but resplendent in amice, stole, and violet cope. His white mitre was trimmed with gold.

On both sides of the pope sat twelve prelates, each with a lit candle before him, and at the far end of the altar, wearing a worn garment of dark serge, sat the longhaired and bearded Robert, his eyes fixed on the flame of a candle. One of the men, his mitre listing slightly to the left, struck the floor three times with a staff. The booms rolled through the cathedral and quieted the crowd.

"In nomine Patri et Filii et Sancti Spiritus," he began. "I, Cardinal Benedict, legate of the holiest of holies, do solemnly call this day's proceedings to order."

Unsmiling, he looked out over the congregation. "Cardinal John," he instructed in a haughty voice, "please review the charges against Philip, King of France."

An elderly man with a palsied right arm hanging limply at his side rose from his seat behind the altar and began reading a document. His frail voice was barely audible and his Latin words were lost on most of his listeners.

Cardinal Benedict, still standing near the pulpit, translated the words into French, speaking loudly so all could hear. "Because of King Philip's illicit and unsanctified liaison with countess Bertrad, the rightful wife of Fulk, Count of Anjou, we hereby re-issue the bans of excommunication…"

At the mention of her sister's name, Isabelle de Montfort began fidgeting with her prayer beads. For the first time, it occurred to Philippa that King Philip's infidelity affected many people beyond his queen.

The twelve holy men sitting behind the altars stood, raised their candles and walked to the front of the altar. The pope, assisted by a servant, rose and read the writ of anathema.

"Wherefore in the name of God the all-powerful, Father, Son, and Holy Ghost, of the blessed Peter, prince of the apostles, and of all his saints, in virtue of the power which has been given us of binding and loosing in Heaven and on earth, we deprive King Philip and all his accomplices and all his abettors of the communion of the body and blood of our Lord, we separate him from the society of all Christians, we exclude him from the bosom of our holy mother the Church in heaven and on earth..."

"Long live the King!" someone shouted from the tribune. Others joined in. "Long live the King!" the crowd repeated, their voices building in volume and intensity. A rock was hurled from above. One of the standing prelates reeled back, knocked his head on the altar, and fell to the ground, still clutching the sputtering candle in his hand. Another rock the size of a man's bounced once and skittered across the marble floor.

The mob responded in a cacophony of boisterous cheers. Pendants and buckles were thrown from all directions. A prayer book careened into the vase of roses, sending flowers, splinters of glass, and spilt water onto the tiles. The prelates fell to their knees. Several crawled under the altar, one pausing long enough to help the pope. Smoke from extinguished candles billowed in great plumes.

Isabelle was the first to hurl her rosary beads.

"We should leave," Sibyl whispered. Licking her lips, she plucked at her chemise before reaching out to take her niece's hand.

Sophie nodded. "This is sheer madness!"

"Not yet," Philippa said, for suddenly the events before her took on personal dimensions. Were she to go before the council seeking to excommunicate William, would the men she had defeated in skirmishes or bettered in land deals defend him as boisterously as this crowd defended their king?

"Stop!" a voice thundered. Robert rose from his seat and raised his arms high in the air. Barefoot and clothed in a simple robe, he looked every bit the ascetic leader who had led hundreds of pilgrims through western France.

"What the Vicar binds on earth shall be bound in heaven, what he looses on earth shall be loosed in heaven," Robert cried out.

The shower ceased. Philippa marveled that such a gentle man could quell a crowd with the power of his voice.

"God told Moses, thou shalt not commit adultery. And yet," he paused and surveyed the congregation before him, "some among you have risked murdering the supreme head of God's church in support of a man who has committed adultery!" He lowered his arms to indicate the rosaries and rocks spread across the marble tiles.

"We shall not see our king excommunicated!" shouted a nobleman. A roiling chorus of voices chanted, "Long live the King!"

"King Philip has already been excommunicated," Robert said, "twice. He now must suffer anathema, which separates him from the body of Christ, which is the Church. If any of you do not wish to witness this sentencing, leave now, for it is God's will!"

There followed a great scrape and thump of kneelers pushed hastily aside. A rush of nobleman erupted from the pews into the central aisle, shouting invocations and swearing allegiance to the crown. For a moment Philippa wavered in her convictions. Philip was her liege as well, yet was he not guilty of the same crime as her husband? How could she support the king's adultery and object to William's? Other nobles followed suit, as did those prelates appointed by the king, exiting the cathedral through the arm of the transept. When the heavy door whooshed shut behind them, a spasm of air belched through the cathedral, guttering devotional candles and blowing rose petals into the pew where Philippa knelt clutching her prayer beads.

Isabelle and the two Agneses stood. "Aren't you coming, Philippa?" one of the Agneses asked.

"No. I shall stay to see the outcome."

"But my lady!' Isabelle whispered, "they are condemning the king and my sister before God and the holy angels!" Her feet crushed a rose petal, releasing the scent Philippa would forever associate with Dangerosa. "Surely," Isabelle continued in a wheedling tone, "you do not approve of such harsh judgment!"

Philippa trembled with righteous anger. "Your sister," she said, "is no innocent."

Isabelle gasped and turned on her heels.

Philippa wondered at her unnecessary cruelty toward Isabelle, a trifling woman of no import. Was she becoming the kind of bitter woman she abhorred?

Robert held his arms out to the pope. A prelate crawled out from under the altar. Smoothing the edges of his fine garments, he attempted to recover his dignity while his servant retrieved and relit the fallen candles.

For a third time Pope Pascal rose to enact the close of the ceremony. "We declare King Philip excommunicated and anathematized and we condemn him to eternal fire with Satan and all the reprobates…"

More people exited the side door, sending another flurry of rose petals against Philippa's ankles. Bending to push aside the tickle of blossoms, she remembered her aunts' story of the miraculous red flower that revived Guilliadun. Her breast swelled with a sudden realization that revenge would neither revive her marriage nor assuage her sorrow.

Pope Pascal took a labored breath and read the closing words of the holy writ. "We deliver King Philip to Satan to mortify his body, so that his soul may be saved on the Day of Judgment." The twelve religious standing before the altar chanted, "Fiat! Fiat! Fiat!" throwing their candles onto the marble floor.

Robert's eyes met Philippa's and she knew what she must do. Just as Eliduc's wronged wife entered the nunnery so would she. At least until William came to his senses and she could find forgiveness in her heart.

Madeleine lit on the edge of the bench beside Robert, her nervous energy reminding him of the hummingbirds that appeared out of nowhere to buzz the salvia. During confinement her hair had darkened and her freckles had faded to pale hemp. Otherwise, she looked much the same. The butterfly fluttering the pulse of her neck still jarred his soul.

Robert had been attending council the day Madeleine gave birth, and afterwards he had remained in Poitiers to meet with prelates and potential donors. He had raised considerable monies for the abbey, but judged his counseling of Philippa less successful. Her decision to enter the abbey seemed hasty.

"Marie is failing," Madeleine said, her eyes full of purpose and sorrow. "She needs your blessing."

Clasping his hands beneath his robe, he concentrated on steadying his voice. "I will administer Last Rites. Let me gather my things," he said simply. Then, because he so dearly wanted to touch Madeleine, he did not. Silently, he followed Madeleine to the new abbey building, into which many of the women had moved during the time that he had been in Poitiers. Madeleine and Marie still shared a small room, but even half-finished, the cells offered more protection than the rustic huts.

"Marie, you've a visitor," Madeleine said, opening the door and stepping aside so that he might enter. Marie lay on a cot, her breathing strained and pronounced, her gray head turned towards the cradle in the corner where Robert could just make out the bundled form of Madeleine's sleeping babe.

"Peace be to this house," Robert said. At the sound of his voice the old tomcat, Bodkins, looked up from where he lay curled near the door.

"And to all who live within," Marie responded in a weary voice.

"May I use the table?" Robert asked Madeleine, removing the satchel he carried on his back.

Madeleine nodded, removing several dried bundles of herbs from the low table beside Marie's bed.

Robert spread a white cloth and arranged a crucifix flanked by two blessed candles.

Madeleine propped Marie up with a pillow. Marie smiled and touched Madeleine's cheek. "You're a good girl," she said, her eyes lingering on Madeleine's. "Now leave an old woman alone with her priest."

Madeleine wrinkled her brow. "Are you sure?"

Marie nodded.

"All right. I'll be at Bertrad's cell." She kissed Marie's cheek and turned to lift the babe from her cradle.

"Leave her be," Marie said.

Madeleine hesitated before re-tucking the corners of Little's blanket. "I won't be gone long then." Robert withdrew clean linen, a vial of holy water, and the Eucharist from his satchel and placed them on the table. Marie studied him with expressionless eyes.

"Ah," she said, "then you have plans to save me?"

Robert nodded. He knew his task would not be easy. Of all the Rouen converts, Marie was most resistant to his teachings. "Only the Lord can do that," Robert said, "and you, if you seek redemption."

"I'm not opposed to redemption," she said, "only leery. But first, we talk. Will you do that Robert? Will you talk to me using your own words?"

"The words of the Bible are…"

"Easier than coming up with your own?" she challenged.

"Better than my own, I was going to say. The Bible's holy words are pearls polished to perfection."

"And what would you know of polishing?" she asked. "Have

you ever worried a rag between the tines of a fork?"

He shook his head and sat on a low stool beside Marie's pallet.

"No. I thought not. I may be dying, but I know when someone's speaking from the heart. She paused to catch her breath. "So here are the rules. And I should be allowed to make the rules, no? Before you perform your last rites we talk. You can speak only what you know. If you agree, then you can stay. Otherwise, leave now." She closed her eyes and her breath came as though she had run a great distance.

Robert thought of all the chores he had fumbled through, the passions he had pursued and those he had fled, and it occurred to him that he had experienced enough to talk for all eternity. "I borrow biblical words not because they are polished, but because they are the word of God and fill me with the same calm I know listening to a bubbling spring."

Marie nodded. "My turn," she said in a matter of fact tone. "Do you think my death will be easy?"

Without the Bible's words to guide him, he felt lost. Over the years he had witnessed godly men die painful, horrible deaths and unrepentant sinners pass peacefully in their sleep. "Death is a miracle and a mystery," he said. "I cannot know what God has in store for you, Marie, only that something wonderful awaits you on the other side."

Marie shivered as though she felt a sudden chill.

"Shall I bring more blankets?"

"The cold is inside," she said, laying her hand against her chest and pausing for a labored breath. "Blankets won't help."

"I have an idea," he said, rising from his stool and lifting Bodkins from his place near the door. The old tom turned as if to bite his wrist, but settled into a fierce purr once Robert laid him at Marie's feet.

Marie smiled. "Better," she said.

"The best is yet to come." As Robert approached Little Marie's cradle he was overcome with curiosity. It was not their mismatched color that startled him but rather their intensity. Hers was not the wobbly unfocussed gaze of an infant struggling to make sense of shapes, but the appraising look of a much older soul. He lifted her awkwardly to his shoulder.

Marie laughed a ragged wheeze. "You hold the poor child like she's a bundle of rags. Cup her head and pull her close." Her shallow breathing sounded hollow and strained, like air passing through water.

Robert placed Little in the crock of Marie's arm near her failing heart. She sighed. "Warmer than down ticking or rabbit fur," she said, closing her eyes.

Robert sat back down in the rocker and allowed the sorrow to pass over him. Marie woke suddenly, her eyes opening in one blink. "You…see it, don't…you?" she asked. The space between her words was long, as though meaning had traveled a great distance. "Our Little … someone to be reckoned with… smart like her mother… but not so apt to… get tangled up in her own thoughts. Nor," Marie said, looking pointedly at him, "seduced by…a soothing voice."

"I never deceived Madeleine," Robert said. "Every word I've spoken to her has come straight from my heart."

Marie took a deep breath, as though gathering all her strength for one last stand. "You think I would be talking to you if I thought otherwise? I'm old and dying, but I still have my senses about me." Her words sounded sopping wet and weighted down.

She drifted away then, whether in sleep or contemplation, Robert could not say. He prayed, "Hear us, holy Lord, almighty Father, eternal God, and be pleased to send thy holy angel from heaven to guard, cherish, protect, visit, and defend all that dwell in this house."

After a few moments, Marie opened her eyes. "I know the dying are supposed to confess their sins and beg forgiveness," she said, "but I don't believe I can atone for a life of sin, not even if I had time to do it." She took a few deep breaths until her breathing slowed.

"If Christ forgave a thief on a cross, surely he can forgive you," Robert said.

The confident trill of a chouh brought a smile to Marie's face.

"I was in love once, did you know that?" She smiled, perhaps lingering a while in the memory of that love. "It was Maddy's father that I loved and for no good reason. He was a scoundrel through and through." She shook her head. Little stirred and settled back into a deep sleep. "Maybe what I liked best about him was that he didn't try to hide his selfishness, didn't pretend any future beyond the boundaries of my cot. But he had a crocked smile and a laugh that's lingered in my heart. Oh Lord, the man could laugh! You think love should be about something, should come in response to goodness or courage or grace. But it isn't like that, and thinking too hard on the why of it is just a waste of time."

The telling seemed to lessen some heaviness inside of her. Robert felt the energy of something important gathering between them.

"What would comfort me is to know that Maddy and Little will be properly cared for after I'm gone."

"All the other pilgrims have a home here for as long as they desire," Robert said.

"That's not what I mean and you know it," Marie said, a note of impatience entering her voice. "Either you're lying to yourself or you're lying to me, and I don't have time for either."

However much he wanted to believe that each and every pilgrim held an equal piece of his heart, it was not true. "You are right. Madeleine is special," he said, wondering if Marie knew how truly special. "I pledge my word that I will look after her and her daughter."

"Thank you. Now I will meet your honesty with some of my own. You're a fine man, Robert, but I worry that tales of your sainthood will turn your head and weaken your resolve. You've work to do. You cannot afford distraction. Believe in yourself, Robert, but don't presume a holiness that isn't yours."

"It's true I suffer from the sin of pride, but I have never imagined any of my actions warrant sainthood," he said with a steely conviction that seemed to settle Marie.

"Good," she said. "You are a good man, Robert."

He knew from the hollow sound of her voice that Marie was weakening. "Should I get Madeleine now?" he asked.

"If I let my sweet Maddy into the room, I'm afraid the strength of her will could keep me tethered to this old body. I'm tired, Robert," she whispered, her breathing as splintery as shale, "tired and ready to move on."

Bodkins meowed and settled more fully against Marie's feet. "Tell Maddy she was the daughter of my soul," Marie said. "Say that loving her was enough. Repeat it so I know you won't go polishing my words."

"Loving Madeleine was enough," Robert said, thinking, *in loving her you also loved the Lord.*

Marie nodded, satisfied.

Robert took the host from the tray and held it out. "Open your mouth, Marie, repent and receive the Body of Our Lord Jesus Christ."

Nodding once, she opened her mouth.

"May the Lord keep you from the malignant foe," Robert prayed, "and bring you to life everlasting."

Her energy depleted, Marie closed her eyes and entered a fitful sleep. Then, because she could not speak the words of the prayer herself, Robert spoke them for her.

"I confess to almighty God, to blessed Mary ever virgin, to blessed Michael the Archangel, to blessed John the Baptist, to the holy apostles Peter and Paul, to all the saints, and to you Father, that I have sinned exceedingly, in thought, word, and deed: through my fault, through my fault, through my most grievous fault."

Marie woke one final time, struggling to get air into her lungs, opening her mouth and turning her head from side to side. Robert took the holy oil and anointed her.

"By this holy unction and his own most gracious mercy, may the Lord pardon you whatever sins you have committed," he prayed. And while Robert could not be sure Marie would hear him, he took her hand and leaned in close. "You are loved and you are safe," he said, his voice confident and strong. "May almighty

God open the gates of paradise and lead you to joys everlasting." Bringing Marie's hand to his lips, he kissed her palm and imagined her death—a deep and mysterious surrender to love, an embrace with God that was filled with peace.

Marie's skin and lips turned milky blue. Robert placed the hand not holding hers against Little's chest, felt the heat of their three bodies braiding them together, and he could not tell where he left off and they began.

"It's all right to let go, Marie," he said, just as Little began to stir.

"I don't know how to do this," Marie whispered, a feathery sound full of curiosity and wonder. "I've never died before."

"May almighty God bless you in the name of the Father, Son, and Holy Spirit," Robert prayed.

Her final breath—a startled puff of air—moved effortlessly past Little's piercing wail.

Philippa and William sat before the fire in Philippa's chambers, two mugs of spiced cider and a silver tray of William's favorite fig tourteletes on the table between them. Philippa broke the silence. "I would like your permission to leave Poiters and take up residence at Robert's Abbey," she said.

Williams continued to stare into the fire, but the scar that slashed his left cheek—that pink rise that Philippa had traced with her tongue and caressed with trailing fingers—stretched white and menacing.

"And," Philippa continued, "I would like to take the children with me."

William took a deep breath before turning to face his wife. "Will stays with me!" he said, bringing his fist down hard on the upholstered arm of the chair.

Snout, asleep at on the hearth, lifted his head at the sound of his master's angry bellow. The old hound's jowls swayed as he sniffed the air. Rising on arthritic legs, he hobbled to Philippa's side and nuzzled her palm before returning to the hearth and settling with a snort and a sigh.

Even then Philippa believed that with a little patience and flattery she could persuade her husband to see the wisdom of her request. "Of course," she said, dropping her eyes. "It's your decision. But there's much to be said for an abbey education."

Somewhere in the corridor a servant opened a door. The draft of air that whooshed into Philippa's chambers carried the sweet fragrance of one of the flower arrangements. The scent of roses triggered Philippa's memory of Dangerosa's red hair and slim ankles. Her fingers clutched the arm of her chair.

William sighed, a long drawn out sound that reminded Philippa of the exaggerated length of the train on her rival's Parisian gown.

Instead of reminding William that his son was but a toddler, that once he was old enough to learn the manly arts of hunting and battle, he could return to Poitiers and learn these at his father's side, she recalled how Dangerosa had entered the grand hall with her hand tucked comfortably in the crock of her husband's arm.

"Why, William?" Philippa whispered, asking the question that had been there all along. "Why did you betray me?"

William stared at her with the same look Philippa saw when she reprimanded young Will. "No like you!" her son would say, his little back ramrod stiff. "No like you!"

How easily she forgave Will. If only she could be so generous with his father. But William was a man, not a child, and fully capable of understanding the consequence of his actions.

"Why, William, why?" she repeated.

"*You* changed, Philippa," he said in an oddly unfamiliar, almost diffident tone that startled her far more than his words. "*You* did."

The accusation made her dizzy. She took a breath. She knew the effect of silence, for she had used it often to trip up bartering merchants or force consensus in a messy land dispute. Silent and composed, she studied the tapestry hanging on the wall above his head, focused her attention on the dark power of a rearing stallion. William had more to say, and her silence might coax it out of him. Her heart beat madly, for she knew that a single wrong move could change the course of her son's life.

"Perhaps," he said, "if you had loved me as much as you loved ruling my estate…"

All of the air seemed to leave the room. Philippa heard resentment in William's voice, but also sorrow and disappointment.

She waited for anger to ignite some fiery defense inside of her, but it did not come. Instead, she shivered with cold. If William was right, if the joy she took in ruling his estate trumped the love she felt for him, then maybe he was justified in taking Dangerosa as his lover. But even as she considered this possibility, she wondered why she was forced to choose one role over another, why the same traits celebrated in men were judged appalling in women. She had ruled his estate with skill and authority, and he did not love her enough to get over it. Even as her mind churned with righteous anger, she heard her aunts' admonishment as clearly as if they were speaking the words aloud—*Hold your tongue, Philippa. Do not let your pride interfere with your judgment.*

Perhaps she would have followed her aunts' advice if only William had not chosen that moment to reach for a tourtelete. Something in the way his thumb dimpled the small pie reminded her of his hand claiming ownership of Dangerosa. He slipped the sweet between his lips, and a look of animal pleasure transformed his features. When he licked the flakes of honey-basted crust from his fingertips, Philippa heard the buzz of a thousand swarming bees inside her skull.

"Go to your mistress," she said, rising from her chair. "I will take the children and go to Fontevrand."

Standing, William seemed to take up all of the space in the

room. "No son of mine is growing up in a nunnery coddled by widows and virgins!"

She knew she should apologize, but pride and anger overrode her better judgment. "Better widows and virgins," she said, "than an adulterous father who shames his mother in public!"

William slapped her face with his open hand. More startled than hurt, Philippa gasped aloud and covered her stinging cheek with her palm. Snout stumbled to his feet. "What kind of man hits his wife!" Philippa said in a quivering, defiant voice that rose above Snout's barking. For now that she had released her anger, she could not contain it.

William's second blow was fisted and harder. Philippa reeled back, tripped on Snout's water bowl and hit her head against the edge of the table, falling unconscious to the floor. She lay there, unattended, until Snout's frantic barking woke her and she opened her eyes to the sight of desiccated clouds ghosting past the turret window.

Water from Snout's overturned bowl soaked through her bodice and chilled her skin. William knelt and touched her cheek, a twinge of shame or regret momentarily softening his features.

Philippa jerked her head away from her husband's touch just as Snout, nudged his muzzle against her arm. "It's all right, boy," she whispered, kissing his wrinkled forehead and rising unsteadily onto one elbow.

William's face assumed the hardened look of a soldier. Rising, he looked down at his wife. "You will not talk to me in that manner. Ever! Do you hear me, woman?" he said in a voice clotted with rage.

Snout growled the fierce guttural warning of a much younger animal. Hackles raised and snarling, he grabbed the hem of William's robe in his mouth and tugged weakly at the cloth. In a flash of annoyance and misdirected anger, William kicked Snout with the toe of his boot. The hound's legs buckled. He slid across the marble on his side, hitting the wall with a yelp of pain.

Giseld entered Philippa's chambers, saw Snout sliding the

length of the room and ran into the hall screaming for Guiscard.

Too dizzy to stand, Philippa crawled to where old Snout lay. The animal's eyes were vacant, but she could see the shallow rise and fall of his chest. "Please, William," she begged, "don't hurt him! He means only to protect me!"

"Leave the mutt where he lies," he said. "He's as thankless as his mistress. He attacks the hand that feeds him."

Philippa rested a soothing hand on Snout's haunch. The old hound stirred. "It's all right, boy," she said. Grabbing the side of the table, she pulled herself to her feet. William watched her struggle with a look of indifference.

"I want you packed by tomorrow afternoon," he said. "You may take Anne, but Will stays with me." His look struck terror in Philippa's heart. Her fingers tingled and she feared that she would pass out.

"I beg you to forgive me! If Will cannot go with me, then let me stay. I will never question your authority again," she said, placing her hand on his arm.

"No," William said, and this time he was the one to pull away.

The room which moments earlier seemed ablaze with William's anger grew chilly. Philippa shivered in her wet gown.

"You will go to your holy man, and you will go without our son." William stared at Philippa with an odd detachment that frightened her more than his anger.

No longer able to stand on her own, she fell to her knees and wrapped her arms around Snout, whose tail thumped half-heartedly.

Giseld and Guiscard entered the room. "Oh, my Lady!" Giseld said, clutching the edge of her apron as she walked swiftly to her side. "Are you hurt?"

"I am fine," Philippa said, fingering her jaw.

"Tomorrow you leave for Fontevraud," William said.

Lord, she prayed, *what have I done! Where has my boldness taken me?*

⊡

After Marie died, Madeleine did not see color for two winters. A sodden grey stripped her life of beauty and meaning. And while she continued to work in the kitchen, salting cod, shelling peas, and peeling onions until her eyes teared, monotonous routine blanched her life of beauty. She worked because she was expected to and because her hands possessed a memory of their own, lifting cutlery, kneading dough, moving through the dreary days without any direction or encouragement.

Then one morning in early summer color surprised her in the root cellar. She was lifting a misplaced carrot from a bin of lentils, running her thumb against the ridged skin, when a vapor of orange climbed the vegetable and warmed her hand. Startled, she slipped the carrot into an apron pocket and returned to her cell in the convent where dust motes blinked copper in the open door and a hinged-legged spider spun silver gossamer in a twilit corner. When the ribbon in Little's hair blushed red against her dark curls Madeleine understood that she had reentered the world of the living.

At Hersend's urging, she returned to her studies with Brother Girard, who taught her to read step-by-step, first the alphabet, then pronunciation, and then grammar, the mortar that glued words into sentences.

Sometimes Brother Peter was also present in the newly completed scriptorium, an oak-paneled room with high windows letting in a diffuse light. Humming while he patiently illustrated manuscripts, Peter spent an hour drawing a scarlet snake peeking from behind the green shaft of a letter *R*. He labored days on a sequence of ornate squares framing robed aristocrats sitting on thrones. Fascinated with the process, Madeleine often lingered after the others had left, watching him use lead plummet to outline a design he would later paint.

Gradually Madeleine became part of the community. But it was color that made the days worth living and gave her the courage to befriend Philippa.

Moriuht's blossoming hyacinths were nothing compared to the tumultuous hues that floated the curves of Philippa's body. Madeleine studied the knotted strands and concluded that Philippa was both complicated and sad. Her hands, noticeably free of blisters and scars, revealed her position. Philippa was a lady.

A dozen aristocrats, widows and women fleeing bad marriages, entered the abbey that spring. Bertrad told Madeleine that a rift had developed between these wealthy novitiates, many of whom donated huge sums to the abbey, and the poor but committed congregants who had been with Robert from the beginning.

"We slept in open fields and lived on tubers and faith!" Bertrad said, a note of pride creeping into her voice. "And now these new-comers enter the order and occupy the best beds."

When Robert began taking his meals with the reformed prostitutes and the other lay clergy, a chasm opened up between the aristocrats and the commoners.

But Madeleine was not thinking of politics the day she approached Philippa in the garden, but of friendship, a desire she saw reflected in the young novitiate's nimbus.

Philippa, seated on a bench with her face lifted towards sunlight, turned to the sound of Madeleine's sandals crunching against the pea gravel path separating a bed of herbs from a mound of flowers. "Why, you're Madeleine, aren't you? Sister Hersend has told me that you are the one responsible for all this beauty!" Philippa's words seemed to acknowledge the glory of each flowering bush, herb and vegetable in the garden.

Madeleine felt an unfamiliar pleasure. Like a winter fire or the summer sun, Philippa's words filled her with warmth. She surprised herself with a smile that felt as spontaneous and sincere as the ones she shared with Little.

"Please, have a seat," the Lady said, patting a space beside her on the bench.

Despite Philippa ease, Madeleine felt a cool whisper of reservation. Philippa was an aristocrat, and even the invitation to sit carried an air of authority.

"You have a daughter, yes?" Philippa asked.

Because the repentant sinners, widows and married women lived apart from the nuns, it did not seem odd to Madeleine that Philippa knew so little of her life. For while the women of the Magdalene Convent enjoyed gossiping, Madeleine imagined that the holy women of the Grand Moutier felt no desire to engage in such frivolous activity.

"Yes. Little Marie is two."

A few golden ringlets escaped Philippa's veil, bouncing against her forehead as though they processed a vigor and independence at odds with the calm demeanor.

"My Anne is a few months older." At the mention of her daughter's name, Philippa's halo glowed with such brightness that Madeleine could only study it at a slant. "I've another child," Philippa said, hands clinched in her lap "a son who lives with his father." Philippa's color flickered and dimmed.

Madeleine thought of a day without Little and her belly heaved. She felt Philippa's pain deeply. The realization startled and amazed her. "You must miss him." Philippa nodded. She looked beyond the garden to something only she could see. At the toll of the church bell, she rose from the bench, nudging her curls under her head cloth. "I must leave you now," she said, straightening her shoulders, "but perhaps we could meet again with our daughters?"

"Yes," Madeleine said, and surprised herself by looking directly into Philippa's gray eyes. "I would like that."

"When Robert thinks no one is looking he stares at Madeleine," Agnes said, her eyes moving up and down Girard's withered arm. Arsen nodded in agreement, a wickedly seductive smile transforming her face. "The man has lust in his heart!" she said, gripping the handle of a knife pinning vellum to a block of wood.

The scriptorium smelled of bee's wax and iron-gall. A gummy residue of paint splattered the stone floor and adhered to the calluses on Girard's feet. He stepped away from the twins, embarrassed by the vulgar sucking sound of his sticky soles pulling free of the stone.

Slipping his withered arm into his cassock, Girard placed his left hand on the day's lesson, an unadorned sheet of letters resting on a small table. He disliked teaching women, particularly comely ones who confused beauty with virtue and thought themselves good Christians despite their whorish ways. Daily contact with such women placed men in constant and, Girard could not help thinking, unnecessary temptation.

And yet Girard had been thrilled by Robert's request that he help the women learn to read, for he took it as a sign that the master looked beyond his corpulence and deformity and saw the worthiness of his soul.

Agnes tugged at Girard's sleeve. "If there's anything we know it's a man's—"

"—lust." Arsen laughed and cupped the knife's pommel with her palm.

Since Marie's death, the twins' behavior had grown crass and inappropriate. Why should he believe two silly girls who could not be bothered to learn their letters? But even then his mind unwillingly retrieved a memory of Robert and Madeleine in the garden.

"They say that your holy master spends nights in Madeleine's cell." Releasing her grip on the knife, Arsen moved with the stealth of a barn cat, skulking between the half dozen small tables and benches. "Madeleine's babe sleeps with Bertrad and her son while Madeleine waits for Robert's knock!"

Girard cleared his throat in an attempt to disguise his alarm. "He does not touch her," he said.

"Perhaps not in the beginning. But that was before Madeleine seduced him," Agnes said.

He turned away, pretending to straighten a sheaf of vellum on his desk. He did not want to believe that Madeleine, who approached her studies with the focus and fervor of a man, was capable of such rank behavior.

"She's strange," Agnes said, palming her robe smooth against her hips.

"Sometimes we talk to her and she doesn't hear our words. She looks *around* us not *at* us," Arsen said, returning to where Agnes and Girard stood. "And once she did this." Raising her hands, she traced the curve of her sister's form. "Madeleine's fingers never touched me, but the air between us ached."

"And she talks to mayflies. I've seen her with my own eyes."

"She's odd," Arsen said, batting her hand through a flicker of airborne dust, "and she isn't even pretty."

Agnes nodded. "She's freckled and too skinny. We were always the first ones chosen at Marie's."

Arsen brought her mouth to Girard's ear. He smelled the scorched sugary scent of her breath. "We have seen Robert enter Madeleine's cell after Matins. He stays there 'til Lauds," she whispered.

Girard reassured himself that their ramblings were nothing

more than jealous gossip. They missed the focused attention of lust. Churning up emotion in others satisfied their enormous vanity.

"Robert asked that I teach you to read," he said. "I intend to do so."

The twins giggled, an inexplicable jittery sound that deflated Girard. Perhaps He was a cripple, assigned to the scriptorium because he was incapable of performing more manly tasks. "Enough!" Girard said in a firm, assertive voice.

Arsen smiled and tilted her head flirtatiously. Girard noted how sunlight slanting through a cutout stroked her dark hair mahogany. In that moment of distraction his crippled arm slipped free of his robe and Arsen's perfect fingers tickled his deformity. Girard pulled away, a grimace affixed to his face. The twins laughed a high jagged sound that mingled meanness with vanity.

"Stop your foolish talk and focus on your letters!" he said, bringing his good fist down hard on the table.

With sly glances and flickering smiles, the twins moved obediently to either side of Girard.

That night Girard hid, squeezing behind a stone sink in the unfinished lavatorium of the Magdalene Convent. He intended to put to rest the scandalous rumors regarding Robert and Madeleine, for he needed to believe that the master he served lived a life worthy of his admiration.

After the women had snuffed their candles and retreated to their cells, he entered a dimly lit hall leading to the women's dorter and crept into a recessed nook with an unobstructed view of Madeleine's door. Then he waited.

In the first hour he attempted to occupy his mind by meditating on the seven spiritual works of mercy. But again and again he found himself distracted by the smell of tallow and the buttery scent of female flesh. He felt certain that Robert would not allow his mind to wander with such loathsome lack of self-control.

In the second hour he grew hungry and nibbled on a loaf of

three-grain bread he had stolen from the kitchen and hidden in his robe. The dry bread tasted oddly acrid, but chewing provided a respite from boredom.

No longer hungry, Girard worried about the state of his soul, questioning his right to spy on the master's interactions with congregants.

Just as he prepared to return to his cell, he heard the swish of bare feet on marble tile. Hidden by darkness and squatting on aching knees, Girard watched moonlight toss Robert's cowled shadow against Madeleine's door. The Master knocked once. His shadow assumed an animal tension.

"Robert," Madeleine whispered, closing the door behind him.

Girard stepped from his hiding place into a pulse of energy that flowed from a gap beneath her door. Melon-scented and lemon-edged, it bristled a raspy-tongued pleasure that reminded him of the ecstatic look on Madeleine's face the first time she saw a gilded manuscript. Girard suspected that whatever transpired behind the closed door was more personal than spiritual, but he could not bring himself to pass judgment on a holy man who had saved so many souls. He had all but justified Robert's secretive behavior when he smelled the bittersweet tang of pomegranate seeds. In the time it took to swallow, he tasted a distillation of every dish he had ever known. The flavor of woodcock, pigeon, turtledove, venison, and pig left him hungry for more. In this ungodly state of gluttonous rapture, Girard closed his eyes and, just like that, he was transported back to the chestnut grove. Once again he watched transfixed as Evraud tore away Madeleine's chemise to reveal her small breasts, the sparse, copper-colored hair of her triangle, and the delicious cleft of her sex. Beading, swirling, then pulling tight, the separate strands of Girard's and Evraud's lust blurred, braided and became one. Together they licked the wine-splashed hollow at Madeleine's neck.

The sound of his own labored breathing brought Girard back to the present. Nauseous and disoriented, he crept back into his hiding place. When his stomach cramped, he lamented having eaten the odd-tasting bread. Hidden in the shadows, he prayed for strength—*Blessed is the man who stands up under trial; when he has stood the test, he will receive the crown of life that God has promised to those who love Him*—repeating the words until they were wrung dry of meaning. Weak-kneed, feverish and dry-mouthed, he dropped to his knees just as the hour of Lauds sounded and Robert slipped through the door of Madeleine's cell.

Girard's stomach roiled and heaved. After the pain subsided enough for him to stand, he crept from his hiding place. Pausing outside of Madeleine's door, Girard heard the whisper of bare feet followed by the creak of a trunk lid. He imagined the gauzy flutter of a linen nightgown caressing her shoulders.

If only she had not sighed, he might have left the cloister then. But the thought of Madeleine's fruity breath stirred his loins and dismantled his soul. A common whore had taken his rightful place in the Master's heart!

He must confront Madeleine and convince her to release Robert from her evil clutches. Having found an action large enough to contain his rage, Girard took a deep breath and pushed open the door to Madeleine's cell. Even in the dim light he could see the swell of her body beneath the thin blanket that covered her.

"Robert?"

"No."

"Brother Girard?" she asked, rising up on one elbow. "Is that you?"

Her quivering voice evoked in him a greasy pleasure that soured his already aching belly. *Let not my heart incline toward her way,* he prayed, closing the door and stepping nearer her cot. "You do not belong at Fontevraud!" he whispered, throwing back the blanket. The stench of burnt sugar replaced the scent of ripe berries, and Madeleine's form took on the comely shape of the twins. *God do not tempt me beyond my ability. Provide me a way out, so I may withstand sin!* Girard prayed to no avail, for evil had hold of his soul. He did not need two arms to pin the demon to the bed because she did not struggle or call out. "Whore," he whispered, "shameless Jezabel." Anger and lust pooled in Girard's groin. He lifted his body atop hers.

"Please," she whispered, "Please stop."

But her words served only to inflame him. He fumbled for the hem of her nightgown, his mouth inches from hers.

"Help! Someone help!" Something seemed to shift within Madeleine and she fought him, pummeling his back with one hand and clawing at his face with the other.

Robert burst though the room with a roar. "Wait, Master, I can explain," Girard said, lifting his crippled hand.

Without a word, Robert crossed the room, grabbed Girard by the shoulders and flung him to the floor.

PART THREE

✣

Then he said to them, "Know this, my dearest brethren, that whatever I constructed in this world, I made for the benefit of our nuns; I offered all the power of my faculties to them; and what is more, I have submitted myself and my disciples, for the salvation of our souls, to their service."

Anonymous, *Life of Robert of Arbrissel*

"Sister," Hersend whispered, touching Philippa's shoulder, "I thought I would find you here. I need your help in the infirmary, dear."

Philippa crossed herself and rose from the kneeler. This night, as on other nights sleep eluded her, she had retreated to the empty church. The bare beauty of its stone interior afforded the same pleasure she had known as a child surrounded by the rose-colored buildings of Toulouse. Raising her eyes to the upward stretch of the chancel's three austere stories, she was newly amazed by the simplicity of Fontevraud, the subtle way in which the architecture reflected a life of independence from material objects.

"Follow me," Hersend said, leading her through a door in the south transept into that hushed tranquility that proceeds the day. Tucking an errant curl beneath her veil, Philippa followed close behind the Abbess, mindful of the slippery gravel beneath her feet. "Look," Hersend said, pausing to point out a rim of gold shimmering against the horizon. "Here comes the dawn, the day's first and most compelling reminder that Christ is the true Light." Her voice registered joy, but her expression remained strained and preoccupied.

"Is it Beatrice?" Philippa asked. "Are her joints bothering her again?" After Philippa entered the order, Hersend assigned her work with the elderly and the ailing sisters. Daily she brought them food, read them psalms and listened to their prayers. And while Philippa's heart continued to ache for her son and, more days than not, long for a more active life, she took comfort in Anne and in her own contributions to the community of women.

"No, dear," Hersend said, "not Beatrice. There has been an … incident." Crossing herself, she took a deep breath. "Madeleine was attacked in her cell."

"Attacked?" Philippa asked, covering her heart with her hand. "Is she all right?"

"She is … traumatized," Hersend explained. "You were lucky," she said, reaching out and cupping Philippa's jaw in her hand. "Let's hope Madeleine fairs as well."

The day Philippa arrived at Fontevraud, she had told Hersend that her bruised jaw was the result of a careless stumble down a stairwell. Until this moment she had assumed the Abbess believed her lie.

"Come," Hersend said. "Madeleine is waiting."

The women's infirmary held a dozen cots, which lined the east wall. Opposite the cots, a fireplace jutted out between two narrow windows, a statue of Mary atop the mantle. Tucked into one corner of the room, a triangular table held a basket of rags and a tray of ointments and lotions. On a ledge beneath the table, a sooty kettle rested on a metal trivet beside a jar of loose tea and a jug of water.

"My child, are you feeling any better?" the Abbess asked.

Madeleine studied the dying fire with vacant eyes.

"I will ask one of the brothers to haul a few more logs," Hersend said.

"No," Madeleine said, gripping Hersend's arm with a force that made the Abbess wince.

"But my dear, aren't you cold? Your fingers are like ice."

"No … men," Madeleine whispered.

"Of course, dear," Hersend said. "Forgive me. I will wake a few of the postulants. Soon enough you will be toasty." She kissed Madeleine lightly on the forehead. "Philippa will keep you company while I'm gone." Nodding at Philippa, she left the infirmary.

Philippa pulled a stool to the edge of Madeleine's cot. She

recalled the guilt that had followed her own beating, remembered the emotional pain that deepened along with her bruises, and she understood Madeleine's suffering in the pit of her belly. "Madeleine, Hersend has told me that you were attacked in your cell."

Madeleine remained fixed on the smoldering fire. Philippa recognized the odd detachment, the stony denial.

"My husband once attacked me," Philippa said, touching her jaw. "The next day he sent me to Fontevraud … without my son. My bruises faded quickly, but my heart continues to ache for my little Will. You are not alone, my friend," Philippa said. "You are not the only one who's suffered at the hands of a man."

Three young postulants entered with their arms full of logs. Silently they replenished the fire. After they left, Philippa poured water from the jug into the kettle and hung it on a metal arm that swung over the crackling fire. Hiding her shaking hands in the folds of her gown, she returned to the stool beside Madeleine's cot. If she was to be of any help to Madeleine, she must compose herself and be patient. She focused her thoughts on her favorite time of day at the abbey, the afternoon meal, an occasion that blended ritual and female intimacy. Lay brothers carried ewers of water to the refectory so the nuns could dip their fingers into them before the meal began while other servants set the tables with cups, flasks of water and wine, and baskets of bread. Soon bowls of soup were brought first to the commoners, then to the nuns' tables, and finally to the tables reserved for the laywomen. Since talking was banned during most meals, the only sounds were the footsteps of the men carrying food to the tables, the thud of cups and bowls on wood, an occasional scrape of a stool on the floor. Yet even in silence the nuns managed to communicate. Philippa watched the movement of the sisters' fingers with rapt attention until she learned to cut one finger over the other if she needed a knife and to shimmy her hand in the manner of a fish moving through water should she require a serving of trout. These signs unified their community even as silence taught them discipline. Gradually, over time, Philippa learned to appreciate how silence and ritual calmed her fluttery pulse and opened her soul to prayer.

"Philippa?" Madeleine whispered.

"I'm right here," Philippa said, pulling her stool nearer the cot.

"Girard tried to rape me."

A ripple of shock climbed Philippa's backbone. She strived to reconcile the kindly monk she knew with the monster Madeleine described. But then had not William's battering hand once stroked her cheek with tenderness?

"I stopped him," Madeleine said, curling her fingers into fists. "I fought back." Her voice held an unexpected note of pride.

"Good. Good for you! You did all that any woman can do," Philippa said, covering one of Madeleine's fists with her hand. Madeleine flinched and started to pull away, but Philippa held fast.

"Is it possible that something in my manner or dress provoked his behavior?"

"You are not your brother's keeper, Madeleine. You cannot hold yourself responsible for another man's sins. That said, I understand what you are feeling. I have spent far too much time wondering if I prompted William's beating. Believe me, such thoughts will get you nowhere. Brother Girard is at fault here, not you. Nothing, absolutely nothing warrants what happened to you."

Madeleine's face relaxed. Her fists opened. Her hands were small and insubstantial. Blood darkened the underside of her fingernails.

"Let me bathe your hands," Philippa said, pouring water from the kettle into a bowl on the floor beside Madeleine's cot. Philippa soaped one of the linen rags then slowly, carefully she ran the rag under each of Madeleine's nails before patting her hands dry and massaging them with lotion.

"You sleep now, my friend. I will be here when you wake."

"Lady Philippa!" Girard called, his blustery walk slowing to a breathless waddle. The blush that suffused his entire body ignited the rash beneath the apron of his belly and in the dank hollows of his armpits. Since the night of the incident in the convent he had been plagued by prickly heat that would not go away despite his attentive application of herbal packs and astringent oils. The simples dried his skin but did nothing to assuage the burning discomfort.

"What is it?" Philippa asked in an impatient voice. The young postulant accompanying her shifted a large woven basket from one arm to the other.

"I need to speak with you."

"Wait for me here," Philippa said to the other woman. Walking a few paces she stopped and indicated with a wave of her hand that Girard should join her. He saw by her stony expression that she had heard the rumors. Panic rendered him speechless.

The morning following his vigil outside Madeleine's door, Girard had awakened with a bruised shoulder and a face cross-hatched with scratches. For five whole days he had lain on a pallet in the men's infirmary, his wounds throbbing, his mind as knotted as his stomach. A series of claustrophobic dreams had weakened his mind. He remembered little of his evening in the cloisters, but given the Master's reaction, Girard knew he must have committed a horrible sin.

"The Master wants me to leave the abbey and seek a life else-where," he told Philippa. "You have shown kindness to me in the past. If you could talk with him, explain that ..."

"I cannot explain what I don't understand," she said, crossing her arms over her chest.

Girard's stomach gurgled alarmingly. That morning in the scriptorium Peter had wrinkled his nose and proffered a rhizome of ginger on the palm of his hand, saying it would fortify a cold stomach and cure an evil humor. And while the root had calmed Girard's queasy stomach, it had not eliminated his flatulence. Now standing in the presence of this great and beautiful lady, he feared his body might humiliate him.

"You must believe me when I say I remember very little of what happened that night. I've heard the rumors that I attacked Madeleine, but I cannot believe that I would ..." He bit his lip and blinked back tears.

She glanced to the basket the novitiate held. "We are taking supplies to the lepers. I have only a moment."

"The truth is," Girard said, fumbling for each word, "I'm not sure what happened. Taking a deep breath, he rested his crippled hand on Philippa's sleeve. "Please," he said. "Help me make sense of the terrifying confusion that clouds my mind."

Phillipa's gaze seemed to penetrate Girard's very being and settle somewhere near his heart. Girard took a deep breath and told her about the gossip the twins had spread, how he had not wanted to believe the Master was guilty of such indiscretions. "For a long time I waited for Robert to appear outside Madeleine's cell door, praying that he would not, meditating as best I could until hunger pangs distracted me." Girard blushed at this awful admission. His body felt branded by the burn of prickly heat, yet he continued, for something about this woman demanded honestly. "I ate from a loaf of bread," he said, and because it seemed to him that he must tell her everything, he continued. "A loaf I had stolen from the pantry."

"Go on," she said, her face a smooth mask.

"The bread tasted grainy and acrid and left my stomach bloated." He slipped his crippled hand into the sleeve of his robe and paused. He felt winded, as though he had run a great distance. "I saw Robert's shadow tossed against a wall. After that I remember only sensations. The convent seemed awash with smells. I felt bathed, no, drowned by the scent of tallow, butter, pomegranates and musk."

Nearby a trio of dogs barked a series of high, playful yelps that seemed to mock the seriousness of Girard's words. Philippa furrowed her brow. He wondered if she was questioning the veracity of his tale. "I know this must sound like madness," Girard said. He could hear the womanish need in his voice, a tight hysterical rise he abhorred but could not control. "I remember feeling nauseous and then this pounding, brilliant scent engulfed me." His words galloped forward and he could not rein them in. "I say scent, but it was more like a barrage of sensation, a suffocating delight ... " The air filled with the buzz of silence. Girard felt an oily sensation in his gut, the slip and slide of a memory, and he waited for it to come to him...*Can't be too careful these days,* the Blois Innkeeper had said. *A fortnight past Vital from Bourges served bread made from grain milled the previous spring, and his guest fell grievously ill with fevers and powerful visions.*

"The bread!" Girard said, "The bread was tainted!" And just like that he remembered his hand pushing open Madeleine's door. "Dear Lord! I'm no better than Evraud!" he said, dropping to the ground before Philippa. "Thank God the Master interceded. But for him I would have committed a most grievous sin." His jowls pressed the soil and he tasted clay. The sobs that rocked his body were nothing compared to the great convulsion of his soul. He felt turned inside out and emptied. A great shame settled on him, weighting him to the earth.

"Get up, Brother Girard," Philippa said. Her voice, though not unkind, offered no forgiveness.

Keeping his eyes trained on a pebble tilted precariously in a tuft of grass, he rose with an awkwardness that embarrassed him almost as much as his tears.

"Even if the bread was tainted, what you did was horrible,"

Philippa said, shaking her head from side to side. "Madeleine is a good woman ..." Her eyes darkened with anger.

Girard felt the slow crawl of prickly heat between his thighs. He deserved both her judgment and his own humiliation. Philippa paused and looked toward the base of the valley where the skeleton of Saint Lazare monastery broke through the trees. Turning her head slightly, she studied the ribbons of smoke rising from the nearby lepers' encampment. "That said, and it must be said because tainted bread only freed an impulse that was there all along ..."

"I was weak," Girard interrupted, dropping his head. "The serpent tricked me and I ate. For this I repent most heartily."

Philippa raised her hand to silence him. "Redemption is not as simple as confessing a wrong," she said.

Although her voice had softened, her expression remained inscrutable. He feared words might shatter any compassion she felt for him, so he said nothing.

"And yet," she continued, "all living creatures are sparks from the radiation of God's brilliance, emerging from God like the rays of sun. It is my duty to seek out God's brilliance in you."

"Bless you, Lady!" Girard cried. "Bless you!"

"But even if you are one of God's rays, you still must pay for your transgressions, suffer the consequences of your sin."

Philippa's voice assumed a gravity that unnerved him. He feared that she had drifted into a consideration of some personal matter. Whatever it was that occupied her thoughts, he prayed that it would not eclipse her kindness.

"I will speak to Robert," Philippa said, "but I make no promises. I will tell him about the tainted bread, your regret and willingness to atone for your sins. Beyond that ... " She lifted her hands and shrugged.

For the first time in his life he felt truly humble. "I am grateful for your kindness," he said.

She nodded a brisk farewell and turned to the postulant who readjusted the basket in the crock of her arm and followed Phillipa's descent to the base of the valley.

Girard lifted his rosary to his face and trailed the beads across his lips. "Thank you Our Lady of Mercy. Thank you!"

To the right of him, just there in a thicket of brush, Girard heard a soft animal sound. But before he could investigate, the unmistakable tinkle of the leper's bells drifted up from the valley. *The sound of the unclean!* he thought and shivered. *To die in pieces is a horrible fate!* A wave of heat passed through Girard, who glanced furtively around before reaching between his legs and scratching his blistered thighs well past the time relief turned to pain.

Robert stepped into the oak-paneled scriptorium where Girard sat hunched over a sheet of vellum. *Help me see past my anger,* he prayed silently. *Grant me compassion to hear this man's words with an open heart.* Straightening his shoulders, he spoke in a measured and controlled voice. "Brother, I've come at Lady Philippa's request to hear your confession."

Startled, Girard eased his bulk off the high stool and dropped to his knees still clutching a stylus in his hand. "Father," he said, his face blanched of color, "I have sinned exceedingly, in thought, word and deed."

Robert heard the tremble in Girard's voice, noted the proud monk did not try to hide his deformity in the folds of his robes, and he felt a surge of pity.

"Although I do not remember every detail of … the incident in the cloister …" Girard began.

Robert stiffened. "*I* do," he said, in a thundering voice. Walking briskly across the room, he stood beside Girard who blushed and cleared his throat.

"I was not trying to deny my culpability," Girard said. "I know that I entered Madeleine's cell and attacked her." He raised his hand, as though to brush his fingers against the fading scratches on his cheek. Then he seemed to remember the stylus and laid it carefully on the floor beside him. "My sin against Madeleine is an abomination! I beseech blessed Mary ever Virgin, blessed Michael the Archangel, blessed John the Baptist, the holy apostles Peter and Paul, all the saints, and you, Father, to pray to the Lord our God on my behalf."

Robert looked at Girard bent in prayer and judged the monk's remorse sincere. He, himself, he judged more harshly. Twice he had failed to protect Madeleine.

"Brother Girard," he said, "You must learn to gird your faith with discernment and self control."

Girard nodded, "I will do anything you ask," he said, "for my contrition is motivated by love of God, not fear of punishment." His voice deepened with conviction.

Outside the high-pitched call of a sparrow hawk mingled with the laughter of children. A warm breeze blew through the open door, rustling a sheaf of vellum atop the table. If he shaped Girard's punishment to address the needs of the community, everyone would benefit. *O Lord,* he prayed, *what is the appropriate action?*

Just then the tinkling reverberation of leper bells climbed the valley walls. A lip curl of disgust replaced Girard's sorrowful look of regret, and Robert had his answer. "In retribution for your sins, you will minister to the lepers, bathing their bodies, bandaging their ulcers, and tending to their spiritual needs." Girard's eyes widened. His mouth, which had been pinched in disgust, opened in silent horror. "May our Lord Jesus Christ absolve you."

The following day Girard packed a leather script with a worn Bible, his mother's rosary beads, and a tattered piece of St. Giles's robe. Slinging the leather strap over his shoulder, he descended into the valley of the lepers. The trail sloped through brush abuzz with insects, and as he drew nearer the encampment, he heard children at play. Accustomed to the muted and predictable sounds of the scriptorium—Brother Peter's mournful humming, his own labored breathing and the inevitable rustle of vellum—the rippling glee of children's laughter lifted his spirits. Despite the horror of what awaited him, a gentle breeze cooled his body and soothed his prickly heat.

Sister Petronilla, a short compact woman with a high chirpy voice, was waiting for Girard by an abbreviated wall, an exceptional job of masonry that reminded Girard of the chancel at Holy Trinity and prompted a wave of longing for the contemplative life he had abandoned.

In later years, Moriuht and a crew of young brothers would plant the valley walls with grape vine and olives trees. But for now, only a dusty ridge of earth, hoed into place by the leper Thomas, and a six-foot section of a waist-high wall of stone, separated the *malades* and the others. Robert had put a stop to the wall, announcing that he wanted no barriers at Fontervand. Thomas reputedly argued with the master, reminding him that while none of the sisters who worked among the lepers had yet contracted the disease, as a safety precaution a line should be drawn between the sick and healthy. Robert had repeated that there would be no barriers.

"You must be Brother Girard," Petronilla called out in greeting. "You're just in time to help me with the baskets!"

Every day novitiates carried food and supplies to the edge of the encampment. A dozen baskets rested atop the wall. "Good morning Sister." He prayed that Petronilla, who lived outside the slippery realm of gossip, did not know the nature of his sin.

As though reading his mind, she lifted her hand before he could speak another word. "The Master told me everything," she said.

Girard blushed and looked away.

"Here," she said, removing a vial from her habit, "dab some of this beneath your nose. It helps cover the smell of the lepers."

Though Petronilla's bluntness startled Girard, he nodded obligingly. Keeping his crippled arm well hidden, he reached for the vial with his good hand, removing the stopper with a flip of his thumb. The spicy scent of clove oil reminded him of Moriuht's diseased gums and he shivered slightly.

"It's possible to find relief from the leper's twisted limbs and contorted faces in the beauty of the morning sky," Petronilla said in a matter-of-fact voice. Smiling, she lifted her wimpled face to the scattered clouds. "But there's no escaping the stench of rotting flesh," she said, lowering her eyes to meet his.

Girard clutched the open vial and blanched. He could feel the bile roiling in his belly.

"You are disgusted," Sister Petronilla said. "Don't be. The disease is ugly. To pretend otherwise would be a lie. But people are not their disease." She pointed to the vial and ran a finger lightly across her upper lip. Girard turned slightly so as to conceal his deformity and quickly smeared the oil beneath his nose.

"In time you'll learn to ignore the smell and to focus your attention on the leper's souls. But for the time being," she said, "keep the vial with you."

Girard turned to face her, clove oil glistening beneath his nostrils. "Thank you," he said.

"Now, if you're ready, I suggest we get started. Grab two baskets and follow me."

"Two?" he asked, slipping the vial into his robe.

She furrowed her brow. "Even then, it will take a considerable time."

"I cannot carry more than one basket at a time," he said.

"Of course you can," she said. "Your fat will hamper you, but I'll slow my pace to match yours."

"It isn't that," he said. Pulling back the sleeve of his robe, he exposed his left arm. "The limb is quite useless," he said.

She appeared neither moved nor repelled, and for this Girard felt gratitude. "Let me see." Using both of her hands, she assessed the strength of his flaccid arm with a gentle probe and slide of her competent fingers. "True enough," she said with the smallest of sighs. "Well then, transporting the baskets will take a bit longer than I had planned. But you needn't worry. There's plenty of time before the midday meal, and if we're lucky, we can cajole some of the urchins to help us!" The mention of children seemed to reignite her spirit. Lifting two of the fullest baskets, she smiled. While she waited for Girard to take up his burden, she broke into a cheerful song about sweet cherry tarts and gingerbread squares.

Madeleine's first illustration was an imitation of an ornate letter she observed Peter painting for a book of hours. Once he understood the depths of her fascination, the usually laconic Peter spoke eloquently of the artistic process, both the practical and the mystical. "You must first imagine the layout," he said, indicating, with a wave of his brush, the text, border, initial, and miniature. Using a mixture of flake white and ochre, he added texture to the green vines banding the stem of his letter P to its vermillion globe. "Above all else," he said, meeting her eyes, "the illuminator should create images that look alive and active." With a few deft strokes, he transformed the base of the initial into a flare of roots. "Even the borders should add beauty and meaning."

And, indeed, Peter's border contained a symbolic maze of serpents, lambs, and purple demons. But what held Madeleine's attention was the miniature within the globe of the letter—Mary Magdalene and the Virgin Mother sitting at the foot of the cross.

Shortly after completing her first drawing Madeleine noticed a sheet of vellum lying in the trash. A small area had been scraped so many times that a hole had worn through. She salvaged a quarter of the page and took it back to her cell.

Later that night, Madeleine sketched a lead plummet outline of the two Marys. Exhausted but exhilarated, she hid her efforts at the bottom of her trunk before climbing into the pallet alongside the slumbering Little.

Each time she cleaned the scriptorium thereafter, Madeleine pilfered colors, small portions that wouldn't be noticed, dull olive green for the dead Christ, azure for his mother's robe, and carmine for Mary Magdalene's, for whom Madeleine felt a special affinity.

She began the illustration shortly after Girard was dispatched to the leper camp, but it was not until the beginning of Lent that she finished. She did not think her work well crafted. Her Christ was a reluctant martyr. Her Virgin did not elicit compassion. But Madeleine was proud of her rendering of Mary Magdalene, who sat in sorrow, one hand resting on her knee, the other lifted to wipe a tear from her cheek. The work came alive, however, when Madeleine added details not contained in Peter's illustration. First, she layered brown onto the stem of the initial P, transforming it into a tree with bony limbs. Next, she painted several leaves within the frame of the miniature. Little more than spots of pigment, the leaves rested at the foot of the cross. Even before she fully understood her reason for including them, she knew their presence was essential.

But the most gratifying aspect of the process was her luck in capturing Marie's colors in the arc of Mary's halo. When Madeleine first met Marie, greens and yellows dominated her palette. As she aged, a splattering of orange and a thin corrosive layer of murky olive muddled their purity and foreshadowed her slow and painful death. All this Madeleine managed. The effect she could not duplicate was the very quality that she felt distinguished Marie's nimbus from all others—an egg-shaped band of light that sparked silver and gold and pressed her vibrant hues against the contours of her body. In the end, Mary's halo only hinted at Marie's energy.

Madeleine did not share her miniature with anyone until shortly after Pentecost. Placing the illustration between the pages of a prayer book, she tucked the book into the pocket of her cape and woke Little from her nap. "Come, sleepy head. Let's walk to the garden."

Philippa and Madeleine met nearly every day after the none office so that Little Marie and Anne could play together among the perennials and early spring vegetables. That day, though chilly, was unseasonably bright. The Loire river fog had burned off early, and the sun was clearly visible. Madeleine removed the prayer book from her robe and placed it on the bench.

Madeleine's friendship with Philippa had deepened following Girard's attack. Philippa talked of her difficult marriage and cried openly when she discussed the child she was forced to leave behind. Madeleine, who was by nature more reserved, talked more than was her custom, discussing her childhood in Rouen and Marie's death. Gradually and over time they came to feel comfortable in each other's presence, in part because their daughters so enjoyed each other's company.

Madeleine heard Philippa and Anne's approach before she saw them, the unmistakable thump of Anne's feet hitting the soil. Anne, a child in love with words, captivated Little. "What hurts?" Little asked, pointing to a scab on Anne's knuckle.

"I fell down!" Anne said, her eyes large with the drama of her wound.

Little nodded solemnly and bent to examine the scab more closely before taking Anne's hand and pointing to a trellis of climbing vines gone to seed.

Philippa greeted Madeleine and joined her on the bench. Their conversation wove in and out of the children's words, forming what Madeleine had come to think of as the fabric of their time together.

"Little and Anne are going to see the dead beans," Little said, to no one in particular. She had an odd way of narrating her experiences, as though in the telling she could enter the moment more fully. A small, compact child with exceptionally fine features, Little possessed curiosity and insight that far exceeded her mother's. While random details distracted Madeleine, Little saw the larger picture. Bright and willful, she was also a skillful dissembler.

When Philippa spotted the prayer book, she tilted her head and asked, "What's this?"

"I've attempted an illustration," Madeleine said. She removed the miniature from between the pages of the prayer book and passed it to her friend.

"How did you manage?" Philippa asked, examining the image closely.

The children had made their way to the beans before Madeleine answered. "I found the damaged vellum in the trash."

"What I meant was how did you manage such beauty? Who taught you?"

"Brother Peter showed me how to mix just the right amounts of pigment and medium and how to apply each color in turn and then allow it to dry."

"I know what pigment is, but what is medium?" Philippa asked.

From anyone else, the barrage of questions might have struck Madeleine as intrusive, even threatening. But Philippa's curiosity was a compliment. "My definition of boredom," Philippa once told Madeleine, "is sitting in a room full of people who share my every thought and experience. Why, it's the differences in people which make life fascinating!"

"The medium turns pigment into liquid paint," Madeleine said. "I mix egg whites and water to make it. Sometimes I added honey to vary the consistency. See?" She said, pointing to the texture in the fold of Marie's gown.

"Yes, I see," Philippa said. And Madeleine could tell by Philippa's rapt expression that she was trying to enter her life, straining to imagine the process of mixing paints and then applying them to vellum. Philippa's momentary silence was not so much the absence of sound as it was a comfortable space. "And what of the halo?" she asked. "How did you manage the colors?"

"Mommy, Mommy," Little cried out, "I'm stuck!"

"I'll be right back," Madeleine said and went to rescue her daughter, who had managed to wedge herself between the trellis and the snap bean's vegetation. After Madeleine had freed her (no easy task as Little wriggled in her frustration and would not be still), she picked up both girls, one in each arm, and carried them to the bench. "Play nearby for a while," she said, pointing to the lamb's ear. The girls loved the velvety feel of the plant.

"Little and Anne find snails!" Little proclaimed.

The hoods of the girls' capes slipped off their heads and gathered against their shoulders. Little's curls were black and shiny as wet pebbles while Anne's blonde waves blanched white against the glare of the winter sun. Madeleine thought, not for the first time, that Anne's coloring was closer to hers than her own daughter's.

"The tree is beautifully rendered," Philippa said. Madeleine smiled and sat beside her on the bench. "But menacing, unsettling in some way I cannot name except to say it makes me fearful." There was a trace of awe in Philippa's voice. "Tell me, will you do more?"

"I don't know," Madeleine said, taking the miniature from Philippa's hands. "Vellum is costly, and Brother Peter is not likely to throw out more anytime soon."

"Where does it come from?"

"We make our own."

"How?"

Madeleine looked to the children, who seemed content, so she answered Philippa's question as fully as she could, proud of her knowledge. "We soak calfskin for three to ten days in a lime solution. When Peter determines the skins are ready, we rinse them in water and stretch them on round frames to dry. Then we scrape both sides of the skin with a special knife and pounce the vellum with pumice stone."

"Perhaps I can help you obtain more calf skins. My husband makes generous donations to the abbey."

"Then you don't think my desire strange?" Madeleine asked.

"Strange? All the women at Fontervand are strange, if by strange you mean we are at odds with convention." Her brow furrowed. "We are oddities," she said with a sigh, "the ones who don't fit easily into the roles we've been assigned. We make people uncomfortable, so we end up relegated to convents." Her tone was decisive.

"Some come by choice," Madeleine said, thinking, *there are worse places to live.* She had never spoken, even obliquely of the particulars of her life in Rouen. She was not ashamed, only hesitant to recall them, fearful of being pulled back into that place and time.

"You are right," Philippa said, touching Madeleine's hand. "I have made this discussion about me, a common fault of privileged Lords and Ladies. The issue is, of course, more complicated. Some women enter the abbey seeking refuge; others are sent against our wills. In either case, we are all displaced from a world that cannot contain us."

Madeleine did not fully understand Phillipa's insistence that the women at Fontervand were all one in their strangeness. She felt little affinity with the novitiates and none at all with the twins. Except for Bertrad and Philippa, she felt isolated from the other women, but she remained silent. "Thank you for offering to secure calfskin," she said.

The bell for sext rang. Madeleine slipped the miniature between the pages of her prayer book and tucked the book into the pocket of her robe. "Time to go," she said to Little.

"You too, Anne," Philippa called. Before they walked their separate ways, Philippa rested her hand on Madeleine's shoulder. "I will write to arrange for the calf skin," she said. "You have a special gift which should not be wasted."

The clove oil proved ineffective. Each morning Girard woke to the same realization: He would spend the rest of his life swallowing the fetid odor of lepers. For Sister Petronilla had been right, the stench of the disease was far worse than the sight of disfiguring nodules and skin lesions. Assigned the undignified job of washer of wraps, he spent his endless days behind Saint Lazare laundering soiled strips of linen, stirring the stinking mess with a hazel stick then hanging the simmering lot to dry on a wooden scaffolding that he thought of as the leper tree because even boiled clean the wraps blossomed pink. The soap, an astringent concoction of animal fat and lye, chapped his hands and burned the insides of his nose without ever completely eliminating bloodstains.

The smell caused Girard to lose his appetite. Even to think of food made him gag. For the first time since his father's death he ate out of necessity, forcing sops of bread past a tight gullet into a roiling belly that grew smaller and less demanding every day. Without the haunting presence of gluttony, he hardly knew what to do with his mind.

Over the years he had spent hours plotting ways to sneak an extra serving of broth or bowl of pudding. Once, during the early days of Fontevraud, he had pilfered half a dozen pippins from a barrel in the kitchen. Under the cover of darkness, he sneaked through the cloisters to the chapel where he hid the forbidden fruits in the statue of Saint Benedict, tucking them one by one behind the stone book of rules held open in the icon's hands. The next night, after the others had fallen asleep, Girard returned to feast on the apples, luxuriating in each tart mouthful. And while his secrecy had shamed him, it had also been oddly gratifying. That he could so easily deceive his fellow man convinced him of his own superior intelligence. During his time at the abbey, Girard had, he understood, grown even more contemptuous of human nature and come to question the motives and sincerity of others.

But after six months of sharing meals with the lepers, his cynicism had been replaced by empathy, a less dependable, more dangerous emotion. When one of the afflicted, an old crone with a splayed and twisted nose, pushed aside her bowl of broth and announced, "For me, taste is but a memory," Girard felt her pain in the sinews of his being.

Shortly after the feast of James the Apostle, Girard stood at the leper tree, stirring a caldron of soap and lye as it emitted putrid clouds of yellow steam. He was imagining the miasma of damp hopes that floated the souls of the sinners assigned to purgatory when Petronilla appeared out of nowhere. Omnipresent in the valley, she lived among the unclean, holding their collapsed fingers, bathing their bodies grown hairless and polished as river stones.

"Good afternoon, Brother!" Petronilla said, as though it was the most natural thing in the world to issue greetings over a cauldron of stewing leper rags!

"Your work is greatly appreciated," she said, briefly resting a hand on his shoulder. Her warm, uncomplicated touch soothed a need he had not known he had had. Sunlight funneled through the clouds. Petronilla closed her eyes and turned her body towards the warmth. All of his life Girard had longed to live in a world of pure sensations, and watching someone so comfortable with her own physical being filled him with awe. Opening her eyes with one blink, Petronilla turned and met his startled gaze. The plain wimple that framed her face lent gravity to her words. "Why is it that you've not once asked about Madeleine or Master Robert?"

Girard stepped away from the cauldron, setting his hickory stick against the trunk of a tree. "I was afraid, not indifferent," he said in barely audible tones. In the distance a child's voice trilled an edgy excitement that could any minute escalate into whooping exhilaration or tears. "How are they?" he asked.

"Madeleine takes joy in her child. And Master Robert, as you well know, is a disciplined and holy man whose faith is far stronger than some passing anger." Practical and pragmatic, there was something spiritually settled about Petronilla. In this place of death and dying, she had found a way for her own soul to flourish. She saw the worse, prayed for the best, and accepted whatever came her way. Never self-righteous, always well meaning, she confronted sinners without appearing to judge them. With a kind word and a gentle nudge, she urged them forward on the cobbled road towards redemption. A whirlwind of good intentions, Petronilla both inspired and intimidated the people she cared about.

A dragonfly flashed the air between them. Petronilla smiled, and her happiness reminded Girard of the joy that lit his mother's face when she cooked her specialty—roasted game marinated in wine and marjoram. Both women delighted in small pleasures and modest triumphs.

"I'm glad to hear that Madeleine and the Master are doing well," Girard said.

"Well enough," she said. "It's you I worry about, Girard. It's your soul that occupies my thoughts. How *is* your soul doing?" she asked him as casually as one might ask about the weather.

Girard imagined an object the size and shape of a dove's breast covered with sores. Touching the sparse ring of hair surrounding his tonsure, he tried to translate this image into something less offensive. "I have come to think of my soul as … unwell," he said.

Petronilla's nod seemed less a response to Girard's words than an acknowledgement of human weakness. "Let me ask you something, Brother Girard," she said. "Do you ever surprise yourself? Do you ever thrill to an unfamiliar act or consider a thought that seems borrowed from some other being?"

Guilt crushed him, and he avoided her eyes. "What happened between Madeleine and me was a mistake, a terrible mistake. I never meant …"

"You misunderstand," she said, resting a firm hand on his shoulder. "I'm not talking about the occasions of sin. I'm talking about impulses that reveal our best intentions. Those spontaneous moments that feel like pure indulgence, but which sometimes turn out to be so much more."

"No," Girard said. "I don't believe I've ever done anything that surprised me, at least not in a good way." Evasiveness and secrecy were so habitual that the truth sounded oddly insincere to his ears. Or maybe it was not the words themselves, but the tone, completely unlike the commanding tone he had assiduously adapted at seminary.

"I didn't think so," she said, her voice thick with emotion he could not immediately identify. Not pity, for Petronilla did not have it in her to pity anyone. No, Girard felt certain that her words contained something so much more. When Petronilla next spoke, she assumed a more cheerful tone. "I've arranged for a friend of yours to visit. Selfishly, I'm hoping he'll agree to stay and work among us."

A friend? Who could she mean? For Girard was not so deluded as to think he had any real friends. "Brother Peter?" he asked, recalling the oddly compelling scratch of the monk's pen moving across vellum.

"Oh no, no!" Petronilla laughed. "A studious and devout man, by any standards, but hardly fit to work among the lepers! It takes a special sort to do that," she said. And for the briefest of moments Girard basked in Petronilla's compliment.

"No, dear, not Peter, but Moriuht! I have always liked the man, and I hear he's become a great favorite among the children. Quite the jester, I understand. If nothing else, your friend will upset our routine, shake things up a bit!"

Of all people, Girard thought, *why Moriuht?* Where on earth did she get the idea that Moriuht was a friend? Smiling politely, he silently recited the *Agnus Dei—Lamb of God, who takest away the sins of the world, have mercy on us.*

"Ah, here he is now," she said pointing to the twisting trail that descended from the main monastery. Motes of pollen floated the bands of sunlight pressing through the canopy of hawthorn trees.

Ah, yes, Girard thought, *I would recognize the creature's lopping, erratic gait anywhere.*

"Welcome, Brother," Petronilla called out. "He does take joy in life, does he not?" she asked Girard. "Look how he dances!"

Before he could respond, Moriuht was upon them, breathless and disheveled. "I've brought you the jaw bone of a hare," he said. Reaching into the deep pocket of his robe, he retrieved his gift, running his fingers along the mandible's curve before handing it to Petronilla with a toothless grin.

"Ah, such stark beauty!" she said, turning the bone in her hands, examining it from every angle. When she looked up it was clear to Girard that her praise was heart felt. "Well, I've work to do. You two enjoy your time together." Clutching the bone in one hand, she waved with the other.

Moriuht watched her disappear into Saint Lazare before turning his attention to Girard. "Look at us!" he bellowed. "You've lost your blubber, and I've lost my teeth!" He strode towards Girard with opened arms. Buried in Moriuht's embrace, Girard could not help wondering if chiggers and lice still infested his gold-streaked beard and the ragged snarls of his hair. Certainly he still reeked of garlic and leeks.

"You know what I'd like?" Moriuht said, slapping Girard's back before releasing him. "I'd like to splash about a bit before vespers. Come. The rags will wait," he said, dismissing the steaming caldron with a wave of his hand. Tired and ready for a break, Girard nodded, following Moriuht into the copse of boxwood that sheltered the fount of Evraud.

When they reached the pond, the silly fool pulled his robe

over his head and leapt in with a whoop that set a whole limb of sparrows to flight. Standing chest high in water, Moriuht raised his arms above his head and swayed, an awkward but exhilarating gyration that left Girard appalled and vaguely envious. What kind of courage must a man possess to engage in such absurdity?

"Come in, Brother Girard," he yelled before diving shallow and resurfacing a few yards away. Water beaded his beard and streamed down his neck and shoulders.

When Moriuht smiled, all gums and exuberance, Girard felt an envy that was as potent as lust. *I would like to stand as he stands, fearless and steady.*

"Take off your robes and join me," Moriuht shouted. "The water is sweet and restorative."

Standing on the shore beneath an overhang of tree limbs, Girard considered the possibility. It was true he had lost a great deal of weight. The apron of flesh that had for years obscured his sex was all but gone, and when he touched his chest he could feel an unfamiliar ripple of rib cage. Still, Girard had not disrobed in front of anyone since his mother bathed him as a child and he was not at all sure he was prepared to do so now. What if one of the women should come upon them? Or Robert? The whole venture seemed wildly inappropriate. After all, there were wraps to be laundered and anyway, he could not swim.

"I think I shall remain safely on the shore," he said, thinking, *I am afraid of so many things.*

Moriuht nodded. Between tumbling submersions, he discussed Robert's goodness, Madeleine's child, the industry of bees, and the grace implicit in a sunset. What he lacked in eloquence, he made up for in passion, urged on by the sheer momentum of his joyful appreciation of life. Girard began to feel it too. He felt it in the buzz of insects and in the chatter of magpies. By the time Moriuht had shared a plotless dream involving rabbits and marigolds, the still clothed Girard was ankle deep in water.

"Come on, Brother. You're half way there," Moriuht urged.

Perhaps for a minute, Girard thought, mesmerized by the

graceful weave of Moriuht's hands parting water. *Just to give my aching muscles a rest.* Modestly turning his back to Moriuht, he peeled off his robe and tossed it onto shore before covering his genitals and wading cautiously into the pond. He watched a water bug skitter the surface and thought that he had never known anything as uncomplicated as the squish of mud between his toes.

"It's wonderful, isn't it?" Moriuht bellowed.

Submerged shoulder-high in pond water, Girard smiled. Not his usual obsequious smile, the one bracketing a hollow need, a bottomless desire, but a smile full of joy and greedy for more. "Yes," Girard said. "Oh, yes!" When the laughter came it was as powerful as it was unexpected, an ecstatic sound—loud, raucous and rippling with delight.

Philippa took her final vows on the first Sunday in Advent. At her clothing ceremony where she received her habit, she felt as though she were coming home. If she could only see her son and venture out into the world now and then, her life would be perfect. Despite these restrictions, Philippa found peace at Fontevraud. The ordinary and extraordinary individuals who made up the community of women supported Philippa in her decision to pursue a life of study, contemplation and prayer by offering both their guidance and their friendship. But every now and then, she felt a sorrow that extinguished joy. Her heart pounded against her ribcage which such force she felt the beat in her fingertips.

On one such day in early summer, Philippa sat by the window of her cell, watching the cloisters gradually emerge in the morning light. Their lush lawns squared by hedges, crossed by gravel paths and framed by arched galleries reflected the order and serenity of a life of solitude. Usually the sight comforted and consoled Philippa, but this morning it only contributed to her anxiety. The previous night she had dreamed of demons, longbows, and lightening strikes, and now she worried that she was growing morbid in her seclusion.

A flurry of activity in the gallery below interrupted her thoughts. She had grown so accustomed to the whisper of bare feet and sandals that at first she could not make sense of the clump of leather-soled shoes taking the stairs. Aunt Sibyl was first through the door. "My dear Philippa! My child!" she said. Thumbs brushing fingertips, she bustled across the room and wrapped her arms around her niece.

Not a fortnight had passed since her arrival at Fontevraud without a letter from Sophie and Sibyl appraising Philippa of young Will's doings and assuring her that as soon as they were given leave, they would journey to see her in her new home, but after three long years, Philippa had almost given up hope of ever seeing her family again.

Philippa kissed her aunt's wrinkled cheeks, breathed in her powdery scent and thought how long it had been since she had touched anyone but Anne.

"Have you come alone, Auntie?" she asked.

"Alone? My dear child, Sophie and I have brought your son!"

As a young girl Philippa saw the Garonne River overflow its banks and surge across the land, swallowing scrub brush and furrowed fields alike. The idea that she might be swept away in the swelling tide had filled her with joy. When Sophie entered the room with young Will in tow, Philippa looked at the sturdy seven-year-old before her and felt awash in a love as fierce as raging floodwaters. She wanted to wade in, immerse herself wholly in its power.

Sophie embraced Philippa, rising up on tiptoes to whisper in her lovely gruff voice, "Give the boy time to take you in, dear."

The air shimmered with silence Philippa did not break, not

even to whisper a prayer, for life at Fontevraud had taught her that patience is a kind of generosity. She was not altogether surprised when Will avoided her eyes and studied her cell instead. When Philippa managed Aquitaine and traveled from dependency to dependency, she too had paid careful attention to the houses she visited, for she had learned early on that a brass candle holder, a crystal vase arranged just so to catch the morning light, even something as seemingly inconsequential as a scattering of cake crumbs revealed much about the occupant.

Her cot, covered with a bleached linen spread folded and tucked precisely at the corners, suggested a fastidious nature but also, she feared, a certain rigidity of temperament, a need for constancy and routine. On the pine table beside the cot was one of Madeleine's miniatures, Our Lady in all her glory. When Will glanced at it, a scrim of apprehension veiled his eyes, and Philippa worried that he might think her overly devout. In fact, she admired the beauty of the composition—Mary's warm luminous flesh and crisp blue robe—as much as she revered the subject. But neither the cot nor the miniature held Will's attention for long. His eyes remained fixed on the silver crucifix, a gift from Philippa's father on her first communion, which hung on the wall opposite her cot. The cross had once graced the wall of Philippa's chambers in Poitiers.

While her son studied the crucifix, Philippa studied him. Will was both taller and stronger than the child she had imagined. To have lost out on these growing years filled her with sorrow. Consciously, deliberately she turned her attention outward, focused on the way sunlight warmed the tiny space of her cell and bathed the room in pearly shades.

When at last Will looked at her, he examined her thoroughly. His eyes were the same blue as his father's. But whereas William's glance was full of fire and heat, Will's was cool, cautious, and even more difficult to decipher. "That expression will bedevil the women who love you," she said, "and there will be many woman, for you have grown handsome as your father, tall and fine limbed." When she touched his cheek he surprised her by closing his eyes.

Dropping to her knees, Philippa scooped him into her arms. And while he did not return her embrace, neither did he pull away. Philippa pressed her mouth against Will's crown and breathed in his grassy scent. His light hair had turned a darker shade of russet, but it still tickled baby soft against her lips. When Will stepped out of Philippa's embrace and touched her wimple, she held her breath and dared not blink for fear of frightening him away.

"Father says your hair is gold, but I say it is more yellow than gold." His voice, though deeper than the one she remembered, was still demanding, though more playful in tone, she thought.

Philippa tugged off her wimple. Her hair was cropped short as a man's, but even the weight of her starched head cloth could not flatten the curl. A breeze wafted through a casement window, cooling her nape and tickling her scalp, but Philippa remained entirely composed, allowing Will a good long look before she rubbed her itchy scalp with such vigor that the curls bounced crazily in every direction.

Will's laughter, an unguarded, breathy trill, made Philippa's throat ache. "I think your hair is neither gold or yellow. I think it's more the straw color of my pony's mane!" he said.

Sophie snorted, a sound more appreciative than disapproving, but Philippa could tell by the way Sibyl's nervous fingers plucked at her bodice that she was not amused. "Oh, Will," she said. "A lady does not want to be compared to a pony!"

Momentarily abashed, Will blushed and dropped his head.

Still kneeling, Philippa rested her hands on Will's shoulders and waited for him to look up. When he did, his eyes had hardened. For though his expression was a grave copy of his father's, Philippa knew that Will did not yet possess the fortitude and resilience of a man. "What's your pony's name?" she asked.

"Sebastian," he said, his eyes flashed excitement and the muscles around his mouth relaxed.

"Is he a handsome pony?" she asked.

"Oh, yes, very handsome! Sebastian has brown eyes and a black muzzle that's soft as pussy willows. And he's ever so smart.

He comes when I call, and when I ask him his name he whinnies and prances about the stable!"

Neighing softly, Will circled Philippa's cell with lively springing steps, ignoring Sibyl's titter and grinning at Sophie and Philippa. When Will's high-pitched neighs tumbled into boyish laughter, Philippa clapped her hands like a young girl. If William broke her heart, then the sound of his son's laughter would meld it back together.

Will, his face flushed and his breathing rapid, cantered to a stop beside Philippa. Lifting his hand to his mother's cropped hair, he pinched one curl, lazily rubbing thumb against forefinger. Philippa's chest ached, for her body recognized the gesture before her mind could piece together the memory it evoked. Closing her eyes, she gave herself over to the sweet pull of Will's fingers. And then it came to her—Will's fisted baby hand buried in her hair, his fingers opening and closing, grabbing hold a curl as she suckled him at her breast. *Thank you Holy Mother,* she prayed silently. *Thank you for this moment.*

When Philippa's boy released her curl, she opened her eyes and smiled. "Sebastian sounds wonderful," she said. "And while I agree with Aunt Sophie that most ladies would not enjoy being likened to an animal, I am honored to be compared to such a fine pony."

This time when Philippa wrapped her arms around Will he hugged her back. "And does my sister also have pony hair?" he asked, his words warm against her neck.

"Come," she said, rising and holding out her hand, "you will see for yourself."

Will and Anne's reunion contained no shyness or hesitancy. Physically reserved, Anne was by temperament and situation a solitary child, and Philippa knew from her aunts' letters that Will would rather curry his pony in the silence of the stables than climb fences with his friends. But both had adventuresome minds, and within the hour they were concocting elaborate tales to entertain each other, stories involving ladies, knights and golden-haired stallions, instructive stories, Philippa noted, that sounded remarkably like the tales favored by Sibyl and Sophie.

Philippa's family stayed for a fortnight, and during that time she told many tales of her own. Anne and Will's favorite by far was the story of the three weeks their great aunts and their mother bumped along the slick winter roads of northern France, navigating swampy puddles and muddy quagmires on the journey to meet their father. In the telling, Philippa recalled her own fluttery excitement and also how certain she had been that William was her destiny. Sitting between their two children, their bodies leaning into hers, she realized that she had been right. Nothing she would ever do in life would exceed the miracle of Will and Anne.

Shortly after Philippa's family visited, Hersend approached her in her cell. "The Master would like to speak with you before he leaves for business in Anjou," she said. "He is waiting in the chapel." She took her leave before Philippa had a chance to ask questions.

Since Will's visit, Philippa had been filled with girlish energy. Hastening to the chapel, she entered through the south door of the transept where she found Robert deep in prayer, his rosary beads draped over his fingers, his eyes affixed on a marble statue of the Virgin. One of the novices placed a vase of lilies at Our Lady's feet, and while the long-stemmed flowers were lovely, Philippa could not help thinking, quite uncharitably she knew, that Madeleine's arrangements had always been more interesting. Her fragrant bouquets of roses and wildflowers were often spiked with sprigs of juniper or foxglove, unexpected additions that delighted Philippa. Not everyone agreed with her. Sister Beatrice complained to the abbess that Madeleine's "odd arrangements" were a "spiritual distraction." Mother Hersend replied simply, "Well then sister, don't look at them."

When Robert sensed Philippa's presence, he rose from the

kneeler. "Please," he said, indicating with a gracious sweep of his hand that she should enter the pew. He waited until she was seated before taking a place beside her. "So," he said, smiling, "you enjoyed your visit with your family?"

"Oh, yes! More than I can possibly say. Will is a fine young man, bright and well mannered. I would be lying if I didn't say I resent the years of separation. But I thank the Lord that he is thriving."

Robert squeezed Philippa's hand. "Good," he said.

His voice was as powerful as ever, but Philippa detected fatigue in the shadows beneath his eyes. "You look tired, Master," she said. "The balance between the active life and the contemplative one is never easy, is it?"

"Ah," he sat, patting her hand with his own. "Of course you would understand. You and I have similar temperaments, Philippa."

Philippa could not imagine what she had in common with a holy man who worked miracles. Surely Robert's humours were in perfect balance while hers, as William had so often reminded her, were dominated by an overabundance of bile. One of the lay brothers furiously swept the nave. Philippa waited for the swish of reed bristles to subside before responding. "While I am deeply flattered that you think us similar, I'm not sure I understand."

"We are ambitious people whose interests are varied. You've married, supervised a household, managed an estate, and now you've found the love of God and entered into a new marriage to the church. And, of course, without your generous contributions, there would be no abbey."

When the Master looked into Philippa's eyes she remembered the first time she had heard him preach, at the Cathedral of St. Sernin. The young barefoot priest had been a bundle of contradictions, his broad shoulders and muscular limbs at odds with his humble bearing; his somber expression a contrast to the zeal that lit his eyes. But it was his voice that held Philippa's attention—then and now—and prompted her to look honestly at her life.

"William's money helped fund the building of Fontevraud," she said, "not mine."

"Without your urging I doubt William would have made such generous donations, and had you not acted as his regent, there might not be monies to bequeath."

"Thank you, Master Robert, but I think you give me more credit than I'm due. When I ruled Poitiers in my husband's stead I made grievous errors that resulted in the loss of land and lives."

"I suspect your story is more involved than the one you tell yourself," Robert said.

Quite suddenly the chapel seemed dreary and contained. Philippa rearranged the folds of her robe, but only because her fidgety fingers needed something to do. "What do you mean?" she asked.

"People or events may bring difficulties and complications, but they also herald new possibilities. Sometimes in working though the unforeseen, we discover strengths of character previously held in reserve."

As was his way, Robert paused. Philippa did not feel pressured to articulate some epiphany she had had in response to his learned words. Indeed, Robert seemed entirely absorbed in the vase of lilies at Our Lady's feet.

"Augustine says that when we enjoy the beauty of nature, we are really taking pleasure in God. For it was through God's Light that all colors and luminosity, in heaven and on earth, came into being."

The lazy droop of fluted petals filled Philippa with appreciation for His divine grace.

"Sometimes, Philippa," Robert continued in the low, vibrant tone she associated with the confessional, "the din of our daily activity prevents us from knowing what is truly important. We hear our thoughts, but we do not listen to their meaning. If we have the courage to accept life in all its complexity, if we can view the disappointments and the triumphs as a single strand that binds us irrevocably to Our Maker, we are that much closer to deciphering the cryptic language of our souls."

"The truth is," she said, "I loved the challenge of decision making. Perhaps I thought if I succeeded in managing William's affairs, he would see me as an equal. But life is more complicated than one imagines, is it not? For even as I gloated over my success, I was not happy, for I resented the time I spent away from my child. And then, when William returned from his crusade and took back control of his estate, I resented that as well."

"You are not alone, Philippa. It's not unusual for one desire to be yoked to its opposite." She understood from his furrowed brow that his words, while meant for her, were relevant to his own life as well. "It's important to keep in mind that all things in human experience can be used in service of the soul's return to God," Robert said.

A line of monks carrying chant books entered the central aisle of the church and began practicing the gradual, an elaborate Gregorian chant of enormous difficulty. Robert and Philippa returned to a prayerful contemplation of their own thoughts until the choir paused to discuss the execution of a particularly difficult musical phrase.

"What I want to discuss with you is not the past but the future," Robert said. "I propose that you begin leading a more active life, one that takes you beyond the walls of the abbey into the larger world where you would act as my ambassador, soliciting funds from the nobles. You have lived and worked among the lords and ladies. You know the circumstance of their estates and the character of their minds. You could be of tremendous help."

"The larger world?" Philippa said and felt a tumbling excitement in the pit of her stomach. "And what of Anne?"

"Your daughter may accompany you and your entourage. Your travel would be seasonal—when the weather is fair and the roads accessible. In the inclement months, you would be free to pursue a life of study and prayer."

Philippa thrilled at Robert's proposal. In serving him she could also serve herself! And yet, she felt a hesitancy of spirit, for she had lived apart from the bustle of secular life for a very long time and feared she would not remember how to navigate the social rules and expectations. Here among the holy men and woman she had found peace of mind. What if she were to run across her husband and his mistress, what then?

Robert placed his hand on her arm. "I know you are afraid," he said. "But our Lord will not allow your feet to slip. Whatever you decide, He will keep you from all harm; He will preserve your soul. Trust in His goodness and His grace, and He will show you the way. And Philippa," Robert added. "Your travels would take you quite often to Poitiers. You could see your son."

"Yes!" she said, smiling broadly. "I will act as your ambassador, Robert." Throwing her arms around him, Philippa gave Robert a quick hug. "I will not disappoint you," she said.

"Benite exultemus domino," Robert said. "Come let us praise the Lord."

Girard almost lost his balance on the gravel path descending to Saint Lazare when Petronilla suggested that he minister to Evraud. "Evraud, the robber, do you mean?"

"*Reformed* robber," Petronilla said. "He is not the same man who led the thugs who attacked your party."

Girard wondered if it was God's will or a nun's fancy that his penance should be so excruciating.

"Evraud is dying a painful death, and you have the capacity to ease his suffering, bring peace to his final days."

While the others at Saint Lazare had joined the pilgrimage already afflicted with leprosy, Evraud alone had contracted the disease at Fontevraud. Girard was not the first to wonder if the robber's illness were an act of divine retribution, but none pondered the possibility with greater self-interest, for while Girard had not accosted innocent travelers, he would have raped Madeleine if Robert had not intervened. Evraud and he were similarly depraved, so perhaps it followed that they would suffer the same horrendous death.

Looking at the steeple of Saint Lazare's chapel rising from the valley floor, Girard's gut clinched at the thought of becoming one of the scaly unclean fated to die by degrees. Until now, the possibility had seemed remote, for while he resided at Saint Lazare, except for devotions and meals, he seldom interacted with the lepers. His position as washer of wraps provided distance between himself and the disease, even if only the length of a hickory stick. But daily physical contact with the dying seemed fraught with danger.

Not only did he fear contracting the disease, he feared disgracing himself before Petronilla and, more importantly, the Master. A good caretaker must intuit the needs of his patient, and Girard was not sure he possessed the capacity to know anything without careful thought and deliberation. Somewhere in his long journey from his father's house to Fontevraud, Girard had come to see himself as a cripple with a blustering tone and a mind for memorizing psalms, an educated man fluent in Latin but unschooled in the nuances of the heart.

"I have no experience caring for the sick," Girard said, coming to a stop, "and my deformity," he continued, uncovering his flaccid arm, "will make the task impossible."

"Difficult perhaps, but not impossible," Petronilla said. "No need to worry, Brother Girard. We are all fallible and flawed."

Girard blushed, and covered his deformity.

"And yet, we must persevere, offering ourselves up, making use of our God-given gifts. You, my friend, have the gifts of compassion and fortitude, admirable qualities best put to use helping others."

Petronilla's praise startled Girard. Since arriving at Saint Lazare he occasionally felt the pinch of an individual's despair or recognized the kindness implicit in another's generosity. And sometimes while watching the children play, he knew the same joy he had known submerged in the pond with Moriuht. But he viewed these experiences as lucky anomalies rather than reasoned proof that he had learned to identify with and understand other people's feelings. More often he was disgusted by his fellow man. Instead of empathizing with their suffering, he focused on their careless hygiene and bad manners. He tried to replace judgment with acceptance, but the substitution did not come easily. As to fortitude, Girard simply did not associate strength and endurance with his character. True, he worked diligently and without complaint, but what choice did he have? It was that or, scorned by the Master, take leave of Fontevraud.

"Come, there's much to learn and I will help you." Petronilla tapped Girard's shoulder and the two resumed their descent toward Saint Lazare.

His eyes trained on the steep path, Girard walked in silence broken only by the intermittent coo of a dove and the crunch of gravel beneath their sandals. When Petronilla resumed speaking, her voice was low and measured.

"Many of the dying fear a loss of dignity and harbor a deep desire to be alone with their pain. They will not tell you what their needs are, so you must learn to recognize them on your own. Discovering what's best for each individual is not easy. What comforts one may annoy another. It's a matter of trial and error."

Girard stopped beside a spindly bush and turned to face her. "Trial and error?"

"For instance, Evraud's humors are out of balance," she said, wobbling her hand back and forth. "He is nearly blind and has very little feeling in his arms and legs." Petronilla glanced up, squinting at the bright fog that was beginning to lift. "Never the less," she continued, "he likes me to look into his eyes when I speak and to massage his arms and legs daily. You, Brother Girard must do the same," she said, quickening her pace.

"But if the man cannot see or feel," Girard said, stumbling to catch up, "I don't understand the benefit of either act."

"Evraud will sense when he has your full attention," she said before stopping in a hazy pool of sunlight and taking Girard's hand in her own. "And even though he cannot feel the slide of your flesh against his, the mere gesture will evoke a recollection of some other touch and that memory will console and comfort him. Just be gentle," she cautioned, the pad of her thumb stroking the back of his hand. "For a leper's skin is fragile and tears as readily as parchment."

Girard recalled an afternoon spent working in the scriptorium. Distracted by hunger, he had pressed too vigorously while copying a minime, forcing the tip of his stylus through the vellum. He imaged his clumsy fingers ripping through leper skin and he shuddered. "I cannot do what you are asking." When he raised his eyes to meet Petronilla's, she released his hand and lifted her face to the heavens. Together they watched a wisp of fog drift across the skies. While the sweeping motion seemed to settle Petronilla, it left Girard dizzy and disoriented.

"Of course you can," she said, dropping her gaze to meet his, "but first you must understand and believe in the power of memory. Close your eyes, Brother Girard. Recall a touch that settled you, calmed your nerves or made you feel loved."

Girard closed his eyes and struggled to do what she asked. But the truth was, except for Moriuht's bear hug, he could not remember the last time anyone besides Petronilla had touched him.

"Think back to childhood," she said. "Think back to a time that was, perhaps, less complicated."

With his eyes closed, Girard's other senses were heightened. Distant sounds—the slurred notes and short trills of a sparrow's call, the rustle of wind through high grass—seemed amplified. He inhaled the earthy scent of damp brush and conifers. But try as he might, he could not retrieve a single childhood memory, not one. He was about to explain his failure to Petronilla, when there it was—his mother giving him a back rub, a memory so vivid that he could feel the warmth of her trailing fingers easing him into sleep. If he thought anything at all it was *yes*, simply, *yes*, so happy was he to have arrived at this comfortable place.

Petronilla's voice came from a great distance. "There, you've found it, haven't you?"

He nodded, not wanting to let go of the moment, knowing that he already had. When he opened his eyes the world was as it had always been, and Girard felt naked and cold. "Sister, I still don't know if I can do what you're asking, for I am a weak and sinful man."

"Your uncertainty only confirms my belief that you are the right person for the job, for the person who works in the service of the Lord even as he entertains doubts is a true man of faith," Petronilla said, indicating with a wave of her hand that they should continue their journey toward Saint Lazare. "I have no concerns regarding the strength of your character. I do, however, think it presumptuous to assume you are the only one to wrestle daily with a troubled conscience. We must all learn to bear the pain of our past transgressions without dwelling on the bleak knowledge of our failures. Self-reflection is the nature of man. It is both our sorrow and our greatest gift, for while it makes us aware of our defects, it also allows for the transformation of our characters. The ability to recognize and address our faults is what separates man from beast."

Petronilla stopped before the main door of Saint Lazare, an imposing building constructed of the same white brick and blue tiled roof as the rest of Fontevraud. In addition to a chapter house, lavatorium, cloister, and chapel, the building also housed an infirmary for the lepers.

"I hope that someday you will achieve a measure of peace in your life," she said, "but that is not something I can control. And, quite frankly, neither is it the point. What you can do, what you *are* doing, is to act on your beliefs, to work tirelessly in the service of the Lord. Beyond that, Brother Girard, what is there?"

Children played marbles in a clearing near the lavatorium. They spotted Petronilla and abandoned their game, squealing with delight, as they ran towards her. Laughing, Petronilla reached into her robe for the sack of ginger snaps she always carried, dispensing them with much laughter.

Girard took a deep breath and considered Petronilla's words. When had he ever acted on his beliefs or worked tirelessly in the service of the Lord? His decision to enter the Benedictine seminary had been as much a retreat from life as a spiritual calling. Fear as much as faith had prompted him to pursue a contemplative life. But perhaps he was being too hard on himself, for it was also true that having found holy purpose in the timbre and pitch of the Master's words, Girard had willingly abandoned his comfortable life at Holy Trinity for the hardships of the road.

The children, having finished their treats, ran to the clearing to gather up their marbles. When Petronilla turned to Girard, she was still smiling.

"And now, my friend," she said, "I must leave you, but Moriuht is inside and he's expecting you." Resting her hand on Girard's shoulder, she looked into his eyes. "You are a good man," she said, "and I know you will open your heart to the men and women of Saint Lazare. Ministering to the sick and dying is not only your penance, it is your salvation."

Girard looked at the stone façade of the building before him and felt a hardening of resolve. "I shall try my best," he said.

"And that, my friend, is all the Lord asks of anyone."

By the time the afflicted retreated to the infirmary, the disease had progressed to its final stage. Some, suffering from gangrene, were missing fingers and toes. Others were covered in sores that completely obscured their features. But the sight of the disease was nothing compared to the stench of rotting flesh.

"Imagine the sweet scent of myrtle," Moriuht told Girard as they stood poised at the entrance to the men's ward. "Think of lavender and roses."

Girard nodded and followed Moriuht into a long narrow room. A bank of high windows offered little in the way of ventilation or light. Despite the cool breeze outside, inside the air was fetid and close. Girard silently recited the twenty-third Psalm. *"Yes, though I walk through the valley of the shadow of death, I will fear no harm; for Thou art with me; Thy rod and Thy staff, they comfort me."*

Moriuht paused before a trestle table pushed against the west wall. A statue of Saint Lazare, a bearded and mustached man of serious mien, rested in the center.

"They say he laughed only once in his life," Moriuht said, nodding in the direction of the statue, "and that was when he witnessed a man stealing a clay pot. Pointing to the man he chuckled, 'Why, look! Clay stealing clay!'"

Girard smiled, not because he thought the tale amusing but because Moriuht took such joy in the telling.

"Here are supplies," Moriuht said, pointing to either side of the statue where baskets of dried herbs, jars of balm and bottles of infusions crowded the tabletop. In willow baskets beneath the table, linen wraps Girard had boiled and hung to dry were arranged in ordered stacks that he found satisfying.

"Herbs rich in volatile oils such as ginger and bergamot make wonderful teas which are quite effective in stimulating digestion and eliminating pain," Moriuht said, repeating word for word what Petronilla had told him.

The careful recitation unaccountably moved Girard. "Is there a schedule of when the potions should be administered?" he asked, scanning the layout of the ward. A dozen pallets covered in bleached linen lined the white walls. Above each station hung a simple wooden cross.

Moriuht shook his head. "We give the patients what they want whenever they need it." Then, patting Girard's shoulder and smiling, he said, "Come, let's get started." But before Girard had a chance to take a step, Moriuht cried out, "Oh, but wait! I almost forgot! I've a gift for you!"

Girard smiled. For even though he fully expected Moriuht to hand him a shard of polished bone or a variegated rock, the gesture brought him enormous pleasure.

"Oh, where did I put it?" Moriuht muttered, patting his robe. "Ah, here!" he said. Reaching deep into a pocket, he withdrew a silver medallion hung on a leather cord. "Saint Lazarus," he said, draping the medal around Girard's neck.

"No one has ever given me a gift before!" Girard said, as stunned as he was gratified. "Thank you." He fingered the cord and then the medal itself, turning the disk so he could see the script imprinted on the circumference. "Saint Lazare Pray For Us," he read aloud.

Moriuht wrapped his arms around Girard, swaying from side to side before slapping him heartily on the back with both hands. "Ready?" Moriuht asked, and began ministering with an enthusiasm that amazed Girard.

While changing the bloody, pus-stained wraps of Raymond, an elderly leper whose collapsed nose exposed gristle and bone, Moriuht discussed the latest antics of the camp dogs. Girard knew he did not have it in him to adapt Moriuht's garrulous manner, but he paid close attention to his matter-of-fact nursing. Lifting a corner of the sheet to expose only a small swatch of skin, Moriuht dipped a clean rag into a bowl of scented water and bathed the man's body in sections, as attentive to his modesty as he was to his lesions.

"Those camp dogs remind me of a mutt I once owned," Raymond said, air whistling through the ruins of his nose. The man's windy words tightened Girard's throat and made it difficult for him to breath. Moriuht, seemingly oblivious to the grotesque sight and sound before him, leaned forward with a rag and wiped the corner of his patient's mouth. When Raymond laughed— *and how could the man laugh?* Girard wondered—spittle flew everywhere, splattering the front of Moriuht's robe.

When he had finished applying new wraps, Moriuht patted Raymond's thigh. "One of the sisters will be along soon with an infusion. You've just enough time for morning devotions." He lifted a rosary from the table and handed it to Raymond who smiled before turning his attention to prayer. "Come, Brother

Girard, I'll introduce you to your patient." Moriuht said, nodding to a pile of blankets heaped on a pallet in the far corner.

Girard nodded, bile rising in his throat. Evraud and Girard had not spoken since that day in the chestnut grove, and Girard feared what the man might say to him. While Petronilla insisted that Evraud had mended his ways, Girard knew that reformed sinners behaved in remarkably dissimilar ways. Some became generous in their estimations of humanity while others grew leery and suspicious. Girard had no way of knowing how redemption had affected Evraud.

Girard could not have been more shocked when the pile of blankets sighed and revealed a face disfigured by disease. The scar that had cleft the robber's lower lip and slashed his jaw was covered by lesions, and the little hair left on his head was grey not black. When Evraud turned his milky eyes towards the sound of Moriuht's greeting, Girard saw that they were without lashes or brows. *Why, everything about the man is diminished!* he thought, a spasm of pity and fear clinching his gut.

"Ah, Moriuht, you've come at last." When Evraud blinked, his lids closed only partially. "Sit."

Moriuht sat on the edge of the pallet and took Evraud's hand, cupping the stubby fingers in his palm.

"A red spot, a tiny blemish on my thumb, that's how it began," Evraud said. His words had the measured beat of a story told many times. "I thought at first I might have scraped it. We were cutting stone that week and I have always been clumsy with a chisel."

Evraud's fingers were so twisted that his hands appeared half the size of the ones that ravished Madeleine.

"The spot looked painful, but it wasn't. That was the odd thing. The numbness. The absence of pain."

Moriuht repositioned Evraud's blanket. "Yes, yes," he said, nodding vigorously as though greatly fascinated. "So you have told me many times before. But what of last night?" he asked in a coaxing voice intended to distract. "Did you sleep well?"

Girard shifted his weight from one leg to the other. The

movement must have caught Evraud's eye, although surely he saw little more than shadowy shapes. "Who is there?" he asked, reaching with a gnarled hand. Girard could not speak because he was holding his breath, willing himself not to flinch or turn away.

"This is Brother Girard come to nurse you," Moriuht said.

Evraud's hands flailed about until, locating the hem of Girard's robe, he pinched a bit of cloth between two fleshy knobs that had once been a powerful thumb and forefinger.

On a nearby pallet, a leper moaned and called out for water. "I will get that," Moriuht said, bounding off without another word.

Girard's stomach balled into a knot. Then he remembered Petronilla's and Moriuht's faith in him, and he busied himself adjusting his patient's pillows. "You were there!" Evraud said. Dropping the hem of Girard's robe, he pulled himself up on wobbly elbows. "You saw!"

"Yes," Girard said, feelings of disgrace rendering him nearly breathless.

"Do you think often of that day, Brother Girard? Does it linger with you as it does with me?"

A memory flashed before him—Madeleine thrown to the ground, her robe and chemise torn away to reveal her naked form. His underarms were damp and a bead of sweat trickled down his chest. "I try not to," Girard said simply, honestly.

"Try not to? Why, what can you mean?" Evraud asked, his blind eyes darting the room, his useless hands moving restlessly against the blanket. "Didn't you see what I saw? Didn't you see the Master call forth a thunderbolt that broke open the heavens and split the trunk of a chestnut tree?"

It was not the dreadful deeds of that day that agitated Evraud so, but his recollection of the Master's miracle! Momentarily startled, Girard was without words. He felt relief, yes, but also embarrassment.

Evraud's sightless gaze bore down on him with such intensity that he grew frightened. Girard had lived a quiet life of solitude and contemplation, and he knew little of people and their emotions.

He searched the room for Moriuht, but he was so intent upon his duties that he did not see Girard's hand lifted in a silent bid for assistance.

"What is this wasting disease, this agonizing death compared to the miraculous events of that day?" Evraud continued, the words spewing from his mouth with a power that recalled the manner in which he had shouted orders to his brigands. "I have lived and worked beside a saint, and I am grateful for that blessing. Robert of Arbrissel changed my life, brought me to a place of grace. Everything else is meaningless."

Girard felt a dreamy realization. *I understand my role here!* What Evraud wanted, what he needed was what we all need— reassurance that his life has not been lived in vain. Girard dropped to his knees and took the dying man's hand in his own. His skin felt dry and fragile, but also warm, and that warmth traveled the length of Girard's arm and settled somewhere in his chest.

"Yes," Girard said, "We two were part of something meaningful and great."

Evraud nodded. A calm settled over both men.

Girard continued holding his patient's hand even after he fell asleep. Having found a point of connection, a bridge between his heart and Evraud's, Girard was hesitant to let go.

Across the room Moriuht fed a young man whose arms had been amputated just above the elbows while another brother read psalms in a low, sonorous voice.

Girard closed his eyes and remembered his first glimpse of Fontevraud. He recalled that when their party of five (seven, if he counted Evraud and Thomas) reached the ridge, Robert thanked Jesus, Mary and Joseph and then, pointing to a valley lush with golden scrub, reedy hemlock and a cool spattering of grass, proclaimed, "Here we will build our monastery." And except for completion of the main Cathedral, they had done just that. *How far we have come since that day,* Girard thought, cradling Evraud's hand in his palm. In a few short winters the brush has been cleared and replaced by a stone monument to God, a double monastery that housed Robert's vision and his dream. And how appropriate that it should be named for a reformed sinner and a true believer. Girard did not know if Robert was a saint, perhaps he would never know. He did know that the Master, a holy man of courage, had achieved great things.

When Girard's shift ended shortly before compline, he set out to walk in the fresh air and, although he had not planned it, he was not surprised when he found himself at the spring. Squatting beside the blessed waters, he cupped his hands and drank, barely pausing for a breath between gulps. His thirst satisfied, he eased back onto his haunches. The setting sun tossed a waning beam across the surface of the pond producing a glassy wink that prompted Girard to take off his sandals and step into the water.

Algae tickled the soles of his feet and sent a shiver down his spine, a surprisingly pleasant sensation. Without a thought to modesty or decorum, he removed his heavy robe and tossed it onto the branching willows that lined the shore. For one brief moment Girard considered checking his body for red spots, but just as quickly he thought, *either I will die in pieces or I will not, in any case there is nothing I can do about it.* He took another step. The cool water tightened his scrotum and lifted the hair on the back of his neck. Girard wriggled his toes in mud and listened to the sharp kew-wit and tremulous hoo-hoo-hoooo of a tawny owl. And though he could not see the bird, he had no trouble imagining its swooping flight across the evening sky, a flight that filled Girard with awe and gave him the courage to take another step and then another. The water rose past his calves, splashed his shins and sloshed against his waist. Spreading his arms and legs, Girard took a deep breath, and leaned back. As soon as his body met the surface of the pond he was floating.

Enthralled by this new feeling of buoyancy, he closed his eyes and, listening to the hollow lap against his ears, marveled at the Lord's mysterious ways. For in the end, it was not the Master who transformed his life but, rather, a tiny, passionate nun and a garrulous, vermin-infested gatherer of bones and feathers, modest people of compassion who simply understood the heart's compulsion to know joy.

I must replace remorse with action, Girard thought, and immediately began developing a plan. Nothing too grand, for he knew he did not possess Petronilla's insight or Robert's courage. Some simple task that he could set his mind to and accomplish in a day.

A light breeze rustled through willow branches, whispered against his chest and filled the air with a clean, grassy scent. Tomorrow he would tuck sprigs of mint and dried lavender beneath Evraud's pillow and massage his limbs with warm oils. It was a simple plan, a tentative step in a new direction. But it was the right direction, of this Girard felt certain.

R obert returned to the abbey, weak with hunger and tired from his journey. On the long walk from Anjou to Fontevraud, he had grown so accustomed to the silence of his own thoughts that it took him a moment to process Mother Hersend's words. "It arrived in your absence," she explained, handing him an epistle. "I thought it might be important."

"From Abbot Geoffrey!" Robert said, recognizing the letter's seal, and the imprint of Trinity Church. He ran his finger over the dried ridge of wax. His heart filled with joy, for he had not received any correspondence from his old friend in some time.

"You must be tired," Hersend said, directing him to a bench in the garden.

For a full fortnight Robert had fasted and discussed his plans for establishing daughter houses with interested clergy and nobles in Anjou. Though the meetings proved inconclusive, he hoped the fasting had cleansed his soul and prepared him for the next phase of his life. For now that Philippa had agreed to act as his ambassador, Robert could focus more fully on his ministry.

"Why not sit for a while and read your letter? We can meet later in the day to discuss abbey business," Hersend said.

"Thank you, Reverend Mother. As always, you are sensitive to my needs."

Hersend nodded and took her leave. Robert eased himself onto the bench. He pressed the small of his back against the slats and heaved a sigh of relief. The sun shone high in the sky. A lone wood pigeon bobbed among the herbs. Nearby a trio of novitiates pulled weeds and watered flowers, their low chatter disturbing his concentration. Slipping Geoffrey's letter into his robe, Robert rose slowly, flexing the muscles of his legs, rolling his shoulders and tilting his head from side to side before retreating to the relative quiet of the Great Church.

Pausing in the vestibule, he dipped his fingers into the marble stoup of holy water and crossed himself. After his eyes adjusted to the dim light, he studied the cathedral. Perhaps because of his time away from Fontevraud, he felt newly struck by the building's austere beauty. No ornamentation whatsoever—no statues, paintings, tapestries, or foliated capitals—distracted the eye from the stark magnificence of sleek white columns rising to expansive vaulted ceilings. In the unfinished chapel no stained glass smudged the purity of the altar. Instead, a beam of sunlight shot through a clear window above a balustrade, a brilliant reminder of God's goodness and His glory. Taking a seat in an unstained pew, Robert withdrew Geoffrey's missive from his robe, slid his thumb beneath the vellum flap and broke the seal. Following an unusually formal greeting, the abbot launched into an angry attack on Robert's character:

We have heard malicious reports about you. You allow certain women to abide with you in too familiar a manner,

often exchanging private conversations with them, and at
night you do not refrain from sleeping with them.

Stunned by his friend's accusation, Robert recalled rumors of
Saint Scothine, a so-called holy man, who engaged in white martyrdom by holding two naked girls to his breast while purported-
ly thinking only of our Lord Jesus Christ. His heart pounding in
his ears, Robert wondered if Geoffrey thought him capable of such
scurrilous indulgence. Relaxing his clinched fingers so as not to tear
the vellum, he scanned the rest of the letter, a document riddled
with malicious reports and false allegations, and then, too agitated
to remain seated, he rose from the pew, placed Geoffrey's correspondence in his robe and left the church by a small door in the
transept. Entering one of the galleries that framed the cloisters, he
glimpsed the courtyard though an arched window. The lawn reminded him of the enclosed garden at Vendôme. Much time had
passed since he had last entered the hallowed halls of Trinity, but
he easily recalled Geoffrey's kindness to the pilgrims and could not
imagine his compassionate friend penning such a vicious epistle.
Following the galleries around the cloisters, he passed the chapter
house, the common room, and the passageway leading to the men's
monastery. He paused by the stone stairs leading to the nun's dorters, took a deep breath and prayed for the strength to turn the other
cheek before exiting through the south door of the novices' house
and descending to the fount. Sitting among the reeds that circled
the pond, he listened to the rush of wind and watched sunlight skitter the surface of the pond until his pulse slowed and the muscles in
his shoulders relaxed enough for him to decipher his heart's desire.
Only then did he rise and go where he had longed to be since returning from Anjou.

As he drew near the commoners' priory, Robert spotted Little
Marie and a bevy of children playing under the watchful eye of
Bertrad. Little squealed and jumped into his arms with an exuber-

ance that never failed to charm him. In promising Marie to care for Little and her mother, he had opened up a piece of his heart previously held in reserve. The child buried her hands in the snarls of his beard and pulled his face closer to hers until their noses touched. In Little's spirit, if not her looks, Robert saw a resemblance to Madeleine. Both were independent thinkers; both saw past his priestly façade to the man beneath.

"Bodkins has run away," Little said, her breath warm against his face. "My mother says that sometimes old cats go away to die. She says that Bodkins was Mother Marie's cat and that he has lived a very long life. Do you think Bodkins has gone away to die?"

Robert had never spoken with the tip of his nose pressed firmly against another's, but he found the sensation surprisingly pleasant. "Most likely," he said, for he did not patronize Little. When she turned her head and blinked, her lashes fluttered against his cheek.

"But you were gone for a very long time. And here you are!" Leaning back in his arms, Little patted his chest with her hands. "So maybe Bodkins will return as well?"

"Maybe," Robert said, "but probably not."

Her body tensed. He pulled her close, kissed her wild curls and breathed in the clean scent of her new life. When she looked up at him with her oddly colored eyes so full of trust, he longed to be the person she saw, a man capable of resurrecting dead cats and healing grief. "I have heard that Brother Justin's tabby birthed a litter of kittens," he said. "Shall I ask him if I might bring you one?"

Little's brow furrowed. She leaned back in Robert's arms and studied his expression. The weight and warmth of her small body delighted him beyond reason.

"Not to replace Bodkins of course, for no kitten could do that," he reassured her, "but to sleep at the end of your cot and keep your feet warm." He tickled the sole of her bare foot until a tentative smile gave way to giggles. When he stopped, Little held out the other foot and wriggled her toes.

"Do it again," she said.

Robert obliged, the two of them laughing together. When finally Little had enough, she rested her cheek against his shoulder and asked, "But what if Bodkins should return? What then?"

"Then he'll have a friend," Robert said.

Satisfied, she kissed him head on, nose pressed to nose and eyes wide open, before wriggling to be put down so that she might rejoin her friends.

As he neared the cloisters, Robert felt a new urgency. Giving no thought to convention or propriety he quickened his pace and mounted the stone steps two at a time.

When he arrived at Madeleine's open door, she stood haloed in sunlight. Separating her long hair into three bunches, she plaited and tossed the braid over her shoulder. The intimacy of these simple gestures sent a shiver down his spine. Robert contemplated Augustine's rejection of the passions of the flesh and wondered if this simple act of denial was beyond his capacity. He did not exhale until Madeleine turned her head and spotted him.

For a moment she said nothing, only stared with the befuddled look of someone deep in thought.

"I didn't mean to startle you, Madeleine," he said.

She scanned the air around his head. Her ability to see and smell color had not waned after she had given birth. If anything, her extraordinary senses had heightened. Whatever she saw now disturbed her. Madeleine blushed and dropped her eyes. "Have you seen Little Marie?" she asked.

"Just now," he said, marveling at the love he felt for this woman. What was it that set her apart from all others? How was it that their two pulses seemed to beat as one?

"The child missed you so," she said. "It seemed to her that you were gone much longer than a fortnight."

Robert studied Madeleine's face hoping to detect a greater meaning in her words. She was not a flirtatious woman, but perhaps she spoke obliquely of her own loneliness? "And how about you, Madeleine? Did it seem to you that I was gone for a very long time?"

Madeleine stroked the plait of her braid. "I used the time well,

Master. While you were in Anjou I studied the gospels." Her eyes shifted to a Bible on her cot.

The hesitancy in her voice filled him with hope. There was no logic in love. Love was not a puzzling passage of scripture to be studied and deciphered. Like the flash of sunlight through foliage or the shared exhalation of a chant, love required nothing beyond an accepting heart. "Brother Peter tells me you are an apt and able student."

Madeleine blushed and the freckles that scattered her cheeks grew darker. "I'm a hard worker," she said simply, examining his face. "Sit down. You don't look well. Have you eaten today?"

Hunger was as familiar to Robert as the oblivion of sleep. Unless someone drew attention to his body's need for nourishment or sleep, he scarcely gave either a thought. He shook his head. "Bertrad has just this morning brought me a basket of apples. I'll cut one for you," Madeleine said, and went to retrieve a woven basket stashed next to the nightstand.

Robert settled into one of two chairs on either end of a small table. Above the table was a wooden crucifix, and on the wall opposite hung Marie's unicorn tapestry, the sight of which sparked a sense of loss in Robert, for he missed Marie's kind heart and common sense. Gradually, and over time, Robert had come to understand that Marie's practicality as much as his own faith had brought him to this place. It was Marie who had reminded him that masons needed coins in their pockets and sharp tools in their hands if he expected them to carve steeples out of stone. And when he skipped meals, Marie reprimanded him, the kindness in her eyes softening the gritty truth wedged between her words—"You must eat if you hope to live long enough to turn widows into nuns and godless whores into true believers." Without Marie, Robert might still be wandering the countryside, speaking endlessly, if eloquently, of his rain-drenched vision in the forest of Craon.

"Do you think Mother Marie knew happiness at Fontevraud?" Robert asked.

Madeleine set the basket on the table. Nudging a curl off her forehead with the back of her hand, she nodded. "Yes," she said. "Just before Marie died she told me that her life had never been so free of worry." She picked up and discarded several apples before selecting a near perfect specimen. "How about you, Robert? Are you happy?" She paused, one hand holding the apple aloft.

Her question startled him, for Madeleine's questions were few and seldom personal. *When I'm near you*, he thought, *I'm as happy as I will ever be in this life.* He readjusted his weight in the chair. "Today I'm worried about a letter I received from Abbot Geoffrey," he said, fingering a dried smear of red paint on the tabletop. "In his letter Geoffrey makes false accusations against my character!" Robert said, slamming his fist against the table with more force than he had intended. He understood his anger, though real enough, also served as a convenient diversion, for complaining about the injustice of Geoffrey's letter was far easier than confronting his love for Madeleine.

"You're a good man, Robert. Who would know that better than I?" Madeleine said and quickly glanced away before he could read the expression on her face. She glossed the apple against her robe, and Robert felt a wave of desire that left him light-headed and ashamed.

"I'm not so sure," he said, studying his fist.

"What do you mean?"

What was it about this woman that gave him leave to reveal his deepest fears? Taking a deep breath, he continued. "The abbot says I show preference to certain women."

"Certain women?" Madeleine laid the apple on a wooden trencher.

Robert nodded. "Geoffrey accuses me of favoring the reformed sinners over the widows and nuns."

Madeleine placed the trencher on the table between them. "You care deeply for the unfortunates, we who've known hunger and poverty. But you are also attentive to the needs of the widows and nuns," she said.

"I believe that the truth of any man is manifest in his deeds, and my deeds have taken me to far more brothels and huts than palaces or cathedrals." Robert 's voice surprised him. Halting, fumbling, it barely rose above a whisper.

She pursed her lips and shook her head. "Many clergy eagerly serve gentlemen and ladies. Fewer feel called to minister to the poor and the needy!" The sight of Madeleine's anger excited him. "You're too hard on yourself, Master Robert," she said. Taking a paring knife from a drawer, she quartered and sliced the apple, releasing a sweet scent into the room. She took a piece for herself before fanning the remaining slices across the trencher.

Robert imagined her fingers trailing his skin and his belly tightened. "The abbot says also that he fears a man cannot be chaste in mind living among women," he said.

Madeleine met his eyes and held them. Lowering her voice, she spoke softly, "I know the man is a great favorite of yours, but surely you must see that he is not always right. It's possible to feel desire and not act upon it," she said. And while her hands shook ever so slightly, her face remained as beautifully composed as a prayer.

The bell for vespers rang. Robert heard the shuffled steps of the nuns on the way to chapel.

"You really must eat now," Madeleine said. She took a few steps until she stood directly in front of him. Sunlight spilling from a high window lit her face and shoulders, highlighting the amber streaks in her hair. "Apples hold the scent of autumn in their peels and the taste of summer in their pulp," she said.

A soft compliance engulfed Robert. Even the memory of the snake whispering evil into Eve's ear did not dissuade him from accepting the apple from Madeleine's hand. Closing his eyes, Robert luxuriated in the slide of his tongue against the fruit's firm skin before biting down and releasing its tart juices.

Madeleine reached for another slice. Her arm brushed Robert's chest, and he felt himself unraveling. *My Lord God help me see the road ahead of me*, he prayed silently. *Grant me the will to abstain from this temptation, which surely Madeleine does not intend and righteousness forbids.*

She motioned to the trencher. Robert took another slice. Madeleine's attention remained fixed on him until the clink of a chisel cutting stone startled her and she lifted her eyes to the window.

As he studied her profile it occurred to Robert that if he set about establishing daughter houses, the greater share of his life would be lived apart from her, and it was all he could do to stop himself from weeping.

"Madeleine…" he said, his voice reedy with impending loss.

"What is it Robert?" He felt a vibration of her words in his chest, they were that close. "Tell me," she whispered and tentatively placed her hand against his bearded cheek.

A great whooshing sound filled his head, battering his thoughts against his skull until he could no longer distinguish God's will from the agony of his own desire. *Oh my Madeleine, is it possible your touch will be my undoing?* he wondered, just as the room began to spin out of control.

"Robert!" The alarm in Madeleine's voice rang fierce and protective. "You are white as a ghost! Fasting has made you weak. Come, lie down," she said, taking hold of his arm and leading him to her cot.

The cot smelled of soap, sunlight and Madeleine's hair. *Her hands have gathered these very linens and wrapped them tight around her shoulders,* Robert thought, recalling that long ago day in the grove when he had covered her naked body with his alb and lifted her onto the back of Philippa's stallion. *The soul exists in opposition to the wishes of the flesh. When we live according to our soul's desire, we become strangers to lust,* the words echoed in his mind, as if uttering scripture could make it so. But Madeleine's nearness, the milky length of her arms, the bluish underside of her wrists, even the crescent moons of her nails conspired against him. *This one time, O Lord, let me have this one time and I will rededicate my life to you.*

"Close your eyes, Robert," Madeleine said in a raspy, uneven voice.

"Perhaps I will rest for a moment," he said.

Pulling a stool nearer the cot, she began to hum softly. Outside, the world went on without them. Skylarks wheeled across the heavens and mallards waddled among willows and floated the pond. In the kitchen the cook prepared the next meal with silent efficiency amidst the noisy clang of pots and pans while the brothers set places in the refectory. Beyond that, in the heart of the Loire valley, fishermen stood among creeping brambles, completely absorbed in snagging bass. And none of it, Robert realized with a kind of wonder, was dependent on what happened in Madeleine's cell.

Her song ended and she began another, and though Robert wanted to compliment her voice, he had not the energy to speak. Weary of body and mind, he tumbled into the most vivid dream of his life.

An orchard of apple trees, lush with rain-polished leaves and ripe fruit, surrounded him. Above his head wispy clouds netted an indigo sky. Beneath his bare feet, in place of dark loam was a planked wooden floor covered in flowers. A pair of white rabbits poked their pink noses into a river of periwinkle.

"Where am I?" Robert asked.

He felt her presence before he saw her—a younger, more vigorous Marie than the woman he had known, how she must have looked before age and disease stooped her shoulders and melted away her flesh. Instead of the simple chemise she had worn at Fontevraud, she was dressed in a tightly girdled gown of the finest silk. "Marie? Is that you?"

"And who were you expecting?" she said in her gruff, no nonsense voice. She approached with her arms spread wide and her cheeks flushed pink as a young girl's. A luminous glow, not soft, but blinding like the sun at its zenith, lit Marie.

When Robert stepped into her embrace, he smelled the flowery aroma of his mother's carefully tended delphiniums and the earthy scent of his father's simples.

"I was measuring ingredients for sweet rolls," she said, patting the flour that dusted her bodice and sleeves.

While wearing a silk gown? Robert wondered, but did not ask, for surely there were more important questions.

"Maddy always loved my sweet rolls. Before I left I taught her to make them. She's good with her hands, you know."

A great mélange of images floated the air above them—Madeleine's hands kneading dough, digging loam, snapping beans, tying bows in Little's hair—and Robert wanted to grab her wrists and suck each capable finger one by one. The more he tried to divest himself of lascivious thoughts, the faster they came.

"You've seen her illustrations?" Marie asked.

"They show great talent. Brother Peter tells me she has an interest in painting saintly women."

Marie nodded. "At last, Maddy's found her art form! But artists need more than talent and interesting subjects, no? They must also possess a commitment of the heart," Marie said in a voice so low he was not sure she had spoken until he saw the set of her jaw.

"Marie, what are you saying?"

"Oh Robert, I thought we agreed, you and I, not to play dumb. Not to pretend to be anything other than who we are." She shook her head and let out an exhausted sigh. "It's funny. I live in a timeless world, and still I haven't time for nonsense."

Hands clinched, Robert fixed his eyes on a tangle of periwinkle vines. Taking a deep breath he exhaled slowly. "It's true that I care for Madeleine above all others," he said. "Which is why I have always hoped that with time the damage inflicted on her in Rouen could be undone. In any case," he said, assuming a tone of moral conviction, "I would not, I will not…"

"I think you would, Robert," Marie said, patting his arm. "I think you would."

Realization struck Robert with the force of a blow. Geoffrey's allegations held a grain of truth, for while he remained celibate in body, his desire for Madeleine frequently waylaid his spirit. Lust had fueled his early life, lust and pride. And now that Fontevraud was nearly built, the two demons renewed their struggle to gain a piece of his soul.

"In truth," he told Marie, "there are moments when I would

barter my soul for one night with Madeleine."

The scent of ripe fruit and anticipation hung heavy in the air. Marie nodded before plucking an apple from the canopy of branches above her head. "There are some surprises ahead for you, my friend."

"Heavenly surprises, do you mean?" he asked. He saw no point in continuing their discussion of Madeleine. Each knew the truth of the other's heart. "Is this planked orchard the Kingdom of God?"

Marie laughed, a joyous sound that rustled leaves and left him more bewildered. "Look at this beauty," she said, admiring the apple's perfect symmetry. She bit into the apple and chewed at a leisurely pace. Robert could not say precisely how long she took to eat the fruit, for time was not measurable in this place. After swallowing the last of it, she sighed. "Wonderful!" she declared, tossing the core and wiping her mouth on the hem of her gown.

A chough erupted with a shrill chee-ow that sent rabbits scurrying for cover. In the time it took for him to blink, Marie aged twenty years. She looked as she had before her death—grey, shrunken, a diminished body housing a powerful will. But far more startling than her change in appearance was the change in her sound. When Marie opened her mouth to speak, a chorus burst forth. His father's deep bass and Abbot Geoffrey's windy baritone rose and fell with a biblical cadence—"There can be only one love in life that burns with such intensity!"

Robert's shoulders ached and he had to remind himself to breathe. Even as he aspired to a holier intimacy with God, Robert longed to place his lips against the pulse of his Madeleine's neck.

"Wrap yourself in the cloak of prayer, Robert. Consider the consequences of your actions." The voices unraveled, separating strand by strand until all that remained was Marie's singular tone. "I am a woman who lived her life selling flesh and catering to men's dreams. I know men, Robert. For better or worse, I know men. And you, Robert, are a good man." She studied the horizon as though waiting impatiently for someone to appear.

Robert listened to the fragile beat of his own heart until the clump of hooves against planking startled him and he opened his eyes to the sight of Marie's hands cupping the muzzle of a unicorn! "You've come at last, my beauty," Marie murmured. Her hands slid from forelock to withers, a mesmerizing motion that inexplicably reminded Robert of the grace that follows a good deed.

A church bell sounded and a golden seam of lightening split the sky. Robert heard the rain before he felt it—not the gentle patter of spring showers but the great whooshing flood of a downpour. And while his feet remained firmly planted in the apple orchard, he heard the deep gurgling of rain flushing the dorter drains at Fontevraud and tasted the cold sweet water of the fount when he swallowed. "Marie, what if I am not the man you think? What then?" he whispered.

Marie smiled. "Oh, but you are Robert. You are." She nuzzled the unicorn's cheek before slapping the animal's croup. "Off with you," she said. The horned beast whinnied once and cantered to a wooded area where he disappeared from sight.

"Marie . . . " Robert began and faltered. There were so many questions; he hardly knew where to begin. Just as his confusion coalesced into words, Marie began to fade. Her image flickered and then blurred, beginning at the hem of her gown and moving upward like the swirl of mist rising from a pond. Robert's breath came in shallow bursts. His palms grew damp. When Marie's shimmering shadow rose and merged with the smudge of clouds above his head, Robert's whole body tingled. He felt the stringy mass of his muscles, the warmth of his skin, the pulse of each and every heartbeat. He was not thinking. He was plunging into the deepest part of his being. When Robert surfaced, drenched in sweat and gasping for air, he clutched the hem of Madeleine's robe.

"I'm right here, Robert," Madeleine said, placing a cool palm on his brow.

Robert's hands trembled. Putting Madeleine's needs above his own would be his greatest act of martyrdom. He imagined the scratch of haircloth wrapping his heart and prayed that he might know the impartial love of a holy man.

"Has the storm passed, Madeleine?" he asked in a sleep-drenched voice.

"There was no storm, Robert," she said, confusion creasing her forehead. "You must have dreamed it."

"I saw Marie…"

"Marie?"

Robert laughed aloud. "Dressed in a satin gown and petting her unicorn. We spoke of you. She approves of your paintings, called you an artist who had found her art form."

Madeleine smiled and turned her head to the window, a far away look in her eyes.

Robert heard the lazy coo of a dove, the tinkle of a leper's bell and the voices of the women singing hymns. *The sounds of Fontevraud*, he thought.

"The day is clear and warm," Madeleine said. "Look how sun lights the steeple of the church!" she said, in a voice filled with wonder. "Your dreams and your faith built this place, Robert." The expression on her face was not the distracted glance of the young girl he had met in Rouen, but the focused gaze of a mature woman, a mother and an artist.

He admired the reach of the steeple before responding. "I can't take credit for Fontevraud. The spirit of God and the faith and hard work of many men and women built this abbey."

Madeleine's unblinking gaze projected sincerity and gratitude. "*You* had the vision, Robert. *You* did."

Robert recalled the pitched ceiling of the Rouen whorehouse giving way to a bank of clouds nestling the majestic white-walled buildings of Fontevraud, and joy filled his chest.

Madeleine took his hand in hers. Bending forward, she brought her face to his. "I called you on my day of trouble and you delivered me, Robert," she said, her breath mingling with his.

It is said that when two souls are perfectly matched all the good that exists in the world plays out in their love. And while Geoffrey would call such an idea blasphemy, Robert knew it to be true. His love for Madeleine went beyond the lusts of the flesh, for it held a shimmer of holiness, a golden restraint. A mantle of peace settled over him, and he sensed a shift in the energy of the room, as though desire had been replaced by something more enduring. "Thank you," he said. Sliding his hands free of hers he knew that he would never love another human being with so much of his heart. "Now I must leave you, for there is much work to be done. I will return, but it may not be for many months."

When he rose from her cot, Madeleine examined his face. "You are still weak, Master. You must eat more than apples and sleep longer than a nap before resuming your work."

"I feel neither hungry nor tired," he said and indeed he felt infused with energy. *The world with its desire passes away like grass, but he who does God's will remains,* he thought.

"Wait!" Bending to the chest at the foot of the cot, she dug through lavender scented blankets, unearthing a miniature wrapped in linen. "Take this," she said, removing the cloth and handing it to him. "So that you won't forget us."

The painting exploded with color. Saffron marigolds, orange poppies, and powder-blue cornflowers spilled out of the frame into the miniature's border where green vines trailed a copper-tinted trellis. In the center of this sumptuous garden Madeleine and Little Marie sat on a rough-hewn bench. Madeleine's robe was the color of mulberry juice, and Little's loose smock pulsed the scarlet of summer crocus. One of Madeleine's hands wrapped her child's waist and the other held a tiny rosebud. Both pairs of eyes looked past the flower and beyond the leaf of vellum as though they could see the very shape of Robert's soul.

"It's beautiful, Madeleine. Beautiful," he said, understanding for the first time that in this place with her daughter and her brushes Madeleine had found peace. "My heart needs no drawing to recall your faces, but I will cherish your gift and carry it with me always." He tucked it safely into his robe and stood for a quiet moment at her side.

"Little and I shall miss you," she said running her hand along the plait of her braid.

"The grace of our Lord Jesus Christ be with your spirit," Robert said, signing the cross. He walked slowly across the cell and paused with his hand on the door latch. He did not think he could put into words the depths of his feelings for her, but he must try. "Before I met you, Madeleine, while I was awake, truly my heart slept. In loving you I have loved the Lord," he said, and quickly, before she had a chance to respond, he closed the door softly behind him.

Thereafter whenever Robert's conscience was troubled or he felt confused about his life's direction he would hold Madeleine's miniature in his hands and recall that moment of clarity when his love was cleansed of cupidity and born anew in charity, and that memory would fill him with the faith and courage to continue God's work which, he came to understand, was his destiny.

But one's destiny is not always easy. Even as Robert resumed his mission, wandering rural roads and cobbled city streets, entering cramped cottages and houses of prostitution, there were many nights when he lay awake on rocky, uneven soil or tossed atop a farmer's musty pallet and wondered—*If Marie had not interceded, would I have forfeited my soul for one night with Madeleine?* That question, that tiny kernel of uncertainty, kept him humble all the days of his life. And if there were moments amidst the fervent activity of his ministry when his upright spirit faltered and he longed to smell the fruity tangle of Madeleine's hair or feel again the flutter of her fingers against his cheek, he accepted, even embraced the pain that his longing aroused, for Robert understood that an easy faith is no faith at all.

fter Robert left Fontevraud, Madeleine spent very little time in the garden. Although beans obligingly climbed the arbors and yarrow bloomed plentifully, no clutch of poppies flamed red against a silver patch of lambs' ear or burst suddenly from beneath an artfully placed slab of granite. Clove-scented gillyflowers no longer bumped blossoms with violets. The young novitiates pruned the bushes to conform to arbitrary borders of stacked river rock, segregated the hyacinth bulbs by hue, and plucked all volunteer seedlings, whether fiddle fern or dandelion, and tossed them aside like weeds. And while Madeleine dearly missed the bold clash of colors, the sloppy cascade of bridal wreath and the careless creep of periwinkle, her new work afforded her a different and far greater pleasure.

Initially Hersend had objected when Robert established a women's scriptorium and placed Brother Peter in charge. With few exceptions, the monks believed creativity was a male prerogative, and she worried that they would see female scribes as rivals and this rivalry, whether real or imagined, would distract them from their duties. But Robert, with Philippa's assistance, argued that an abbey established to serve the needs of women must embrace a larger notion of creativity. "Freedom and salvation comes to us in many forms," he said, "why not through rubricating manuscripts and painting miniatures?"

Hersend relented. The women's scriptorium, much smaller than the men's, found a home in the Abbess's residence. What the room lacked in size it made up for in light. Two large windows caught the morning sun and held it fast until late afternoon, and even on cloudy days, a dozen tapers and a large fireplace tossed a warm glow onto the pine tables and benches arranged against the walls. After a while Hersend assigned Hildegard, a commoner from Jumièges, and Eleanor, a reformed sinner from Orléans, to work in the Abbess's scriptorium as it came to be called. But in the beginning only Peter and Madeleine worked daily in the small room.

The moment Peter took Madeleine under his wing she felt born anew. Even before she picked up a brush, she saw in her mind's eye the infinite possibilities of color. She started out as a rubricator, highlighting chapter headings and capital letters in the body of the text. Initially she relied on pattern books and stencils, but as she grew more confident, she creating her own style of initials. After applying a base coat, she made outlines in lead plummet that Peter, if he judged the image satisfactory, filled in with color. When she grew proficient, Peter allowed her to paint portions of his miniatures—the feathery wings of an angel or the gilded garment of a saint. Gradually he granted her permission to compose her own illustrations.

Peter never commented on Madeleine's affinity for painting biblical women of virtue and courage, but he complemented her bright and varied pallet. In response to his encouragement, she dared to experiment, grinding carmine and azurite, mixing the powdery pigment with glair or gum Arabic. He also praised her attention to details, noting the folds in a robe or the sinewy slide of a serpent's tail brought the spirit of the gospels to the page.

Early in her apprenticeship Madeleine realized that painting, much like gardening, celebrated God's glory through the beauty of color. But while a garden bloomed only briefly, a fickle splendor that withered and died in a matter of weeks, a miniature's beauty lasted far longer.

In addition to satisfying Madeleine's urge to create and to spread the word of God, painting allowed her to hide her oddity. She remained ill at ease around people. With few exceptions, she continued to distrust men and her infrequent contact with the monks of Fontevraud did little to change that. For while the monks willingly served aristocratic nuns as penance for their sins, they balked at sharing the privilege of their position with commoners. They were outraged when she began illustrating manuscripts. In response to their angry whispers and scathing glances, Madeleine concealed her true emotions with a modest drop of her eyes, for she believed that the appearance of timidity and compliance in woman calmed most men. She felt certain that Marie, a pragmatic soul who understood that success is sometimes achieved in circuitous ways, would approve of this deception.

As for the women of Fontevraud, the reformed sinners lived apart from the nuns cloistered in the Grand Moutier. Madeleine spoke daily with Bertrad, but seldom saw the twins. She heard talk that Agnes had fallen in love with a stone cutter from Tours, and suspected that she and her sister would very soon take leave of the abbey. Madeleine and Philippa remained friendly, but Philippa was by birth a woman of great power and Madeleine never completely relaxed in her presence.

Although Madeleine's distrust of people limited the number and nature of her relationships, it seemed to benefit her art. All of her unexpressed emotions found their way into her illustrations.

Of course she had a life apart from the scriptorium. Little Marie, a sturdy, confident child with a sharp mind, exhibited none of her mother's timidity. More fearless than most girls, Little spoke forcefully at times, but always with kindness. Robert said that in loving her daughter Madeleine had forgiven Evraud, and she suspected he was right, for she knew that without Evraud's unwanted seed there would be no Little, and Madeleine did not want to imagine that life. While not as expressive as Philippa's or as attentive as Bertrand's, Madeleine's love for her child deepened with each passing day.

Aside from Little, Robert was the only living person ever-present in Madeleine's thoughts. He once told her that redemption was a long journey of the soul. And while he spoke of his own journey, Madeleine understood that his words applied to hers as well.

That day when the Master returned from Anjou, Madeleine had been preoccupied with thoughts of Saint Lucy, the subject of her next miniature. Deeply immersed in her private world of inspiration, Madeleine momentarily mistook Robert's nimbus for the one she envisioned glorifying Lucy.

Usually the movement back from the flexible world of the imagination happened gradually, a cautious re-entry that, nevertheless, left Madeleine confused. But when Robert said her name, her confusion evaporated and her breath caught in her throat. Blushing, Madeleine dropped her eyes, but not before she noticed the look in Robert's eyes.

Ignoring his evasive words, she sought the cause of his distress in the cloud of light surrounding his head. What she gleaned sent a shudder through her body, for amidst the bands of color she recognized the ruby glow of lust. Taking a deep breath, she focused on the long slow rush of air into her lungs and willed herself calm. When she had regained her composure, she took a closer look.

Unlike the men she had known in Rouen, Robert's lust did not dominate his colors. Instead, bands of blue, turquoise, and pink joined and intertwined with the ruby creating a rainbow of compassion. Robert's desire was not separate from his love, but prompted and tempered by its presence. Once she understood the meaning of his halo, her feelings for him became translucent. When she placed her hand against Robert's beard, their love for each other lit the room and wrapped them in its glory. Then fate interceded, and Robert, weak from fasting, grew faint.

Sitting beside him while he slept, Madeleine hummed softly and considered the possibilities implicit in their love. By the time Robert woke, she had made a decision. And while she could not have rendered her resolve into words, she recalled the emotion that prompted it when she painted Saint Lucy's hands cleansing the wounds of Saint Sebastian. Sooner or later Robert would judge any love that distracted him from his love of God as adulterous, and that betrayal would destroy him. With this realization, waves of loss washed over her. In their wake she felt a ripple of relief, for she suspected that she did not have it in her to love as a woman loves a man. What she felt for Robert, the tenderness of unrealized passion, contained a purity of restraint that comforted and sustained her. She prayed it was the same for him.

Madeleine thought often of the night she met Robert, She remembered a solemn man with a bright halo and a persuasive voice who took her breath away. When he spoke of the abbey he hoped to build, she remembered entering the grand portal into a place of light.

But who can tell with memories what is real and what is imagined? Time is an unreliable storyteller, shifting focus, providing details where none exist and filling in lapses with fancy and lies. Regardless of what happened in Rouen, the scriptorium was Madeleine's place of light.

Marie would have argued that miracles are few and far between, that most of what happens in life is a result of hard work and good luck. Robert would insist that happiness is a matter of grace. Madeleine did not pretend to understand the workings of grace, but she knew for certain that she had found her life's purpose at Fontevraud. In this she felt truly blessed.